Cinnamon Bun

· Volume 6 ·

Cinnamon Bun

· Volume 6 ·

RavensDagger

Podium

Cover design by Yanhong Lu

ISBN: 978-1-0394-8731-4

Published in 2025 by Podium Publishing
www.podiumentertainment.com

Podium

Cinnamon Bun

· Volume 6 ·

· Chapter One ·

Adventurers for Hire

We're back!" I cheered while hanging off the airship's side.

Below me was Goldenalden, the great big capital city of the Kingdom of Sylphfree, lit by the first clear rays of morning sunlight. It stuck off the side of a huge mountain, with sylph-made plateaus and carved-out sections of the mountain giving the city plenty of room. The sylph liked building things tall, on account of being able to fly.

A familiar taloned hand grabbed me by the scruff and pulled me back onto the deck. "Get away from the edge, you doofus, you're going to trip off the side. I don't care how good you are at jumping, you'll splatter yourself at this height," Amaryllis said.

I laughed. I couldn't help it. I was filled with this great manic energy, and no amount of worrying from Amaryllis was going to rob me of it. "I was holding on," I protested.

"Yes, and I'm sure you've never dropped anything before," Amaryllis said with a huff. "You would feel quite stupid if you tripped off the side of the ship. At least for the few seconds it would take for you to hit the ground."

I grinned, but she was probably right. "Okay, fine. Thanks for worrying."

Amaryllis's cheeks puffed and she strutted off in a huff.

"If you want," Awen's more timid voice said from next to me, "I could get some ropes and straps. That way you can hang off the edge of the ship all you want."

I shook my head. "It's fine," I said. "Besides, it's a bit windy." I had to keep adjusting my ears and hair because both kept getting flicked around by stray gusts.

The ship—a sylph military vessel commandeered to get us to and from the Dungeon of the Lullaby Knight—was about as aerodynamic as any sylph ship, which is to say that it was basically a flying brick with sharply angled sides and a partially armored balloon.

The ship sailed past the busiest parts of Goldenalden, over the Blue and Red and Gold Districts, before we finally glided down toward the military port where sylphs in uniform flew up to meet the ship with long cables behind them.

Amaryllis returned, carrying her things as well as mine and Awen's. "Here. I figured I would grab all of our things while I was below deck."

"Thanks!" I said. I hadn't brought too much on our last adventure. A small bag and Weedbane, my new scythe, were about it. Awen had a bunch more stuff, but she was a mechanic and she needed her tools and such.

The ship docked, a gangplank was fixed to its side, and after the first few sailors moved across it we squeezed past them and onto the docks.

"Okay," I said as I walked with a bounce to my step. The docks clunked and bobbed beneath me. "Where to now?"

The sun had just come up after our overnight trip back to the capital, so we had a whole day ahead of us. I hadn't slept a wink all night. Our guide in the Lullaby Knight Dungeon—Lieutenant Petalwrought—had given us potions that were meant to make us resistant to Sleep magic.

They definitely did, and they worked really well against normal sleep too. My friends and I had spent the night in a little cabin just chitchatting about everything and nothing.

"I suppose since this mission was given to us by the king, we ought to report back to him," Amaryllis said. "But it would be somewhat unusual for three contractors to report directly to the king unless he specifically ordered us to do so."

"We could pop over to the palace anyway and leave a message," I suggested. "I bet he's got secretaries."

"When you're a king they're called stewards, but yes, he definitely has people who can take care of appointments for him," Amaryllis said.

I glanced around, got my bearings thanks to the mountain peak poking out above the city, and then we set off to cross Goldenalden. Last time we'd come with a carriage, but this time we simply walked. It was early enough in the morning that most of the city was still sleeping, though birds were darting around after one another and the first townspeople to wake were already out and about.

We stuck to the ground level, where the traffic was even quieter. Most sylphs liked to fly around, or at least flutter from rooftop to rooftop, so the streets were relatively quiet except for the occasional donkey-drawn cart.

As we moved north toward the Gold District, the streets widened and apartment buildings gave way to stately homes and eventually small estates before we reached the walls surrounding the palace.

Two guards stood on either side of the gate, and more waited in the towers above. These weren't city guards; they had much nicer armor and a lot more feathers and fluff on their helmets.

"Hello, sir," I said as we came over. "I'm Captain Bunch, and this is Lady Bristlecone and Lady Albatross. We're here to deliver a message to the king."

The guard stared at me, then blinked. I think he might have been close to his change of shift, because it took a moment for him to realize that I was asking for something. "Ah, one moment, ma'am," he said.

A cord was pulled, a bell was rung, and soon enough a butler-looking sylph flew over the front gate and greeted us with a bow. "I'm afraid His Majesty was not yet expecting you, though we do have orders to expect your arrival sometime today. If it would please you, we may extend the royal family's hospitality to you and offer you one of the guest lounges until His Majesty is ready to receive supplicants and guests."

"That would be fine," Amaryllis said.

"Could we have snacks while we wait?" I asked.

The butler stared.

"We could pay you back. I'm really hungry."

"Ah, yes, something could be arranged, of course. Please, follow me."

The butler led us—and a complement of two guards—through the front gate and across the palace grounds. We entered, and then I immediately got lost as we navigated through an unfamiliar part of the palace.

The butler dropped us off in a room with a few lounge chairs, a couch, a low table, and a little bookcase next to a window overlooking one of the greenhouses next to the palace. "I shall return with refreshments in a moment," he said before heading off.

The guards stayed on either side of the entrance to the room. They were really good at staring blankly ahead.

"Awa, do you think the king will want us to do more work with dungeons?" Awen asked.

"It's a possibility," Amaryllis said. "It's good work, at least as far as pay and reputation goes, but I doubt it would last for very long. Training people to use Cleaning magic the way Broccoli does shouldn't take too long. A few weeks at most. Sylphfree won't lack for volunteers. Grab a few soldiers with appropriate classes, have them clean the latrines until they get the skill, then escort them through a few fights until they level up enough to pour points into Cleaning magic, and voila, you have a new person able to clear out Evil Roots."

"It took me . . . about two months?" I said. I wasn't great with keeping track of the date, so I just guesstimated how long I'd been on Dirt for.

"Which is impressive," Amaryllis said. I puffed up with pride, but then she shattered that with her next words. "But I suspect that soldiers undergoing strenuous training could fairly easily go from level one to ten in as little as a month. Less, if risk is put aside in favor of speed."

"Soldiers train that quickly?" Awen asked.

"Oh no," Amaryllis said. "Soldiers can *level* that quickly. Given access to dungeons with guides, and able to face appropriate threats, they can definitely spend days at a time fighting and working to level up. The training to learn how to fight as a group, though? That can take several more months."

"You know a lot about this," I said.

She shrugged. "I had a passing interest in the matter back home. I recall that most career soldiers take six months to a year to train before they're deployed anywhere, with frequent retraining and additional classes needed if they specialize in anything. If there's a draft, though, the average training time is reduced to a handful of weeks."

"That's not very long," Awen said.

"No, it isn't, and so you can imagine that the quality will be similarly impacted."

I tapped my chin, then turned to one of the guards. "Hey, mister guard. How much training did you get?"

He blinked, then glanced at his companion. "Ah, forgive me, ma'am, we . . . uh, aren't meant to interact with guests."

"Not even to answer questions?" I asked.

He nodded slightly.

"What if I need to use the ladies' room and don't know where it is?" I asked. "Would you just stand there while I did the have-to-pee dance?"

The guard's cheeks definitely took on a reddish hue. He was saved from having to explain himself when someone appeared at the doorway. "Stop bullying the guards, Broccoli."

"Caprica!" I said as the princess entered the room. She was in one of her usual outfits, a tight red uniform not too dissimilar to the one on the guard I'd been talking to—*not bullying!*—a moment ago, though hers was tailored very neatly, and the gold-colored gilding looked like actual gold as opposed to yellow thread. "It's good to see you."

"Has it even been more than a day?" she asked.

"Does it matter how long it's been? I'm still happy to see you," I said. I pulled Caprica into a tight-tight hug, making sure to be careful where I placed my hands on her back. I didn't want to squish her wings.

Caprica patted my back in return. She was still a bit awkward about hugs, but I'd wear her down eventually. "Well, regardless of all that . . . how did it go?" She turned to Amaryllis and Awen, who gave her greetings of their own, though no hugs . . . yet.

"Dungeon cleared!" I cheered at an indoor-voice level.

"Broccoli's right, the dungeon was cleared," Amaryllis said. "She took out the Evil Roots. We'll have to wait and see whether the dungeon itself will heal after this. I imagine some of the people who went down with us will be writing reports on the entire event for you to peruse."

"They will," Caprica said, "but it might take some time before I get access to those. Still, if you say the dungeon was cleared, I'll believe you."

"Awa, thank you," Awen said.

Caprica found a seat on the plush couch and looked ready to say something when the butler sylph returned with a tray before him. He paused a bit on seeing the princess in the room, but then collected himself and placed his tray down on the coffee table before leaving the room with a bow.

There were slices of toast and pots of jam and little cream-filled pastries dusted in sugar. Sylph food was always super sweet.

"So, what's the next step?" Amaryllis asked as she plucked a pastry off the platter and ate it in one bite.

"That depends," Caprica said. She grabbed a piece of toast—which looked like it was still warm—and started spreading jam on it. "Mostly on what you want to do next. I imagine Father wouldn't mind continuing to pay you to clean out our dungeons."

"That could be fun," I said. "But it sounds a bit too much like doing the same thing over and over."

"Could be good for leveling," Amaryllis pointed out.

I frowned, then picked one of the pastries for myself. It was gooey and yummy and I was lucky I had Cleaning magic or else I'd need to get my gambeson cleaned, because some cream spilled out of the back of the pastry when I bit into it and fell into my lap. "Mmm, yeah, but we're here to save the World *and* have fun. Not just grind and get stronger."

Awen giggled. "I guess not."

"In that case," Caprica said, "I think there's another job you could do. But I'll have to ask Father about it first. This is a somewhat politically sensitive issue and one that I think you'd be well suited to take care of."

"Do tell," Amaryllis said.

Caprica grinned.

· Chapter Two ·

Broccoli & Friends Mercenary Company

Caprica took a moment more to make sure we were all comfortable, which meant asking about our tea preferences and what kinds of pastries we liked, then repeating that to one of her butlers. Once we were all comfy and settled, she got down to business. "You're familiar with the harpy delegation that was meant to be at the summit?" Caprica asked.

My friends and I all nodded. "What's going on with that, by the way?" I asked.

"The summit? For the moment it has been postponed. We haven't set any sort of date for the second attempt. It would be a faux pas to organize something too hastily. I imagine that it will be a few weeks until we start planning another summit, this time with greater security."

Amaryllis sighed. "And to think I wasted all that time preparing."

Caprica chuckled. "I wouldn't consider it entirely a waste. Your group left a much better impression on the nobility of Sylphfree than any speech could have."

With a proud sort of huff, Amaryllis gestured for Caprica to continue. "You were talking about the delegation. Has the airship been discovered?"

"Not quite," Caprica said. "We have an idea of where it was when it disappeared, but not an exact location. The army scoured the areas it was supposed to pass through, but nothing was found. Then they expanded their search to other routes the ship might've diverted to— but still, nothing."

"Which either means that the army is incompetent beyond measure or the ship never made it to Sylphfree in the first place," Amaryllis said.

"Maybe it flew too far east?" I suggested, trying to remember what Dirt looked like on a map.

"That would be very unlikely," Caprica said. "We did receive confirmation of a sighting to the north of the Golden Peak. The path the ship should have taken would have brought it farther north, then around through a well-marked passage between the northwestern mountains of Sylphfree. But the ship never arrived at the passage, so we now believe it likely disappeared in the territory of the Trenten Flats."

"So you want us to grab the *Beaver Cleaver*, head out there, and find the ship and all its passengers?" I asked.

Caprica hesitated, then nodded. "Partially correct. Though there are several details we'd need to work out beforehand, and I'm not certain if your vessel would be suitable for the quest at hand."

I crossed my arms. "The *Beaver*'s an excellent ship," I defended.

"I'm certain that it's a fine vessel. However, this quest would require a certain amount of . . . discretion, which wouldn't be easy to obtain if you were to just fly in with an airship and start searching for a potential crash site."

"Ah," Awen started. "Um, why aren't the sylphs looking? Why send us? If it isn't the *Beaver* that's making us, um, uniquely qualified, then what is it?"

Caprica hummed. "Mostly the issue comes down to politics. The United Republic of the Trenten Flats and the Kingdom of Sylphfree aren't allies. We're not enemies either, but things are tense right now. Having Sylphfreean ships roaming above the Flats would violate their territorial skies."

"Couldn't you explain the situation to them?" I asked. "A whole ship went missing, full of innocent people."

"And politicians," Awen added.

I nodded before continuing. "Even if the sylphs can't get involved, the seriousness of the situation should warrant a search by the cervids, right?"

"You'd think so, but the Trenten Flats have fewer ships than we do, and they're older—they were outdated when they were first launched. Asking them to do the work would raise tensions. Besides, we can't rule out the possibility that the Trenten Flats are the reason the vessel went missing in the first place."

Amaryllis sat up straighter. "You think the Trenten . . . what, *shot down* the harpy delegation?"

"The delegation was escorted," Caprica said. "It's not the case of one ship going down, but several. One vessel having an unfortunate accident and getting lost is plausible. A small fleet is less so. Had the fleet turned around to return to the Harpy Mountains, we would have heard about it by now."

"So, you need someone real discreet and sneaky to look around the Trenten Flats and find the missing delegation fleet. And, naturally, you thought of me and my friends," I said carefully. I was pretty sure Caprica knew that I didn't do sneaky very well.

Amaryllis snorted. "Princess, we're the most conspicuous people that have ever set foot on Dirt."

Caprica chuckled. "To be entirely fair, I wasn't expecting you to go unnoticed. What I *am* expecting is that the Trenten Flats won't know what to do with you. Legally, there is no reason you can't go sniffing around on your own initiative. Politically, it would be hard to blame any nation for your actions. Amaryllis, you have a reason to be looking for the delegation, even if you're not employed by the Nesting Kingdom. Awen, Broccoli, you're both strangers to these parts."

Amaryllis nodded along. She popped another pastry in her mouth, then chewed and swallowed. "I see what you're thinking. I can merely claim that the delegation is needed back to do its job. Broccoli and Awen can be acting as assistants and companions in my . . . let's call it a personal quest to discover what happened to the delegates I had to replace."

"That's exactly what I was hoping for, yes," Caprica said.

"I'm in," I said.

"We've barely heard all the details, Broccoli," Amaryllis said. "Besides, we need to discuss compensation."

There was a knock at the door to the lounge, and one of the guards reached over and opened it. A second later, both of them somehow went even more stiff than they had already been.

The reason why stepped into the room, followed by a pair of paladins who scanned the space as if any one of us might be a threat. "Hi, Reggie," I said to the king.

The king grinned and made his way to the couch Caprica was on. She slid to the side, making room for him next to her as he sat down across from us. "This is a less formal gathering than I'm used to," he noted.

I wasn't too sure about that. There were nearly as many guards in the room as there were non-guards.

"Formality isn't our strong suit," Amaryllis admitted.

"That's fine," the king replied. "I imagine that if Caprica is here, she has already highlighted the request I had?"

"You want us to sneak over to the Trenten Flats and find the delegation," I said. "Or . . . maybe not sneak over, but at least get there without people knowing that Sylphfree is involved?"

He nodded. "I would have embellished the mission a little more, but essentially, yes. The location of the delegation needs to be sussed out. The sooner the better. The Nesting Kingdom could level accusations against us any day now about their missing diplomats. I'm certain that news of their disappearance has already reached some ears on the Harpy Mountains."

"No doubt," Amaryllis said. "Are you doing anything to cover it up?"

"No," he said. "Innocence in matters like these can be difficult to prove, but I've found that covering up details and masking the truth only tends to make the truth stand out all the more. There are people with skills and classes who are exceptionally talented at discovering and connecting disparate facts together to draw an accurate conclusion."

That sounded really neat. Magic-empowered detectives!

"Wait!" I said. "Why haven't you used *them* to find the delegates?"

The king grinned. "Clever. But we thought of that already. Our own analysts haven't been able to discover any more of the delegation's trail. We have a few ideas, some theories—it is partially thanks to such analysts that we are confident the delegation vanished outside our territory—but nothing solid. We've also tried to scry for their location. The army, as you can imagine, has ample reason to keep a number of capable scryers around. So far though, we've found nothing conclusive."

Awen raised a hand like a schoolgirl asking a question. The king nodded to her, and she asked, "Um, what are the limitations of the scrying?"

"I would have a number of generals quite angry with me if I divulged that. Suffice to say, though, that there are issues of range. We cannot, for example, scry from here to the Harpy Mountains. The distance is too great. Nor can we pinpoint a person's location with great precision. There are spells that will point you toward a person, but they usually have two to three degrees of inaccuracy. Even triangulating from a few stations will point to a large possible range of locations a person could be in."

"Um," Awen said, "wouldn't that mean that, based on the range, you'd know where the delegation . . . isn't?"

The king tilted his head to the side. "Yes, we used that to mark out areas where the delegation ships aren't located. That will narrow down the area you'd need to search."

"Before we agree to all of this," Amaryllis started, "is this mission something you want us to organize on our own?"

"I was going to suggest that you team up with a few choice sylphs. I believe there is a paladin ready to escort you to the Trenten Flats, though I'm afraid the search, once there, will be up to you."

I rubbed at my chin. "We're going to need to bring the *Beaver Cleaver* closer," I said. "Not to do the actual search, but if we discover that the delegation left to go somewhere else and we need to chase it down, we need a fast, reliable ship that can do that." The *Beaver* wasn't the fastest ship, but it was very reliable!

"That can be arranged. I'll have someone bring the ship to the capital. If you could write a letter addressing your crew, that would be helpful," the king said.

I nodded along. That made perfect sense.

"And now on to the more interesting topic," Amaryllis said. "Remuneration."

The king chuckled. "How very mercenary. Yes, I wouldn't imagine giving anyone a quest like this without paying them back for their last one. Speaking of which . . ." He gestured to one of the paladins. The sylph reached under his armored cuirass and pulled out a lacquered wooden box, which he handed to the king. How did that box fit under his armor? I had no idea, unless the paladin was very, very thin under there. The box seemed heavy, especially as the king placed it on the coffee table with a *thunk*.

He undid a latch on the front of the box, opened it, then turned it around for us to see.

"Three hundred sylph ducats, as promised for a job well done," he said. "There will be more if this next mission is a success, of course."

The box had three rows of coins, all neatly placed in grooves obviously meant to hold them in place. I reached out and plucked one. It was heavy, which I expected of gold, and about the size of the circle I could make by touching my index finger to the tip of my thumb.

I held the coin up before me, face-side lined up next to the king's face. "Were these stamped a while ago?" I asked

One of his eyebrows rose. "Some years ago, yes. Have I aged poorly?"

I giggled and shook my head. "No, no. But you had more hair once."

"Broccoli!" Caprica gasped.

The king laughed. "Yes! I did! My wife reminds me frequently. Mostly I blame my overabundance of daughters."

"Father!"

"Broccoli, stop insulting the guy who can chop our heads off on a whim," Amaryllis said.

"Oh, oops. Sorry!" I said before placing the coin back into its box.

The king waved the apology away. "It's nothing. I do own a mirror or two and can see the truth for myself. Now, this is the promised reward for the last task you completed for us. A handsome reward, I'm certain."

I glanced at Amaryllis. I had no idea if this much gold was a lot or not. I figured it was, but my frame of reference wasn't ideal. Since arriving on Dirt I hadn't made much gold, but I didn't really need it either.

Amaryllis caught on to what I was wondering with just a look. "Yes, Broccoli, it's a lot. The sylph ducat is perhaps the most valuable coin on Dirt, or at least the parts I'm aware of. It's pure gold, not mixed with anything else. Three hundred gold is enough to purchase a small house in most cities."

"Oh, that's nice then," I said. "We can spend it on the *Beaver*! Make the ship even cooler, right Awen?"

"Ah? Yes, I can think of a few modifications that would cost about that much," Awen said. "A new engine wouldn't be cheap. But we don't really need much. The *Beaver Cleaver* is still very new."

The king cleared his throat. "I'll let you ladies discuss things further. You're invited to stay the night, if you wish. I wouldn't want you to start this mission without a good night's rest. Let Caprica know what you think."

And with that, the king was off, leaving us to make our choice.

· Chapter Three ·

Early to Bed and Early to Rise

We spent the rest of that day walking across Goldenalden, eating at the inn, and generally wasting time and having fun. The weather was nice and chilly, and we even got a flurry of snow that quickly melted away.

When noon hit, all of us started to feel really tired, and I think we were reminded that we hadn't slept at all the previous night.

We did end up spending the night at the palace, though only after returning to the inn where our stuff was. I might have been able to clean all of our clothes really well, but my friends still insisted on changing their underthings and grabbing their stuff.

We went to bed early in one of the guest wings of the palace.

I slept like a rock, blacking out for who knows how long, until a knock at the door woke me up.

"Miss, I was told by Lady Amaryllis to awaken your group at this hour," an unfamiliar voice said from the other side of the door.

I yawned. "Thank you!" I called back.

Then, because I could, I stretched my arms and legs out until every bit of me was shivering with tension, then melted back into the floofy mattress. The sylphs really knew how to make a good bed.

After lazing about for a bit until the sun's light reached the edge of the mattress, I rolled over and off the bed. Then I found my things where I'd dropped them on a clothing-chair (the chair that belonged in every bedroom, where clean clothes were piled) and got dressed for the day. I found Awen in the corridor, walking the slow shuffle of someone who wasn't entirely awake yet. "Good morning!" I cheered before giving her a morning hug.

"Awa?" Awen mumbled weakly. She stuffed her face against the crook of my neck. "Hmm. Morning."

"Did you sleep well?" I asked as I backed off.

She nodded. "I guess so. The bed was nice."

"I know! We should get a few of them for the *Beaver*. Do you think Caprica would help us grab a few?"

"You . . . want to steal beds from the royal palace to put on our airship?" Awen asked.

"Of course not. The beds here are nearly as big as our cabins. We'd need much smaller ones. Besides, stealing is wrong."

Awen nodded along, then stifled a yawn. "Did you see where Amaryllis went?"

I shook my head. "Just came out of my room, sorry. Let's wander around until we find her."

That turned out to be a very inefficient way of finding our harpy friend, though we did end up meandering into that big dining room where we'd spoken to the king the other day. Caprica, her little sister Gabrielle, her older sister Stephania, and the queen were all at the table having breakfast.

"Good morning! Have you seen Amaryllis anywhere?" I said.

Caprica looked up from her meal. It seemed like some sort of porridge with lots of sweet sauce and jam on it. "No, I haven't," she said. "But you can wait here and eat breakfast. There should be enough for a few more. Unless anyone minds?" She glanced at her family.

"Of course we don't," Gabrielle said. She grinned and gestured to the seat across from hers. "Come, sit! There's enough for everyone."

I noticed that they all sat a bit apart from one another, and that all four of them also had books and papers out on the table. Stephania was looking over a newspaper and the queen was reviewing some reports. Gabrielle was the only one not working while eating.

"I'm sure Amaryllis will show up eventually," Caprica said. She frowned at the breakfast laid out before her. "Should we hide the eggs?"

"Ah," I said. "I guess? I don't know if Amaryllis is all that easy to offend . . . Well, actually, yes, she *is* easy to offend, and she did say that eating eggs is quite taboo among the harpies, but I don't think she'd make a fuss over it."

"Aren't there eggs in all of our pastries?" Gabrielle asked. "I haven't spent a lot of time in the kitchens, but I think they use eggs there for baking."

"Oh," I said. "Well, I don't think she's allergic to them?"

I sat down across from Gabrielle and Awen took a seat next to me. She kept glancing at the queen, but the older sylph woman was focused on her paperwork and her jam-covered toast.

Caprica gestured to one of the butlers hiding in a nook next to a pillar, and he swept in and plucked the eggs away with one hand while laying out fresh plates for Awen and I, with little folded napkins and shiny silverware.

Butlers were so cool!

"Please, serve yourselves," Caprica said.

"Thank you!" I said before I did just that. Sylph breakfasts were heavy on the bread, pastries, and jams, with a few meats here and there that I avoided. They smelled nice, but I didn't need a tummy ache so early in the day.

"I heard that you went on a big adventure at the Dungeon of the Lullaby Knight," Gabrielle said. "Was it scary?"

I nodded. "Oh yes, very. Some of the floors were easy, but there's this one floor where you have to cross a room that's filled with all of your worst nightmares. It was awful!"

Gabrielle gasped, hands over her mouth, but for all that, she still looked interested. "But you braved past those, right?"

"Yeah!" I said. "Me and my friends are real brave."

"And humble," Stephania mumbled.

"We'll be putting that bravery to the test later," Caprica said. "We found a way to carry you to the location of that quest Father gave you."

"Caprica," the queen said, without looking up from her papers. "Is it wise to discuss secretive matters over breakfast?"

"Usually, no, but Broccoli can't keep a secret. All a spy would have to do is ask and she'd spill it all. Besides, we're in the heart of the palace. If we can't speak here, then nowhere is safe."

My cheeks, already filled with a mouthful of toast, puffed out even more. I could *totally* keep a secret! I . . . just didn't have any secrets to keep, was all.

"How are we going to get to the Trenten Flats?" Awen asked carefully, still glancing at the queen.

Caprica grinned. "I recall you mentioning that Paladin Bastion"—she ignored Stephania's snort and Gabrielle's sigh—"promised to let you ride some wyverns. We have some knights who would be more than willing to fly over the Trenten Flats to escort you and your companions to a predetermined location."

"Oh, that sounds fun," I said. "Is riding a wyvern anything like riding a dragon?"

"You'd have to ask someone who rode a dragon to learn the difference," Caprica said with a grin. Then her eyes narrowed. "You . . . don't know anyone who has ridden a dragon, do you?"

I had kind of forgotten that the sylphs really didn't like dragons. That dislike wasn't mutual, though. From what I gathered, dragons loved the sylphs. As in-flight snacks.

"Of–Of course not?" I stammered while cringing away from Caprica's curious look.

"You were right," the queen said. "She can't keep a secret."

"She really can't," Amaryllis agreed as she entered the room. She crossed the space, paused to bow to the queen—wait, were Awen and I supposed to do that too?—then continued on and pulled out a seat next to Awen. "What is Broccoli failing to keep secret now?"

"Amaryllis! You could have distracted them by changing the topic, at least," I said.

"I didn't feel like it," she said. The butler swept by and placed another plate before her, and she started loading it up with food.

"I was just telling Awen and Broccoli about our plan to get you to the Trenten Flats quickly. It involves taking a flight of wyverns over the Flats," Caprica said.

"Not exactly inconspicuous," Amaryllis said.

"More so than you'd imagine," Caprica said. "Wyverns are native to the Sylphfree mountains, but the wild ones range over the Flats in search of prey. Seeing a group of them isn't common, but it isn't unheard of. From the ground, it's difficult to tell that a wyvern has a rider at all."

Amaryllis considered it, then nodded. "That's one way to make it there. How do we return? On foot? Can we charter a ship back from one of the towns in the Trenten Flats?"

"We can give you a magical device to signal us," Caprica said.

"You have long-range magical signaling devices?" I asked. If that was the case, why didn't they have telephones and the like?

"I was thinking of giving you a special banking ring," Caprica said.

Oh! Like the one Amaryllis had that connected to the bank in the Harpy Mountains. That was less a communication device and more one that let people teleport things back and forth. I'd considered getting one for myself, but we kept traveling far from any central banks—too far for their limited range.

"That could work," Amaryllis said. "Do you have any more details for us, other than 'go to the Trenten Flats and find the diplomats'? That's a little too vast of a region for just three people to cover."

"Three very talented people," Caprica said. "But yes, we have a few potential leads you can follow up on. I'd suggest that you travel to Fort Middlesfaire. It's one of the many fortress-cities the cervids built as they pushed north. One of the first ones, actually. From what I've read, it's a prosperous enough little city now, centering around the fort. There are dozens of smaller towns around it that provide the food and supplies needed for the city to function."

"You think we'll learn about the delegation there?" I asked.

Caprica nodded. "If you ask around, most likely. Fort Middlesfaire is a central hub for the region, and an important stop for the trade caravans circling around the Harpy Mountains. Keep in mind that most commodities in the Trenten Flats are transported over land. Traders have long convoys that require frequent stops, so they enjoy having forts less than a day's travel apart. Bandits are an issue as well."

Bandits? That sounded awful. And a little exciting.

"Don't worry! I'm sure we'll make lots of new friends that can help us figure out what happened to the diplomats," I said.

"Your conviction is appreciated," Caprica said. "The wyverns should be ready to take off within a few hours. I know it's on short notice, but I think haste might be more important here than caution."

"That's okay, we're always ready for adventure, right girls?" I asked.

Awen was finally looking awake, and Amaryllis just made a vague *so-so* gesture in the air.

I pouted. So much for that. "Well, *I'm* always ready, in any case. Just let me get Weedbane and . . . do you think we'll have time to prepare a lunch-box or two?"

"Of course," Caprica said. "I'll have the cooks prepare a meal that you can carry with you. We'll have some packs with ready-to-eat-meals as well. They're . . . frankly, barely edible, but they keep for a long time and do provide all of the necessary nutrition. Perhaps you can even just bring a normal soldier's kit with you. It will have everything you need."

"And it will paint them as coming from Sylphfree," Stephania pointed out idly.

"Ah, that is true," Caprica said. "I'm not well versed in this kind of subterfuge."

Stephania nodded. "Even Gabrielle is subtler than you."

Gabrielle giggled. "No one expects the Gabquisition!" she said before her giggles cut off with a cough. She still laughed though, even as Caprica patted her back.

"Right, once you're done with breakfast, you can head out to the wyvern tower. That's where you'll find the wyvern knights and Paladin Bastion, who is no doubt dutifully waiting for you."

"I can't wait," I said.

Awen and Amaryllis both perked up a little. I think they were almost as excited to fly on wyvernback as I was!

· Chapter Four ·

Introductions Are in Order

The carriage rattled and shook as we rode up toward the edge of the city. We weren't going to any of the sections that hung off the side of the mountain, or even one of the many ports surrounding Goldenalden. No, we were heading up, toward the higher parts of the city where it more or less disappeared into the mountain.

Even after just twenty minutes of riding along steep switchback roads, I could tell that the air had grown a little bit thinner. It was certainly colder. Awen was stuck between Amaryllis and me with a heap of blankets on top of herself, and she was still shivering a little.

I shifted around and wrapped an arm over her shoulder. "There, that'll warm you up a little," I said.

"Thank you," Awen said.

"You know, it's only going to get colder once we're in the air," Amaryllis noted. "And the air will only grow thinner."

"I'm used to it on board a ship," Awen said. "But being on the ground is different somehow. Also, I don't think we usually flew all that high with the *Beaver*."

I grinned. "I'm kind of excited about this. Last time, when we flew with Rhawrexdee, I could barely tell what was happening. I spent the entire flight focusing on not falling off his back."

Amaryllis gave me a look. "You're so reckless," she said.

"I'm sure the sylphs have a bunch of safety precautions. They seem like very safety-minded people," I said.

"Yes, probably because they had a few people like you in their ranks before they slipped out of the gene pool," Amaryllis said.

I harrumphed at her. "You know, what you're doing now isn't legal here."

"What?" Amaryllis asked, her grin shifting away in place of confusion. "What are you talking about?"

"Being so smug isn't allowed here."

"I doubt they made a law about it," Amaryllis said, rather smugly at that. "It's called smuggling, and it's not allowed."

Amaryllis stared at me, then she looked to Awen. "Can we switch seats? I need to smack Broccoli around a bit."

We tussled for a minute, filling the carriage with laughter and Awen's squeaky giggles. Eventually though, the carriage rolled to a stop and we all paused to look out and see what was going on. We were at a gatehouse next to the roadway. It was manned by a single young sylph dressed in an ill-fitting guard's outfit. He spoke to the carriage driver, and we were quickly let through.

Our carriage circled around a driveway, then stopped in front of a tower that stuck out from the mountainside. This had to be built with magic. There was careful stonework on the outside, but the rearmost wall seemed to almost melt into the mountain itself. It reminded me of the old palace where the summit had taken place.

"I suppose this is it," Amaryllis said. She pushed the door open, peeked outside, then jumped out. Awen shed her blankets and did the same, with me following right behind her.

"I guess we go to the tower," I said with a gesture to the building in question. There were a few other places nearby, some newer-looking barracks and a warehouse with a tin roof, but there didn't seem to be too much going on up here.

"I'll be heading back down, as ordered," the carriage driver said. "Do you need any help with your belongings?"

I shook my head, jumped up onto the back of the carriage, and then tossed our stuff down to Awen and Amaryllis, who caught all of our gear. We didn't have all that much. A few tools, some weapons, and the packs that Caprica had found for us with survival meals and tents and such.

After saying goodbye to the carriage driver, we started toward the tower only for the front doors to glide open, letting a few sylphs spill out. One of them was immediately recognizable.

"Bastion!" I cheered.

The paladin smiled. "Hello, Broccoli. Awen, Amaryllis," he greeted with a nod to my friends. He planted his feet in place so that my hug wouldn't bowl him over, patting my back while chuckling. "It hasn't been that long. I don't know if I deserve such treatment."

"Of course you do," I said as I backed out of the hug. "You're a friend, and I haven't seen you in over three hours; that's enough reason for a proper hugging. It's been days. So much has happened!"

Bastion conceded the point with a nod. "I suppose we have all been rather busy," he said. He half turned to gesture to the two sylphs who had come out with him. "Let me introduce my companions here. This is Menos Salvonote and Winnow Underwing."

Menos was a very young sylph knight with a breastplate that looked a tiny bit too big for his chest. He was also wearing a leather uniform, with fur ruffs at the neck and sleeves and I think also around the holes for his wings. He nodded, which made the leather-and-plate cap on his head (with big goggles) bounce a bit. "Pleasure," he said.

"Hello," Winnow replied. She was older and just a pinch shorter than Bastion, with a serious set to her brow but bright eyes that seemed curious and happy. She had on the same sort of uniform as Menos, though she lacked the breastplate and cap.

"These are Ladies Awen Bristlecone and Amaryllis Albatross, and this is Captain Broccoli Bunch," Bastion introduced us. Amaryllis nodded curtly and Awen gave them a little wave. "Captain Willow and Knight Menos here will be accompanying me in escorting you to the Trenten Flats."

"Oh?" I asked. "You're both . . . What do we call people who fly on wyverns here?"

"Wyvern knights," Menos said. It was clear he was pretty proud of his job. "The few and the brave. The kings of the open skies."

Winnow chuckled. "We're hardly the kings of the sky. We are knights, though, which ought to suggest a certain pattern of behavior." The last was very pointedly aimed right at Menos, who straightened.

I nodded along. "That sounds really cool. Will we be flying together? Two to a wyvern?"

"That was the plan, yes," Bastion said. "It's safer that way. Having someone inexperienced leading a wyvern, especially so far from the usual training airspace, would be unwise."

"So, you'll be adventuring with us again," Amaryllis said to Bastion.

The paladin nodded. "One more time, at least," he said. "Though this time we are merely bringing you to your destination. It isn't much of an adventure at all."

"Oh, don't worry," I said. "There are always plenty of things that can go wrong: monsters showing up, bad guys to fight . . ."

Amaryllis whapped me behind the head with her feathers. "Don't go begging for trouble, Broccoli. The World is liable to give you more than you can handle."

I pouted at her, but she was probably right.

"Do you want to meet the wyverns?" Winnow asked. And just like that, she had all of my attention.

We walked into the tower, which turned out to look more like an office building on the inside, with the first couple of floors obviously dedicated to all the paperwork and bureaucracy needed to take care of a group of wyvern knights.

"This is the Goldenalden wyvern tower," Winnow said. "We have one of these towers next to most of the important cities, and there are a few more dotted here and there across the mountains, some in secret locations, others out in the open."

"How many wyverns are here?" I asked.

"You mean those bred in captivity? Fewer than a thousand across the nation. Half of those aren't ever going to be used for any sort of fighting. We do have courier positions and other jobs for those wyverns who don't pass the training to do aerial combat," Winnow explained.

"What about in the wild?" Awen asked.

"Far fewer," Winnow said. "Unfortunately, wyverns are a threat to a lone sylph, and they can even cause damage to small airships. They'll avoid cities unless something has disturbed them, but they're still a threat. The only wild flights are far to the north and east, where settlements are sparse and there's no real air traffic."

That was a little sad, but probably understandable. We continued to climb up the stairs while Winnow told us more about the wyverns. They were apparently gluttonous eaters if you let them be. They were also lizards, so they were cold-blooded and really enjoyed a bit of warmth. Fire was one of the rewards they gave to a well-behaved wyvern, so we didn't need to panic if we saw a knight spraying one with some magical fire.

We reached the top floor of the tower. One half of the room was a ramp leading up onto the flat roof, where I imagined wyverns could take off. The base of the tower was dug into the mountain and was filled with big pens with metal bars between them.

Wyverns were sleeping inside those, and I started to feel nervous about our flight for the first time. They were so big! Each wyvern had a pen big enough that we could have parked the *Beaver* inside it. Well, if we were willing to squish it in a little.

A wyvern raised its head up from the bed of straw it was resting on and watched us walk past. Its head was taller than I was, even with my ears. It could have chomped me in half if it wanted to, I think.

"We'll be taking Bloodfang, Greencrest, and Little Doug today," Winnow said.

I blinked. "Those are the names of the wyverns?" I asked.

She nodded. "They are. They should be saddled up for us already, but we'll go and meet them first. It's good form to let them get used to you before a flight. Especially since none of you are sylph. You'll look and smell different from what they're used to."

We stopped by Little Doug's pen first. Menos stepped up, opened the slim door to the cage, and walked in without hesitation.

Little Doug had a chest bigger around than the carriage we'd used to get to the tower and was as long as the *Beaver Cleaver* was wide. "Hey there, little guy," Menos said as he patted the wyvern's snout.

"Why is he called Little Doug?" I asked.

"Oh, he was the runt," Winnow said. "Almost failed every test. By all rights he shouldn't have been trained any further, but we discovered that he's one of the most docile wyverns we've ever raised. Not optimal for an aerial combatant, but he doesn't mind new riders flying on him. So he's the training mount for a lot of newer knights, and when we need to escort VIPs around, Little Doug's our go-to."

"Oh," I said. So he was just a friendly little guy. I liked him already!

"He seems nice," Awen said.

"Good, then you can ride on him with Knight Menos. Go on in, he'll show you how to greet Doug, and then we'll have some of the stable hands load your gear up," Winnow said.

A wide-eyed Awen was ushered into the wyvern's cage. She stood back for a bit, but Awen was quite brave when she wanted to be (and when the situation wasn't a social one), so she walked over to the wyvern and gave it her hand to sniff as if it were a big dog.

"A wyvern's sense of smell isn't great," Winnow said, "but their eyesight is second to none. Their hearing is awful, though it's just good enough that they can hear orders."

"How long have you been working with them?" I asked as we continued on.

"Oh, nearly a decade now. Which is a long time for a wyvern knight. It's very much a young person's career."

"How long do wyverns . . . work for?" I asked.

"Three, maybe four decades," Winnow said. "Depending on injuries and how gracefully they age. We train them to be comfortable with multiple knights, but they do have favorites. Come, this is Greencrest; Paladin Bastion will be flying her."

"Broccoli," Bastion said, his tone very serious. "You cannot keep the wyverns as pets."

I blinked. Why would he even say that?

· Chapter Five ·

Flight of the Wyverns

You're a good little almost-dragon, aren't you? Yes you are! Yes you *are!*" I cooed to Miss Greencrest the wyvern. The big beastie's emotions were hard to read. It didn't have as expressive a face as most mammals, or even the few dragons I'd met, but I think Miss Greencrest was still quite happy with the way I scritched her under the chin, if the way she pressed down on my hand was any indication.

"She seems to like you," Winnow said. "That's good. You can ride her along with Paladin Bastion."

"Oh? I don't mind which wyvern I fly with. They all seem very sweet and friendly. Isn't that right, Miss Greencrest? Do you want to be my friend?"

```
Greencrest
Desired Quality: Someone who will give her meat
Dream: To fly and hunt
```

I chuckled, then glanced around. There was a metal bucket in the central corridor with the words *Bones and Gristle* painted on the side. I'd bet those were snacks. "Can I give her a treat?" I asked.

"Certainly," Winnow said. "But she'll have to be saddled in a moment, so do so quickly. And take care not to have your hand bitten off."

"Okay!" I said.

Winnow led Amaryllis deeper in, toward the cage of the third wyvern we'd be flying. Bloodfang was a big boy of a wyvern with reddish scales. He bumped his head against the cage as Winnow approached, looking pretty excited to see the knight.

I got a honking big chunk of meat for Greencrest, who gobbled it up greedily while the other wyverns in the cages around us looked on with jealousy. (I *did* want to give them all snacks, but I wasn't sure if I was allowed to do that. Maybe they were on a specific diet?) Then I had to leave her cage as a group of pages and squires came around with harnesses and nets and big leather pieces that they started to strap over Greencrest.

The other two wyverns were being prepared too. I noted that the barding had chainmail between layers of padding and leather. It covered a lot of the wyvern's sternum and ribs, and they also had a sort of metal helmet that fit around their heads, giving them a fearsome appearance.

The saddle was at the front, just above the wyvern's wing joints. There was a lot of flexible material there, probably so the wyvern could move their wings unimpeded. The seats looked like they were padded, but I suspected it wasn't going to be super comfy.

The door to Little Doug's cage was opened and Menos led him out. Awen clutched on to the saddle while the wyvern moved with careful grace. A few more squires approached with some last bits of equipment that were probably too tricky to fit while the wyvern was still in its enclosure.

Greencrest was led out next. I moved back so that I wouldn't be in anyone's way and watched as the wyvern slithered—well, as much as a reptile as long as a bus could slither—out of her cage and allowed the sylph working with the wyvern knights to equip her properly. Allowed, because I had no doubt that things would be quite different if she didn't want to be fussed over.

The wyverns all had thick, corded muscles just beneath their scaly-cool skin, especially along their backs and flanks. I walked over to Greencrest's front with another snack, then patted her on the snoot while she munched through what I suspected was a goat's femur bone.

"Will you need a hand climbing aboard?" Bastion asked.

He had changed while I wasn't paying attention. He still wore his shiny paladin breastplate, as well as the greaves and vambraces, but he had removed most of the rest of his armor. The sylphs around him were acting a bit more carefully now that he was there. A paladin was a big deal in Sylphfree.

"I think I can manage," I said. "But we should probably wait until we're outside?"

He nodded. "Indeed," he said before reaching up to Greencrest's head and giving it a rub. We both had to move back as a squire stepped up apologetically and started to strap a helmet on the wyvern's head. There was lots of padding, and it looked custom-made, so it was probably fairly comfortable.

Another sylph passed by and handed Bastion a set of reins that led up to the bridle around the wyvern's head. Once Greencrest was fully equipped, we started walking toward the exit, only I was stopped a few steps away.

"Ma'am," a young sylph in armor similar to Menos's and Winnow's said.

"Yes?" I asked.

"Ah, we have some equipment for you and your companions," she said. "It was interesting, finding things in your . . . approximate size range."

"Will I need to change?" I asked with a tap to my breastplate.

She shook her head. "No, no, the harnesses are meant to go over a knight's armor, so you'll be fine. The overcoat will give you another layer for the journey. Trust me, you'll appreciate it—unless you happen to have self-heating magic."

"I don't think I have any magic like that," I admitted.

The nice knight brought me aside to a small room with all sorts of other equipment, then helped me into a harness made of tough leather straps. It ran around my chest and over my arms and between my legs, with parts strapped to my thighs and upper arms. There were lots of buckles that clinked and jingled, and I had to squish up my skirts to be able to fit into the bottom part of the harness.

I probably looked silly, but then the knight gave me a big coat made of some very long fur. It had slits for my arms and more slits so that I could access the harness buckles through the furry material.

"Oh, this is cozy," I said as I hugged myself. I was now the softest bun ever.

"You'll need it. It gets cold midflight, especially with any metal armor on," the knight said. "Here, the caps aren't fashionable, but they'll keep your hair out of your face, and the goggles will let you actually see."

She handed me a leather cap with thick cloth pads around the outside of it. The inside was filled with more of the same fur, and the front of the cap had a half-mask that could be buttoned up on one side to cover everything from my nose down. It even had goggles with thick glass. It was a good thing I didn't wear glasses or else that bit would have been tricky.

I did encounter one big problem, though. Or rather, two of them. "What do I do with my ears?" I asked.

The knight blinked, then slowly looked up above my head. "Ah," she said.

A couple of minutes and a couple of holes later, I pulled the cap on tight, ears wiggling around out of the modifications we'd brought to the cap. "Thanks," I said.

New skill acquired: Wyvern Riding

Rank: D

Oh, that was neat!

"No problem. Please make sure you're well hooked onto the harnesses before you take off. It would shame us all if you were blown off your wyvern's back midflight. Not to mention search-and-rescue missions aren't any fun."

I nodded. I wouldn't want to inconvenience anyone by splattering myself against the countryside somewhere.

I left the room and a grinning Awen went in after me, followed by Amaryllis, who was led by another knight.

"This isn't going to be as quiet an event as I had wished," Bastion said as I returned to his side.

"What do you mean?" I asked.

He gestured to the many sylphs loitering around. They didn't seem to have much to do anymore. Too many of them were sweeping the floor with brooms just to look busy. At least the place would be very clean if they continued to stick around.

"Oh," I said.

"Oh indeed," Bastion replied. "I think we're all gaining a fair bit of attention. I had hoped that the mission would be discreet."

"Well, they don't know where we're going, do they?"

"That's true. Still, if the rumor goes around, it might reach the ears of someone who'll feed it to the cervids, and when they get reports of your rather distinct group in the Trenten Flats it won't be difficult for them to put two and two together."

"Is that a bad thing?" I asked.

Bastion rubbed at his chin. "Not necessarily. Even if the wrong cervid learns about you, it doesn't mean they'll act in a way that would be immediately detrimental. But that's asking for the mission to go without a hitch. Never rely on your adversary doing what's convenient for you."

"They're not really our adversary, though."

"If you're trying to talk sense into her, I'd just give it up as a lost cause," Amaryllis said as she stalked over with a jingle of metal on metal from all the belts she wore.

I blinked. That had been surprisingly mean of her. She was always a bit snarky, and didn't mind calling me a moron, but . . . "Are you nervous about flying?" I asked her.

Her chest puffed out, feathers going poofy. "I'm part bird, Broccoli, I'm hardly going to be nervous about flying."

"It's okay to be a little afraid about something new," I soothed her. "Flying like this is something you've never done. Well, besides that one time with Rhawrexdee, but that was different." I nodded. "When I'm scared, I find that hugs make the scary feelings go away. Do you want a hug?"

Amaryllis was glaring at me, but her puffiness had changed in quality, and I think I had the measure of her. A moment later, she as much as confirmed it when she huffed a *yes-you're-right-but-I'll-never-in-a-million-years-admit-it* sort of huff.

So I gave her a big tight hug and Amaryllis pretended that no one was watching as she returned it.

"Oh, we're doing hugs now?" Awen asked.

She didn't look the least bit nervous about the flight. Meeting so many new people might have made her a little nervous, but I think Awen was really excited about taking off and flying around.

"All right, everyone," Winnow said. "Everything's packed up. Last chance to reconsider."

"I think we'll be okay," I said.

The knight nodded, and we followed her outside. The three wyverns we were going to ride were lined up to one side, their big talons gripping onto a set of logs bolted to the edge of the tower roof. Judging by all the scratches on the wood, I guessed that was where most wyverns launched from.

Bastion fluttered up onto Greencrest's back with a few flaps of his wings and I hopped up behind him. There were a lot of buckles to clamp on to my harness, and we took our time making sure all of them were properly secured while a couple of sylphs packed our things away in big saddlebags near the wyvern's flanks.

"We'll be flying at a brisk but easy pace," Winnow called out over the wind. "Nothing showy. Understood, Menos?"

"Yes, ma'am!" the other knight said.

"All right then." Winnow tugged at Bloodfang's reins and the wyvern growled eagerly as he spread his wings wide. "Let's go!"

I gasped as Greencrest spread her own wings, bunched her legs up, then threw us up and forward.

The wyvern's wings flapped hard and fast, with great big *whups* that snapped out at every beat. My tummy did a little flip as we started to rise. Then we hit some sort of updraft and our slow ascent became a lot faster.

I laughed as we circled over the tower. Goldenalden was spread out below us, and only the highest of the airships were even with us.

I heard Awen laughing too, and noticed Amaryllis's very white face as she gripped on to Knight Winnow atop Bloodfang.

"Follow me," Winnow shouted over the wind. And with that, we banked around and started across Sylphfree.

· Chapter Six ·

Successful Insertion

Flying wyvernback was awesome!

It was also, I realized after a few minutes, a literal pain in the behind. The saddles we had were designed more to prevent chafing against the tough scales on the wyvern's neck than to provide a soft cushion.

The wyverns, or at least Greencrest, shifted their necks up and down slightly with every big, sweeping wingbeat, which meant that we were constantly moving in our saddles. The multitude of straps now made a lot more sense; they kept us in place even as we were forced to shift with the wyvern's movements.

Bastion leaned down ahead of me with a rein in each hand, head lowered so that he was almost hugging Greencrest's neck. I saw him glance back quickly, as if to make sure I was still there. "Are you well?" he asked.

"Yuppers!" I called back against the blowing wind.

"If you need to warm yourself, use Fire mana. Though be careful with it, you could burn yourself internally or externally."

"It's fine," I said. "I'm from Canada."

I think Bastion didn't quite understand what that meant, but he just shrugged and refocused on flying.

We were in the middle of the formation of three. Ahead of us, Winnow and Amaryllis were pushing forward with Bloodfang, and Little Doug took up the rear with Menos and Awen. If I understood things correctly, at some point we'd switch around so each wyvern could take turns acting as windbreak for the others.

"Are we going faster than if we were on an airship?" I asked.

Bastion shook his head. "Not really. A fast airship will outpace the fastest wyvern. The advantage with wyverns tends to be their mobility and size, as well as their acceleration. The average wyvern can fly circles around even the most maneuverable airship, and they're much smaller targets. They're discreet too."

"Discreet?"

Bastion gestured to his ear. "Not nearly as loud as an airship. The wyvern knights are excellent at hunting down air and sea pirates, especially at night. A wyvern with a handler and a mage riding it can deliver a pretty heavy blow to a ship, coming in from angles where an airship might not be able to defend itself."

I supposed that ships like the *Beaver* were pretty noisy, especially compared to a lizard of prey like a wyvern. "Hey, can wyverns fly on airships?"

Bastion shrugged. "It's happened before. The wyvern knights have a ship or two in their employ that are built to house and launch wyverns, though the wyverns take up a lot of space and tend to dislike roosting onboard a ship. At least, that's what I understood from the experiments."

"That's still kind of neat," I said. I shifted my bum again to try and find a comfortable position. "How long will it take to reach our destination?" I asked.

"We'll be arriving by late afternoon or early evening," Bastion said. "It'll depend on the winds and weather. Though, the skies are predicted to be calm. We have stations all around the nation that report back to the capital, and some talented individuals have skills that let them predict the weather."

That sounded very useful. "I guess we're using wyverns because they're sneakier, otherwise it would be better to use an airship, right?" I asked.

"This mission is supposed to be quiet, yes," he replied. "Having a whole crew in on it would spread the news around a lot more. And airships are noticeable. The Trenten Flats aren't the most observant, but they'll see a ship landing on their territory."

We continued to fly, and after a while I tucked my hands into the big fur coat I'd been given to keep my fingers warm. I was regretting not wearing thicker socks, or maybe some boots too. My toes were freezing. My ear-tips weren't any better, especially as they flapped in the passing wind.

It wasn't all that bad, though. I got to hang out with Bastion after not seeing him for a whole couple of days, and the slow trip gave me plenty of time and reason to practice circulating mana. I turned some of my raw mana into Fire mana, then with a bit of help from Way of the Mystic Bun, I pushed it toward my feet, then into my hands and back again, as if I was going to launch an attack but then pulled back.

The warmth was nice, thawing out my toes and warming my shoes.

At the same time, I took in the passing scenery. The mountains of Sylph-free were quite beautiful. Dozens of peaks, all jammed in together with deep valleys between them. I saw countless plateaus where little fields were growing, and I noticed a few villages next to rivers near the lowlands. Just little spots with a couple of dozen homes, some fields, and maybe a mill by the river.

The towns hadn't been on any of the maps of Sylphfree I'd seen, but maybe they were too small to be noteworthy.

I let my imagination run wild for a bit, putting myself in the shoes of some normal farmer living in a peaceful little town like that, barely more than a hamlet, where you'd grow up knowing everyone and where you'd dream of maybe visiting the city one day.

Then I shook my head and recalled that I was currently riding what was basically a small dragon. Anything my imagination could come up with was objectively less cool than what I was currently doing.

The flight continued on through the afternoon. My tummy protested a bit after so long without a snack, but I didn't complain. I was glad I didn't drink much before leaving either. We couldn't exactly make a pitstop along the way.

The sun was right overhead as we finally escaped the grasp of the mountainous terrain around Sylphfree. The land below us dipped down into rocky crags, then leveled off, with only the occasional bumpy hill below. The world of ice and gray rock was replaced by verdant fields and open plains with a few clumps of trees growing where they could find respite from the wind.

"See that little mountain to the north?" Bastion asked. He pointed to our right.

"I see it," I said. It would have been an impressive peak anywhere else, but with the Sylphfree mountains as a backdrop it was kind of underwhelming.

"That's Mount Goldshire. Once we're to the west of that, we'll start looking for a place to drop you off."

I nodded. "Okay!" I said, since he couldn't see me. "Any tips for when we're in the Trenten Flats?"

Bastion didn't reply for a minute, thinking. "I know you like trusting people, but be careful with the locals. They're superstitious, and they don't trust strangers easily."

I'd have to win them over the hard way, then, with lots of patience and niceness. I could work with a bit of a challenge, I was sure. "And what about our mission?"

"Get to the fort, ask around," Bastion said. "Then leave before you wear out your welcome. If it comes to it, you can likely divulge that you've come from Goldenalden. We don't have excellent political or diplomatic ties with the Trenten Flats, but at worst, you will only be *temporarily* imprisoned."

"That makes it sound a lot more dangerous than I expected," I admitted. I'd been hoping for a fun time, not something overly dangerous. I knew there were risks, of course, but still.

"You'll be in a foreign land. Keep your guard up. And while you're there, you might want to consider practicing your magic and combat where you can. It's a little late to hone those kinds of skills, but some added proficiency is better than none."

"Is the wildlife around here dangerous?" I asked.

"Somewhat. Lots of large predatory cats, some very territorial land beasts, and a few nasty local creatures. There's a kind of snake common to the region, and slimes are abundant during the right time of the year too. Stick to the roads if you want to avoid them, though that will mean that you'll encounter more guard patrols than otherwise."

"Okay. We'll do our best to stay safe. Or at least safe-ish."

Bastion glanced back at me. "You're an honest girl, so I'll take your word for it."

Our flight continued, though only for another half hour or so. Eventually, we started to circle over a particularly hilly bit of terrain. The wyverns shifted, and then, on Winnow's command, we swooped downward.

I heard Amaryllis and Awen screaming, so I joined in too, arms loose above me as if I were on a big roller coaster. The dive leveled off soon enough, then we skimmed the top of a hill and the wyverns flared out their wings to arrest our momentum.

With big meaty thumps, our rides landed at a run with their taloned feet racing below. Finally, we came to a full stop near the bottom of a valley nestled between a few hills.

"All right, let's unbuckle you," Bastion said.

I helped him undo the clasps holding me in place. Once I was free, I leapt off Greencrest's back and landed with bent knees next to the wyvern. "Thanks for the ride," I told her as I gave the underside of her chin a proper scritching.

The wyvern huffed contentedly at my face and I had to wipe off some drool with a bit of Cleaning magic.

My friends were dropped off too, and we started to collect our equipment. Mostly those were the backpacks from Caprica with plenty of survival stuff and of course our various weapons and other things. I slipped out of my harness and handed it back to Bastion, who stuffed it into one of Greencrest's saddlebags.

"This is the last we'll see of each other for a couple of days, I think," Bastion said. "If I don't hear from you for longer than that, I'll start looking for any major signs of trouble. Burnt down villages, destroyed dungeons, that sort of thing."

"I'll be sure to leave a super-obvious trail if we're in trouble," I said.

"That is less reassuring than you probably thought it was," Bastion said.

I grinned up at him. "I'm kidding," I said. With a little hop to reach him up in the saddle, I gave my sylph friend a quick goodbye hug. "Stay safe too, okay Bastion?"

"Always," he said.

"And watch over Caprica while we're off. I bet she gets lonely."

"I'll see what I can do," he replied.

And with that, I rejoined my friends. Amaryllis was fixing her feathers back into place—the long flight had mussed them up—and Awen was swapping out the loaner fur coat for her regular blue trench coat.

"Are the both of you ready?" Amaryllis asked.

Awen nodded.

"I think so. Where are we heading to?"

Awen pulled out a small compass, then tugged a folded-up map from her pack. "Awa, I think we're about . . . here. Which means that if we're going to Fort Middlesfaire, we need to go west and a little bit south."

Amaryllis glanced at the map, then at the compass, then she stood taller and looked westward. "I noticed a river over there while we were in the air. It's quite a ways off. We'll need to find a way to cross it."

The three of us paused as our friends took off without much fanfare other than a few heavy wingbeats from the wyverns.

"Okay," I said as they became distant specks above. "Let's get started?"

"Yes. The sooner we move away from here, the better," Amaryllis said. "Someone might try to investigate the area if they saw the wyverns coming down."

"And we need to find a place for a camp," I pointed out.

"So soon?" Amaryllis asked.

"Well, I don't know about you two, but I'm real hungry, and we flew right past lunchtime, literally!"

· Chapter Seven ·

Campfire Ladies

We didn't end up setting camp so much as we just found a comfy-enough spot to rest and rummage through our packs for food. We had a bunch of sylph rations that came in enclosed packages made of something like wax paper with a few simple instructions written on the side.

The ready-to-eat meals were . . . edible.

On opening one of them ("Vegetable Lunch"), I found a couple of little tin boxes and a small pouch with some water in it. The instructions said to pour the water into one of the little boxes, then apply some Fire-aspect mana to the circle on the side of the box.

After doing what it said, I discovered that the box had little wires in it that conducted the heat through the package and warmed up its contents, producing a sort of stout soup with veggies and pasta.

The meal was fun to prepare, and a lot less fun to eat.

I think some of the metal might have rubbed up against the veggies, because they tasted like tin.

"Well, that was an experience," Amaryllis said as she chucked the meal package aside.

I shook my head at the casual littering and picked the tin up. In the end, we dug a little hole and shoved all of our waste into it. Amaryllis claimed that it was a good idea to mask our tracks.

With a glance at one of our provided maps, and another look at Awen's compass, we aligned ourselves westward and headed off again.

We knew we weren't going to make it too far today. It was midafternoon already, and Fort Middlesfaire was quite a ways to the west, so we wouldn't make it there today no matter how fast we walked.

The hilly landscape leveled off after a while, which really just meant that there were now fewer hills, but each hill was much broader, like a huge grassy plateau with drooping sides that were a bit of a pain to climb up.

The grass reached up to mid-thigh, whipping against my legs with every step. It was actually kind of nice, though. At some point we crossed through a huge patch of wildflowers, all of them white with pretty yellow dots in their centers. The air was filled with their perfume, and happy little bees bumbled past, fat with pollen.

My friends and I chitchatted as we walked along; there wasn't much else to do out in the open fields. All it took was a quick glance around to prove that we were all alone. Amaryllis went over the political implications of what had happened recently and tried to imagine what the various factions would do now. Awen, when it was her turn, talked at length about her ideas. She was planning on building a wyvern-inspired flying machine one day, fitted with a bunch of repeating crossbows and maybe some rocket propulsion.

With all of our talking, the day slipped by. We'd done enough long-range trekking that I figured our legs were going to be fine, but to someone unused to it, the long walk might have been exhausting.

By the time the sun was starting to set, we'd crossed a good chunk of the distance westward between our landing spot and Fort Middlesfaire.

"That's the river," Amaryllis said with a wing over her head to shade her eyes.

"Looks like there are some trees around it," I said. "Should we camp near here?"

"If we can find a high, flat spot to set up our tents, I don't see why not. We'll be able to gather some kindling at least," Amaryllis said.

We climbed up one last hill, then headed down the other side toward the riverbank. Being tucked between the hillsides provided the river with shelter from the wind, which meant that the trees growing around there had plenty of water and sun and not too much wind pushing against them.

My friends and I found a spot where a few big flat stones stuck out of the hillside. I could tell someone had used the place to camp before, because there was a fire pit dug into the ground and an old lean-to made of branches had been left off to one side. It had fallen apart, and the leaves on the branches had blown away, but it was a clear sign that someone had passed here once.

Our packs had little tents, but instead of erecting three of them, we decided to snuggle up into a single one. It would be warmer, and besides, the tents were all a mess of poles and ropes and pins that had even Awen confused and frustrated.

While Awen set the least-tangled tent up, Amaryllis and I scoured the area for fallen branches and twigs. Soon enough, we had a nice big pile of them. I used some Cleaning magic to wash out the fire pit (after removing some charcoaled wood from the bottom), which uncovered a little tunnel dug into the bottom.

"That's to suck in air from below," Amaryllis said. "Look, the other hole's right here. I think a fire pit like this will create less smoke too."

She might have been right. Once we got a fire started, it didn't create all that much smoke. I had fun plugging up the hole with my palm, then popping my hand off the entrance to watch the fire shift.

We ate more rations, fished out some blankets from our packs to keep our backs warm, and then stared at the starry sky above through the faint sheen of smoke rising from our fire.

We drew straws to decide the watches—Awen was first, then poor Amaryllis in the unenviable middle watch, and myself for the last slot.

I guess all that walking had tired me out more than I'd assumed, because almost as soon as I snuggled in next to Amaryllis and closed my eyes, I fell into a deep slumber.

I was awoken a few hours before dawn by a grumpy Amaryllis shaking me awake. Sometime in the night, she had managed to swap places with Awen without disturbing me, and now I did the same with Amaryllis, vacating my warm bedding for the cool of the night.

Nothing much happened. Some more magic practice, a bit of staring at the night until the sun started to rise. I kept the fire company in the morning and got my tea stuff out as well as some rations, which I cooked over the fire. A few curious birds gathered on some of the nearby trees to watch us prepare for our morning trek.

"We're going to have to go north along the river, I think," Amaryllis said between bites. She had the map on her lap and was occasionally glancing at the river while her talon-tip traced a path.

I looked through the sparse trees between us and the river. It was pretty wide, maybe as wide as a hockey rink was long, and the water was moving along at a steady clip. There'd be no jumping over that, and I didn't trust that I could swim across easily, especially not with all of our gear.

"All right, let's find a spot where we can cross, then. Maybe there're some shallower parts downstream."

Amaryllis nodded. "The river will end eventually. But I think we should move upstream, not down, at least if we hope to ford it and not end up at a lake."

"Oh," I said. That made sense.

Once the tent was taken down and we'd packed everything away, we started off along the river's edge.

The morning walk was fun. I got to see a fox who scampered away when we got closer, and there were a bunch of long-legged heron-like birds with bright green plumage standing very still on the river bank, only moving their long necks when they spotted a fish darting below the water.

We had to cross a few streams that joined into the river. Most of them were small enough that we could just step over, but a few were wide enough that we needed to splash through or carefully walk across some logs that had been put in place by previous travelers.

By early afternoon, after stopping for a break in the shade of a big willow-y tree for a snack, we were all quite sweaty.

I offered to use Cleaning magic on my friends, but wiping away the sweat would just make us hotter.

I think that after spending a week or so in the cool weather around Goldenalden, we'd gotten so used to the cold that the moderate warmth of the Trenten Flats was really hard to deal with.

"How far do we have to go still?" I asked as I knelt next to the river and splashed some water against my face.

"Not too far, I don't think," Amaryllis said. "Here, can you fill this?"

She handed me her waterskin, and I dutifully filled it up with river water, then pushed some Cleaning magic into it to clean out anything too icky. Fish pooped in that water, after all.

Amaryllis's predictions ended up proving true. An hour or so later, with the river thinning down until I could almost jump across it, we came upon a little village.

There was a squat wall around it, only about as tall as I was, with maybe two dozen homes on either side of the river. A bridge crossed the water, and further into the town was a long building with a mill and big stacks of wood cut lengthwise next to it. A sawmill, maybe?

The homes looked like pretty cottages, with wooden walls and thatched roofs with chimneys poking out here and there.

"Do you think they'll have an inn?" I asked.

"Doubtful," Amaryllis said. "It doesn't look like all that many people live here. We're on the frontier, far from the center of the Trenten Flats. This is hardly a metropolis."

"Ah, maybe they'll have a general store, at least," Awen said. "We could buy fresher food. Our rations are meant to be kept for a long time, but they're not very tasty."

I nodded. "And I want to meet the locals too. Maybe they'll know something about the ships we're looking for?"

Amaryllis shrugged. "If we can't use their bridge, we'll have to go all the way around. No harm in stopping by, I suppose."

Grinning, I bounced ahead of my friends, flaring out a bit of Cleaning magic to freshen up. I hardly wanted to meet new friends while stinky and dirty. Bastion had said that the locals might be hard to win over, so it was probably a good idea to put our best foot forward. We reached the edge of the town's walls and found well-plowed fields with irrigation ditches running all the way over to the river. There wasn't much growing except for some tiny, hand-high sprouts of . . . something set a few centimeters apart.

Going around the fields, we made it to a big gate that had been left wide open. The town was shaped like an H. There were two roads with houses on either side, then the bridge in the middle of the town joined the two halves together.

When my friends and I walked in, we immediately became the center of attention.

Cervids paused on the street, and some of them, especially the younger ones, ran off to hide in their homes. No one called out to us or said a friendly hello; instead, they watched us as if we were twenty-foot-tall monsters bent on eating all of them.

Undaunted, I pushed on through. I'd met plenty of people who had been harder to befriend, and I wasn't about to be intimidated so easily! It looked like there was a store on the other side of the bridge, one right next to a smithy and what might have been a church of some sort.

"Hello!" I called out to one cervid, a well-built man with a hat made of woven grass. He was carrying a stack of baskets, which he dropped when I addressed him.

"Warm welcome," Amaryllis muttered.

"Maybe they're shy?" I asked.

"You!"

I spun around at the voice. It came from an older cervid lady, one carrying a cane that she was using to point right at me.

"Hello?" I tried.

"You! Strangers!" she barked. "You're the ones who kidnapped my son!"

· Chapter Eight ·

Smother

I'm sorry, ma'am, but I think you've made a small mistake," I said carefully. It wouldn't do to insult a worried mom. The older cervid lady was clearly distressed. She was also gathering a crowd.

Those cervids who'd previously been watching us secretively and from the corner of their eyes now had an excuse to stare, and they were using it to the fullest.

The older cervid lady waved her cane around, then brought it down onto the wood of the bridge with a hard *clack*. She stomped forward with only the slightest limp of one of her forelimbs. "Where's my Deiter? What've you done with him?"

I glanced at my friends, then back to the lady. "I'm sorry, miss, but I don't know who Deiter is."

"My son!" she shouted. "My son that *you* fawnnapped."

I pointed to myself. "Me? I'd never kidnap . . . Okay, look, miss, I haven't kidnapped anyone today. If you need help looking for your son, then maybe we can help you? We're pretty handy!"

There was a lot of murmuring going on in the crowd of cervids around us, and I had the impression they weren't overly happy with the scene going on. A lot of mean looks were directed at us.

The cervid lady stomped closer, raising her cane over her head. "Give me back my Deiter or I swear on the gods and the World that I'll beat you myself!"

I raised my hands before me, empty so that it was clear I didn't mean any harm. "Miss, I don't know who Deiter is. We didn't kid—fawnnap anyone."

The lady screeched and I winced as her cane came racing down toward me.

It smacked into Amaryllis's outstretched talon with a meaty *thwap*. My friend closed her hand around the long wooden stick and an electrical arc snapped in the air. A moment later, the cane cracked apart at the middle, bits of wooden shrapnel pinwheeling to the ground. "Ma'am, we are travelers passing through your town. Nothing more. Calm yourself," Amaryllis said.

That was a bit direct, but I suppose she had been about to smack me.

"Fawnnappers! You heard the bird! She admits it!"

"What?" Amaryllis snapped in stupefied amazement. "I did no such thing! Have you gone senile? You look too old by half to have a child!"

The lady *was* a little more elderly, but that didn't mean anything. Maybe she adopted?

"All right, all right, what's going on here?" a deep voice said. An older cervid stepped up. He was tall and barrel-chested, with a bit of a paunch. I think if he were a human, he'd have what they called a "dad bod." But he wasn't human, so I really wasn't sure how to describe the cervid stepping onto the bridge. "Myrtle, what are you doing?"

"They're the ones who kidnapped Deiter!" the old cervid lady, Myrtle, said. She stabbed a finger at me and my friends with what was left of her cane. There were more murmurs from the crowd.

The big cervid crossed his arms. "All right. Do you have any proof?"

"They're strangers!" Myrtle said.

"True," he replied, his eyes turning toward us. "Do you have anything to say for yourselves, strangers?"

"What?" Amaryllis asked. "That's enough for you? Someone shows up who you don't know and you just assume the worst of them? What kind of backward, uneducated, hovel-filled heap is this?"

The cervid snorted. "You seem to be making your own assumptions, miss," he replied.

Amaryllis's mouth shut with a click.

The cervid eyed us some more, then sighed. "Myrtle, how heavy is your son?"

"What?" the older lady asked. "I don't know. He weighs more than my old bones, certainly."

"I don't believe these three waifs could carry him off, then," he replied. "They're too thin, and not nearly muscled enough to manage such a feat."

I wasn't sure if I should feel insulted by that or not. I was plenty strong! Over a month of constant physical activity was doing great things to keep me in shape. I wasn't sure if I could lift a cervid, but maybe if it was a small one? They were all four-legged, with human-sized torsos and the lower bodies of large deer. That couldn't be light.

"We didn't fawnnap anyone," I repeated. "We've only just arrived in the area, following along that river. Besides, why would we fawnnap someone?"

"To eat him!" the lady said.

I blinked. "But I'm a vegetarian."

"It's true that buns don't eat meat," the big cervid said. He shook his head. "I'm sorry, Myrtle, I don't see these youths being the ones to take your son out of the town. Still, I wonder what you three are doing here in Riverstart?"

This place was called Riverstart? That was a very utilitarian name. "We're members of the Exploration Guild," Amaryllis said. She tapped her chest where she wore her Exploration guild pin. I had my own fixed to the strap of my backpack. I'd kind of forgotten about it, to be honest.

"We're pretty good at finding things," I said, mostly addressing Myrtle. "If you want, we can look for your son, maybe?"

"First you fawnnap him, now you'll extort me to bring him back?" she asked.

"Damnation Myrtle, Deiter is twenty-nine summers old. He ought to be able to handle himself."

"Twenty-nine," Awen muttered confusedly.

I was a little confused too. That sounded a bit old for a mom to be so worried. Then again, maybe that was normal? I wasn't in Myrtle's shoes. Or horseshoes, as the case may be.

"Does it matter?" Myrtle asked. "Someone's taken him! Half of his things were missing from his room!"

"Wait," Amaryllis said. She had her hands on her hips and didn't look amused at all. "So your son was kidnapped, but he's very much an adult, and he packed his things up before leaving? Were there any signs of a scuffle? Did anyone *hear* him being kidnapped? Who was the last one to see him?"

"I was!" a cervid on the sidelines spoke up. Everyone turned to him, and he wilted at all the sudden attention. "Ah, well, he was walking out toward the north with his saddles full, and he said . . . bye to me?"

Amaryllis threw her arms up. "He wasn't kidnapped, he ran away!"

"He might still be in trouble, though," I said. "We could help."

"Broccoli, we're only traveling through this town," Amaryllis said. "We have business elsewhere. I know you love your detours and pointless stops, but we can't help with every little problem we run across. Especially not when the problem comes from people who like to accuse others without any proof or reason." That last part was very clearly aimed at Myrtle, who bristled at the accusation.

"You broke my cane! Everyone here saw that!"

"You assaulted one of us! Everyone here saw that, too!" Amaryllis snapped back.

"All right, calm down, both of you." The bigger cervid stepped up next to Myrtle and laid a hand on her shoulder. "We'll figure out what happened to Deiter, Myrtle. Maybe we can set up a search party. Judging by the amount of people lollygagging here, we have plenty of fine cervids with nothing better to do. Now, you three. Are you really just passing through?"

I nodded. "That was our intent, mister. We're trying to head to Fort Middlesfaire, but we couldn't find a place to cross the river." I remembered that we were trying to be a bit subtle about what we were up to. "Uh, we might have gotten a little lost?"

"Hmm," he said. "I'm Cody, what passes for a mayor in this fine little town. We can point you toward the fort, if you want. We head over there every so often to trade. It's a good day's walk from here. Two if you leave at this hour."

I glanced up. It wasn't noon yet, but it was getting closer to it. My tummy was also starting to feel a bit empty, which was as good an indicator of the time as any. "Is there an inn here?" I asked.

"Sorry, I'm afraid not. We have a general store, the old church, and a smithy that I run. That's about the whole of it. Riverstart is mostly farmers, lumberjacks, and a few odds and ends. Good folk trying to make a life for themselves on the old frontier."

"Oh. Well, it looks like a very nice town," I said.

Cody regarded us for a moment, and I felt as though we were being judged. "Say, you're explorers, aren't you? You think you could handle our Myrtle problem?"

"What do you mean, 'Myrtle problem'?" Myrtle asked, seemingly incensed. "I'm not a problem, my missing son is the problem!"

"We don't actually know that it's an issue," Amaryllis pointed out.

"Ah, we might be able to ask around here about . . . you know, our diplomat problem," Awen said quietly enough that only the two of us would hear. "Or maybe someone here knows someone who might know better in Fort Middlesfaire."

One of the mayor's eyebrows perked. "What's this, then?"

"Can we discuss this in a more private setting, perhaps?" Amaryllis asked. "I think we've entertained the town enough for one day."

Mayor Cody nodded, then gestured to the general store and smithy on the other side of the bridge. "Come, we'll talk by the forge. I need to keep stoking it, anyway."

"What about my son?" Myrtle asked.

"I'll talk to these misses about it, Myrtle."

"They're just children," she snapped. "And girls besides."

Amaryllis puffed out. "And a minute ago you thought we'd fawnnapped your son? Did your egg crack before you hatched, you—"

I placed a hand over Amaryllis's mouth, which didn't stop her from ranting but it did turn her rather mean words into mumbles that no one could understand.

"I think that maybe we should go our separate ways for now, Miss Myrtle," I said. "It was nice meeting you . . . I guess?"

I dragged Amaryllis across the bridge. My friend looked quite ready to smack the elderly cervid lady around, but I tugged her along before she could do anything regrettable.

"I am sorry about Myrtle," the mayor said. "For what it's worth, I don't think anyone sensible in town will actually listen to her. We've seen her behavior for long enough to be used to it. It's good drama, which is hard to come by in these parts, and most folk don't put much credit in what she says."

"Then why do you allow her to continue?" Awen asked.

"What else are we to do? Kick her out of the town? She's not healthy enough to be on her own, nor would it be honorable to leave a woman to fend for herself in the wilds. This may no longer be the heyday of the frontier anymore, but it's no less dangerous at times. Her son keeps her in line. Or he did."

Amaryllis huffed. "He probably ran off just to get away from her."

"Good for him. Still, it would behoove us to make sure he's well," Cody said as we approached the blacksmith's shop. The side was built with a big sliding door that opened up into the forge itself. Even with such a big opening, the space around the forge was smoky. At least it smelled nice, like fire and leather and that weird smell that burning metal had. "So, what is it that the guild sent you here to find?" he asked.

It wasn't quite accurate, but it was a good guess on his part. I wanted to correct him, but I held back. We were supposed to be subtle. Amaryllis spoke up before I could make up my mind about what to say. "An airship crashed in the plains, and the owners of it would like to know where and how. So we were dispatched to explore the area."

Not quite the truth, but not entirely untrue.

"Huh." Cody scratched his chin, staring off into the distance. "Well, I think I know someone who might know a thing or two about that," he said. "And it just so happens to be in roughly the direction I think Deiter went."

· Chapter Nine ·

Fortune Seeker

Where are you thinking of sending us?" Amaryllis asked. She sounded suspicious, which I supposed was only fair.

Mayor Cody rubbed at his cheek, then made a vague gesture off to one side. I assumed that he was pointing more in the general direction than at the back wall of his forge. "North and west a ways."

"What's that way?" I asked.

"Honestly, not very much. Most of the time, there's nothing at all up north until you reach the badlands. Past that you're in the Snowlands. But every year there are big hunter-gatherer groups that pass by chasing after the cockatrice herds."

"The what?" I asked. I'd never heard of a cockatrice before.

The mayor shook his head. "Cockatrices. They're these birds, though I've been told they're related to dragons somehow. Big ugly things, usually covered in skin and nasty as sin. About as tall as any of you girls to boot."

That sounded like a lot of trouble. "Are they an issue?" Amaryllis asked.

"Not usually. They avoid folk for the most part. They'll fight if you get close to their nests, and you'll want to avoid being anywhere near them during mating season. The males will pick a fight with anything that time of year."

"Deiter went to see the cockatrices?" I asked, confused. "I didn't get that impression about him."

Cody snorted. "Nay, he likely went to see the harvester's caravan. Cockatrices have all sorts of useful things to them. Feathers and the like. Well . . . so I hear. It's not my line of business. People say you can't ranch them; can't keep them on a farm. So, every year, the harvesters follow after them and grab what they can. It's hard work, but it pays, from what I hear."

"Oh," I said. "Do you think he joined them for work, then?"

"Possibly. A caravan stopped by here about three days ago. They needed the forge to whip up some new axle fittings for one of their wagons and they bought up a few supplies. I suspect Deiter got to talking to them and saw an opportunity to leave."

I nodded along. "All right. And you want us to go meet these harvesters?"

"That's up to you, though I'd appreciate it if someone checked on Deiter. Besides, you said you were looking for something out in the plains, weren't you? No one better than the harvesters to ask. They range across the entire prairie chasing after the cockatrices."

"That's . . . actually reasonable," Amaryllis said. "If we do find Deiter, though, how are we going to tell you about it?"

"Honestly, just guilt him into sending his mother a letter. I understand his wanting to run off, trust me, but he owes her that much, I imagine," Cody said.

I considered things while Amaryllis asked Cody a few more questions, mostly about the area and if he'd seen any passing airships lately. It didn't look like she'd find the answers she was looking for, but that was okay.

We were heading to Fort Middlesfaire to find out if anyone had seen the diplomatic convoy of airships. From what I remembered of its trajectory, it was supposed to have passed far to the north of the fort, not over it. It was unlikely anyone at Fort Middlesfaire could have spotted the ships, but we were assuming that others might have and that they'd have told people at the fort.

On the other hand, these harvesters were to the north, where the ships likely *had* passed.

"How far north are the harvesters?" I asked.

Cody shrugged. "I can't rightly say. They were here three days ago, but that wasn't the main group of them, just a few that came down for supplies. Maybe a day's trot to the north? A little more, perhaps."

I glanced at my friends and didn't see a consensus there. "Well, I'm down to try it," I said. "It's in the direction we're supposed to be looking anyway, and they might have seen something. How long do the harvesters stick around one area for?"

"Two, maybe three weeks," Cody said. "That's how long it takes them to scout their surroundings and grab what they can. Mostly it's cockatrice feathers from right after their molt and some meat from hunting, and there are usually a good number of herbalists along too, looking to grab anything valuable that grows in the prairie."

If they had been there for a week already, then they might have seen the airships! "If we run into Deiter, I promise we'll tell him to send a letter back," I said.

"Thank you," the mayor said. "Now, I won't pressure you to follow the harvesters. You said you were heading off toward the old fort, so I won't stop you. Do you need any supplies for the route?"

"We have some things," I said. "Field rations and that kind of stuff. But if you have anything better . . ."

"Bah, come, we have fresh bread and you'll want to refill your canteens for the road. We have well water here that's less likely to sicken you than water from the river. Not that the river water is bad."

Cody led us into the little general store, which, while it had a high ceiling, wasn't all that spacious. They had a few essentials, though, and we did end up picking some things. There was indeed bread, which smelled much nicer than anything in our sylph food packs, and little bags of nuts and locally-picked berries, which Cody explained were pretty commonly found along shaded riverbanks in the plains.

We paid for everything, and I suspected that the price was much lighter than it should have been. Was Cody giving us a discount because of the kerfuffle with Miss Myrtle earlier?

With everything packed away, we slipped out of Riverstart just as easily as we'd entered the little town. We still got a few stares, but they were more curious than hostile now that we were escorted by the mayor. "Have safe travels," he called to us.

"Bye-bye!" I shouted as I waved at him from some ways down the packed dirt road. I was happy that we made at least one friend in the little town!

The midday sun slanted down on us as we trekked down the path. After a few minutes of walking, Amaryllis spoke. "I'm inclined to veer north. The harvesters there might know something, but even if they don't, we'll at least be on the same route the airships took. We can likely swing around and follow the ship's path for a while. If the ships crashed, we might be able to discover them," Amaryllis said.

"I don't mind wandering around aimlessly for a while," I said. "It's fun as long as you're with friends."

Amaryllis shook her head.

The break at Riverstart had been enough to recharge our batteries. Just not walking for an hour had been nice, though I could have used a sit. We continued vaguely northward, occasionally veering off the road until Awen pulled out her compass to point us back in the right direction.

It was hard to walk in a straight line once we were out of the little woods around the river. Sure, there wasn't much around us, just sweeping hills and open plains, but somehow we always ended up going just a little bit off course.

I was sure that if we plotted out our trajectory on a map, it would look zigzaggy the entire time.

When my tummy started to rumble again later on, and I noticed that the sun was starting to dip toward the horizon, I asked my friends if we should find a place to relax and grab a bite to eat. Amaryllis pointed ahead to a small patch of trees on the downwind side of a hill. Just four trees with wind-bent trunks and swept branches.

We made it there and sat down with our backs to a tree. Awen split apart a loaf of bread and we shared it between us with some cheese and a small jar of very sweet preserves from our sylph rations. "How much farther do you think we can go today?" I asked.

"Not very," Amaryllis said. "We have another two hours of sunlight. I'd rather not waste those. We'll just need to keep an eye out for a good spot to set up camp."

I nodded as I chewed.

"Ah, do you think there's anything dangerous around here?" Awen asked.

"Cockatrices should be plenty dangerous," Amaryllis said. "I suspect we could take one on with the three of us working together. If we see a group of them, though, walking away might be the wisest course."

"What's a cockatrice anyway?" I finally asked. The mayor had mentioned them, but that didn't mean I knew what they were.

Amaryllis entered lecturing mode. "A cockatrice is a large draconic bird. They're primarily omnivorous, mostly subsisting on grains and grasses and seeds, though they'll hunt down any small creature they come across. Think rabbits and foxes and flying birds. They're relatively large, with great talons and . . . strange beaks."

"How strange?" Awen asked.

"They have teeth," Amaryllis said. "Well, the females do. The males have sharper, longer beaks. At least, I believe that's the case. We don't have any in the Harpy Mountains, so what I'm saying is mostly coming from what I've read. Their main weapon, though, is their eyes. If a cockatrice locks eyes with you, you'll freeze up. I believe the bigger ones have more powerful gazes. Some can turn you to stone in an instant."

"That's terrifying," I said.

"Fortunately, those have likely all been hunted down. Cockatrice parts are valuable alchemical reagents, especially from the older, bigger ones, and the meat of the younger ones is supposed to be a delicacy," Amaryllis said. "The current wild herds have been trimmed and hunted every year for decades now; I doubt they're as formidable as they once were."

I shook my head. "That doesn't sound good. They'll be hunted to extinction if that goes on for too long."

"I suppose," Amaryllis said. She didn't seem terribly bothered by the idea. "Anyway, it needed to be done. The cervids have large overland caravans that loop around the northern end of the Harpy Mountains toward their western frontier. They do some trade with the independent cities there and the Snowlands as well. The cockatrices were a threat to those caravans, once."

We finished up our late lunch, got up, then headed out once more.

The day was really nice for a walk. The skies were nearly empty of clouds except for a few white wisps far, far above, and the sun was warm on our faces. There was a brisk wind coming from the north that kept us cool despite the sunlight. It was very much appreciated.

Walking up hills all day was a chore, but it was wholesome exercise and it meant that the route down the hills would be all the easier later.

We chitchatted about nothing with great enthusiasm until the hour grew late and we all became quite tired. The hills had grown smaller and the grass taller as we headed north. We couldn't find a spot with any trees or even a stream, so we ended up settling down in a spot where a few large boulders would cut the wind.

There was nothing to burn, so we didn't get to build a fire, but Amaryllis was good with magic so she warmed things up for us while Awen and I struggled with the tent.

We ate with our backs to the boulder. Somehow, Awen convinced Amaryllis to tell stories about her sisters, then we talked about our schooling. Explaining how school worked back home was weird, but my friends had received very different sorts of education.

And then it was bedtime.

I took the first watch, sitting atop the boulder and watching the plains fade to utter darkness with only my one tiny magical light ball for illumination. In that breathtaking stillness, I lost myself in the glittering sea of stars until Amaryllis came to replace me.

So far, our trip had gone pretty well. I was looking forward to the next day!

· Chapter Ten ·

Meat New People

I liked taking the first watch because it let me sleep uninterrupted until it was time to wake up. Plus, I didn't really feel like cooking, and the last watch was always the one to start breakfast.

I don't think my friends were big fans of cooking either, but we muddled along decently enough.

So yeah, I wouldn't admit it to my friends, but I was being a little bit selfish when I took first watch to avoid having to do morning chores. I felt a teensy bit bad about it too. Maybe we'd set up a rotation, so that way I only had to do the breakfast stuff one day in three?

Those were the kinds of hazy thoughts I was dreaming up when I felt Awen shaking my shoulder. "Mmm? Already?" I asked.

"No, Broccoli, you need to wake up," Awen hissed. "Amaryllis, you too, come on."

I blinked a few times. There was some urgency there, and I couldn't smell any breakfast in the air. Why was Awen worried?

I sat up, rubbed my face, then looked around. Early morning sunlight was staining the outside of the tent a pale blue. "What's going on?" I muttered.

"There's someone here!" Awen whispered. "I saw them in the grass. They saw me too, I think."

"Oh," I said. Then, with a bit more urgency: *"Oh!"*

Amaryllis was up too. My poor harpy friend had the middle watch, so she'd probably only gotten an hour or two of sleep so far, but she still moved fast.

Awen snuck back out of the tent, grabbing her crossbow on the way out as well as a bundle of bolts.

Nightclothes flew around the tent as Amaryllis and I got dressed in a hurry. Usually we did that one at a time for privacy's sake, but there was no time for that now. I set down my breastplate with my gambeson still in it, then with a twist of mana near my tummy, made myself smaller.

It was a neat trick I'd figured out with my new Proportion Distortion skill. I was now a good few centimeters shorter and thinner, which made it easy to slip into my armor, shove my hands through the armholes, then let go of the magic so that I returned to my normal size. I'd just saved myself a couple of minutes of strapping pieces on, and with a pulse of Cleaning magic, I wasn't even gross from sleep sweat and stuff!

Amaryllis snorted as she shrugged her coat on, then she gestured to the outside of the tent. "How do you want to play this?"

"We don't know what's out there," I said. "Maybe it's friendly?"

"Ah yes, friendly people love sneaking up on others," Amaryllis said as she walked out of the tent, talons still working to buckle on her strange harpy pants.

I stumbled out after her, grabbing Weedbane on the way out and laying the still-folded scythe onto my shoulder. A glance around revealed . . . not much at all. There was still that large boulder right next to the place we'd chosen to camp at. It was serving as a decent windbreak, preventing the constant breeze blowing across the plains from ripping our tent away. Around us were two hills with nothing much on them except for hip-high grass.

Anything could be hiding in that grass.

Or nearly anything, I supposed. Anything within a certain size range.

"Where did you see them?" Amaryllis asked in a low whisper.

"Just one person," Awen whispered back. She gestured with a nod to the west, the same direction the wind was blowing toward. "I saw them over there, maybe fifty paces away. They poked their head out above the grass, then ducked back down."

"Any details?" I asked. "Was it a cervid?" That would have been impressive. Cervid were kind of tall, though I supposed they could be crouching. Or it could be a small cervid.

Awen shook her head. "No. They were humanoid."

"Harpyoid," Amaryllis corrected absently. I snorted, which earned me a *look* from Amaryllis but no comment.

"Awa, I didn't get a good look at them? They had a hat on. Like a brown hat with a wide brim. I didn't see any weapons, but they could have something."

"If all you saw was their upper torso, then they could have anything. A bow, a sword, even a spear if it wasn't raised," Amaryllis muttered. "To say nothing of combat magic."

"Or no weapons at all if they're just friendly," I pointed out.

Amaryllis huffed an *I'll believe it when I see it* sort of huff. "All right, well, this is cutting into my sleeping time, so let's get it over with." Amaryllis took a deep breath. "We know you're out there!" she called out. "If you want to cause trouble, come out and cause it. If you're peaceful, then you have nothing to worry about from us."

"I don't?"

All three of us jumped and spun around. There was someone standing on the boulder. Or maybe they were laying on it; all I could see was their upper body. It was a young woman, I think. She had a cowboy hat on, which cast a deep shadow over her face, and a leather vest over her torso.

She was also covered in beige fur and had a pair of feline ears squished down by the brim of her hat. And a bow. I couldn't ignore the shortbow currently pointed in our direction, even if the bowstring wasn't drawn back.

"Uh, hi!" I said.

The young woman stared at me for a moment, then at my companions. She pointed to Awen. "Human person," she said. Then she pointed to Amaryllis. "Talking chicken meat." Then she pointed to me. "Talking rabbit meat."

"Uh," I said.

"Meat's not supposed to wear clothes like people," the cat-person said. She fiddled with the string of her bow, whiskers twitching as she looked at us with narrowed eyes.

"We're not meat," I said. "Well . . . okay, I guess technically we are."

"Broccoli," Amaryllis warned.

"No, that's a vegetable, those are gross," the furry-faced cowgirl said.

I sighed. "Can we start this over? My name is Broccoli Bunch, and these are my friends, Awen and Amaryllis. We're from the Exploration Guild."

The person on the rock stared at us for a long moment before dropping her hold on the bowstring. "I'm Savan," she said. "Hello, rabbit meat Broccoli and chicken meat Amaryllis. Also human Awen."

"Hello, Savan," I replied with a little wave. "What are you doing out here in the plains?"

"Hunting for meat," Savan said.

I was really hoping she didn't plan on adding us to the menu there, because otherwise things might get a little awkward. "Well, we're just camping here on our way north. We're looking for a group that's chasing after cockatrices that way. The harvesters?"

"Harvesters?" Savan's expression lit up. "Oh! The hunter caravan. I know where they are."

"You do?" I asked.

She nodded. "They buy my meat."

"That's great," I said. "Um. I hope you understand that we're not . . . meat, right? Because I'm sure they wouldn't want to eat us. I'm very bony, and Amaryllis here probably tastes sour."

"Pardon me, what does that mean, exactly?" Amaryllis asked.

"See?"

"She's spoiled too," Awen added.

That earned her a weak swat from Amaryllis and a muttered "Look who's talking."

Savan laughed and lowered her bow fully. "It's okay. Calamity told me not to shoot people that talk unless they shoot first or are rude. You're not rude for meat, so I won't shoot you."

"Great!" I said. "Did you have breakfast yet, Savan? I think Awen was about to start preparing something. We have enough to share with a new friend!"

```
Savan Ah
Desired Quality: Someone who'll keep her fed and scratch
her on that one spot next to her ears
Dream: To eat so much meat she explodes, then nap
```

Savan seemed like a . . . very simple kind of girl. She bounced down from her rock, revealing that she wore tall boots and jean-like pants dyed a pale brown that actually matched some of the more faded grass. A quiver hung by her waist from a belt, with cloth stuffed between the arrows so they didn't rattle when she moved. In fact, I bet Savan had a few stealth skills, because she hardly made a sound as she approached us.

"What're we eating?"

Awen was the one who replied, mostly by listing off what we had in our ration packs. Savan looked dubious about some of the options, but she lit up when Awen offered to warm a can of salted meat paste for her.

Amaryllis provided the heat while Awen tended to the food under Savan's watchful eye. Since it was unlikely we'd get any more sleep, I got to packing up the tent and the rest of our stuff.

"So, do you think you could lead us back to the hunters' caravan?" I asked. "We're looking for someone called Deiter, and also maybe some information while we're at it."

"I can do that," Savan said. "But Calamity sent me out to hunt."

"Who's that?" I asked. Once our stuff was packed away again, I sat down on the grass next to Savan. I noticed that my friends were a little slower to pack. They kept eyeing Savan the entire time, as if expecting her to jump out and take a nibble. "Also, if it isn't mean . . . what are you, exactly? I've met all sorts of people, but you're the first one like you I've met!"

Savan laughed. "I'm a big cat. We come from around here, and I heard that there's packs of us to the west too, across the mountains."

"Cat folk aren't too uncommon," Awen said as she tipped the contents of the pan onto some plates. It looked like she was preparing a big portion for Savan and a few smaller ones for the rest of us. Savan got my share of the meat, of course. "There's a lot of differences in the . . . subspecies of them. I guess that's what you'd call the different groups."

"Yup," Savan said. She grinned as she took her plate and then, after searching inside her vest, she pulled out a small leather kit which she opened to reveal a few tools. Including a fork. She dug in with gusto right after. "Mm-hmm, there's a lot of us here, and around the Flats. We hunt because it's fun and we like to eat, and we do what we want because we can."

"Oh? Do you have your own nation?" I asked.

Savan snorted. "As if."

"From what I recall the cat folk are notoriously . . . catlike when it comes to matters of state," Amaryllis said.

"They have a weird reputation," Awen added. "Some people call them lazy"—Savan laughed at that while nodding—"but some of the cat folk are really hard workers. They just don't really do . . . bosses and such."

"Oh, we will," Savan said. "I work for people all the time! But only if I like them. I like you. You gave me meat. Want to hire me? I kill things good."

"Aren't you working for that Calamity person?" Amaryllis asked.

"He didn't give me breakfast."

I held back a giggle of my own. "Maybe we can trade the food you're eating for your help getting us to the caravan? We might get lost otherwise."

Savan shrugged. "Okay. I don't ever get lost, so I'll show you how to get there." She nodded while her tail, which was long and whippy, flicked from side to side behind her.

I'd spent enough time with Orange to know that meant she was probably in a good mood. "Oh, I have a spirit kitten!" I said. "Would you like to meet her?" I'd left Orange in Caprica's care, mostly because it made Caprica and Gabrielle really happy.

"A spirit kitty? I've never eaten spirit meat before!"

Or maybe I could leave Orange in their care for a while longer.

· Chapter Eleven ·

Catching Up

Savan definitely knew her way across the plains. She didn't use any maps or a compass, just the occasional glance at the sun, or a squint at some rocks in the distance. The path she led us on wasn't straight either, being a meandering route that followed the edges of hills and crossed rocky crags with the occasional skip across a rivulet.

"This way, meat friends!" Savan said with a gesture ahead.

I was trying to convince Savan to stop calling us meat, but she kept slipping. In the end I gave up. At least "meat friends" was a nice alternative to just "meat."

"There's dust ahead," Amaryllis said with a gesture of a wing toward the sky.

I shaded my eyes with a hand and squinted ahead. She was right, there was a plume of smoky dust rising above the nearest hill's horizon and into the sky. Something big was moving up ahead. Or a lot of medium-sized things, maybe.

"That's the hunters," Savan said. "This time of sun, they should be out."

It was still pretty early in the morning, though the sun was fully up and shining above. If Savan had run into us after leaving her camp, then she couldn't have started too far away unless she hunted at night.

Then again, she was a cat-person, so maybe she did. I wondered if she could see in the dark really well.

I asked her about it, which quickly snowballed into a conversation about the various advantages of the different intelligent species. Amaryllis, of course, gloated about how great harpies were, until Savan asked her if she tasted more like turkey or chicken, which set Awen and I off in a giggle fit that annoyed Amaryllis a bunch.

Just as Awen was mentioning humanity's reputation for being able to eat just about anything, we crested a hill. Out ahead of us, the land flattened out considerably for a long ways, with nothing but a sea of grass in greens and browns and yellows stretching out nearly to the horizon.

After staring for a while, I noticed that the land wasn't quite flat, though. There were still bumps and dips in the landscape, but the ever-present grass made it hard to see them.

A few trees dotted the area, though they were few and far between, mostly big windswept trees that seemed very picturesque in the distance.

"There are the hunters," Saven said. "There's a camp farther out that way." She pointed to what I thought was the west. I couldn't see anything that way, so her vision must've been better than mine.

"Should we go to the camp or the hunters?" I asked.

"Hunters!" Savan said. "That's where my friends are. Calamity will know what to do. He's smart."

With that pronouncement, she started off once more, and the rest of us scrambled to keep up. Savan moved through the grass with much greater ease than the rest of us. She had a way to zigzag through that didn't leave a clear trail showing where she came from and that seemed to require less resistance to push through the tall grass.

I was tempted to just bounce along, but the ground under the grass was uneven and filled with little holes. I was worried I might sprain my ankles if I wasn't careful.

As we approached the hunters, I began to make out more details.

The group had maybe fifty or so members, all either cervid jogging along or cat-people like Savan riding on ponyback. Some were actually riding the cervid. A few of the hunters had long staffs which they were using to bat away the grass, and others nearer to the back were planting poles down with different-colored flags. Several carts and wagons were being pulled along with the group.

"What are they doing?" Awen asked.

"Hunting!" Savan said. "Cockatrices can be very sneaky. They'll lay down in the grass and only pop up when they feel like eating your meat or if they feel like running. The poles are to tell the gatherers where the hunters found poop."

"Droppings," Amaryllis corrected.

"From cockatrices. For potions," Savan explained.

I blinked, then considered the few potions I'd drunk in the past. Had any of those contained dragon-monster poop? Should I have been worried?

"Wait, if the hunters are out in a group, then what were you doing?" Amaryllis asked Savan.

"Scouting," Savan answered easily. "I'm small and sneaky, and the cocka-trices aren't going to be scared by just me. If I find them, then I can tell the hunters, and then we take them down as a big group."

Savan paused her explanation to jump up onto a rock that I hadn't seen through the grass. She tied a kerchief on the end of her bow with a lazy knot, then stood at her full height and waved it around over her head.

There were a few whistles from the hunters, and I noticed a few pointing our way.

"What was that for?" Amaryllis asked.

"To tell them we're here," Savan said.

"Yes," Amaryllis said. "I had gathered that, but why?"

Savan jumped off the rock and untied the kerchief before stuffing it away. "Because I don't wanna surprise anyone and get shot," she said.

That seemed like a perfectly valid reason to me.

We continued toward the group, and I saw what Savan meant by sneaking up on them. Some of the grass we pushed through was taller than I was, ears and all. Big stalks of dry yellow grass whipped to and fro as we moved through it. We burst out of the tall grass into . . . less tall grass, right in front of a group of three hunters. Two cat people on ponies and a young cervid.

"Hello!" Savan said. "I found meat friends!"

"Hello, Savan," one of the cat people said. He was a handsome young man, maybe a few years older than my friends and I, with a nice chin and bright green eyes. He tipped his hat at us. "Howdy, ny'all, what're you doin' round these parts?"

I held back a snort. That would have been impolite. "Hi!" I said instead. "We're looking for someone, and also something."

"Well, we've got a bit of both," he said with a grin. "Savan, where'd you find this lot?"

"They were camping to the southeast," Savan said. "They're looking for a lost cervid boy."

"And an airship," I added before Amaryllis gave me a smack.

The leader of the little band perked up. "An airship?" he asked, excited.

"Oh boy," his two companions said in stereo before they shook their heads.

"Ny'all are lookin' for a ship round these parts?" he asked. "Because I swear on the dirt we're standing on that I've seen one. It crashed . . . 'bout that way. Maybe a day's ride yonder." He pointed to what I suspected was north.

"You saw a crashed ship?" Amaryllis asked.

"Two of 'em!" he said. "But where're my manners; my name's Calamity. Calamity Danger, at yer service, ma'ams. Best shot in the Trenten Flats. I can swat a fly off yer nose with the feather of an arrow from a hundred paces."

I clapped. He was very cool.

"I'm Broccoli Bunch, and these are my best friends, Amaryllis Albatross and Awen Bristlecone."

"Albatross," Calamity said. "Like the airship manufacturers?"

Amaryllis blinked twice. "Yes, in fact, just like them." Her chest puffed out a little.

"Calamity, we should get back to it," the cervid said. "Daylight's burning."

Calamity nodded. "Fair. Now, I don't want to leave you misses standing out here all on your lonesome." He swung his leg over to dismount his pony. "Savan, can you lead Blinky here back to the others? We'll follow along shortly."

Savan grinned. "Horse meat!" she cheered as she scrambled up onto the pony and grabbed its reins. She *hyah*-ed quite loudly and took off at a gallop back toward the main formation of hunters.

The other two ran after her, obviously somewhat annoyed.

"Is she . . . normal?" Amaryllis asked.

"Savan? She's as normal as she wants to be, I suspect. Which isn't very normal at all, no," Calamity said. He grinned and raised his hat to comb his fingers through the fur atop his head. Unlike Savan, Calamity was more of a calico, with black bands of fur on his face over more grayish-brown fur with a few odd white speckles. "But she's good folk."

"Are you in charge of the hunters, then?" Amaryllis asked.

Calamity laughed. "Goodness no. I just stick my whiskers where they don't belong often enough that folk turn to me to fix things. I'm just along for the pay and the adventure. Now, you were looking for some ships?"

"As well as a cervid called Deiter," I said. "He's from Riverstart, a little village to the south."

"I know the place," Calamity said with a nod. "I think I even remember the lad you're talking about. Tall, gawky fellow, bit on the skinny side? Mom had lungs like a banshee that got its tail stepped on?"

"Banshees don't have tails," Amaryllis said. "But yes, that sounds like the right person."

Calamity grinned. "Poor lad saw one of the hunter does and fell in love with her on sight. I think she insulted his mom too. Might've seen him around the main camp."

"Thank you!" I said. "That helps a lot. And the airships?"

"Hmm, those came down way off to the north. Gonna be hard to point you in the right direction, honestly. Might be able to guide you over, if nya tell me why nyer looking."

I glanced at my friends and earned two shrugs. "Well, a whole bunch of important people—a diplomatic envoy—were taking a big airship to Sylph-free, but it never arrived. It should have had an escort. We're out here look-ing for it now."

"Huh, that's mighty interesting," Calamity said. He glanced back at the other two hunters, then back at us. "All right, look, misses. I'm keen on showing nya to the spot where I saw those ships go down. I have been curious to see 'em ever since I saw them from afar. Everyone here knows I've got a real love for airships."

"Which is normal," I said. "They're awesome."

Calamity nodded seriously. "That's right. Can't just shirk my duties, though. If you misses don't mind, you can trail along with the rest of the group. We stop at around high noon to find shade and fill up. I'm sure I could lead you off northwards around then."

"So, what, you just want us to follow you until noon?" Amaryllis asked.

"If we leave then, I bet we can make it to the crash site and back before sunfall. If nya want, we can borrow a couple of ponies. It'll make the ride a fair bit faster. I've got Blinky, of course. If we can't all ride, then at least we won't need to lug yer gear around."

"That sounds really great," I said.

"Really convenient," Amaryllis muttered. She eyed Calamity suspiciously, but didn't say much.

So I stepped up and extended a hand to the cat . . . man. "I'd love to work with you, if you don't mind."

"Ah, but before that, we need to talk remuneration," Calamity said.

"Of course," Amaryllis said. I think it actually made her less suspicious to know that Calamity wanted to be paid. "Let's haggle now before Broccoli starts insisting on . . . reverse-friend-discounts or something."

"Wha—?" I asked. "But I haven't even asked Calamity if he wants to be friends yet! Though since she mentioned it . . . do you?"

Calamity laughed. "Sure! But a good friend's a payin' one!"

```
Calamity Danger
Desired Quality: Someone who'll be by his side through
thick and thin
Dream: To become the coolest sky pirate
```

Whoa! He was so cool!

· Chapter Twelve ·

Our Little Ponies

The hunting party spent the rest of the pre-afternoon moving along at a decent pace. My friends and I had to jog to keep up at times, but not too often. A group of this size could move so fast through the tall grasses, especially with their wagons and cargo.

Once Calamity introduced us as a group of wandering explorers, we were welcomed with open arms. I think our jobs were similar enough without overlapping that the hunters didn't mind our company, though there wasn't much time to talk and make friends since they all had to work.

About an hour after we joined the group, Calamity and a bunch of others conferred together, then charged off into the distance. No one else panicked, so I assumed that was pretty normal.

Half an hour later, we came upon them tying the legs of what looked like a particularly orange lion together. The poor thing was clearly dead, with a few hook-tipped spears poking through its hide.

"That looks a little like a sandcat," Awen said. "They're big stealthy cats that hunt in the deserts close to my home."

The hunters loaded the lion onto one of the carts, then tied it down so that it wouldn't bounce around too much. They didn't seem particularly proud of their catch, or disappointed by it either. I had the impression that this was just work as usual for them.

That didn't change the fact that the lion was longer than I was tall and weighed enough to make the cart groan a bit.

The caravan continued, following some twists and turns in the landscape that seemed entirely random to me. By the time the sun was near its zenith, the group had only paused a few times, either to load up a few more animals onto the carts—they caught some that looked like tiny buffalo, smaller than a pony but with thick hair—or to collect herbs and cuttings from some bushes and flowers as we moved.

Finally, the group stopped within a copse of trees next to a large oasis formed downwind of a slight rise. The hunters warned us that there were monsters in the water, and that we should only approach it once it was safe.

The animals pulling the carts were unhitched and given water pulled from the pond by some hunters who had water magic, and then someone started a small fire and the hunters began to cook up some lunch.

Calamity approached us then. "I've gotten two more ponies," he said. "With Blinky that makes three. The hunters will be heading back early today. Our meteomagist sensed a rainstorm coming this evening and we can't be caught out in the grasslands when the ground gets wet."

"So we can go?" I asked.

The catboy cowboy nodded. "That's right. We can leave right meow if nya want."

I held back a snort. "Sure thing!" I said. I wasn't going to laugh. My friends were treating Calamity's verbal tic as if it were entirely normal, so maybe it was just me who found it weird.

The ponies Calamity had secured were waiting for us on the edge of the camp. They'd been fed and watered already, and had little satchels on their backs with some grain and water bags in them. "This is Tassels, and that's Shanks," Calamity said. He turned toward us. "You understand that I had to rent their services, yes?"

Amaryllis sighed. "We do. Do you accept sylph gold?"

Calamity grinned. "I accept all gold, my lady."

That started a quick round of haggling between Amaryllis and Calamity. "Fine," Amaryllis said before she fished out some coins from a purse hidden in her coat. "Now, how much for your services as a guide?"

Calamity took the coins, bit into one, then slid it away into a hip pouch. "That'll depend. Quite honestly, I've been meaning to look into it myself, but I couldn't quite justify leaving the caravan on my own for an evening. Still, having to guide nya might slow me down a whole lot."

"We're not slow," I said. "Although I'm not sure exactly how riding a pony works." All I had to do was hang on and scream *hyah!*, right?

Calamity gave me a look, then shrugged. "Fine. Then how about this: I'll charge nya half of what I usually would, but I get finder's rights on whatever we run across once we reach the crash site."

Amaryllis hummed. "That seems far more profitable for you than for us. We'd essentially just be bankrolling your own venture at that point. We've already covered the cost of the ponies and their feed."

The catboy shrugged. "Do you have the means to grab whatever valuables are left at the wreck if we do find something?" he asked. "If the ships are really there, I can ask the caravan to make the trip. My word's worth enough that if I promise it's worth it, they'll come. I don't know if you can manage carrying the loot off so easily. Or if nya could, then it would take some time. You'd need to head to the fort and hire teamsters and guides and a whole troop of folk."

"You might be correct, but I won't give up so easily. We'll give you the right to exploit the crash site, but we can leave with anything we can carry. Papers, maps, the ship's manifest, even including things like tools or any gold aboard the vessel," Amaryllis said.

"But only what you can carry?" Calamity asked.

"We can hardly carry off an entire ship with a few ponies," Amaryllis said.

Calamity thought about it for a moment, then nodded his head and extended a hand to shake. All three of us shook, then he nodded to the ponies. "Two of nya will have to ride double. I'll let nya sort yourselves out."

In the end, Amaryllis and I climbed onto Tassels, the biggest of the three ponies. We were both pretty light, so it wasn't a big deal. Amaryllis had a hard time with the reins, which weren't designed for talons, so I sat in the front, which meant that Amaryllis had to wrap her arms around me to hold on.

"Why are you grinning so much?" Amaryllis asked quietly. "We just rode wyverns. Why are you so happy about being on a pony?"

"It's less the pony and more the hour-long hug I'm gonna get."

Amaryllis squeezed me, then huffed a very *you're silly, Broccoli* kind of huff. "Figures you'd get excited about something so juvenile."

I pulled her wings forward so that she was hugging me even tighter, and Amaryllis laughed for a whole two seconds before she remembered that she was supposed to be all serious and unfunny all the time.

"All right," Calamity said. "Tassels and Shanks should be used to following along. We'll try to make good time without tiring the ponies out."

With that, we took off out of the shady copse and into the hot day. The sun shone above, bathing everything in bright warmth while a few puffy clouds lingered above in a blue-blue sky.

Calamity set a strong pace, not quite a trot but faster than a normal walk. We pushed through where the grass was shortest, taking an occasional turn as Calamity guided us around obstacles that I didn't see until we were right on top of them.

At one point, we crossed a bridge that just showed up suddenly as we pushed through the grass. The bridge crossed a long cut in the hillside. It was only a few meters deep, but it would have been a heck of a surprise to anyone running through the grass who didn't see the fall coming.

"So, Calamity," I asked once I got bored. It took a whole ten minutes after leaving the camp, so I was pretty proud of myself. "Where are you from?"

"Me? Right around here. My family's all from Fort Middlesfaire. Or at least, that's where we've lived for a while. My grandpa was from the Endless Swells. He was a mariner."

"Oh," I said. "What's that?"

Calamity laughed. "A sailor, but for one of them ships that's on water instead of in the air. He used to tell me all sorts of stories when I was just a wee kitten. Always wanted to head out that way and see what was what."

"That's cool!" I said. "Is that why you're so interested in airships?"

Calamity grinned. "Nyeah! I want to ride one someday."

"They are really neat," I agreed.

The catboy cowboy half-turned in his saddle. "You've been on one?" he asked.

Awen giggled. "Broccoli is a captain," she said.

I nodded as Calamity's eyes locked onto me. My chest puffed out with pride and my ears straightened up. "Yup! It's true. I'm Captain Broccoli Bunch of the *Beaver Cleaver*, the nicest ship in all the skies."

"What kind of ship?" Calamity asked. He was clearly excited, as anyone should be when the topic of airships came up.

"An owl-built ship, a special commission by some fancy harpy lord who didn't want it in the end. I don't even know if it had a class name," I said.

"A one-off," Calamity said. "That's properly fancy. What sort of ship is she?"

"He!" I said.

"Aren't ships usually shes?" he asked.

I shook my head. "The *Beaver*'s a boy, I think."

"Don't argue with her, she'll just confuse you," Amaryllis said.

"Oh, don't worry, I understand," he said with a nod.

Amaryllis sniffed. "The ship's a modified full-body catamaran. Single balloon, two hulls."

Awen nodded along from her spot atop Shanks. "It has a type-two-sixteen Albatross engine, with a three-meter prop-span and custom cam-work. The original engine was an Owl-wright model seven, I think. Some of the parts were left over, including a lot of the transmission and gearing, which is probably for the best. They are better than the Albatross models."

"Pardon me?" Amaryllis asked.

"So, you think maybe an aspiring young man could get his hands on a ship? Like, a small one?" Calamity asked.

Amaryllis laughed. "Oh no, you sound like Broccoli did when I met her. She asked the same question. Well, it was worded differently, I suppose, but the idea was the same. I'll tell you the same thing I told her: If you have the gold, you can have a ship."

"If you become Amaryllis's best friend forever you get a cool discount too," I pointed out.

"What? No you don't," Amaryllis said.

"I got the *Beaver* with a one-hundred-percent-off friend-discount," I pointed out.

Amaryllis was quiet for a moment, then she squeezed me tighter. "All right. I'll give you that one. But don't you ever tell our competitors."

"What could they do? Convince you they're your best friend just to steal a ship?" I asked.

"Yes. I'm sure they wouldn't blink at the idea of planting a false friend next to me or one of my sisters just to steal a ship or two."

I gasped. That . . . that was horrible! What kind of sad person would pretend to be someone's friend? Worse, who would pretend to be someone's friend just to steal from them? That was . . . it was despicable! It was beyond the pale! *Unforgivable!*

. . . Ah, so this is hatred.

That sobered me right up. "I don't like that. Let's talk about something more fun." I scrambled for an idea before latching onto the first that came to mind. "Hey, Calamity, how'd you become a hunter?"

"Well, it was something of a natural evolution," he said. "I'm the best shot with a bow in the World—I was back then too—so naturally all I needed to do was turn those skills toward hunting. Then, as it turns out, I'm a great leader. So, obviously, I was quickly promoted up the ranks. Not that we have any sort of formal ranking, really."

"And your incredible humility makes you the humblest person in the World too," Amaryllis snarked.

Calamity laughed. "Humility? Nya, I don't have any of that!"

· Chapter Thirteen ·

Raindrops Keep Fallin' on My Head

The warm afternoon turned into an early evening that wasn't much cooler. Some gray clouds rolled in from the west, traveling toward the Sylphfree mountains to our right. They looked like they were heavy with rain, but for the moment all we got was rising humidity to go with the heat we had.

We stopped by a rivulet along the way, and after Calamity checked around it for predators we let Blinky, Tassels, and Shanks have turns at drinking some water. We did the same, emptying our waterskins before refilling them in the stream. I threw in some Cleaning magic to keep the water pure of gunk and stuff.

Once our break was over, we continued on. Calamity kept up a good chunk of the conversation, talking about his experiences as a hunter while occasionally asking questions about airships.

Awen was being a lot more sociable than usual. I shouldn't have been too surprised, but I still kind of was. It was nice seeing her break out of her introspective nature for a bit. I think it mostly had to do with the topic at hand; Awen loved talking shop and Calamity was a huge fan of airships, so they were on the same wavelength when it came to that.

The trip continued, with the four of us charting a zigzaggy route across the plains. Calamity seemed to know where he was going, and he had hinted that he had a skill that prevented him from getting lost out in the open.

Then, just as Calamity finished saying that we were only an hour out, the sky opened up.

Something touching my ear had me wincing. I reached up and noticed that my ear fur was a bit wet. All day, a few flies had been buzzing about me, but usually a quick flick of my ear was enough to send them off. The thwap of another raindrop smacking my helmet told me this wasn't a bugging bug. "Huh, I think it might be raining," I said.

A half-second later the skies opened up and it was as if a million buckets had just been flipped upside down over our heads.

Awen squeaked and Amaryllis squawked as a deluge came pouring down atop us. Calamity reached up to hang on to his hat and the ponies shifted under us. "Well, looks like that storm's come around. You ladies good to ride through this, or should we look for shelter?"

"What shelter? There's nothing but grass around here!" Amaryllis shouted.

"There's always something," Calamity yelled back. I had a hard time hearing him over the constant rush of water. It was like standing next to a waterfall. Or maybe under it. I was pretty sure if I tilted my head back and opened my mouth, I could drown just standing still.

"Let's find shelter!" I called out.

"Right! Stay close!" Calamity said. He reached into his saddlebags, pulled out a length of rope, and tossed both ends at us. I caught one and Awen, on the other pony, grabbed the other. "Tie it to the saddle," he shouted while looping the middle around the horn on his saddle.

We did as he asked. I think Awen's knot was much nicer than my own, but it wasn't the time to compare that kind of thing. I didn't have time to ask why we'd done that, but it became obvious as Calamity rode forward and the lines went taut. I could only barely see him out ahead of us through the sheets of rain.

My armor, which had a lot of padded cloth to it, was soaking up water like a sponge and clinging to me in an icky way. I felt way heavier than usual as my ears, which were too waterlogged to stand, flopped down.

At this rate, someone would have to hang me out to dry for a while once it stopped raining.

A strong gust of wind whipped by, making the water swell around us in great big sheets. That cleared things up for a bit, and I could make out the open plains around us for just a moment before the rain returned in force. The grass was forced down flat and there was a fog rising from the ground.

We pushed into the rain, Calamity leading us despite the constant downpour, though he had a hand on his hat the entire time to keep it from blowing off.

A bright light flashed in the distance, then, maybe some ten seconds later, a heavy rumble washed over the sound of the rain.

"Thunder!" Amaryllis shouted.

"Means there's a proper storm coming," Calamity said. "We'll need to find cover sooner than I thought!"

"This isn't a proper storm already?" Amaryllis asked.

Calamity's laughter carried back to us. "Ladies, this is just a light shower! Now hang on, we'll be moving a trot faster."

Calamity *nyah*-ed and the ponies started to move much faster, with a pace that had us bouncing on the saddles. We reached the end of a cliff that

I hadn't seen coming and Calamity turned, then had us follow the edge until we descended into a gully. A stream ran through the bottom, full to bursting with rapid water that we crossed with plenty of splashing.

As we started to move along the edge of the cliff, Calamity pointed ahead. "Look!" he shouted.

I squinted, then brushed a lock of sopping hair away from my face. There was something out ahead, but I couldn't tell what it was. Poles and bars loomed out of the downpour at odd angles, and I glimpsed what looked like a house-sized boulder, but I couldn't make out much more than that.

As we came closer, the details became clear.

It was an airship. Or half an airship, at least. One that was tilted onto its side, with entire chunks of its hull ripped out and some of the main beams half-driven into the earth like lawn darts. The tattered remains of the balloon lay across the wreck, just as sodden by the rain as we were, while some lighter material flapped wildly in the wind.

"That's one of the ships you saw crashing?" Amaryllis asked.

"About the right place!" Calamity called back. "Is it one of the ones you're looking for?"

"We'll see," Amaryllis replied.

We did see, once we got closer. The ship had been, if I had to guess—which was made hard since half the ship was missing—about half the width of the *Beaver Cleaver*. Its hull was still much larger than either of the *Beaver*'s own hulls, though. There was a main deck and a bilge deck below that, both of which had been crushed into the ground on landing.

We made our way around to the back of the ship, where the entire aft section was conveniently missing, which left a large opening for us to wander into.

Amaryllis and I cast some light balls ahead to illuminate the interior, in case something had decided to make their home inside the wreck. Fortunately, other than a few creepy-crawlies, the ship was empty of anything alive.

We pulled the ponies in after us and all let out contented sighs as we finally got out of the constant downpour. I placed a hand against my breastplate and pushed it in, which squished the gambeson underneath and sent water pouring out of me. "I think I'm soaked through," I said. "I'm like, eighty percent water now."

"Well, at least no one's thirsty," Calamity chuckled. He removed his hat, then ran his hands through his fur. "I'm going to smell like wet cat all day now."

"Should we, ah, look around?" Awen said with a gesture to the crashed ship.

"Before that, we need to tend to the ponies," Calamity said. "I imagine we'll be waiting the storm out in here, and at this hour, I don't fancy riding back to camp. Unless nya really want to brave the storm, it'll be best to wait in here." He walked up to Blinky and started to undo the straps on the pony's saddle, which was just as waterlogged as the rest of us.

I rolled up and twisted the side of my skirt to wring out some water, realized it was pointless since I'd just get wet again, then gave up and went to help Calamity.

Soon, we had the ponies set up in a corner of the wreck, far from the hole we'd entered, where they could stay nice and dry. The food we'd brought for them had stayed mostly dry thanks to the leather of the satchel it was in.

Our bags weren't so lucky. They were more canvas than leather, and not quite as waterproof. The packages the food came in were somewhat better, but not by much.

"We'll eat those that got hit the worst," Amaryllis said as she stacked the food to one side. The stack looked . . . kinda saggy and sad. Still, the sylph rations came in little boxes that had resisted the weather. It was too bad that they weren't tasty even fresh.

Awen was collecting bits of wood and stacking them along the wall while Calamity and I dragged a big metal plate over. I think it was once part of the baseplate the anchor's pulley was fixed to, but now it was just a big bent chunk of metal. Good enough for a makeshift fire pit.

We didn't have to worry about the smoke pooling above us, because the side of the ship that was now the "top" had a few shattered portholes. At the moment they were letting in plenty of rainwater, but after the soaking we'd had, it was nothing.

It took a good twenty minutes to set up camp. In the end, we had cleared out a space for a pair of tents and found some actual benches to sit on around our fire pit.

"This is definitely a harpy ship," Amaryllis said once we sat down. She eyed Calamity for a moment, and I felt like she was deciding how much to reveal or not. I think she chose to trust him in the end.

"You recognize the design?" I asked.

Amaryllis nodded and pointed to the ceiling of the hold. "The trusses there, the way they're jointed, that's one of my family's techniques. This ship was made in our shipyard. It's a patrol frigate, I think."

"Think we can find out more about it?" I asked.

"We'd need the logs for that," Amaryllis said.

"There's still a lot to explore," Calamity said. "They might turn up somewhere we haven't checked yet." He seemed quite excited to look around. We'd checked for survivors already but hadn't found anyone, living or otherwise. We did find bunks, though, and storage rooms by the keel. They were on their sides, but that just meant it was trickier to look around.

Awen was handling the cooking while we tried to dry off. A cord strung across the ship was being used as a clothesline where a lot of our clothing was left to dry.

Amaryllis shook her head. "The logs would be in the officers' quarters, which should be right about . . . there." She pointed toward the big chunk of the ship that was missing.

"Oh," Calamity said.

"The engines would be there too," Awen said. "And most of the heavier sections of the ship. Harpy ships are typically back-heavy."

"We compensate for that in the design," Amaryllis said.

Awen shrugged. "It's probably why the ship was ripped in half. I'm guessing here, but I think this part still had the balloon hooked to it when it crashed. That would have slowed it down a little. But the gravity generator and other equipment would have been in the back, where they'd work best."

"Would they be far from here?" I asked.

"Maybe. If the generator was still working when the ship broke in half, it could have flown off for quite a ways," Awen speculated.

"Most of the crashing bits I saw fell near enough to each other," Calamity said. "But that was 'near enough' from a long ways off. Nya can't judge distances well like that."

"We can look around once all of this clears up," Amaryllis said with a gesture to the storm outside. The flashes were a lot more frequent now, and there was a constant bass-y rumble occasionally accentuated by a loud *crack-boom* that made the ground shake.

I nodded. "I'd rather not be out there right now, no. We can look around in the morning! I bet we'll figure the whole thing out, no problem!"

· Chapter Fourteen ·

Crash Scene Investigators

We spent the night hiding from the storm inside the ship. The worst of it took an hour or so to arrive, then hung above us for twice that long. There were constant flashes of light as lightning struck nearby, and the ground shook almost constantly with the echoing thunder.

Calamity pointed to something glowing in the distance at some point and said that part of the grassland was on fire. Apparently that was pretty common during storms like these. I could barely see it at all, but I took his word for it.

I was mostly impressed that anything could burn in the pelting rain, though the glow did disappear after a few minutes.

We drew lots for the order of watches, then settled in for the night. Thanks to my Cleaning magic we didn't need to freshen up much, so we mostly all just slept in our gear on a blanket or three. We were still soaked for the first half of the night, but the warm fire eventually left us just uncomfortably moist and finally dry-ish by the time morning came around.

I slept fitfully, but it wasn't the worst sleep I'd ever gotten. It helped when I had my friends close so that I could use them as warm pillows to keep away the chill.

Awen cooked up a simple breakfast in the morning, using a few chunks of the ship's floor as kindling. The storm had passed but there was still a faint drizzle outside. Nothing at all like the deluge of the night before.

"The rain will pass in a few hours," Calamity said. "We'll be a bit muddy, but we'll manage, I think. Let's finish up eating first though. Let the earth soak up more of yesterday's rain."

I waited another hour before stepping out of the ship after breakfast to see the wreck from the outside—since I hadn't actually looked all that hard the night before—and almost immediately lost a shoe as it was slorped up by a patch of mud. After ripping it out and tying it back on tighter, I found that the best way to move was to step on the grassiest patches. Maybe my friends and Calamity had been smart to stay inside. Awen and Amaryllis were packing up our camp, and Calamity was giving the ship another search during the daylight to see what else he could find.

The ship was called the *er's Eye*. Or at least, that was the part of the name that was left. The rest was probably on the other half of the airship, wherever that was. It was, as I'd suspected, a bit wider than either one of the *Beaver Cleaver*'s hulls, but not wider than both. It also wasn't nearly as fancy, though there was a beautifully carved figurehead of a harpy girl with her wings spread wide wearing a very windswept dress. A chunk of one wing was outright missing.

I noticed something on the hull. A long metal harpoon was jutting out of the side, the metal bent and a cut-off rope dangling from an eyelet at the back of it.

Someone had jammed that in there, probably before the ship crashed.

It had been attacked!

When I reported my findings to my friends, I got some other possibilities. "That's plausible, but it's not unheard of for ships to harpoon each other in times of need," Amaryllis said. "If this ship was losing ballast, for example, it's possible an allied vessel harpooned it to prevent it from rising too quickly. Or to tow it in an emergency. Both unlikely but plausible explanations. It certainly lends credence to there being an attack, but it's not a sure thing."

"No bodies, either," Calamity said. "I spied some blood here and there, but honestly, I imagine the folk onboard this thing took quite the tumble on the way down, so it's anyone's guess if they were hurt from that or from an attack."

"Did anyone find anything salvageable?" Awen asked. After packing up most of our things with Amaryllis, she'd loitered around one of the rooms currently above us: the mechanic's room, which I imagined was meant to be connected to the missing engine room.

Calamity nodded. "Yes, but nothing worth taking now. Plenty of provisions, some tools, a few odds and ends. All the stuff I guess you'd expect to find on a ship. The hunters are going to love scavenging this thing. Usually we bring back meat and pelts, not finished goods."

"I found the mechanic's log," Awen said. "It has details on all the recent repairs and maintenance. There was a mechanic and two apprentices. Um. The maintenance log seems pretty up to date? Unless the mechanic was lying or cutting corners, then this ship should have been in decent shape."

"Which doesn't rule out mechanical failure, but *does* make it unlikely," Amaryllis concluded. She frowned, and was clearly thinking about something before she nodded. "Maybe the other half of the ship will tell us more. Let's head out."

We did just that, climbing onto Blinky, Tassel, and Shanks and heading out of the wreck. We didn't try to hide that we'd been there. Maybe another adventurer walking by would use the fire pit we'd made. I kind of liked the idea of the wreck being turned into a landmark. The hunters would take anything salvageable, like Calamity had said, but I couldn't imagine it being easy to move the entire hull.

Calamity rode in a strange sort of spiraling pattern that had us sweeping outward, then ranging further in the other direction. It was a little weird, but an hour or so after we took off, the pattern proved its worth.

We found the other half of the airship, and another ship besides.

They were both planted at the junction between two hills, where they would be somewhat hard to spot from afar, especially once the grass straightened up post-storm. The rear of the first ship (which, from the stenciling on the side, I could now guess was called the *Hunter's Eye*) was jutting out of the side of the hill. It was planted nose-down in something of a crater.

A few hundred meters away was the other ship, which looked like it had crashed more gently. The balloon's internals were slumped across the top of the hull, metal ribs jutting through the torn fabric. Even though it was half-crumpled like a soda can, its shape was still recognizable, so I guessed the landing wasn't as harsh as it could've been. Based on the gouge trailing behind it, it seemed the ship had crashed atop one hill, then plowed down the side of it until it came to rest at the bottom, tilted at a good thirty-degree angle.

Planks and bits of its keel radiated out from the scar in the landscape.

"Engine section first," Amaryllis decided. "We'll piece together what we can from the *Hunter's Eye* before looking for clues elsewhere."

"All right," I agreed. She was the expert here when it came to harpy ships. And it was the closer one to us anyway.

Any doubts about enemy action faded as we approached the ship's rear. A gaping hole in the side of the ship poked right through the top deck and into the officers' quarters beneath. There were scorch marks too, so whatever caused that had been hot, probably some kind of magic.

There was some netting caught in the propellers at the rear. The ropes were tangled into the shafts and looked like they'd done a good job of seizing up the propulsion.

Because the *Hunter's Eye* was standing up on end, we couldn't get inside easily, and Awen pointed out that it was probably not a good idea anyway. The storm hadn't tipped it over, but if we poked around inside it, we might jostle it loose and bring it down on our heads. Unlike the forward section, this half was resting at a precarious angle, with all the heavy parts at the top and nothing but dirt below it.

If it was the only ship to explore, then maybe we'd take the risk, but it wasn't.

The second ship was a short pony ride away. Its name was the *Remiges Crown*, and I suspected it had been a warship from the moment it was designed. The ship wasn't too much longer than the *Beaver Cleaver* but its middle section bulged out, giving the impression that the ship was rather chubby.

The reason for that was the ballista platforms on either side. They weren't just little ones either. Each bowstave was half as long as I was tall. There were more of the bows at the aft of the ship, but they were much smaller.

"That's an escort corvette," Amaryllis said. "An older model at that. Half of these have been retired or sold to the independent cities by now."

"The prop of this one is also tangled in a net," Awen pointed out. "I'll have to look at the net, but it's probably the same kind."

The ship had a ladder set into the side, little handholds cut into the wood, so when we reached it and finished tying off the ponies, it only took a bit of jumping to be able to climb aboard.

Walking on the deck was strange since it was tipped to one side at a bit of an angle, but it wasn't impossible.

"More blood," Calamity pointed out. "There was fighting on this one."

"And casting," Amaryllis said. She gestured to the deck where a long scorch mark had darkened the wood. A bit farther on, the wood's grain was burned in a strange, zigzagging pattern that looked a bit like lightning bolts. An electric spell?

There were broken railings on the side, and a few abandoned grappling hooks were hanging off the ship.

"Someone boarded this vessel," Amaryllis said. "I think they were repelled, though."

"How do you know?" I asked.

"The ship's in decent condition other than the obvious. If someone had boarded it to steal it, they would have taken it, I think, or scuttled it. This ship crashed slowly. The lifeboats are missing as well." Amaryllis pointed to a pair of racks in the center of the deck where I imagined two long boats were supposed to sit.

"Maybe the people boarding the ship took them?" I asked.

"That's possible, I suppose," Amaryllis said.

As it turned out, Amaryllis was right about the ship being evacuated before it crashed. We couldn't explore most of the decks on the ship—the bottom one was ripped apart, and the main deck was a mess of broken floors and splintered wood, though it was possible to travel through it. There weren't any signs of fighting there.

Awen spent a couple of minutes at the captain's door with a few tools before she finally unlocked it and opened the door wide for us.

Calamity whistled when he entered the cabin. It was quite nice, with drapes over the shattered windows and a beautiful desk in the center of the room. Latched cabinets with glass doors were stacked to one side filled with maps and there were expensive navigational tools strewn across the floor.

There was a door past that leading to a few rooms. On one side was the captain's quarters and across from those were two smaller rooms for the officers.

"Nice!" Calamity said as he returned to the main room with a sword in hand. The grip looked like it was designed for a harpy, but it was still usable. He swung the cutlass around a few times, grinning all the while. "Think I might keep this one."

"We're looking for something a little more important," Amaryllis said. "Books, logs, anything like that." She checked around the room, clearly looking for something that was hidden. I poked around too, but there wasn't anything too shiny. I did find a nice hat, but it was the first mate's, and I preferred my captain's hat over it.

"I think I found it!" Awen called back.

She had discovered a hidden compartment built into the desk in the center of the room. Within it was a thick, leather-bound book and some writing implements.

"It's soul-bound," Amaryllis said as she inspected the book. "The ship's log. Bound to the captain. I think these are linked from captain to captain." The book had a heavy clasp on its front.

"Can you open it?" I asked.

"Only certain people can," she said. "In case the book falls into enemy hands. You need the blood and mana of a willing person taken from a relatively short list. That includes the captain and first mate, who are added to the records, a few admirals, and of course the person who originally built the vessel. It keeps a continuous record of the ship's voyages and actions that can't be tampered with. Well, unless the captain themselves does so."

"Oh," I said. "So we'll need to find an admiral to open it?" I asked.

Amaryllis shrugged, then made a small cut with a talon along the back of her hand. She dripped a drop of blood onto the clasp and it glowed faintly before popping off. "Or, you could find a direct blood-descendant of the person who built the ship," she said.

"That was anticlimactic," I pointed out.

"Yes, well, let's not complain about being lucky one of the few times that it's on our side," Amaryllis said. She opened the manifest, which turned out to be pages and pages of carefully penned notes and navigational information. She leafed over to the last page with writing on it, then stared. "Huh . . . I wasn't expecting actual pirates."

· Chapter Fifteen ·

Piracy in the High Skies

Pirates?" Calamity asked.

"Pirates," Amaryllis confirmed.

"Pirates!" Calamity cheered.

"Pirates!" I cheered with him, because it was fun.

"Pirates?" Awen repeated.

Amaryllis huffed. "Okay, enough of that. I'm aware some of you are excited, but can we please take this seriously? This is an important matter."

I nodded along. That was a fair thing to ask, even if the news was quite exciting. "So, what does the book say?"

Amaryllis held the manifest open in the crook of one wing and ran her talons across the other page. "All right, let's trace this back a little," she said as she flipped back a couple of pages. "Here. This ship was one of the first to meet with the *Royal Plumage*, the main delegation vessel. They took off from Fort Sylphrot, then headed north. They collected new crewmates at Farseeing and waited two days at dock for the fleet to assemble. There are some notes from the quartermaster."

"I think we can skip those," Awen said.

Amaryllis nodded. "All right, here, the ship left Farseeing and headed north again. They stopped by Walker's Rest, where they picked up a few more nobles and another couple of escort ships. The *Hunter's Eye* was one of those, as well as its sister ship, the *Hunter's Fang*."

I nodded along. I could more or less trace the trajectory in my mind. "How many ships does that make?" I asked.

"Including the main delegation ship, which was a government yacht, there were two corvettes, two frigates, and a single cruiser."

Calamity whistled. "That's an awful lot of ships," he said.

"More escorts than you'd ever expect for a commercial venture, but for a political one, this is more or less par for the course." Amaryllis tapped the page. "This ship, the *Remiges Crown*, I think it belonged to a noble of the Canary family. So not a Nesting Kingdom Navy vessel but a privately owned and operated warship."

I looked around the deck, noting all the weapons on it. "Really? This is a private ship?"

"A merchant escort. It explains why it's so lightly armed," Amaryllis said.

This was lightly armed? It had a lot more going for it than the *Beaver* did. Then again, the *Beaver Cleaver* was an adventuring ship first and foremost. "Anyway, then what?"

"So, all six vessels headed further north. They crossed to the east of the mountain range through Walker's Pass, then they headed toward Sylphfree using a fairly circuitous route." Amaryllis turned the page. "Ah, they hit a storm coming from the south maybe . . . a week ago."

"I remember that one," Calamity said. "Nasty storm. Way worse than what we slept through last night."

"That threw the fleet into disarray. They regrouped to the west of Fort Middlesfaire and continued north. I think they were planning on slipping to the south of the Greenstone."

Calamity frowned. "That's daring."

"What's the Greenstone?" I asked.

"It's an area to the north of here, thataways," Calamity said as he pointed. "It's all dead. Like a small desert, with a nearly perfect edge. There's this huge green pillar in the middle of it. All glowy and magical."

"What's it do?"

He shrugged. "Kills nya, mostly. Don't rightly know who put it there or why."

"Giant mysterious pillar, got it." I turned back to Amaryllis. "Then what?"

"Then, the pirates. The fleet was trying to move at double time, but they ran into complications. Doesn't say what. The log only says that they saw . . . well, here, read this passage at the bottom here." She turned the manifest my way and pointed to the very last lines, all done in a neat hand.

0909h: Ships sighted. 340–345 North. Six vessels. No sight on flags.

1017h: Ships approaching. Three vessels turning to intercept. No flags. Unknown vessel type.

1037h: Alarm raised from the Concordance. *Ships are Snowlanders. Two frigate-tonnage vessels. Two corvettes. One cruiser. One heavy vessel (cargo converted?). Bearing on fleet.*

1100h: Flags raised. Pirates. Preparing for boarding and combat. Closing log.

* * *

That was the last entry. The rest of the page was all blank. I was kind of impressed by the steady hand of whoever had written the notes. "So, pirates. For real-real," I said.

Amaryllis nodded. "This ship and the *Hunter's Eye* were taken out. The pirates didn't come down to salvage, by the looks of it. The delegation was going to be late because of the storm. This just made it worse."

"I guess they had bigger things to worry about than being late," Awen said. "Like pirates."

Amaryllis nodded. "Their route is strange. This isn't the fastest path to Sylphfree, not by a long shot. The timing isn't adding up."

"Think someone on the inside told the pirates?" Calamity asked. He was pretty excited by it all.

"It's possible, though I'd hope not. The last thing we need is a political element within the country consorting with pirates and scoundrels." She snapped the manifest shut and locked it up. "We need to report this."

"Going to take a couple days to reach Fort Middlesfaire from here," Calamity said. "Longer, if we intend to loot the ship before we run off."

Amaryllis narrowed her eyes in thought, then shook her head. "No, that's too long. I suggest that we use the ring we have to contact our friends in Sylphfree for pickup."

Calamity looked at her, but didn't comment.

"They'll be able to find us out here?" I asked.

Awen nodded. "It shouldn't be too hard to triangulate where someone is with that kind of ring. Not for a paladin team, I imagine. Also, we'll be telling them where we are, which should help."

Calamity slowly raised a hand to ask a question. "Sorry ny'all, but what are we talking about?"

My friends and I shared a look, and I was silently elected the spokesbun. "Well, we came here to discover what happened to the delegation, right?" He nodded. "Both Sylphfree and the Nesting Kingdom want to know. So we're in contact with Sylphfree for this mission. They're the ones who helped us get all the way over to here."

"Oh," he said. "Well, I'll be. Proper spies from another land."

"We're not spies," I said.

"It's true. At worst we're mercenaries," Amaryllis pointed out. "But in reality it's more that our goals happen to align with Sylphfree's. It's a matter of mutual convenience. The sylphs need to know what happened to the delegation so that the harpies won't be angered by them. Ideally, we'll also be able to prove that the Trenten Flats are innocent in all of this."

"Innocent?" he asked. Then his eyes lit up. "Because the ships went down over the Flats. Right, I can see why that might ring some alarms. Like discovering one of your hens died in the neighbor's yard."

"Not the analogy I'd use, but yes, something like that," Amaryllis said. "I need a moment to pen a response." She glanced around. We were still in the officers' quarters, which happened to have desks and writing implements. Most of the latter were scattered across the floor, but they weren't far.

"Want to keep snooping around while she does all that?" I asked Calamity and Awen.

"Sure, I'd love ta," the cowboy said. Awen nodded. We left the cabins at the rear of the ship and made our way to the center of the lower deck, where a staircase led to the main deck. "So, are nya really an airship captain?" he asked.

I nodded. "I am! I've only been one for a couple of months, though."

"Busy months," Awen said.

"Oh yeah, very. This won't be our first run-in with pirates."

"You've seen pirates before?" he asked. "Like, in the air?"

I nodded. "Awen was kidnapped once!"

"I get kidnapped a lot," Awen noted with a heavy sigh. "Twice since I met Broccoli. But the first time it was by Broccoli, so I'm not sure if it counts."

"I think it technically needs to be involuntary for it to count," I pointed out. I hardly needed Calamity to start thinking I was some sort of evil bun mastermind, kidnapper of cute friends and hug-thief.

"That's incredible. You must know a bunch about airships then, like, ah, what kinda loot we can find in one of these here airships?" he asked with a gesture around himself. The lower deck of the *Remiges Crown* was fairly open, with netted shelves to the sides and an area near the fore that was filled with hammocks.

"Uh, I guess food, some normal supplies, maybe weapons?" I asked. The *Beaver* didn't have much by means of treasure on it. Maybe a few personal items, but that was it.

"A ship this big might have an armory," Awen said.

As it turns out, she was right. We found a heavy metal door at the rear of the ship with three big locks on it. None of them were actually locked, though, and the door had been left half-open. I imagined that the crew had grabbed what they needed when pirates showed up and were a bit too busy to lock up on the way out.

The room was narrow, shoved up against the side of the engine as it was. One wall was entirely made up of racks that had held a bunch of weapons once. Now it was down to a few that had been left behind. Calamity was still excited about it, though. "Oh, crossbows. And grapples." He picked up a cutlass, then compared it to the one he'd grabbed earlier.

I looked around at things too, but I wasn't super interested in weapons, and there wasn't much else there. The kitchen proved a lot more interesting. It was also at the rear and seemed nearly intact.

That made some sense. All the food was in cupboards with strong latches or secured onto racks that were meant to endure a good bit of turbulence. There was a magical rune-powered fridge at the back filled with all sorts of goodies, and the stove was also powered by mana.

Awen and I started cooking, mostly noodles with whatever sauces we found in the fridge. It would let us save up some of our other supplies in case we needed them.

"You're getting the hang of cooking, huh?" I asked Awen as she mixed a pot full of a tomato-like paste.

"It's not too different from assembling something, in a way. And . . . I like it when you and Amaryllis are happy that I cooked something nice."

"Aw!" I cooed before grabbing her for a quick cheek-squishing hug. "I like it when you're happy too!"

Amaryllis came down a few minutes later with a small frown on her face. "Ah, there you are," she said. "Are you cooking?"

"Early lunch!" I said.

"I suppose there's no point in letting anything go to waste. Anyway, I finished contacting Sylphfree. They can have a flight of wyverns here to pick us up by tomorrow afternoon."

"That's a long time away," I said.

"We're not exactly close by. Though I had hoped they would have a ship ready for departure with less delay than that," Amaryllis said.

"So, we hang around here until the sylphs arrive, then I lead the ponies back?" Calamity asked. He was in what I guess was the ship's mess, though the table was clearly meant to fold up against the wall to be out of the way.

"No, not quite," Amaryllis said. "They want us to keep investigating things in the region. Calamity, you said you only saw two ships coming down, right?"

"Yeah, but it was from afar. I don't doubt my eyes, but I know their limits."

"Then maybe we can find a vantage and look around, just in case. We have time to kill before the sylphs take off, and they can home in on us. We don't need to sit around and wait."

"That sounds fine," I said. "But first, let's get something warm into our tummies, huh?"

Amaryllis rolled her eyes, but when Awen came out with a big bowl full of steaming noodles and sauce, her hard expression turned quite eager.

A small break, then a pinch more adventure. Just what we needed to cap off the day!

· Chapter Sixteen ·

Abandoned Ship

After grabbing a few supplies from the *Remiges Crown*—and waiting for Calamity to load up on knick-knacks that he could fit in his pack—we got back onto the ponies and headed out. Calamity pointed us toward a hill to the south of our position. It looked almost like a shelf of earth that jutted out of the ground with a sharp edge. The space beneath it had a small forest's worth of trees growing where the wind couldn't reach them.

We switched things up for fun; Amaryllis rode with Awen, so I had Shanks all to myself as we traveled across the plains. I kind of wished that I was riding with one of my friends. Sharing a saddle was a great excuse to get my daily dose of cuddles in.

The hillside wasn't too far away, but it still took an hour to get to it. The ground being so muddy didn't help any. The poor ponies had splashes of mud all the way up to their tummies, and my shoes were caked in it by the time we reached the hill. A bit of Cleaning magic worked it off, but it was still kind of annoying.

Calamity found a switchback path dug into the side of the hill. "Is this a natural path?" Amaryllis asked.

"Hmm? Oh, nyeah this is ancient. I don't know who dug this out, but it's been here forever. There's a wider, newer way down farther south, with some railings and all, but it's a bit far to travel for us when all we want's a spot to see from. I heard that these were made by an earth mage a long while back. Some folk say that a magic cockatrice that could move earth made them, but I don't rightly believe those tall tales."

Once we were at the top of the hill, I took in the great vista below us. It was, for the most part, just grass. Lots and lots of grass, as far as my bun eyes could see. Some places had muddy pools of water where there was a dip in the land, but even those had grass pushing through the mud, and I didn't doubt that by midafternoon it would all dry up and be absorbed by the thirsty ground.

Calamity had mentioned in passing that it only rained once every week, but when it did, it was always strong.

"That's the *Hunter's Eye*," Awen said as she pointed. I followed her gaze to the distant form of the ship's keel. "And that over there's the other half of the *Eye* and the *Remiges Crown*."

The nearer ship wasn't too difficult to see, being a bit larger, but its position leaning against the hill made it likely that anyone approaching from the opposite side wouldn't notice it as easily. Once the storm-pushed grass returned to its upright position and the ship sank a little deeper into the ground, it could become almost impossible to find.

I didn't doubt that the wind would toss some dirt onto the deck and then grass would grow from that, until it melded into the verdancy. But that hadn't happened just yet and wouldn't happen for a while.

"So, that's two ships in three parts," Amaryllis said. She scanned the horizon. "I don't see any others. I wish we had a spyglass."

"Oh!" Awen said. She brought her hands up, as if holding an invisible tube, then furrowed her brow. Glass formed between her hands with a faint crackle, like crystals growing but a thousand times faster. She focused harder, then squinted as her creation took form. It was a telescope! A single piece of glass forming lenses with bars to hold them in place. "I'm going to need to fiddle with this, and I don't think anyone else will be able to adjust the focus, but . . ." She looked through it at the distant form of the *Remiges Crown*.

"What can you see?" I asked.

"The . . . ship I'm looking at?" she answered, a bit confused. "There's nothing really new. Uh, having this only helps me see, it doesn't really help me find new things to look at."

"Oh, right," I said.

We squinted out into the distance, looking for anything that stood out. Unsurprisingly, it was Calamity who spotted something strange first. "That way," he said. "Along the ridge we're on, about two hours' ride southeast." He was pointing a bit behind us.

I spotted what he was talking about. It was a few kilometers away from the crash site for the *Hunter's Eye*'s fore-section, just a little bit behind the ridge we were standing on. Or maybe it was another ridge? It was hard to tell, but I suspected we were on the lip of a very big, very old crater.

"I see it," Awen said. The telescope clinked and cracked, like someone stepping on a wineglass with heavy boots and shifting their foot around. The lenses twisted a bit, and the telescope adjusted itself minutely. "Got it."

"So, what do you see?" Amaryllis asked. "It looks like a dark lump to me."

That was a pretty accurate description for me too. There was something black in the distance, but because it was barely peeking out of the grass,

I had no way to get a sense of scale. I had probably looked right past it a couple of times already.

"I think it's a ship," Awen said. "No, it's definitely a ship. There's a balloon, I think that's the black part. It's a bit behind the curve of the hill, so I can't see much of it." She passed her telescope to Amaryllis, who plucked it from her and stared into the distance as well.

"That does look like it might be a vessel of some sort. A smaller one. Could be one of the lifeboats. No, no it couldn't be," Amaryllis said.

"It couldn't?" I asked.

"Harpy lifeboats don't have their own balloons. That looks more like a skiff, similar to the *Shady Lady.*"

Abraham's little ship? Flying on the *Shady Lady* had been a blast! Though it had also been kind of terrifying. That ship was held together with tape and happy thoughts.

"Do you think it's part of the delegation or the pirates?" I asked.

"Hard to tell," Amaryllis said. She passed me the telescope while Awen made another in about half the time it had taken her to make the one I now had. I squeezed one eye shut and looked through to search for the ship.

It really was hard to spot, even with a zoomed-in view. The craft looked like it was pretty even with the ground, but its balloon was draped across the hill as if it had ripped, which was probably exactly what had happened.

"It doesn't look like it crashed," I said. "It looks like it's mostly in one piece."

"We'll see once we get closer," Amaryllis said.

That kind of decided our next destination for us, though only after we looked around for more points of interest. We patted down the ponies, I cleaned off the mud from their shoes and flanks, and then we headed out once more. Calamity had us walking a little ways away from the cliff's edge. He said that while it was great for keeping track of where you were going, he'd also seen the cliff fall apart a few times and didn't want to trigger a landslide.

Calamity's guess about the distance was spot-on. It took a bit over an hour to get close enough to the ship to see it without Awen's telescope, and another half hour before we drew near it.

"That's not a harpy design," Amaryllis said as we got closer.

The ship was long and narrow, maybe a third as long as the *Beaver Cleaver* but thin enough that it could easily fit between the *Beaver*'s two hulls. Its hull was shaped a bit like a teardrop, with the rear section being larger and the front tapering to a curved point.

It wasn't made of wood the way harpy ships were or flat metal panels like the sylphs preferred. This was all sleek, curved metal, carefully shaped and riveted together.

"That's a Snowlander ship," Awen said with obvious glee. "Oh, these are super uncommon outside of the Snowlands. They're the *best* airships, period."

I could see why Awen was excited. The ship reminded me a bit of pictures I'd seen of old World War Two aircraft. Compared to this, every other airship I'd seen had more in common with a Blériot or a Wright brothers' aircraft.

The front of the ship lacked a figurehead; instead, the metal wrapped around to form a semi-enclosed turret with a fixed crossbow mounted on a ring. It looked as if someone could stand inside and turn all the way around while aiming the bow. The crossbow was also . . . High-tech wasn't the right word for it, but I couldn't think of anything better. It had big metal bars and a box under it, with a large, visible spring and a chain with linked-together bolts dangling from the side.

Behind that, the ship was mostly enclosed until the larger section at the rear, where a wheel sat in a tiny booth with glass around it and there was some walking space to access the posts and winches the ship likely needed to tie itself at a dock.

The rear of the ship contained a mostly-enclosed propeller. There were openings around it to suck air out from the front and direct it all the way to the propeller itself.

"Oh, look at that!" Awen cooed as she rode closer. She jumped off her pony, leaving Amaryllis to catch the reins. "The air is pulled through those vents on the underside, see, and I bet they'll pass next to the engine. Not only pulling air through, but using it for cooling too! It's so simple, but so clever!"

I dismounted my pony, then gave its reins to Amaryllis, who stared at them, and the other reins, then huffed a very clear *why am I taking care of these?* huff.

"What kind of metal is this?" Awen asked as she tapped the skin of the ship with a knuckle to produce a hollow *clunk*. "Even tin would make this way too heavy."

"Aluminum?" I asked. "It's very light and pretty strong. They use it for airplanes where I'm from, I think."

"Oh . . . but how did they shape it like this? Is every single part cast individually? Unless they have a whole factory making just this kind of skiff, that's a lot of work. It doesn't look hammered."

I watched Awen go. It was cute how enthusiastic she was about the mysterious Snowlander ship.

While she poked and prodded at it, I walked around the ship and took in its position. There were three large landing gears deployed below and sunk into the mud a little. One looked a bit bent, as if the landing had been rougher than ideal, but they weren't broken, I didn't think. So the ship hadn't crashed.

"Is there anyone in there?!" I called out, hands around my mouth.

My friends paused. I don't think they'd considered that possibility.

No one made a sound, so if someone was hiding in the ship, well, then they were *hiding*, not just waiting on board.

"There's a ladder here!" Awen said.

She'd found a panel on the side of the ship which could be opened. It revealed two ladders, one mounted to the hull, and another on rails which dropped with a clack and stopped half a meter off the ground.

Awen was the first to climb aboard, but the rest of us followed soon after, with Amaryllis taking up the rear since she had to tie the ponies to a stake.

The ship's interior was a lot sleeker than any I'd seen, with walls that were padded with leather and wooden floors. Some of the walls had little cabinets built into them for tools and supplies. The ship was too small to have anything on the top deck, but there was a set of trapdoors that Awen pulled open to access the engine below the command console.

The console itself, with the wheel at the back of it, was in the center of the main deck. There was a whole heap of levers and gauges within easy reach. It looked like the sails could all be controlled from that one place by a single pilot.

In front of the console was the covered section of the hull, which looked like a tight tunnel all the way to the crossbow emplacement at the very front. I poked my head in. There were bunks along the sides here, and a tiny compact kitchen and sitting area.

Something felt off about the ship but I didn't figure out what until I came to stand behind the wheel and had to reach my arms up to touch it. This was a ship designed for someone taller than I was. I gave the bunks another look, and they were like that too. About as wide as a normal one-person bunk, but longer by a nearly half a meter.

Whoever had built this thing knew how to pack every necessity in tightly.

"Pirates," Calamity said, pulling me out of my reverie. He was looking up, toward a flag hooked to a ladder that would have reached the balloon if it hadn't collapsed. The flag was black, with a grinning skull.

· Chapter Seventeen ·

Finders Keepers

So, how bad is it?" I asked as Awen pulled herself out of the engine bay. She had a bit of grease on the tip of her nose and some sweat on her brow, but she looked happy all the same.

"It's fantastic," Awen said. "It's also so, *so* simple. Well, no, it's complicated, so many little parts interacting, but it's like whoever designed it wanted every part to be easily replaceable. I think I could make half the parts here out of *glass* and they'd still work. Nothing's under a lot of strain when everything's operating properly. There's nothing new here, exactly, it's all just executed so cleanly."

"That's nice," Amaryllis said. Usually when she said that, it was sarcastic, but this time it didn't sound that way. "But Broccoli was asking if the ship will work?"

"Oh," Awen said. She pulled out a hankie to wipe her nose, but before she could I knelt down, licked my thumb, and rubbed the grease off with a bit of Cleaning magic. She made a face before replying. "If we can get the balloon refilled, then yes. Even without that, I think this one can fly, though it'd be under a lot of strain and we might not get far on the fuel we have."

"Flight-capable without a buoyancy device?" Amaryllis asked. "That's impressive. We've been trying to crack that one for a while, but we always run into issues, at least when it comes to anything larger than a raft. You need a lot of fuel to manage it, which means more weight, which means bigger engines, which means more fuel."

Awen nodded. "They've figured it out here. Which I guess isn't too surprising; the Snowlanders are supposed to be some of the best mechanics around, and it shows. I don't even think this was a mass-produced ship. It's got a few little personal touches that I wouldn't expect from something built in a factory."

Artisanal ship crafters? That was neat. The more I heard about these Snowlanders, the more I wanted to visit them. Although the flag still concerned me. "Nothing piratical in there, right?" I asked.

Awen shook her head. "I don't think a motor can be piratical."

Calamity had found a seat atop the covered part of the hull. Now that I was thinking about it, the ship was kind of shaped like a very sharp shoe with a hole on the heel end. "So, are we going to leave this here? Seems a shame to leave a working airship behind."

"Air*boat*, technically," Amaryllis pointed out. "And . . . yes, actually, you're correct, leaving it behind is a shame. Under most international treaties, capturing a pirate's vessel means that the vessel is now, in part, your property. You have a legal duty to communicate with its previous owners in most countries, whereby they have the right to purchase it from you at half its market value. Which should be covered by any halfway-competent insurance. So, having technically captured this vessel, we can lay a legal claim on it."

"Really?" I asked. "We didn't even beat the pirates ourselves though, so would that be fair?"

"Broccoli, the nice thing about pirates is that they don't show up in court to argue with you," Amaryllis said.

I pouted, a bit of warmth clinging to my cheeks. "Okay, fine," I said. "But it still feels wrong to just up and take this ship."

"Take a quarter of it," Calamity corrected.

We glanced up to him and the catboy grinned a very Cheshire grin. "We are, of course, splitting the find four ways, right? It's only fair."

I nodded. "Yup, that's true."

He blinked. "You're not going to argue?"

"No, it's fair, why would I?" I asked. "Besides, without your help, we wouldn't be here. Did you want me to teach you a bit about handling a ship? I'm not an expert yet, but I think I can qualify as an experienced novice."

"Oh, I'd like that, sure," Calamity said. "But if we're going to take this thing up, how're your sylph friends going to reach us?"

"We could meet them in midair," Amaryllis said. "It might even simplify things greatly."

Calamity nodded along. He was clearly excited, but then his shoulders fell. "We can't. The ponies." He gestured off to the side where the three ponies were grazing on some of the taller grass.

"Oh, right," I said. "What do we do with the ponies? Could we bring them aboard?"

Amaryllis wrinkled her nose. "I don't know about that. Most ships that carry livestock are designed around the idea that they'll have to carry livestock, with stables and cages that have straps designed to hold them in place without too much motion."

"That's true, but this ship should be able to lift them," Awen said. "They're heavy, but not past the total load we could carry."

I looked over at the ponies, who were just happily munching along. "They seem pretty tame."

"I've got a skill that'll keep them from panicking," Calamity said. "We can tie 'em up here, and maybe cover their eyes, just in case. They won't mind the noise, I don't think."

I was pretty sure that Calamity just really wanted to ride on the airship. "What would we need to do?" I asked Awen.

She gestured to the balloon. "It's deflated, but not entirely. So we need to look for holes, and if there are any, we need to plug them. Then we need to inflate the balloon. There's a pair of tanks under the hull, and I'm guessing they're filled with whatever the Snowlanders use for their buoyancy."

"It's a mixture of helium and a few magical gases," Amaryllis said. "They keep the formula somewhat hidden, but not as hidden as their methods for sourcing helium."

It made sense. Helium was pretty much the best gas for airships, with hydrogen being a bit *way too explosive* and other gases having their own problems. If the Snowlanders had easy access to helium, that would give them a leg up. Then again, looking at the little ship, it was clear that helium wasn't their only advantage. I had no idea what the magical stuff was, but it didn't seem as rare, somehow?

I wasn't that well-versed in history and such, but it was pretty clear that this vehicle was a few decades ahead of any other airship I'd seen so far. "Have the Snowlanders always been so advanced?" I asked.

"Technology-wise?" Awen asked. She nodded. "I think so. I remember Uncle talking about them when I was young."

"But that was a few years ago," I pointed out. "Haven't any others caught up?"

"It takes time to catch up," Amaryllis said. "Time which the Snowlanders have used to progress even more. But their technological edge won't hold forever. The Snowlands have plenty of resources, but the area is cold and rather hostile at the best of times. In a few decades we'll catch up to them, I'm sure."

Awen had Calamity and me clambering over the balloon to look for rips or tears while she prepped other things aboard the ship and Amaryllis sent a message to the sylphs with our new location and the information we'd found.

That the pirate idea was entirely verified (the not-quite-Jolly-Roger was a dead giveaway) was troubling. More troubling was that the pirates had access to some really high-tech Snowlander ships.

"Found one!" Calamity said. He was poking a finger through a fist-sized hole in the tarp.

As it turned out, there was a second hole on the opposite end.

"It looked like the balloon got pierced through," Awen said as she brought out a patching kit she'd found in one of the compartments. "Maybe by a magical attack, or a ballista bolt. It doesn't look like it's a big enough hole to ruin the ship, but it would have made it lose altitude."

"So they landed out here and abandoned it," I guessed. "But why?"

"Does it matter? It's good for us, and too bad for them!" Calamity cheered.

Patching the two holes took a good half hour, even with Awen helping. The stuff the ship had for hole-patches were tarp strips with glue on one side covered in a thin piece of paper. By using Fire magic to burn off the paper, the glue became warm and very, very sticky, and it could then be slapped over the hole and pressed on while it dried. The instructions called for cold wind or Ice mana to be pushed against the surface to help it dry, which Amaryllis helped with since she had the easiest time converting her mana to other aspects.

Once I cleared the glue off of our equipment—it really was terribly sticky—we set to reinflating the balloon.

"We don't have enough gas to fill the balloon entirely," Awen said. "We're going to have to mix in normal air."

In the end, we inflated the balloon with what gases the ship had left, then Awen and I undid the rather heavy tanks and tossed them off the side. They were designed to be easy to remove, so it wasn't difficult, and the weight difference would help.

After that, Awen set up a pump to fill the rest of the balloon's space with normal air while Calamity and I coaxed the blindfolded ponies aboard up a lowered gangplank, and then convinced them to lay down onto some blankets while we fed them the rest of the grain we'd brought.

I could see why Amaryllis didn't like the idea of bringing them aboard. They took up a lot of space, and if they panicked, things would get really complicated really fast.

"I think our first stop will have to be somewhere to bring the ponies," I said.

"We can return to the hunters," Calamity said. "There's a fairly large camp. It might have some supplies we need to keep this boat going too. I think a few of the machines we have at the camp use the same kind of fuel."

With that semblance of a plan in place, we spent the rest of the afternoon preparing to fly. There was probably a lot less to do to get this ship airborne than, say, preparing the *Beaver*, but the ship was unfamiliar to us, and we didn't have nearly as big a crew to help set things up.

Awen got the engine started, then, with a box secured to the floor to give her some height, came to stand behind the wheel. "All right. All hands on deck. Gravity engine to half and throttle at idle. Broccoli, sails to neutral. Amaryllis, Calamity, check the rudder sails and start winching the anchors up."

I snapped a salute to Awen, which lit up her cheeks brilliantly. "Aye, aye, Captain Awen!"

"Awa! I'd much rather be the first mate, actually."

"Can I be the captain?" Calamity asked.

"You don't have the hat for it," I replied. Cowboy hats were cool, but not what you were looking for when about to pilot an airship. Not nearly enough feathers.

"This is a boat, not a ship," Amaryllis argued. "Which means we have no need for a captain. Now, will we sit here and argue, or are we going to get this tub into the air?"

Calamity spun the winch to bring up the ship's anchors, and Amaryllis and I busied ourselves adjusting the sails, which was surprisingly easy. They were smaller than those on the *Beaver Cleaver*, so we didn't need to use nearly as much effort to get them deployed and angled correctly.

Awen kicked up the juice on the gravity engine, and then for just a moment, we hovered on the spot. I grinned at the familiar but still strange feeling of momentary weightlessness before we started to climb up very gently.

"Engine seems buoyant at . . . sixty-four percent," Awen said.

"Is that good?"

"It's not exactly fuel-efficient," Awen said. "It's enough to let us move, but we'll be slow."

We rose up a few dozen meters, then Awen slowed the ascent down so that we were hovering on the spot.

"Okay," I said as I glanced over the edge. "Now we only have one more thing to do. What do we name this ship?"

· Chapter Eighteen ·

Redemption Arc

Awa, the, um, *Smooth Sailing*," Awen proposed.
I thought about it for a moment. It wasn't a bad name. Very sweet. Cute, even! But I wasn't entirely sure if it fit the ship. It was too metallic and sharp for that name.

"And here I thought you'd ask to name it the *Rose's Lips*, or something," Amaryllis said.

Awen blushed while a storm of denying *Awa!*'s escaped her.

"Am I missing something there?" Calamity asked. "By the way, clearly this beauty ought to be called something properly enticing. The *Dagger*, or maybe the *Sky Meowderer*."

"I'm not sure about that last one," I said. "What about the *Friend-Ship*?"

"Vetoed," Amaryllis said. "We won't abide pun names. We could call it something like the . . . hmm, it's a warship. The *Strongly Worded Letter*?"

Awen made a noise that was very close to being a huff. Was she trying to get back at Amaryllis? "That's too long. It wouldn't fit on the side. And Broccoli, this is a boat more than a ship."

"I'm guessing the *Friend-Boat* is out too?" I asked.

I got three nods in reply.

"We need something a bit more fierce than that," Calamity said. "Like some sorta predatory animal?"

"The *Angry Moose*?" I tried.

Amaryllis frowned. "What in the World is a moose?"

"Is it like a mouse?" Awen asked.

I shook my head and gave up on the name. "No, never mind."

"Well, how about the *Hermeowne*?" Calamity asked. "It's the name of this girl I was sweet on for a while."

"Let's not name our new boat after one of your no doubt many failed romantic conquests," Amaryllis said.

"Maybe we can name it after something it is?" I asked. I trimmed the sails a bit. We were picking up some speed, but I was pretty sure we didn't want to be moving quite so quickly.

Awen clapped her hands. "Ah! I know. It was a pirate boat before, wasn't it? And now it's ours, and we're the opposite of pirates. Or near enough. So the vessel's being reformed. We could call it the *Redemption*!"

"That's properly intimidating," Calamity said. "I vote aye on that one."

Amaryllis considered it for a moment before replying. "It's . . . suitable."

"I like it!" I chimed in. It was also nice that everyone seemed to agree about the ship's name too.

With that done, we got back to work piloting the newly named *Redemption* across the grassy plains. Awen stood fixed at the back of the wheel for a while, testing the various controls, but eventually she called me over to take the wheel. I had the Captaining skill, which was the only airship-related skill anyone in our group had, at least as far as piloting a ship went.

It didn't take long for me to get a hang of the controls. They reminded me a bit of a car's, actually, but without the foot pedals. There were airbrakes in the form of flaps that could be pulled up with a lever, and the throttle wasn't any more complicated than the throttle on a riding lawn mower.

Amaryllis and Awen checked our position, with Calamity giving a few pointers toward local landmarks, and then we turned south and west a bit, straight toward the hunters' camp.

If we were going to keep the ship, we obviously needed to get the ponies somewhere safe, and we'd need fresh supplies in any case. Once we were prepared, we could head back out and meet our sylph friends up in the air, then figure out where to go from there.

I was a smidge worried about that last part, actually.

The diplomats had been taken by pirates. Actual, hardened pirates. They hadn't issued any ransoms that I knew of, which was concerning. Were the diplomats being treated well? They'd better be! Pirates were cool and all, but only the nice sort who worked to destabilize mean governments and spread art that was otherwise unavailable.

The *Redemption* was a pretty nice boat, though it didn't fly as evenly as the *Beaver Cleaver*. I had to fight it to stay even, and every big gust of wind sent us flying off track. Once we skimmed a bit too close to the top of a hill, which had us dialing back the speed, just in case.

Still, it made up for its strange flight characteristics by being pretty zippy and maneuverable. With a practiced pilot at the wheel and a few good crew-mates, I was certain the *Redemption* could fly circles around some of the larger airships I'd seen.

"Smoke ahead and . . . Uh, which one is right?" Calamity asked.

"Starboard," Amaryllis replied. "I see it. About forty degrees, three klicks as the harpy flies. We might want to slow down. I imagine the hunters below would rather we come in slowly and peacefully rather than spook their horses."

"A few of them are pretty good shots," Calamity said. "Might turn us into pincushions before we have time to identify ourselves."

I pulled back on the throttle until we were basically only moving on momentum. I turned us so that we weren't pointing right at the hunters' camp, which meant I could actually see it. The *Redemption*'s bow was too tall for me to see out ahead, which was maybe something of a design flaw. As we turned a smidge, I could make out the camp. Dozens of tents, some carts, and plenty of people moving around, most of them atop a wide hill surrounded by pressed-down grass.

"Ahoy!" Calamity called as he hung off the side of the boat and waved his hat about.

His pals below shouted back, some waving, others masking their eyes from the sun to see us better as we circled the camp in a tight loop and settled down next to the camp. Awen undid the latch on the anchor and a pair of chains rattled out of the *Redemption*'s rear to hold us in place.

We lowered the landing gear and gently reduced the strength on the gravity generator until the boat touched down with a lurch. "I think that went pretty well, for a maiden flight," I said.

"It wasn't a maiden flight," Amaryllis said. "Unless you consider it this crew's, in which case . . . it still wouldn't count."

I puffed my cheeks out. "Well, I don't know what it is then, but it went well. The boat handled things with no trouble."

"We burned a lot of fuel," Awen said. She closed one of the engine compartments with a hard *thump*. "We wouldn't have been able to fly for much longer. Maybe another hour or two?"

"We made it, didn't we?" Calamity said with a grin. Then he glanced over the railings and grinned. "Heya there, Savan! Come to see my brand-new ship?"

A familiar catlike head poked up from the edge of the ship. Savan was gripping onto the railing, her legs around one of the anchor chains. "Pretty," she said. "But you can't eat ships, Calamity."

"I know, but I bet you can hunt all sorts of things from the skies," he replied. "Is everyone at the camp?"

Savan rolled up onto the edge of the *Redemption*, then bounced to her feet. She looked around as she spoke, obviously curious about the ship. "Two of the teams aren't back yet. We lost a pony to a cockatrice. It stared into its eyes and Mey was catapulted off when it dropped. But she's fine."

"Hah! I'd've loved to see that," Calamity said. "Too bad about the pony. Speaking of which, want to help me unload these three?"

With the help of Savan, and then the other catpeople and cervids from the camp who came to loiter around, it wasn't too complicated to unload the ponies. Calamity was the hero of the hour. He told a greatly exaggerated story about us braving the storm and discovering huge destroyed airships, then the four of us valiantly working together to piece the *Redemption* back into working order.

The story was mostly truthful, at least in the broad strokes. I would have complained, but Calamity was having fun, and his hunter friends seemed happy to rib him and call him out for exaggerating.

Once we were all back on firm ground, I turned to Amaryllis and Awen. "Now what?" I asked.

"Now we ensure that no one steals our ship from us without proper remuneration," Amaryllis said. "And we need to relay our location to the sylphs again. They might not want to meet in a place with so many strangers."

"We could hunt for more clues," Awen suggested.

We turned to her, and she squirmed but continued. "We know the diplomats were attacked by pirates, but at that point the trail goes cold."

"That seems like a good idea to me," I said. "But we'll need supplies to keep searching."

"I can help with that." The three of us jumped and turned to find Savan standing really close to us. She grinned. "I know where to find all the stuff. What are you looking for?"

"Uh, fuel, mostly," Awen said.

Savan blinked. "I don't know how to find that stuff," she admitted. "But I know the people to ask. Come on!"

With that, Savan led us toward the camp proper. It was a loose collection of tents, some large, some small, with a few buildings made of wood and tarps set up here and there and some carriages parked on the flatter ground that had little homes built atop them. It looked like a few of those more temporary buildings had been knocked down by the storm, but they were being fixed in quick order.

A few roads cut through the camp, all made of stomped dirt, packed down by hundreds of passing hunters. There was a large grazing area to one side surrounded by a picket-and-rope fence where horses and ponies were plucking at the grass.

I checked out the temporary buildings as we walked by them. One had a mobile forge in it where a pair of cervids were working the bellows while another held tongs clenching a red-hot bit of metal. Next to that was a small shop with a cat person on a carpet surrounded by knives and walking sticks and tarps for sale. Finally, Savan brought us to a small general store of sorts. She pushed the tent-flap door aside and stuck her head in. "Hello? Do you sell fuel?"

We ended up meeting a nice elderly human, of all things, who didn't have airship fuel but who did have some oils that Awen said would work in a pinch.

Then we crossed over to a set of tents set downwind of the camp where some hunters were working at butchering their catch. They were more than willing to sell us a few tankfuls of grease and fat, which Awen had some use for.

"We won't have enough to get far, but this is more than what we had to begin with," Awen said as we lugged the tanks back to the airship.

On our way back, we met with Calamity, who seemed to have tired out his buddies with his stories. "Heya. So, are we heading out on our ship again?"

"Not quite yet," Amaryllis said. "We wanted to see if anyone here knows anything about the pirates first."

"You'll want to chat with old lady Three Hooves then," he said with confidence. "Come on, she knows everything and everyone. If anyone knows anything, it'll be her."

We finished storing what we'd picked up on the ship, and Awen volunteered to stay behind. She wanted to turn some of the blubber we'd bought into oil, which meant she needed to create a little machine to get everything going.

Calamity led us up the camp's hill toward the topmost part where the nicer carriages were parked. One of those had its sides open to reveal an old cervid woman resting on three legs atop a stack of well-worn cushions and blankets. For all her age, she looked like a tough old cookie, especially with the eyepatch covering half her face.

"What sorta trouble did you bring me here today, Calamity?" she asked.

"Hello, Three Hooves," he said with a bit of a bow. "Just wanted to introduce my new friends." I felt myself smile when he called me his friend. "This is Broccoli, and this is Amaryllis. They have a few questions you might be able to get to the bottom of."

· Chapter Nineteen ·

A Little Bird Told Me

Hello!" I said with a little wave to the old cervid lady. I wondered if it would be impolite to ask about her missing limb and the eyepatch she was wearing. It probably would be, but I bet there was an interesting story behind that. Then again, maybe those weren't the best of memories, and it wouldn't be nice to bring it up.

"Hello," Three Hooves said. She cracked a smile for us. "So, what are your friends going to ask me about, hmm, Calamity?"

"Ah, well, I think I maybe ought to let them talk to nya," he said before backing up a step.

I shared a look with Amaryllis, and she tilted her head a tiny bit toward me. I nodded back and then faced Three Hooves. "We just have a few questions," I said. "My friends and I came over here looking for some lost ships."

"Not many ships in the plains," Three Hooves said.

"They were airships. Apparently they got blown off course and ended up passing by a bit to the north of here. Uh, I don't actually know how far away, exactly, but yeah. Calamity helped us find a few of them."

"That's hardly surprising. He's lived his life with his head in the clouds, that one."

Calamity cleared his throat and looked a bit peevish, but I suspected that maybe the old woman's words weren't far off.

"Oh, don't lose a shoenail about it," Three Hooves said. "You know it's true. Now, ships. Did you find what you were looking for?"

"Kinda," I said. "We found crashed ships, some of the ones we were looking for, but not all of them. We also found a smaller boat that wasn't part of those. Uh, it's a pirate boat, but there weren't any pirates around, so I guess it's ours now. Well, ours and Calamity's."

"A full quarter of it!" Calamity added.

"Oh-hoh, well, that's one of his dreams come true," Three Hooves said. "I imagine you want to hear what we know about the fight?"

"That would be nice," I said. "But more than that, I think we want to know about the pirates. They had to be pretty well equipped, and that means a lot of people working for them, which means they've probably made lots of contact around here. Maybe you've heard something?"

The older cervid rubbed at her chin in thought, then nodded. "I keep abreast of most things. This old body of mine isn't what it used to be, but my mind's never been sharper. I listen, you see. Something you younger folk aren't too apt to do, I've noticed."

I pouted. "Have you seen my ears, ma'am? I'm perfectly good at listening."

"Hah! Maybe you are, at that. We'll see. Now, as I was saying. I listen to folk's problems and whip people about to get things done. I haven't heard of these pirates of yours, and if they were recruiting, I'd have heard it. For that matter, I know what it's like feeding a lot of folk and taking care of equipment. It's a big job, takes all sorts of people and things. I can tell you that there's nothing like that in the plains. How many ships are you talking about?"

I glanced at Amaryllis, since she'd know the exact numbers better. "At least six vessels," she said. "Possibly more than that waiting in ambush. We're talking six decently sized ships, with crews of between ten and thirty aboard."

"And I imagine they'd need more folk back where they're from, just like the hunters need camp folk," Three Hooves said. "So call it two hundred folk, more or less. No, a group that big would leave a mark on the plains. Prices would have been different at the fort too if they were supplying from there."

"So you think that the pirates aren't getting supplied from here?" I asked to confirm.

"They're pirates, couldn't they just steal what they need?" Calamity asked.

Three Hooves gave him a *look,* which had his mouth clamping shut. "Fool boy, if they stole what they needed, the price of those goods would still go up. More so, even. Merchants aren't keen on banditry. We would have more guards being hired to patrol the city and escort merchant caravans. Didn't notice anything of the sort this season, and no one's talking about being robbed, so they're getting their things from elsewhere."

"That leaves the north and Sylphfree," Amaryllis said. "Or a long trade from the Harpy Mountains. Well, thank you, that eliminates a lot of possibilities. We might just have run into some pirates that are either state-funded by the Snowlands, or who are hard-up for resources after buying good Snowlander ships."

"You're welcome," Three Hooves said. "Now, I'm not quite done with you. See, I've heard things that I haven't had time to tell yet, so do yourselves a favor and listen to me for a minute."

We all agreed and came closer to listen properly.

"There's a story that's been circulating around for a while now. I hadn't decided if it was hearsay or some silly overblown rumor, but I'm starting to suspect that there's a grain of truth to it all. That's often how these things are. Stories of a pirate lord who has traveled from the far west, chased by the knights of Pyrowalk across the Endless Swells to come and settle on the edges of our lands."

"We don't hear too much about the Pyrowalk Empire," Amaryllis said. At Calamity's confused look, she continued. "It's far to the west, across the Moonstruck Sea, with the Endless Swells between us and them. They're old. Ancient, even. Mostly human, but not like the humans of Mattergrove. Richer, more set in their ways, I think."

Three Hooves hummed. "As you say, little word of those distant places reaches us. This pirate lord might hail from there, but rumor has it he's come here to escape the wrath of his old lords and to make a new name for himself in our lands. It's been quiet, but some people have followed the rumors. People with very particular trades from the western end of the Trenten Flats."

"What's his name?" I asked, both as tantalized and curious as a bun could be.

"Commodore Megumi. The Sky Killer," Three Hooves said.

"Whoa," I said. That was a scary-sounding name. They even had a cool title! I didn't have one of those. I kinda wished I did, though maybe not something too close to "Sky Killer."

Amaryllis crossed her arms. "What do you know about this Commodore Megumi?" she asked.

"Very little," Three Hooves admitted. "News from so far afield doesn't make it here, like I've said. But it's a name, and there's a reputation attached to it. He's supposed to be a terror in the skies. A man who has reached the third tier, at least."

So he was at or over level thirty, and had two other classes to boot. That was a lot of skills with a lot of potential synergies. Not to mention a lot of health and stamina and all of those other bonuses to go with it. Rainnewt was around that level, I thought, and Bastion too.

"Thanks," I said to Three Hooves. "Just knowing who we're dealing with will be worth a lot." I bet that the sylphs had a file or two on him, even if he was located far, far away from their mountains. They seemed the sort to keep tabs on strong people, just on principle.

Three Hooves nodded. "I wish you the best. Though I do hope you won't be running headlong into trouble. However, if Calamity's coming along, that might well be a moot point. Boy always loved making a mess, hmm?"

"Hey meow, I've matured a pinch since my younger days," Calamity said. But he said it while lowering the brim of his hat so that Three

Hooves couldn't see the expression in his eyes, which cast some doubt on his assertion.

"Well, I haven't matured and I don't plan on it," I said. "But I think I still know better than to just run up to someone called Sky Killer and cause a fuss."

"No, you'd run up to him and ask him to be your friend," Amaryllis grumbled. She turned to Three Hooves and gave the woman a quick bow from the waist. "Thank you, ma'am. I appreciate the information. Rest assured we'll put it to good use."

With that, we said our goodbyes and then stepped away from Three Hooves's carriage to a spot where we could chat with a bit more privacy. The camp was a busy hive of activity, especially since another group of gatherers were now returning with all the goodies they'd found on the plains.

"So, we need to tell Sylphfree about Commodore Megumi," I said.

"Obviously," Amaryllis said. "They might be able to relay information about Megumi back to us. Something's fishy about all of this, though. An infamous sky pirate moving to the Snowlands just in time to cause trouble for the harpy delegation?"

"Nya think it's suspicious?" Calamity asked.

Amaryllis nodded. "Of course it is. The delegation was a big deal. It was well-guarded, more so than any normal trade convoy, and yet it probably carried less valuables than the average trading ship . . . Well, perhaps not. There's no accounting for what a bunch of nobles would think to bring along, but those kinds of goods can be difficult to fence."

"But the nobles themselves are worth something, no?" Calamity asked.

"Yes, that's true," she replied. "It could just be a pirate, new to the area, trying to establish themselves as a big player by capturing an important and valuable bounty. But something tells me that's not the whole of it. The *Redemption* would be worth as much as a small corvette under the right conditions. If the entire pirate fleet is made up of valuable ships like that, then they're not spoiling for more riches. Also, they aren't advertising their deeds, so it's probably not a play for reputation or fear-mongering. Which leaves . . . politics."

"Oh no," I said. I'd gotten my fill of those lately. I was hoping that our secretive adventures in a foreign land at the behest of a foreign king to save foreign nobles would remain nice and non-political.

"Well, I ain't know nothing about that," Calamity said. He stood up taller, which wasn't all that tall really, and puffed his chest out. "But as one-quarter captain of the *Redemption*, I think I ought to accompany you on your quest. To keep my investment safe, nya see?"

Amaryllis huffed the sort of huff that was almost a laugh. "Uh-huh. I'm sure you're not coming along because you have misplaced dreams about fighting sky pirates over the prairie like some dashing prince out of a children's book."

"More of a dashing rogue than a prince, really," he said with a grin. "But I wouldn't mind meeting a princess or two."

"Eh, princesses are mostly just normal girls," I said. "They run around, plot crimes, and do shadowy things in secret just like any other girl."

Calamity blinked. "I think we've been spending time around a different quality of girl, you and me."

I glanced at Amaryllis, then gave her a shrug. "I'm okay with Calamity coming. He seems strong, and I think we're going to need every friend we can find if we end up having to fight an entire crew of sky pirates."

Amaryllis shook her head. "I'm voting nay. He's another variable to calculate, and there's no guarantee he will be useful."

"Hey now," he said.

"You were a great help in the plains," Amaryllis placated. "But I don't know if your skills will translate well to the sort of trouble we tend to land ourselves in. We can let Awen cast the deciding vote."

Calamity grumbled, but I had the impression he thought the criticism was fair enough.

We returned to the *Redemption*, which was still parked next to the camp. A few tents had been moved away, but a few more had popped up nearby. It looked like the camp was constantly changing as new people showed up and others ran off. The airship was a novel change though, judging by the people giving it curious looks.

When we found Awen, she was on the ship's deck with a complex device in front of her that was burning some lamp fuel to heat up a glass bulb that had some liquid pouring into a container to one side. It looked dangerous, but Awen was being pretty casual about it.

After we shared what we learned and asked her for her vote, she gave Calamity a long, searching look, then shrugged. "Yeah, okay."

That, of course, meant that it was time for a round of congratulatory and celebratory hugs!

· Chapter Twenty ·

Message Delivered

Before we could take off again, I had to do a few quick things. The *Redemption* had a bunch of supplies on board, but we were lacking a lot of essentials. Water wasn't as much of a problem on the ground when there were plenty of streams to draw from, but in the air we'd have to use magic to pull water out of the air, which was both tiring and inefficient . . . plus, I couldn't do that spell yet.

Food was also a minor concern. We had plenty of hardtack and such, and some sylph MREs still, but those weren't exactly tasty.

Other than that, we needed a few knickknacks to make the ship feel more like a living space, like a small carpet before entering the crew compartment so that we wouldn't track mud in.

With that in mind, I checked my money pouch to make sure I had a good amount of change, then I set off. Awen had told us that while her oil-making gizmo was working, it was also really slow, so I had a decent amount of time to shop around.

Amaryllis stayed behind to contact Sylphfree, and Calamity was sitting on the ship, looking around and sighing wistfully.

It was weird, heading out all on my own. A few meters away from the *Redemption* I paused, looking back at the ship and second-guessing myself. Did I really need to head out? I could stay with my friends . . .

But no, they'd be fine without Broccoli for a few minutes. And I'd be okay too. It wasn't like I'd lose sight of them, what with the airship's balloon towering above the camp.

So I headed out, though maybe with a bit of a hurried pep to my step.

The first stop was the small market-ish part of the camp. The hunters didn't seem to have much use for a market, but there were still a few carriages of hangers-on who came with supplies and stuff to sell to a hunter in need at a steep markup.

That's where I found most of the things I was looking for. Different fruits and grains wrapped in a sort of papery leaf and tied up with long strips of tough grass, and a tiny bit of salted meat, because I was pretty sure Calamity ate meat and so did my friends.

I got lost looking over some pelts, then poked at a big bucket full of long, sharp-tipped feathers that had been plucked from a cockatrice. They were part feather, part scale, almost.

With a bulging bag full of stuff, I started to head back to the ship when I overheard two cervids talking.

It wasn't my fault that I eavesdropped. With ears as big as mine, that was naturally going to happen, whether I wanted it to or not. Most of the time I just ignored what I could overhear, or listened in on tiny snippets of other's lives, aware, in that little moment, that they had entire lives going on that I wasn't part of, a whole heap of stories I hadn't heard, from the mundane to the extraordinary.

"Come on, I can help," a rather small cervid said. He didn't look young, at a glance—he just wasn't a very big guy. He was tailing after a cervid woman in a thick gambeson with a few spears hooked to her side.

"No, Deiter, you'll only get yourself in trouble."

I blinked. Wait a moment, Deiter?

The couple were deeper into the camp already, so I had to jog to catch up to them. It looked like the girl Deiter was talking to was giving him an earful.

"Hey! Sorry, wait up, please!" I called out. The two of them half-turned, as if to see if I was talking to them. I bounced up ahead of them and smiled my best smile. "Hi! Sorry, my name's Broccoli, Broccoli Bunch, and I was recently over at, uh, Riverstart."

Deiter winced, hard. It was almost a physical blow the way he flinched back. His companion didn't seem to notice. "Yes, and?" she asked.

"Right, sorry. While we were there we ran into this . . . nice . . . lady who was looking for Deiter."

The cervid woman quirked an eyebrow, then half-turned to Deiter. "A wife you haven't told me about?" she asked. She didn't sound angry, so I imagined they weren't in a relationship.

"What? World, no! That's probably my mother. She, ah, lives in River-start," he said without meeting my eye. "Just a quiet old homebody, wouldn't disturb a fly. Haha."

He was really bad at lying.

"Anyway, she was worried, so she asked that if anyone saw you, they'd, uh, ask that you write a letter or something. I understand that sometimes you want to make space between you and your family, but if they're not terrible people, then maybe stay in contact . . . I guess? I don't know how families like that work."

He glanced to the side, biting his lip, then seemed to rally himself. "Uh, yeah, sure. I can do that," he said. "Thanks for the message," he added before slipping past me.

I blinked after him, but I wasn't about to pursue it if he clearly didn't want to continue chatting. I gave a wave in goodbye to the woman he was with, then stepped aside to let her pass. "Well, that's not how I expected all of that to get resolved," I muttered.

Maybe the anticlimax was good, though. One less thing to worry about. With that done, I hitched up my bag of provisions and headed back to the ship. The day was carrying on, what with all the traveling and exploring we'd been up to.

In addition to our provisions, I also picked up some already-cooked meals that a cervid chef was preparing in a big cast-iron pot that had to outweigh me twice over.

Juggling four bowls—which I had to pay extra for, but I figured they might come in handy—I returned to the *Redemption* and climbed up the gangplank onto the ship. "I have lunch!" I called out.

That got everyone's attention.

We ate sitting on the deck right in front of the wheel, and my friends filled me in on what they'd been up to since I ran off. I, of course, told them about meeting Deiter and how we probably didn't have to worry about that particular side quest anymore.

"Ah, well, I've managed to make a whole gallon of oil, and I think it's within the engine's burn tolerance. I don't really have a way to test that, but mixed in with our other fuel, it should be fine. It only adds up to about a tenth more fuel than what we had to start with. It's really not a lot."

"So our range is going to be very limited," I said.

Awen nodded. "If we fly high enough, with minimal wind resistance, and don't push the engine too much, we might be able to fly for six or seven hours."

"Which won't even get us a quarter of the way to Sylphfree," Amaryllis pointed out.

"Is that where we're headed next?" Calamity asked.

Amaryllis nodded and tapped the ring Caprica had given us. "The sylphs said they want us to come back and regroup. Besides which, what can we do against a properly large installation of pirates? Invite them out for tea and hope that they'll give us the delegates back?"

"I guess," I said. I really did want to burst onto the scene like a big hero and save everyone, but Amaryllis was probably right. Just the four of us and one tiny boat wouldn't exactly win the day when it came to fighting a whole heap of pirates. "So, we're returning to Sylphfree?"

"To Goldpass, actually. It's in the northernmost end of Sylphfree. A little farther than the capital, but with fewer mountains to navigate around to get there it's actually quite a bit easier to reach," Amaryllis said.

"Ah, we can't go that far," Awen said. "Not unless the wind is with us the entire way and we find more gas for the balloon. Or we could walk, I guess."

Amaryllis sniffed. "I thought of that, of course. We'll be meeting a group of sylphs in midair this evening. They'll track us by the ring. I told them to bring fuel for the *Redemption*, and you know how good they are with following instructions. I've no doubt they'll bring plenty."

Well, that settled it. "We should get going, then," I said. "We'll cut the amount of time it takes to meet them short, and if they don't show up until later, then we can always just land as soon as we start running low."

Once lunch was tucked away and we'd cleared the deck of anything that might get in the way, we were pretty much ready to head out. Calamity asked for just a few minutes to say his goodbyes, and since we weren't in any big rush, we of course let him climb down the boat and go chat with his friends.

He came back soon enough, and I couldn't tell if he was more sad at the goodbyes or excited to get going. On the ground, Savan and a few of the hunters stood by and waved as we weighed anchor, started up the engine, and then lifted off the ground with only the slightest of lurches.

We floated straight up for a while, letting the wind carry us as it wanted as long as we were still rising. It was coming in from the south, which was neither good nor bad, really, though it might be troublesome later when we had to head due east.

Once we were high enough that the hunters below were nothing more than pinpricks and the air had that familiar chill that came from being so far off the ground, we adjusted the sails and took off eastbound.

Calamity asked Awen a question about the ship, which launched her into a long-winded, rather one-sided discussion that had too many technical terms for me to follow it fully. Calamity was listening intently though, and I think he was hoping to learn as much as he could.

The flight continued at an easy pace for the next couple of hours. We didn't want to push the *Redemption* much, so we allowed the wind to carry us along with just a nudge from the main propeller to keep us going in the right direction.

By the time early evening rolled around, I found myself a bit restless behind the wheel and regretting not bringing something a bit warmer to wear.

"I see something!" Amaryllis called out from ahead. She was in that little basket at the very front of the ship, the one with the repeating crossbows. "South a few degrees." She pointed and I squinted that way.

It took a moment, but eventually I caught on to what she was seeing. Three vague forms so far off they were little more than shadowy smears at a higher altitude than we were at.

Wyverns? If so, then that was probably the sylph party we were supposed to meet. My Identify skill marked them as wyverns soon enough, and Awen whipped out her telescope and confirmed that they were being ridden.

We adjusted our sails, and after checking to see if we still had a good amount of fuel, we picked up the pace and pushed against the wind a bit. Soon enough, we crossed paths with three familiar wyverns.

I recognized Greencrest, of course. A girl ought not to forget the first wyvern she flew on. There was Bloodfang too, but the third wyvern wasn't one I knew. I imagined the rider was different too, though it was hard to tell the riders apart with all the gear they had on to protect them from the cold.

"What now?" I asked Amaryllis.

"Best to land. I don't fancy transferring things in midair," she said.

So we landed. It wasn't hard to find a big, flat space on the open plains. Once we dropped anchors and cut the engine, the wyverns circled around a final time and landed nearby.

I saw Winnow pulling down her hood to reveal a professional smile. "When you set out you were on foot. Now you come back with a trophy ship. Paladin Bastion must be right about you three and your capacity for shenanigans."

· Chapter Twenty-One ·

Hopping the Border

The wyvern riders dismounted and immediately began unpacking the saddles strapped to the almost-dragons' sides.

Winnow was the only wyvern knight I recognized; the other two were new. Once we landed, I hopped off the *Redemption* and bounced over, only stopping once I was just outside of the wyvern's *I can nom you without stretching* range. Just in case.

"Hello!" I cheered. "I'm glad you found us. Was the flight okay?"

"It was fine," Winnow replied. She grunted as she flew up and backward, using the momentum to haul out a large metal can from the satchel she was working on. "We have your fuel, and a few other supplies as well. You'll be surprised to know this isn't the first time we've had to do a refueling."

"It isn't?" I asked.

"Oh no, it happens several times a year. Some cheap merchant tries to make a trip without paying for backup fuel, or a noble who wants to show off their ship forgets to bring enough fuel, or because of bad weather an airship will burn a lot more fuel than it accounted for, and it runs out. Then we get sent over to resupply because they landed somewhere too precarious for a proper ship to land."

Winnow handed me the canister. It was a sort of jerry can that sloshed with every motion. "Thanks! I'll bring this to Awen."

"We have a few other things too. We weren't sure what kind of shape the ship you found would be in."

"It's not that bad. I think it could use a bit of love, but Awen seems excited to start work on that," I said.

Winnow nodded, then looked over at the ship and shook her head. "A proper Snowlander boat. You're lucky you'll be escorted. That crossbow emplacement on the front wouldn't be allowed in civilian hands."

"It wouldn't?" I asked.

"Oh, World no. There're pages and pages of documentation required to even just carry any kind of large ranged weapon on a ship, let alone having it installed and ready to use like that. The only ships with fixed weapon placements allowed in Sylphfree skies are part of the Air Force, and if it was up to the bureaucrats, even the wyvern knights would be reduced to delivering strongly worded letters."

I giggled at the mental image of that. The *Beaver* had Awen's autocrossbow on it, but it had been tucked out of sight when we flew to Sylphfree. And Bastion had been onboard to distract the inspectors. Maybe we'd narrowly avoided a heap of trouble there. Or Bastion knew and did us a favor?

I made a mental note for later: Extra hugs for Bastion.

"So, once we're back in the air, we just follow you?" I asked.

Winnow nodded. "That's the gist of it. We'll escort you back to Goldpass. If the wind keeps up, the trip shouldn't take too long at all. We'll have to fly the wyverns slow to keep pace with your airship."

"We could stop for the night," I suggested. "We don't have a big crew to begin with, and even with the fuel you brought, it might not be enough to coast through the entire night."

Winnow hummed. "We'll think about it. We're meant to have you back at Goldpass as soon as possible, but while I'll always follow my orders I take exception when they fly in the face of proper safety precautions or common sense. If slow is safer, then slow it will be."

With the gangplank lowered, it wasn't hard to get the fuel aboard. The fuel was exactly what Awen was hoping for, and she recruited Calamity to help her empty the can into the ship's bunker—which is what she called the tank under the deck where the fuel went.

The other wyvern knights unloaded a few more cans and I hopped over to help them carry the containers aboard. With two cans per wyvern, we actually had enough to fill the bunker right up to the quarter mark.

"We should be able to make it all the way, I think," Awen said. Then she turned toward me and locked her eyes onto mine. "But we absolutely can't head off in another direction for a side quest."

"Why are you giving me that look?" I asked.

Amaryllis sniffed, which was like a huff, but even more disdainful somehow.

"Hey!" I protested.

"If that's all," Winnow said past our team drama, "we'll be taking off again. If you need to communicate, you should have some flags aboard, right?"

"Oh, we do," Awen said. "Ah, but they're Snowlander. I don't know if they're the same?" We ended up checking, because even Amaryllis wasn't sure, but as it turned out semaphore flags were pretty much international, which I supposed made sense. It wasn't exactly a language with its own dialects and nuances.

Winnow gave us a quick salute, then she and the other wyvern knights quickly inspected their barding, mounted up, and took off.

Getting the *Redemption* up into the air was a bit more involved than taking off on a wyvern, but we weighed anchor and started up the engine without too much trouble. I helped trim the sails, then got behind the wheel again. I kinda missed Clive. The old harpy knew how to pilot so well that I found myself wishing he were here to point out what I was doing wrong.

In fact, I missed the *Beaver Cleaver* as a whole. The ship had become home at some point, though I guessed that was bound to happen. You could only have so many adventures, share so many meals, and sleep in one place so much before it inevitably became home.

The *Redemption* felt different, but that wasn't a bad thing. It'd become part of our family or it wouldn't. Time would tell.

"Broccoli, why are you hugging the wheel?" Amaryllis asked.

"Reasons," I said.

The flight was pretty easy. The wind turned and was now almost directly behind us, which just made us move a bit faster. I was worried about the poor wyverns, of course, but they just floated off way above us and eventually started to fly in long ovals that intercepted our flight path and then ranged out ahead.

As night came around we dipped back down and found a place to settle behind a few big hills that conveniently kept the wind at bay. The *Redemption* had enough buoyancy that we could stay afloat without doing more than idling. The wyverns settled down nearby, and we joined them for a quick meal before returning to the *Redemption* and putting those bunks to use.

The night passed easily enough. I got middle watch, which was annoying—but it was my turn, so I did my part, standing on the deck and looking out into the hillside for trouble while also practicing my magic a little.

I had a lot of spells to learn, but not much time to knuckle down and learn one well, so I practiced my mana manipulation, then I made myself bigger and smaller using my new Proportion Distortion skill. If I was ever going to use that in a fight, then I'd need to have it down to second nature. It was strange to feel like the ship shrank and grew around me, instead of feeling like I was the one whose size was changing.

Amaryllis woke up to take her turn, but instead of moving over to go on watch, she just stood there and stared at me. "Broccoli."

"Hi, Amaryllis," I said.

"I know *how* you're that size, but I don't understand why."

I currently came up to Amaryllis's knee, or I would have if I were standing on the deck. Of course, because I was on watch, I was standing on the railing, which was plenty wide enough now that I was smaller.

"I'm practicing," I said.

"Are you . . . wrapped up in your own ears?" she asked.

I hugged my ears closer. I'd tried, but hadn't figured out how to make them shrink with the rest of me, so they were still as long as normal, which meant they reached down to my feet. Obviously I'd wrapped them around myself like big warm, furry blankets.

I snuggled deeper into the ear fluff. My tail also didn't shrink, so I had a sort of fluffy beanbag to flump onto. "Yes," I said. "They're warm, and it's cold out. I'd make myself all big and cover you in my ears, but they stay the same size when I embiggen myself, so they end up looking tiny."

"I see," Amaryllis said. She rubbed her eyes clean. "Go to bed, Broccoli."

"Okay!"

The next morning we had a quick breakfast of hardtack and tea while the sun hadn't quite risen yet. By the time it did though, we were already lifting off and the wyvern knights were circling around us in the air.

Technically, we were right on the edge of Sylphfree, but according to Amaryllis that depended on whose map you looked at. The Trenten Flats claimed the area just as much as Sylphfree did. Neither group had any use for the land, so it was mostly just another thing for the two nations to argue over. It did mean that the wyvern knights could relax a little bit. They were over home territory, and no longer camping in a foreign land without permission.

We crossed over increasingly hilly terrain, taking a rather circuitous route that confused me a bit. Fortunately, Calamity was there to explain.

"All of the land to the northeast of the Greenstone is dangerous. No one smart travels there if they can avoid it. Not much in the area anyway, so it's not a big deal."

"That sounds weird," I said. The evidence was impossible to miss, though; a huge swath of the grasslands and hills were utterly bare, revealing dull brown dirt. There wasn't a speck of grass or a tree to be seen for kilometers. Off in the distance, a great billowing cloud of dust had been dragged up by the wind and was rolling steadily east.

Calamity said that no one knew what had made the Greenstone or how it worked, and no one seemed eager to find out.

Eventually, a bit before noon came around, we were back in the mountains of Sylphfree and swinging around mountaintops that were taller than the height we dared bring the *Redemption* to with so little fuel.

Goldpass, when it finally came into sight, was revealed to be a surprisingly small city. It didn't even have a wall, and was instead just a sprawl of multi-floored homes packed tightly in a valley surrounded on three sides by mountains.

A broad but shallow-looking river passed by, with tributaries joining it from the various mountains so that it was quite wide before the river just . . . stopped. It was only as we got closer that I realized the entire river tumbled into a big cave-like crack in the ground. Did it fall into an aquifer? An underground river? It was weird.

The city had an airship port to its south that was mostly occupied by commercial ships, though there were a few sylph military vessels parked there as well. And, in the middle of them, a very familiar ship.

"The *Beaver*!" I shouted.

"The what?" Calamity asked.

He followed my pointing finger to the *Beaver Cleaver*. The twin-hulled ship was sitting at port, its prow, with its two top-hatted ducks, looking mighty and proud. The balloons were different, no longer the patched-up ones we'd been using for so long. Instead they'd been replaced by two sky-blue balloons, with a paler blue below.

The wyverns cut out ahead of us and dove toward the port, and I saw Winnow gesturing toward an open landing berth just across the dock from the *Beaver*. Of course, we immediately started to drop down and prepare to land.

I was practically bouncing on the spot. I was so excited! Were all of our friends there? We had so many new stories to share!

The *Redemption* came in for a nice, gentle landing, with all four of us doing our very best and with a bit of help from some dock-working sylphs who flew over with ropes to tie us down with.

By the time we were secured, there was a small crowd waiting for us. Mostly guards, but in the middle of them was Caprica, and by her side, Bastion, which neatly explained why he hadn't come to help refuel us. Protecting the princess was far more important than helping us out.

· Chapter Twenty-Two ·

The Golden Gold Inn of Goldpass

Caprica!" I cheered as I jumped off the *Redemption* and ran across the dock. One of the princess's guards tried to stop me, but I just made myself smaller and slipped under his attempt to grab me.

Then, with a big leap, I launched myself into the air and crashed into Caprica's waist with a giggling *whomp*.

Caprica laughed and patted my back with one arm. The other, I discovered, was busy cradling Orange close to her side. "Orange!" I cheered as I grabbed the spirit cat. I spun around with Orange's lanky frame held out before me, then I pressed my nose against hers and laid a few kisses against her face. "I missed you too," I said.

Orange gave me the long-suffering look of a cat who did miss someone but didn't want that person to know.

"Hello, Broccoli," Caprica said.

"Hi!" I replied. "Wait, I need to hug Bastion too."

Bastion raised his arms up and I flung my arms around him, squishing Orange in between us. His expression softened a bit, even if he did keep his arms raised like he wasn't sure what to do with them.

By the time I was done hugging Bastion, my friends had descended from the tied-down airship and the wyvern knights had come to a landing a bit deeper into the docks where the local dockhands and guards were giving the big almost-dragons a wide berth.

"Hello, Princess Caprica," Amaryllis said. Next to her, Awen gave Caprica a little wave and Calamity hurried to pull his hat off his head, then licked his palm and ran it through his tangled hair.

"Hello, everyone," Caprica said. "So, before anything else, can someone please pry Broccoli off of Bastion?"

"Oh!" I said as I let go of the paladin. Were we making a scene? Bah, that didn't matter. "Did you want more hugs, Caprica?" I asked before walking over and hugging her some more.

Caprica laughed and rubbed my head, which was easier now that I was at the same height as her, minus the ears. "Broccoli, am I losing my mind or have you lost some height?"

"Nope! I have a skill to change sizes," I said. I let go of the skill and popped back to my normal Broccoli-height. "See?"

"That's . . . interesting. I've never seen a skill like that before," she said. "Anyway, how was your trip? I see you've made a new friend?"

"Oh! Right, Princess Caprica, Paladin Bastion, this is Calamity Danger, he's the best hunter ever and when he grows up he wants to be an airship pirate."

"Meow, wait a moment," Calamity said with a startled jump. "Nya might be right about that, Broc, but don't go telling it to crown-folks. That's just trouble."

"I don't know if you've been with Broccoli and her friends for very long," Caprica said. "But you'll discover that Broccoli doesn't treat authorities with any special reverence."

"Well, that's fine by me!" Calamity said with a smirk. "These three have been nice and fair to me so far, so they won't hear any complaints from me."

Caprica smiled. "That's nice to hear. If you three vouch for Calamity, then I'm certain I'll be happy to call him a friend—fantasies of piracy aside. We can't have a royal endorsing that sort of behavior, you understand."

"Yes, ma'am, I understand, ma'am," Calamity rushed to reassure her. I grinned. Calamity was a good guy, and a better friend, so far.

"So, are we going to stand out here all day?" Amaryllis asked. "It's a little warm to be in the sun."

Caprica nodded, then gestured further down the dock. "Come. I have the inn all to myself. I'm the first royal to fly into Goldpass in over a decade, so I'm getting the special treatment. I'd usually discourage that kind of thing, but it does have its advantages. The inn's owner fell over himself to offer us the entire building for as long as we need."

"Won't he lose a bunch of money from that?" I asked.

"He'll likely earn it back once word gets around that a princess found the accommodations acceptable," Amaryllis said. "Besides, I imagine Caprica's guards need to sleep somewhere too."

"Indeed," Caprica said. "Why, with a smaller inn I might have had to ask my guards to sleep three or four to a room. I might even have had to share a room. Perhaps with the diligent Paladin Bastion."

Bastion glanced our way, but he was currently busy doing his *I'm scanning everything for trouble* routine off to the group's side.

We ended up meeting the wyvern knights who had escorted us near the docks' exit. They were waiting in an orderly row, helmets off and tucked under their arms while they stood at parade rest. Their wyverns were sitting on the road behind them, taking up a fair chunk of space, but no one seemed brave enough to complain about it.

Caprica stopped before Winnow and smiled at the knight, who stood a little straighter. "Knight Winnow, was it?" she asked.

"Yes, Your Highness," Winnow replied. Winnow's back could not have been any straighter as Caprica addressed her.

"I heard good things about you. Thank you for escorting my friends back safely. I appreciate that you've gone above and beyond."

"Just doing our duty, Your Highness," Winnow said, as if Caprica was a drill sergeant and not a happily grinning princess.

I smiled but held back a laugh. It was strange to see people get so nervous around Caprica. It was as if they didn't know that under all the princessness she was just a normal—if very motivated—girl, with normal girl problems and a normal girl crush on her friend and paladin guard.

Caprica made a bit of small talk with the wyvern knights before asking them if they could stay in town for a little bit, stating that she might need their help later on. And then we were off again.

The Golden Gold Inn was a pretty establishment set right next to Goldpass's skyport. It was three stories of worked stone, with balconies on the upper floors and big windows with storm shutters painted a brilliant orange-yellow and a steep peaked roof. There wasn't much room for landscaping around the inn, since it was squished in between two other businesses, but the owners had clearly tried their best by putting a few benches out front and some big pots filled with colorful flowers.

The inn's interior was a bit different than what I was used to. There was a sitting room and a dining room, but they looked more appropriate for a big home than a tavern. This wasn't a place that also doubled as a restaurant or anything like that, though I was certain they served food for customers.

"Since we've appropriated the entire inn, in a manner of speaking, I suppose you can all have your own rooms. The third floor is mostly unoccupied," Caprica said.

"Thank you," Amaryllis said. "We appreciate the gesture. And our purses will appreciate the savings as well, I imagine."

Caprica chuckled. "I can't imagine you having a difficult time with gold at the moment, not after the last mission."

Amaryllis shrugged. "You can never have enough, truly."

We ended up sitting around the dining room table after Caprica had dismissed most of her guards. They seemed content to start patrolling around the inn, looking all important and tough in their shiny gear while the inn's proprietor, a sylph called Juley Juleschild, prepared some light snacks for us.

"So, tell me about your latest adventure!" Caprica asked.

We immediately jumped into the story. I tried keeping any exaggeration to a minimum, but I might have gotten a little excited here and there, especially when describing how cool it was to ride on wyverns, something that Caprica, despite having wyverns nearby her entire life, had never done.

I wondered if it was like someone who lived close to an amusement park never visiting it, or if she just really hadn't ever gotten the chance to fly on a wyvern?

Amaryllis ranted at length about the rude mother we'd met in River-start, and then we recounted meeting Savan and then Calamity. Caprica was a lot more interested in the crashed airships than she was about the wyvern flight. "I received your report, of course," she said to Amaryllis. "Or rather, an intelligence officer did, but I made sure to read a copy for myself. Two crashed diplomatic vessels is a big issue. That they crashed on Trenten Flats territory complicates things immensely. We won't be able to bring in inspectors to scour the crash sites."

"I imagine the hunters and other scavengers will be all over the ships soon enough," Amaryllis said. Caprica winced at that. "The only upside is that it's unlikely the government of the Trenten Flats will be able to make a fuss about the slight invasion of their territory."

Caprica nodded, then leaned back into her seat. I wondered if that was comfortable with her wings. "Indeed. So . . . pirates. Or what we're presuming to be pirates. I'm not entirely convinced. A big enough and powerful enough group that they were able to waylay an entire diplomatic convoy . . . That sounds like more than a band of ruffians."

"There's this rumor we heard from Three Hooves," I started.

Caprica gestured for me to continue.

"So, Three Hooves is this cool older cervid lady. She's missing a leg, which I imagine is why she's called that. Unless it was her name before too and it's all a really unfortunate coincidence. Anyway, she said there's rumors about this big scary pirate from way out in the west. He might have come to stay in this area, or maybe in the Snowlands to the north."

"Does this scary pirate have a name?" Bastion asked.

I nodded. "Commodore Megumi. 'The Sky Killer.'"

"That's . . . disturbing," Caprica said.

"Yeah, I know! Why do the bad guys get such cool names?" I smacked the table with impotent fury. Then Awen started to rub my head between the ears to calm me down and I settled back in my seat. "I want a cool name."

"I can imagine," Amaryllis said. "Living your entire life with a name like Broccoli must have a toll."

"What? No, I meant like a title name. Wait, what's wrong with Broccoli?" I sat up a bit. There was nothing wrong with my name. My parents told me so, and they were the ones to pick it, so they'd know!

"Anyway," Caprica said. "Let's bring this back on-topic, shall we? Commodore Megumi. The Sky Killer. I haven't heard of that name before. Bastion?"

"I . . . might have. In reports from the Endless Swells, I think. Distant persons of interest. Those are usually either politically important figures, or people who have gained enough levels to become something of a threat."

"How many levels is that?" I asked.

Bastion hummed. "Usually, the moment a person gains a third class, they're considered interesting as far as the government is concerned. Even three entirely noncombat classes working in tandem might result in some powerful combinations. Most civilians who reach that kind of level are those with high-risk jobs that afford them a fair amount of experience. Adventurers, hunters, classes that encourage them to stay outside of the safety of a city."

"That makes people dangerous?" I asked.

"No, it makes them *interesting*. Which can, in and of itself, be a sign that someone is dangerous," Bastion said. "Don't underestimate lower-leveled people, though. Levels equate to potential, not competence. I've known paladins who were bested by creatures beneath level ten because they just didn't know how to handle them."

Caprica chuckled, and I felt like I was missing out on a joke.

"It's just a rumor," Amaryllis said. "But it might be worth investigating."

"Indeed," Caprica said. "In the meantime, we have a direction to search in. I'll have the wyvern knights patrol the border with the Snowlands; we might be able to spot this pirate camp, especially with the number of ships they'll have to hide."

"And then what?" I asked.

"And then . . . I'm not certain. Our diplomatic channels with the Harpy Mountains have been acting strangely. I suspect that a ransom was finally sent out. What, exactly, these pirates are asking for, though . . . That we'll have to see."

· Chapter Twenty-Three ·

Diplomats in Distress

We woke up bright and early the next morning. Caprica wanted all of us together for breakfast because she'd received some important news that she wanted to share. There was a tasty spread waiting for us, and Caprica had obviously been patiently waiting for everyone to be gathered before she ate.

Orange, who had a majestic bowl of top-grade milk placed at the head of the table, hadn't been so patient, but she was excused on account of being a cat.

So, we all sat around the inn's dining table, again, and ate while Caprica went over a few reports. When most of us were done eating and drinking, she looked up and, with a serious expression, spoke up at last. "There's a ransom," she said.

"How bad is it?" Amaryllis asked.

Caprica lowered the pages. She didn't look very pleased. "It's not ideal. They have a number of politicians, diplomats, and various nobles in their care. The original document was signed by each, and I believe a number of their identities have been confirmed by experts. The ring-seals attached to the ransom note match up as well. It proves that there were alive at the time of the signing."

"We kind of knew that already, didn't we?" I asked.

"Yes," Caprica said. "But now this is becoming a much wider incident. The harpies will be demanding their diplomats back, of course."

"Obviously," Amaryllis said. "If the Nesting Kingdom itself doesn't respond, then it will fall to individual families to reply as they see fit. That might turn messy. I don't want to imagine my countrybirds acting cruelly, but I can still envision some families asking that other hostages not be returned."

I gasped. That was terrible!

"It's worse than you know," Caprica said. "They're not . . . asking for gold."

"Territory? Legitimacy?" Amaryllis guessed at.

Caprica shook her head. "They want a prisoner exchange. Specifically, for a prisoner that's being held by Sylphfree."

"Rainnewt!" Awen gasped.

I glanced at her, then back to Caprica, who was nodding already. "Exactly. How did you make the connection?"

"Well, awa, it sounds like the kind of thing he would do," she said. "He seemed very, ah, invested in his plan to plunge the entire continent into war. So . . . it would make sense for him to have some redundancies in case his original plan failed. He's probably responsible for the diplomats being kidnapped, even though he's been in prison."

"If his bombing plan worked, he could have used the hostages to heighten tensions between our nations," Amaryllis said. "Much of the Nesting Kingdom's best were supposed to be sent to the summit. Removing them from the board only makes it harder to act diplomatically."

Caprica dropped her reports down with a sigh. "I don't know what the Nesting Kingdom is going to do, but I can predict how the Sylphfreean military will react."

"There's no way that you'll surrender him," Amaryllis said.

Caprica shook her head. "He attempted regicide. You could make a case for treason, and you could certainly make a case for mass homicide. Any one of those would make it impossible for us to release him. We certainly wouldn't hand him over only for him to be freed into the care of pirates."

"Are they asking for anything else?" Amaryllis asked.

"So far, no. They'll trade any five hostages for Rainnewt." Caprica pushed the stack of papers toward Amaryllis. "There's a list of them on the third page."

Amaryllis took it, flipped over to the list, then winced. "There are a lot of nobles here, over a dozen. There's an earl, and two barons, though I don't know them. I recognize the names of two harpies who have parents who are dukes. These are some important people, even setting aside the career politicians. The Nesting Kingdom will be under a lot of pressure to get them back."

"What about the crews?" I asked.

"Nothing on them, except for captains and first mates," Amaryllis said.

"There had to be dozens of them," I said. "Those ships were way bigger than the *Beaver*, and even we have a full-time crew of six sailors, not counting those of us here. A bigger ship will need a bigger crew, right?"

"And servants too," Awen said. "Ladies' maids, cooks, cleaning staff, porters, and entertainers. Big-name nobles don't just travel without an entourage. Oh, and guards too."

"Right, for when they arrived in Sylphfree," I said. I nodded. "Welp, in that case, let's go free them all. If they have no hostages, they can't make ransom demands, and Rainnewt will stay in jail where he deserves to be."

Bastion, who had been quietly standing guard two and a half steps behind Caprica's chair, cleared his throat. "I think you may be oversimplifying things somewhat," he said.

"No, she might be right," Amaryllis said. "We know more or less where they are, don't we? North of the Trenten Flats, possibly within the Snowlands, and about as far as you could expect to travel on a normal ship's fuel reserves. That narrows it down. And we're relatively close at the moment. Certainly closer than anyone else. If we can gather a large enough group and move in stealthily, we might be able to surprise the pirates and take back the hostages."

Caprica blinked. "That's quite a reckless plan."

"I like it," I said.

"Of course you do, it was yours," Amaryllis huffed.

"You liked it too!"

"Well, mostly because of the massive clout we'd gain if we succeed," she reasoned. "I can't see how we could manage it, stealth aside."

Caprica tapped the table, then half-turned to Bastion. "How many troops are stationed in Goldpass?"

"It's a frontier town," he replied. "One company. About a hundred flying-fit troops and twice as many in logistics. In addition to perhaps fifty full-time guards working for the city itself."

"That's not nearly enough to take on a pirate's den. I estimate we'd be outnumbered five to one. Even accounting for our superior training, it won't be enough," Caprica muttered. "But . . . perhaps we can bolster those numbers."

"Maybe we don't need to fight at all," I said. "The goal is to free the hostages, right? We don't need to beat up every pirate you find to do that, we just need to grab the hostages and run."

Caprica hummed to herself. "You might be onto something," she said. "A special operation, designed like a smash and grab. A good number of the hostages might well be fighting-capable if freed. Though . . . maybe they won't be. I'll talk to a few people here. We have a number of ships available that we can commandeer."

"A distraction?" I asked. "Send a big fat merchant ship close to the pirates, then have it fly away, and while they chase it, we invade their base!"

"They won't leave it unguarded," Amaryllis said while stroking her chin. "But it could work to divide their forces."

Awen raised a hand. "Um, what about the Snowlanders? The pirates are near them, right? Are they okay with them?"

"Officially, the Snowlands condemn piracy. But . . . it is quite suspicious that the pirates were able to acquire such an advanced Snowlander vessel.

So, I think some level of under-the-table collusion is plausible," Caprica said.

"In any case," Bastion said, "none of this will be possible without a much better understanding of the local area and the forces we're dealing with. I wouldn't want to deploy troops in a foreign nation like that at the best of times."

"Ah, you're correct," Caprica said. "The Snowlanders might take umbrage if we're storming their lands, even if they *are* occupied by pirates."

I crossed my arms. My breakfast had been nice and tasty, but I had a bit of a sour taste in my mouth now. "Well, I don't like the idea of sitting back and doing nothing."

Awen raised her hand again. "That would only be a problem if the troops are Sylphfreean, right? What if, um, they were all privately hired mercenaries?"

"That would violate all sorts of codes of conduct," Bastion said. "But . . . it might be doable. The force would have to be all-volunteer, and it would be a mess no matter the results."

"I'll see what I can do," Caprica said. "On that note, I need a few hours to prepare things. If you want to visit the town, then feel free to do so. Gold-pass is open to you. The docks as well, as I imagine you might want to revisit your ship after so long away."

I nodded vigorously. "Yes! We definitely need to check out the *Beaver* again. It's been forever! I have weeks of overdue hugs to hand out to the crew."

"And I need to see if the repairs pass muster," Awen said. "Um, no offense."

"None taken," Caprica said. "You girls . . . and sir, go and enjoy yourselves. I'll keep what you said in mind."

With that, Caprica stood, nodded to us, then gathered her papers and shuffled off.

"She's got a lot on her plate," I muttered as I stood too.

"Yes, but it's important work," Amaryllis said. "And it's the kind of work that could earn her a lot of political clout. Saving desperate harpy captives of a known pirate would earn her, or at least Sylphfree, a lot of goodwill. It might be the public relations victory we all need to finally put these stories of war to rest."

"I imagine the folk them pirates have captured would be mighty pleased to be saved," Calamity added with a catlike grin. "Meow, you had a ship to show me?"

"Yes!"

I dragged Calamity along after me as I left the inn, and my other friends filed out as well. I really couldn't wait to return to the *Beaver Cleaver* after so long away.

The docks weren't as busy as some I'd seen before. Goldpass was too quiet of a city to really have much air traffic coming and going from it, so it was easy to navigate the many stairs and towers around the docks to reach the level where the *Beaver Cleaver* was currently parked and waiting for us.

I paused as I came close, taking in the ship in all of its splendor.

Someone had clearly taken some time to spruce it up a smidge. Not so much cleaning it—after all, it *was* my ship, so it had had plenty of Cleaning magic splished and splashed across its deck. No, what took me by surprise was the fresh coat of paint on the sides and the patched-up holes in the hull.

I couldn't even tell where he'd been smacked and shot and magicked anymore. I sort of missed the slapdash and kinda terrible paint job I'd given the ship, but there was no denying that he was a lot more handsome now.

The rigging had all been replaced, the balloon was fresh and new, and someone had even taken the time to replace many of the banisters and railings with shiny metal ones that had heaps of whirly bits and decorative metalwork.

"Wow!" Calamity said. "That's a beaut of a ship. When nya said nya were a captain, I didn't rightly believe nya, nya know?" I held back a giggle. It sounded like his accent only got thicker when he was excited.

"I know, right? It's like a dream come true!" I felt myself smiling so big it hurt. "Let me grab my captain's hat. It should be aboard the *Beaver*. Come on!"

I skipped over the gangplank and onto the ship. Almost immediately, Gordon spotted me. He grinned a harpy grin and flapped his wings. "Captain on deck!" he squawked.

There was a rush of boots, and soon the entire crew rushed up from below to join us.

"Scallywags!" I cheered as I launched myself at the crew. There was Two-Eyed Joe, and No-Pegs Oda, and of course Fearsome Sally, our sorta-piratical human crewmates. They'd actually grown a smidge since I'd last seen them. They were certainly looking more fit and fed.

Hugs were had while Amaryllis and Awen followed aboard more calmly.

Then it was time to hug Clive and Steve and Gordon, our more experienced harpy crew. "The *Beaver Cleaver*'s ready to set sail at a moment's notice, ma'am," Clive said. "The stores are full, the fuel bunkers are stocked, and everything's running better than new."

"The *Beaver* looks so good," I said. "What happened?"

Clive puffed his chest out. "The sylphs were mighty insistent on giving him a little bit of a refit. We made sure they didn't mess anything up, but they do know their shipwork and it was only the work of a day or four to get all the holes patched and all our troubles smoothed away. Lady Bristlecone will be wanting to look at the engine. The rooms haven't been touched, of course."

"Well, let's take a look then!"

· Chapter Twenty-Four ·

Fusion Mode

After saying hello to everyone, sharing a whole heap of hugs, and then trading stories of what we'd all been doing over the past couple of weeks, we decided that we should find a way to get the *Redemption* onto the *Beaver*.

That turned out to be a whole lot trickier to do than we initially thought.

It was definitely possible to do it. With a measuring tape and a few trips back and forth, we confirmed that the *Redemption* was thinner in the middle than the space between the *Beaver*'s two hulls. The *Beaver* was also more than long enough to overshadow the *Redemption* if it came to park in its middle.

The problem was twofold. First, we had to secure the smaller ship, which wouldn't be easy. The *Beaver* didn't have anything in its middle designed to grab and hold on to a small boat.

Second, the *Redemption*'s balloon would rub up against the *Beaver*'s in a way that would quickly wear a hole in the material. We couldn't deflate the *Redemption*'s balloon, because the *Beaver* wasn't designed to carry the weight of an entire airboat, even if it was much lighter than the *Beaver*.

In the end, Awen drew up quick plans to lengthen the *Beaver*'s rigging, which would raise its own balloons farther above the hull and essentially give us more headroom to fit in the *Redemption*. It would alter the *Beaver*'s handling a bit, but she assured us it would be manageable. Additionally, she specified latch points that would be retrofitted to both vessels so they could lock together while docked.

Curious sylphs from the port noticed our plans, and by midafternoon we had a small crew of eager engineers and mechanics swarming over the two ships trying to get everything in place. Awen was in her element, giving them orders and showing them what to do with barely a stutter.

I think Caprica showing up during a small break to see what we were up to really encouraged them too. Apparently she'd ridden aboard the *Beaver* on the way over (she took one of the spare bedrooms, and her guards had plenty of space to stay on the other side of the ship, though most of them came in a pair of smaller Sylph Air Force ships anyway). Her riding on the ship made it a "princess's ship" in a way, which somehow translated to a bunch of honor for those working on improving the *Beaver*.

I didn't pretend to understand all of that, exactly, but I was glad for the help. I'd rarely seen Awen so excited to work on something before, and the idea was really cool.

Unfortunately, after a while I discovered that I was mostly in the way.

What they needed were mechanics and manual workers, not someone who was an expert hugger.

So, instead of being in the way, I returned to the inn and had lunch with Caprica and Bastion, then I convinced Amaryllis to help me train my magic a little bit.

"Huh," Amaryllis said as I carefully touched her upper arm and turned a simple light spell she was trying to cast into a strange mix of light and Cleaning mana that dispersed harmlessly next to me. "That . . . feels very strange."

I nodded along. I was practicing my Way of the Mystic Bun on her, though only in small amounts and very carefully. The last thing I wanted to do was hurt a friend.

"It feels rather intrusive. I can feel your mana pressing into my arm and fighting for control, then it subjugates my own." She frowned, then went through the same motions with her hand. "Do it again."

"Okay!" I said. It cost a few points of mana to do the trick, but only a few. I could do it all day, really.

Amaryllis had me repeat the move three more times. The last time, it failed outright. When I had tried to push my own mana into her system through the contact I had on her arm, her magic had slipped by me, and then she cast her spell without any trouble.

"I see," she said. "So, it's resistible. Easily, as well, you just need to actually try and know what to look for."

"How'd you manage that?" I asked.

"Once I felt the intrusion, I shifted my mana around to avoid it. I'm pretty sure someone could brute-force their way past your intrusion too. It's likely not as strong as you think . . . except if your opponent doesn't know what you're doing."

"Oh," I said. That made sense. "It's hard to grab a person's mana, it's kind of like . . . shoving your hand in a bowl of spaghetti and trying to grab one strand in particular."

"That's disgusting," she said. "But yes, I imagine that some well-practiced mages will learn to counter the intrusion in no time at all. It might add a hundredth of a second to their casting time, but that'll be it. Someone who really knows what they're doing might be able to use that to steal your mana as well. Here, touch my talons again."

I grabbed her sorta-hand, then pushed mana in when she instructed me to. Amaryllis concentrated for nearly a full minute in silence, then I felt a strange tugging sensation in my arm, as if someone were slurping out the insides of it.

"Oh, ew!" I said as I pulled my hand back.

Amaryllis grinned. "So, that's doable as well. Interesting."

"Did you just copy my skill?" I asked as I shook my hand.

"No, no nothing of the sort. I don't know how to do the intrusion that you can manage. But since your mana was in my system already, well, it wasn't too hard to figure out how to steal it. And it seems as if I could keep pulling too. It's all Cleaning aspect, though. Or . . . perhaps more accurately, it's Broccoli-aspect magic, which is nearly indistinguishable."

"I guess that makes sense," I said. "So should I continue to use it in a fight?"

"Of course you should," she huffed. "I didn't know how to counter it without thinking about it for a couple of minutes. The average mage who's never encountered that kind of ability won't come up with a counter mid-battle. Even if they do, it's a distraction, and the easier ways to counter the ability still require concentration."

"Cool!" I said. I mostly liked the ability because it made it harder for people to use offensive magic on me or my friends without harming them much. A fight would end a lot sooner if the person I was fighting ran out of mana early.

"Have you been leveling well?" Amaryllis asked.

I winced. "Ah, well, it's been a few days since anything's gone up in level," I admitted.

Amaryllis gave me a very flat look. "Broccoli, you're aware that we're all at very respectable levels for our age, right? It takes most people years to level most of their skills up."

"Yeah, but I was making such good progress before. Also, I still have a bunch of general skill slots open."

"That's normal, Broccoli," Amaryllis said. "Unless you've been specifi-cally training something new, you shouldn't unlock a new general skill. Otherwise everyone would fill all of their free slots in a matter of hours just from . . . breathing and scratching themselves and hugging their family."

"But I got a hugging skill," I pointed out.

"Yes, exactly, because you're bizarre and intentionally put a lot more effort and time into doing that kind of thing than normal people. I suggest you either practice a specific skill a lot more to gain it as a general skill, or just allow yourself to gain skills as they come. They'll usually be for things you're doing already."

I considered it, then shrugged. That seemed fair enough. I didn't have many general skill points left to spend in any case. I only got those from destroying dungeons, and that was a rare occurrence that ideally would never happen again. A couple of skills were nearing the spot where they were ready to level up, so that would be exciting!

Name	Broccoli Bunch
Race	Bun (Riftwalker)
First Class	Cinnamon Bun Bun
First Class Level	13
Second Class	Wonderlander
Second Class Level	4
Age	16
Health	150
Stamina	165
Mana	145
Resilience	65
Flexibility	85
Magic	30
Skills	Rank
Cinnamon Bun Bun Skills	
Cleaning	S - 09%
Way of the Mystic Bun	C - 14%
Gardening	D - 39%
Adorable	D - 100%
Dancing	D - 100%

Wonderlander Skills	
Tea Making	C - 16%
Mad Millinery	D - 94%
Proportion Distortion	C - 07%
General Skills	
Insight	C - 99%
Makeshift Weapon Proficiency	C - 27%
Archeology	D - 49%
Friendmaking	C - 83%
Matchmaking	D - 69%
Hugging Proficiency	D - 89%
Captaining	E - 91%
Cinnamon Bun Bun Skill Points	1
Wonderlander Skill Points	2
General Skill Points	3
First Class Skill Slots	0
Second Class Skill Slots	0
General Skill Slots	3

I hummed as I looked over my skills. By the time we were done dealing with these pirates, I was certain I'd be leveling up a couple of them.

"Right, want to stand over there? I need to practice a few more spells. These are electric spells that track their target. I'll make sure they're weak enough that they only sting a little," Amaryllis said.

"Wait, what?" I asked.

"Don't worry, you can use it as dodging practice!"

When Caprica walked into the inn's backyard an hour later, I was panting for all I was worth and Amaryllis was finally starting to run low on mana. It wasn't fair how quickly her reserves refilled, but I guessed that was only normal since her main class was all about spellcasting.

"Practicing hard?" the princess asked.

"Very!" I said. I tugged my shirt forward a bit and blew some air down the front. It was pretty warm out, despite being so far north.

"Good! I got some news, and I think you might want to come inside for this one. Awen just arrived as well, with your new catfolk friend."

We followed Caprica back inside and into the same dining room we'd been meeting in a lot lately. There were plates out already, so it looked like we were just in time for supper to be served.

"So, how did the ship stuff go?" I asked Awen as I sat next to her.

She grinned. "Well! It'll take a while to finish everything, but we added fixed docking points to the *Beaver* and their opposites on the *Redemption*. It should be possible to undock the two in midair. But I wouldn't want to try docking in midair," Awen said. "It needs a lot more precision than I think we could manage if we're fighting the wind and trying to pilot two ships at once."

"We can always fly the *Redemption* next to the *Beaver* until we reach a port, if we ever need to," I said.

Awen shook her head. "I'm working on it. But we don't have all the facilities to build what I'm thinking of here."

"That might all come in handy sooner than you think," Caprica said. She slapped a few pages down onto the table and grinned. "We have official denial to attempt a rescue."

"Official denial?" Amaryllis asked.

"It means that if we try something, the government will deny it officially. Which is basically giving us approval to actually try," Caprica explained. "We've been looking for volunteers since the order came in, and I think we've found a couple of vessels with brave captains who wouldn't mind acting as troop transports. Finally, we've chartered a merchant ship to fly close enough to the suspected pirate lair to entice them. We'll be loading the ship full of soldiers disguised as sailors, of course."

"As a distraction?" I asked.

She nodded. "Now, all we need is a flagship to lead this operation."

"You want to use the *Beaver*?" I asked.

She nodded.

"You're aware that it's not a warship, right?" Amaryllis asked.

"Oh, yes, but if things go well, your ship should never have to fight at all. I have a whole plan drawn up. I'm certain it will work out just fine!"

She sounded pretty sure of herself. I figured it was worth a shot! There was a whole heap of people that needed saving, so all we had to do was go out, fight off some pirates, and save the heck out of them!

· Chapter Twenty-Five ·

Provisioning

We need more bolts!"

"Where's case eight-seven-five with the provisions?"

"Coming through! Pardon me, coming through."

I stepped aside to let a pair of sylph soldiers stride by who were carrying a case between them with a set of straps. They climbed the gangplank onto the *Beaver*, then brought the case next to the hatch in the top deck leading into our main hold.

I couldn't even begin to imagine what was in that case, but judging by all the other stuff being loaded aboard, it was probably weapons or supplies.

The *Beaver* wasn't the only ship being loaded up, of course. Caprica had managed to "borrow" two sylph frigates, the *Model Twenty-Two Ship G* and the *Model Twenty-Four Ship C*, which were, in my humble opinion, terrible names for ships.

There were two more ships coming along as well, civilian vessels: the *Lunch Box*, which was an unsurprisingly boxy ship about as big as the *Beaver*, and a larger cargo ship called the *Featherfall*.

And, of course, we had our big distraction, a large merchant airship called the *Royal Pride*. It was one of the biggest ships I'd seen up close, with three balloons—a huge one in the center and two smaller ones connected to nacelles that stuck out of the rear of the vessel. It was being armed up for the mission, and there were a lot of weapons being attached to it, which made sense with how big it was.

Now it was going to host a contingent of sylph soldiers in full gear, which I imagined would give any pirates trying to take her a nasty surprise.

Every ship was being prepared to launch all at once, with sailors running along the decks with equipment, tugboats drawing near to guide the larger ships out of their berths, and hoses connected to every ship to replenish their fuel.

I imagined that this was all going to be very, very expensive, but Caprica had asked nicely, and the people of Goldpass seemed more than eager to meet her demands.

My friends and I were relegated to standing out of the way while the entire port buzzed like a kicked beehive. The metaphor was especially apt since the sylphs could fly and were zipping through the air to carry stuff faster.

I was standing behind the *Beaver*'s wheel on the poop deck where I wouldn't be in anyone's way, so I was able to see Caprica arriving with a contingent of guards and, of course, Bastion by her side.

"Hey!" I called out.

"Hello, Captain," she said from just off the gangplank. "Permission to come aboard?"

"Always!" I cheered.

Caprica grinned and flew over to us, landing with a dainty step and accepting my hellohug. Then I gave one to Bastion too, so he wouldn't feel left out. "Things are coming along well," Caprica said.

"There's a lot of motion going on," Amaryllis said. "What did you set off here, exactly?"

"Hopefully, the sort of mission that will go down in the history books for all the right reasons," Caprica replied. "I am as surprised as you are at the numbers we're pulling. When I asked for volunteers I didn't expect literally every soldier to sign on."

Bastion nodded. "It's not as surprising as you might think, Princess. In the minds of the sylph soldiers, there is little more honorable than serving our country, but to be honest, most of us will never see much action unless things go terribly wrong. This is an opportunity to put their hard-earned training to work. Not to mention, the idea of fighting pirates, saving diplomats, and aiding a princess brings the venture from appealing to irresistible."

"I'm impressed," I said. "How many volunteers does all that add up to?"

"Enough that every ship will have as many sylphs as they can safely carry," Caprica said. "We had to refuse people just on the basis that we can't fit them all aboard. Bastion and the local officers ended up drawing the requirements for who would and wouldn't be allowed to come."

"We set the requirements to match age and time of service," Bastion said. "We'll be bringing the best with us. This is a small settlement, so we won't find as many high-quality soldiers as we might find in the capital, but so far they all seem perfectly competent."

That was a big endorsement from Bastion.

"So, we're running straight toward trouble with an entire army of over-eager soldiers," Amaryllis said. "This will go well. Who's legally in charge of all of this?"

Caprica froze up. "Ah, well. Technically, we needed someone of a certain rank to run an operation of this size. Not to mention an operation in foreign territory. It would have to be an admiral."

"There's an admiral around?" I asked.

Caprica nodded. "Yes. In a manner of speaking."

"Uh-oh," Awen muttered.

"See, when you first introduced my sister and me to Orange, you introduced her as a Grand Admiral, and my sister thought this was a great thing. She, might have, perhaps, officiated the rank. As a small joke."

I blinked. "Wait, what?"

Orange strutted onto the *Beaver Cleaver* with her head and tail held high and her chest fur puffed out luxuriously. She was wearing a tiny tricorne with little feathers affixed to it. *Actual* Grand Admiral of Mouse-Chasing Orange Bunch crossed the deck, slipping past feet and once stopping just long enough to send a young sailor tripping forward with a box full of stuff that spilled across the ground.

She jumped up the steps to the poop deck, then leapt up to take her place on the dais holding up the ship's wheel. "Mrow," she said.

Calamity doffed his hat. "Ma'am," he said.

"Hi!" I said to the spirit cat. She lifted her head a bit, so I gave her chin some scritches. "So, you're the one in charge of all of this?"

"Technically, on paper," Caprica said. She cleared her throat. "Which is why we need to make sure this entire operation goes off without a hitch, because if it doesn't, then we're all going to have to answer a lot of really awkward questions."

"You'd think they'd ask those regardless," Amaryllis said.

"Oh, they will, but success overshadows criticism in a very satisfactory way," Caprica said.

Bastion seemed both amused and exasperated by it all. "We should be heading out. By the looks of it, the ships are almost ready to cast off."

He was probably right. The hustle and bustle had died down. Now most of the sylphs on the docks were only sitting back and waiting for us to take off.

"Oh, we're going on this mission too, Bastion," Caprica said. She smiled up at him. "We must go. Your strength will be invaluable in this mission, and I want to see it through myself. Besides, I think the soldiers might fight harder for having me around."

"Princess Caprica," Bastion said warningly.

"No, Bastion. I insist. I'm hardly incapable of taking care of myself. And I can't send people out to fight without being expected to lead them from the front. Besides, my presence there will reinvigorate things back home, I think."

"What's that mean?" I asked.

"It means that it has been a while since a member of my family has stepped out and done anything truly impressive," Caprica said. "Noblesse oblige means that I must where I can, doesn't it?" She nodded to herself. "And on that note, permission to remain aboard your vessel, Captain Bunch?"

"Of course," I said. "I think you already had a room picked out for yourself?"

"Yes. Bastion's former room. I didn't want to bother any of yours," she said. There was a faint touch of red to her cheeks that I imagined meant something more, but it wasn't the time to go poking at that.

"That's fine by me. The *Beaver Cleaver* always has room for more friends. What about you, Calamity, did you want a room?"

"Ah, if nya don't mind, I'll use one of the bunks on the *Redemption*. They're comfortable enough for the likes of me," he said.

I shrugged. If that was what he wanted, then sure. The airboat was currently fixed between the *Beaver*'s twin hulls. It would take some finagling to detach it, but with Awen aboard we'd manage.

In the berth next to ours, the *Model Twenty-Four Ship C* unhooked itself from the docks and started to gently rise up. The frigate was one of those boxy sylph warships, which meant that it was probably way better in any sort of fight than we were. It was going to be handy to have, I suspected.

"I think we ought to get ready to take off ourselves," I said. I adjusted my captain's hat, making sure my bun ears didn't look too silly poking out of the brim, then I reached over and rang the bell next to the ship's wheel. "Everyone, to your positions! Clive, Awen, check the engines. Calamity, go join the Scallywags by the foredeck, we'll need to trim sails in a hurry. Amaryllis, keep an eye on the newbies. Caprica, Bastion . . . uh."

"We'll stay out of the way," Caprica promised.

I grinned. "Thanks!"

Boots thudded across the deck as people took their positions in a hurry. The last of the troops came aboard and were directed to the sides where they wouldn't be in the way.

The ropes anchoring us to the docks were loosened, then coiled up, and then the entire ship lurched as we were let loose. I noticed the cause of the problem right away. "Awen! We need to shift the anchoring on the balloon, we're pitching forward more than we ought to."

"On it!" Awen said before she ran ahead to the cables holding our balloon in place above. With the added weight of the *Redemption* being a little off-center, we were tipping that way a bit more than we should have. We'd have to do the opposite adjustment once the smaller ship was loose.

I cranked up the power to the gravity generator and felt a familiar hum under my feet. The *Beaver* was in fine form. The sylph crew that patched him up really knew what they were doing. The main engine started with a loud bark, and the prop at the back started to *woosh-woosh* as it cut through the air.

"Captain!" Gordon shouted from the side. "Dock tower gives us permission to depart. Heading three-fifty north. We're in the center of the formation."

"Aye!" I called back, because that sounded way cooler than just "okay." I turned the wheel around a bit, then eased up on the gas. We weren't setting out yet, just forming up. We just had to hover up at an appropriate height. And, since we were the flagship, we'd be setting the pace. "Caprica, do you happen to know what kind of speed the other ships in our little fleet can manage?"

"About fifteen knots, Captain Bunch."

"Alrighty, slow and steady it is. Do you know how to send signals to other ships?"

"I do," she said.

"Neat! Want to tell the *Model Twenty-Two Ship G* and the *Model Twenty-Four Ship C* that we'll be circling around Goldpass until the *Lunch Box* and the *Featherfall* have taken off?"

"You know, some people might object to you asking a princess to work," she said.

"They might, but that's silly. You're here because you want to help, no? All are equal under my captainly authority."

Caprica laughed. "It's fine. They'd be silly people to object anyway." She flashed me a quick salute. "I'll be right on it, Captain."

· Chapter Twenty-Six ·

Onto the River and Through the Woods

With Admiral Orange's assent, Caprica and I figured out a formation that our fleet could take as we traveled. The *Beaver Cleaver*, as the fleet's flagship, got to sit pretty in the middle of the formation, with the slightly faster *Featherfall* ahead, and the *Lunch Box* behind. The idea was that we could create an area with less pressure for the *Lunch Box* to keep pace with us.

The two sylph frigates kept pace on either side of the formation. They were the best-armed ships in our fleet and could outpace even the *Featherfall* when they pushed themselves a little.

The *Royal Pride* split from the formation relatively early on. It was going to head west, then circle north and wait for Caprica's signal to fly past the place where we suspected the pirates to be. That was our big decoy.

As for us, our heading was north-northwest, which had us fighting a cool wind from the northeast.

The first day of the trip was simple enough. After a few hours of figuring out optimal speeds and getting used to flying in formation, we made good progress toward our ultimate destination.

As night fell, the air grew colder and I found myself switching out from behind the wheel to let Clive have a turn, though I made sure to bring him a warm blanket because I didn't need him catching a cold.

When it became too dark to see, we slowed down, descended, and came to a stop above an area barren of any sort of grass or shrubbery.

According to Calamity, that was because of the Greenstone. We weren't in the area of its direct effect, but we were close enough that there wasn't anything growing here. It was safe to stay, but not for a long time. If we did, we'd end up lethargic and eventually sick.

I was a little worried about that, so I kept my Cleaning aura up to make sure the ship stayed clean. It was surprisingly hard to do that, though, and after asking around, Amaryllis conducted a test with some spells that showed that the mana in the area was much, much lower than it should have been.

Maybe that explained why nothing was alive around here?

It didn't really matter. The next morning saw us pulling up our anchors and taking to the skies once more under Grand Admiral Orange's careful watch. If everything went well, we would be reaching the Snowlands a few hours before nightfall, hopefully a good ways east of where the pirates were located.

That's when I got a pleasant surprise.

Congratulations! Through repeated actions your Captaining skill has improved and is now eligible for rank up!

Rank D is a Free Rank!

That was a heck of a boost! I wouldn't say no to it, especially not now that we were working with so many other ships.

It gave me a bit of pep in my step to know that I was improving, and I worked extra hard to keep everything in tip-top condition. It wasn't too hard, though. The sylph troops aboard the *Beaver* were already on their best behavior since they were sharing a ship with a princess and a paladin.

The day passed surprisingly quickly. There were a million and one things to take care of, but I still had a few moments to take in the scenery as we continued flying on. There was something nice about the smell of spent fuel in the crisp-cold air. The world below was spread out far and wide, huge plains eventually giving way to old-growth forests.

The biggest change, though, happened when we reached a sheer cliff-side. It was like the whole world was split apart, with a wall of stone rising up a hundred meters off the ground. Above that rise was another forest, but this one was different from the one below.

The trees were much larger around, and significantly taller. They reminded me of maple trees on a scale that dwarfed even a redwood, and I ended up ordering us to climb a bit higher to avoid brushing too close to their tops, even if that meant dealing with slightly thinner air.

It was colder here too. Some of the trees farther north had brushes of snow on their topmost leaves, and the ground I could spy between them was covered in a white blanket protected from the sun by the canopy formed by the trees.

"The pirates should be to the west of here," Caprica said. She had a clipboard out, with a map of the region on it. "If they have as many ships as we think, then they'll need a place to dock them, and the only place like that nearby is the Lightning Watch."

"What is that?" I asked.

"It's an old Snowlander keep. From what I remember of the nation's history, they used to live to the north of here, but they moved into these woods at some point. Then, some fifty years ago, they moved westward and settled their capital near the Bay of Storms."

"For some reason?" I turned to Caprica..

All she gave in answer was a shrug. "I don't have any better information than that, sorry. It's not like I'm carrying the palace library around with me. I could write a request back home." She tapped her ring.

Amaryllis nodded. "That might not be a terrible idea. If we intend to approach this keep on foot, then we might as well learn what we can about the environment."

"I'll pen something in a moment then," Caprica said.

We continued across the forest until a fog started to collect on the ground around us. It was probably the sun's warmth touching the few snow-covered rivers we were passing, combined with the warmer breeze from the east.

One of the lookouts on the *Featherfall* signaled back to us that there was a glade, so I ordered the fleet to slow down to quarter speed, and we coasted ahead until we came to a large river bank.

Two rivers met below us, both shallow but fast-moving, especially where they met and the competing currents splashed against each other.

"Seems like a good enough place to make landfall," I said.

Orange hissed at the ground, but I think it was mostly the idea of taking a dip in all that water that didn't amuse her, rather than her not liking my plan.

We parked ourselves as close to the ground as we could, lowering ladders to splash into the river's edge while our anchors fixed themselves onto the stony ground. The clearing was only barely large enough to fit all of the ships, but we managed to squeeze them all in.

Hiding five airships wouldn't have been doable under normal circumstances, but the trees here were so tall that it might just be possible to go unnoticed if we sat the ships low enough.

Because I was the captain, I had to be one of the last ones off, at least according to the sylphs. The *Beaver Cleaver*'s normal crew—which meant our harpy friends and the Scallywags—were left on board, as well as a team of six sylphs who pulled the short straws. Every ship kept a small crew and a number of soldiers onboard to defend them. The last thing we wanted was for someone to come around and steal our rides back home.

My shoes hit the water with a splash and I gasped as water raced around my legs. It was cold!

I raced to the river bank, sloshing through water that ran all the way up to mid-thigh in places. I used that trick to warm myself up as I left the water . . . and then I realized that I could have embiggened myself once I was on the opposite shore and felt quite silly for not thinking of it earlier. On the shore, a sylph gave me a hand, and I noticed that a few of the soldiers were wet all the way to their shoulders. Their packs were dry though, so they'd prioritized keeping their stuff warm. Some of them were burning mana in their off hands, using self-heating spells that warmed their clothes enough that the water soaked into their armor was wafting off as a light steam.

"I haven't been this cold in a while," I said with good cheer as I found my friends to one side.

"It's not too bad, it gets colder than this in Goldenalden during midwinter," Caprica said.

Awen didn't say anything, but the clatter of her teeth spoke volumes about what she thought of the forest's temperature.

I wrapped an arm around her shoulder to share some of my warmth. "You'll get used to it," I said. It was a partial lie; it took a while to get acclimatized to this kind of cold.

Amaryllis huffed and tugged her jacket tighter. "We should get moving. We have half a day of travel time left if we pace ourselves. We couldn't see the keep from the air, so it's going to be a good distance away."

Bastion nodded. "I'm sending scouts ahead. We don't have many, but those we do have are pretty talented. They'll give us the lay of the land. Otherwise, I suggest we move as a single group. A three-long formation."

"A what?" I asked.

As it turned out, the sylphs had a lot of formations and such that they trained. A three-long was a long column with rows of three soldiers walking side by side. The one in the center would look ahead, and those on the left and right would look to the sides. Each threesome stayed within weapon's reach of the one ahead, so as we started to walk into the tall forest, we did so as a long, thick snake of people.

I ended up somewhere in the middle, with my friends by my side. Caprica was just ahead, flanked by two of the more experienced royal guards who'd come along with us.

The forest was wild, but there was far less underbrush than I expected. Instead, we had to cut our way through fallen branches to walk in a more or less straight path.

The size of the trees made me feel absolutely tiny, and I wasn't even using Proportion Distortion. These weren't the big maples and such I was used to seeing back home. They had more in common with sequoias than anything else. If an animal came out from around a tree, I imagined that it would have to be enormous just to be relative to the trees.

But we didn't see anything.

Not even a squirrel or a wild bird.

In fact, now that I was paying attention, the forest was eerily quiet once we were far enough from the river that the murmuring of the water was far enough back that I couldn't hear it anymore.

"Where are all the little beasties?" I asked.

"Hibernating?" Awen suggested.

I shook my head. "Not cold enough for that."

"It'll get even colder?" Awen asked, aghast.

"Broccoli's right, there's nothing but plant life around. And insects," Amaryllis said. She swatted a few little bugs away with a sweep of her wings. "Nothing bigger than a beetle."

"Could it be that Greenstone thing you mentioned before?" I asked.

Calamity, who was in the group right behind us, spoke up. "I doubt it. The Greenstone's effect doesn't go that far, nor in this direction, I don't think."

"Do you know this area?" I asked.

"Nah, sorry. If I knew nya'd drag us here I'd have asked around a bit more. Heard some stories, but mostly about how the forest is filled with monsters and ancient dungeons."

"Oh," I said.

Monsters and ancient dungeons. Neither sounded good at the moment. We didn't have time to go exploring a dungeon. Especially not an older one, which would undoubtedly have more floors and more dangerous challenges.

I imagined that a dungeon in a forest like this, so far from anything, might have gone unchallenged for a very, very long time. Monsters and ancient dungeons might be okay later, but for now we had to take out *pirates*!

My ears twitched around, and I felt the fine hairs on the back of my neck rising. Was something watching us? I looked around, and noticed some of the soldiers doing the same.

At the very front, Bastion raised a hand and made a few quick gestures.

"Quiet," Caprica muttered for our benefit.

The soldiers carefully shifted, hands casually alighting on hilts and shield arms moving as if to make sure they were limber and ready to move. Any chatter down the line, which wasn't much to begin with because they were professionals, died down to nothing at all.

We didn't stop moving, though, not until something stumbled out ahead of us and we came to a stop without anyone communicating that we should.

One of the scouts returned, covered in sweat, with a gash on his forehead and his wings buzzing loudly in the quiet as he came for a hard landing before the group. "Sir," he gasped.

"Report," Bastion ordered.

"Spiders, sir. Big ones."

Chapter Twenty-Seven

Food for Thought

It took Bastion half a second to come up with a plan. "Phalanx, I want a grid. Spears out ahead. Swordsmen, be ready to take to the air. We're going to need wide sweeps of fire to clear out any webbing."

"Oh no," Calamity said. "Nope, nope, nope."

"What's wrong?" I asked as the formation shuffled around us. We were being positioned near the rear, along with an obviously irate Princess Caprica. She didn't like being pushed back to where it was safest.

"I'm not, ah, fond of spiders. In fact, I'm *very* not-fond of them."

"Really?" I asked.

"Yes, really," he said. He reached for his pack and pulled out his unstrung bow, then quickly and expertly looped a string through one end and over to the other while bending the bow on the ground. "We have spiders out on the plains. They're bigger than both my hands together and will pounce on any birds that fly too close. Whenever I see their nests I go the long way around."

"That is kind of spooky," I agreed. I shucked off my pack and set it down to one side. A lot of the soldiers with extra equipment were doing the same. Then I pulled out Weedbane and held it close, ready to snap the blade out the moment I needed it. Hopefully it wouldn't come to that.

"Broccoli," Bastion called back.

I jumped, then looked over the heads of the sylphs between us to see the paladin waving me over. "I'll be right back," I told my friends before I pushed through the formation and toward Bastion. "What's up?" I asked.

He nodded to me, then gestured to his side. The scout from earlier was there. Up close, I could see that he wasn't in as bad a shape as I'd feared. Sure, his armor was roughed up and a bit dirty, but he didn't seem wounded other than the gash on his forehead.

I pushed some Cleaning magic out, which startled him before he realized that his uniform was clean again.

"Best to keep your magic reserves topped up," Bastion advised. "We might be needing every spell we can muster soon."

"Oh, all right," I said. I was pretty sure my Cleaning magic would work on spiderwebs. It worked on cobwebs well enough. Though maybe those were different, in a way? It wasn't hard to agree to hold back, though. "What did you need me for?" I asked.

"Negotiations," Bastion said.

The scout looked as surprised as I felt.

"I know you well enough," Bastion continued. "You're going to try to talk to the spiders whether or not I tell you not to, so I might as well nip this in the bud. When the spiders arrive, I'd like for you to open a dialogue with them. Maybe it won't come down to a fight."

"That makes sense," I said. And it did sound like something I'd do. "We *are* invading their home, so it's only polite to say hello."

"Yes, I'm sure," Bastion said. "Mostly, my concern is trying to get past the forest without losing any lives or equipment, and perhaps even time. We're on a schedule here."

"Right," I said. "We might be able to ask for permission to peacefully cross their territory. And they might know about the pirates too."

He nodded. "That would be a great boon, yes. But keep in mind, if things don't work out, or if the spiders are mere animals, I don't want you interfering in the fight to protect them over us."

"I know. I'm not that silly." Turning to the scout, I smiled before I asked him a few questions. "Did you see the spiders for yourself?"

"Yes, ma'am," he replied immediately.

"What do they look like, exactly?" I asked.

"They're quite large, ma'am, easily the mass of a sylph, I'd guess. They are brown and black. I believe their . . . chitin might be a natural camouflage in these forests."

"Right. Are they more like ambush predators, like normal spiders, or are they more jump-at-your-face spiders?"

The scout shrugged. "I'm sorry, ma'am, I don't know."

"Either is bad, but ambush predators would be worse," Bastion said. "We need to stay sharp, but if we're constantly expecting an ambush, crossing the forest is going to wear down everyone's nerves."

That sounded about right. The forest was already on the creepy side. I couldn't imagine walking through it while expecting a big spider to drop down from above or spring from a bush at any moment. Dangerous rescue missions were already stressful enough; if we added any extra stress, people might start cracking.

A second scout came hurtling down from above. Not from ahead though, but instead from the side. "Sir," she said as she landed at a jog. "Spiders, left flank."

"We're being surrounded," Bastion said. "All right. Round formation, everyone. Keep the VIPs and our range experts centered. Eyes up. Keep flight to a minimum. Prepare to fight stealthed enemies. I want sense magics on full blast. Buffs up."

I felt a queasy sort of pressure in my tummy, and my skin tingled. I had no idea what had just happened, but I could tell that it was magical, and it was coming from . . . Caprica? The princess was standing tall, eyes closed, a fist over her heart. I noticed most of the soldiers standing a little taller, too.

"That should help a little. Don't rely on it alone, though," Bastion said.

He was too busy forming the sylphs up into a perfect circle to explain what Caprica had done. The sylphs with swords and shields were on the outside, with an inner circle of sylphs with spears ready to poke out of the gaps in the shield wall. In the very middle were my three friends and a few sylphs archers, getting ready to help as best they could.

"Get into the formation," Bastion ordered the two scouts and they both took to the air, flying over and into the center. "Broccoli, if you would stay with me, please."

"Yup," I said.

"If I order you back into the formation, I expect you to listen," he warned.

I nodded. I could do that. Bastion had a lot on his plate, and dealing with a silly bun who couldn't listen to orders—even if that silly bun was me—would just add to his burden in a way that wasn't very kind.

We waited, Bastion with his hand on the hilt of his sword, and me with Weedbane held like a staff while I swiveled my ears around to listen.

When the spiders arrived, they were so quiet it was only someone in the formation saying "Look!" that made me notice them.

The first spider to show up was a big one. They were about as tall as I was, though they seemed much, much wider due to their long, thin limbs that reached way out from their body. Their limbs were quite hairy, all covered in spiky bristles, and they scanned the clearing with eight beady, pupilless eyes that made it impossible to tell what, exactly, they were focusing on.

"Hmm," Bastion hummed. "Second tier."

I winced. "Does that mean that the spiders have access to a dungeon?"

"It's possible," he said. "It could be a natural level. They're all around the same level range. Or the few I've seen have been. It puts them on par with most of our soldiers. I was hoping to have a clear level advantage to leverage against their superior numbers."

The spiders probably had a heap of natural advantages here. Plus, they were on their home terrain. Yeah, I could see why Bastion was worried. "Let me see what I can do," I said.

The big spider was clinging to the side of one of the trees, the claw-tips on the end of their legs hanging on to the bark so that they could stay in place, even if that place was a vertical surface.

I hopped forward and away from the group until I was about halfway between us and the spider. Just one big backward bounce back to the formation, if I had to run. I cleared my throat and looked at the spider.

That's when I realized that this would be one of those weird situations where I couldn't just talk to someone verbally . . . well, not only verbally. I took a deep breath, then clicked my tongue as hard as I could.

The spider paused, their attention turning toward me as I clicked my tongue a few more times and tried to get the right sound and pitch. My ability to speak any language was neat, but sometimes it left my throat sore.

"Got it," I muttered.

Then I bounced into a wide squat, stuck my butt way out, and raised my arms above my head straight up, parallel to my ears.

I clicked twice more while shifting to the side. "Hello, spider friend," I . . . didn't so much *say* as I signed.

The spider turned a little, then one of its rear legs moved up and wiggled while its thorax shifted. It clicked, "Stop. Wait."

That . . . wasn't addressed to me, I don't think. I glanced around, and started to notice that a number of the shadows nearby were moving in a way that didn't match the wind passing through the canopy above.

I shifted my arms again, this time at fixed angles, then I twitched my ears the same way. I was so lucky to be a bun. I was already two limbs short for a proper spider conversation, so my ears were invaluable at the moment. "Hello. We are friends. Not food. Passing through. Hello."

More spiders appeared, scuttling around tree trunks to come and stare with their many eyes.

There was a faint echo of clicks that I would have dismissed as branches creaking if I didn't know any better. It was kind of the equivalent of a crowd murmuring.

"Broccoli?" Bastion asked.

"We're chatting," I said. "Or I'm trying to. They talk in clicks and with their bodies. It's kind of complicated."

"Tell us if they seem to be turning aggressive," he said.

I gave him a thumbs-up and returned my attention to the first spider that had shown up. It eyed me in turn, then it clicked and wiggled its thorax in a way that was actually kind of cute until I parsed what it was saying.

"Food clicks at us. Strange. Dangerous. New food."

I wiggled back as soon as I could, and tried not to think of the group of people behind me watching me shake my bum. "Not food. Friend."

The spider twitched at me. "Look like food. Smell like food. Will taste. See if food." Then it started to skitter down the tree until I danced faster to get it to pause.

"Don't eat. Not food," I said. "Group is passing through trees. Group is looking for other food." I was running into a pretty big problem with spider vocabulary. Also, getting called "food" was giving me flashbacks to meeting Savan.

The spider let out an irate set of clicks. "All food in forest our food."

"Our food not in forest," I replied with some clicks of my own. "Looking for food that looks like us."

"So, you food?"

Oops. I'd fallen into that trap feet-first.

"No. Friend!" I signaled. There was more clicking from the forest, and I had the impression the peanut gallery of giant spiders were finding this exchange very amusing. Hopefully not in the predinner entertainment kind of way.

"Confusing. Is food who says isn't food. Is looking for food in our trees. Small. No webs. Not enough legs, but can still click," the big spider said. "Will bring to Mommy."

"Yes," I agreed. Was Mommy their leader? Maybe they were matriarchal.

In either case, talking to their leader might be helpful. They might be older and wiser, or maybe just be better at communicating. That would be super helpful all on its own.

"Broccoli!"

I gasped as a large web shot out toward me, white silky material spreading out to envelope me. Then, faster than I could blink, Bastion was there with his sword singing and the web was sliced apart into a thousand ribbons.

I gasped and turned to the spider. "Why web?" I signaled.

"Cocoon the food for Mommy," it clicked back.

I had the impression it wouldn't be getting any easier to communicate.

· Chapter Twenty-Eight ·

The Amazing Spider-Mom

It took a bit of back and forth to convince the nice spider *not* to cocoon me to bring me to Mommy. In the end, I managed to convince them that if I was cocooned, I wouldn't be able to speak at all, since speaking in spider required some movement, which I couldn't manage if I was all tied up.

Since they couldn't bring me to their mom, they decided to bring their mom here. One of the smaller spiders was voluntold to go fetch the spider matriarch, and I decided to retreat toward the safety provided by my friends and all the soldiers around them.

"That seems to have gone well," Amaryllis said.

"Really?" Caprica asked. "Because we're still surrounded by obviously hostile forces that we can't number and whose strength we can't determine."

"But Broccoli was able to talk to them," Amaryllis argued. "Which means that either she'll be able to convince them that we're friendly, or they'll presume that we're as innocent and harmless as she is."

"Hey now," I said, defending myself. "I can be harmful."

Amaryllis patted me on the helmet between my ears. "Yes, you're very intimidating and harmful," she said.

I pouted.

"Don't worry, Broccoli, I'm sure you'll be intimidating one day, if you work very hard at it," Awen said comfortingly.

"All of this aside," Caprica said. "What did the spiders have to say? And what was with the . . . dancing you were doing? Is that how they communicate?"

"It is," I said. "They speak with their limbs a lot, and with those clicks. It's a pretty simple language, I think. They don't really have grammar, so to speak, so you kind of need to interpret everything on its own merits."

"Interesting, but not what we're here for," Caprica said.

"Right. They sent a spider off to get their matriarch. Or I think it's their matriarch," I said. "It sounds like someone important to them."

"A leader of some sort," Caprica said. "Maybe we actually *can* negotiate. If we can't, though, I'm certain we have the manpower to press through. We have proper soldiers here, Sylphfreean soldiers, not some untrained rabble."

I noted the backs of the nearby sylphs straightening a bit. So, they were listening in on us. Caprica had to know that. "Uh-huh," I said. "But negotiation would still be better than fighting, I think. If only because I don't want us to get covered in webs and spider ichor. I can probably clean it, but it's gross."

"Time's a concern as well," Amaryllis said. "If things turn hostile, we'll have to fight our way out, which will likely take a while and could even reveal our advance to the pirates. On the other hand, if we can successfully negotiate passage, we will be able to move rapidly, possibly even with a local guide."

"We'll manage either way," I said. Glancing back over the heads of the soldiers around us, I noticed that the spiders were standing a bit less stiff than before. A number of them were rubbing their legs together, which didn't mean anything in their language, so I guessed that they were just quickly grooming themselves, like someone running a hand through their hair before an important meeting. "I think she's arriving."

There was a skittering sound coming from deeper in the forest, just loud enough that it carried over the breathing of the soldiers. Some of the spiders started to click excitedly and sway from side to side, limbs rising and falling in what was almost a dance.

They were chanting one word, over and over again. "Mommy! Mommy! Mommy!"

A dozen new spiders poured into the clearing, clinging to the massive trees. Most were smaller than the spiders we'd seen already, but almost all of them carried a bundle on their backs.

With quick and practiced motions, the smaller spiders laid out long threads of silk which went taut with hard twangs. Others set down what looked like wooden drums with skin tops and still others jingled and jangled as they tied rattles to the trees.

"What are they doing?" Caprica asked.

"Those are musical instruments," Awen said. "A bunch of them."

The clearing quieted down and the spiders retreated, though only far enough that they were half-hidden in the shadows and could still watch us with gleaming eyes. A susurration of shifting sounds came from the ground ahead of us, and soon a spider came walking around the largest of the trees.

She wasn't walking vertically along the trees like her children had done, maybe because despite the enormous size of these trees, she was still too big to grab onto them.

Mommy was three times as tall as I was, with mandibles longer than my arms and eyes as big as my entire head. She was covered in fine, bristly hairs on her legs and back and even around her torsos, which twitched slightly as she moved.

The gigantic spider came to stand in the clearing across from us, then her long limbs reached out and very gently touched the long silken threads connected to the instruments around her.

There was a strange moment where she tested each string, one at a time. The drums thumped and boomed, the strings hummed like violins, and the shakers above rasped and clattered.

"Iiii am . . . Mom-me!" the spider said through the means of drumbeat booms and violin strums.

"Well, that's something I never expected to see," Amaryllis muttered.

"Was that in a language everyone understood?" I asked.

"Yes, if barely," Amaryllis said. "She has a bit of an accent."

"I think she's doing very well, considering," I said. "Let me go talk to her."

Amaryllis touched my shoulder. "Be careful, please."

"I will," I promised. "Besides, if she went through all of this trouble to come and talk, then she must have something to say, right?" Stepping out from between the soldiers, I took a few steps toward Mommy, the huge spider, then I made a few quick gestures, with some clicks added in for good measure. Just to be safe though, I spoke to her aloud at the same time. "Hello, Mommy, I am . . . uh, Broccoli Bunch, a non-food friend."

"Yooou . . . arre innn myyy trreeees," Mommy said with her many instruments. Her eight eyes were focused on me. "Yooou arre . . . NOT uusssssual foooood."

"That's because we're not food at all," I replied.

Mommy the spider tilted her entire body slightly. "Yooou look smaaall . . . like fooood," she said. "Buuuut not liike ouur fooood."

"That's because we're not from around here."

"Frrooom beyooond the treees," she said.

"Exactly!" I cheered. "We're looking for people who are from here. A group of stealers. People who have flying . . . uh . . ." I hesitated. There wasn't a word for "airship" in spider, which probably made sense. "Houses," I settled on.

Mommy bobbed her entire body up and down. "The prooomise-breaakers," she said with a click.

The click was repeated by all of her many spider friends as a short-lived cacophony.

"Who are the promise-breakers?" I asked.

Mommy turned and pointed behind her toward the south, more or less in the direction we were headed. "Theeey aree froom the stooone home."

"And they broke a promise?" I asked.

She bobbed again. "Theey saaaid they wooould neeever reeeetuuurn. Yet, theeeey are heeeere."

"Are they people like us?" I half turned and gestured to the group behind me.

"Smaaaall foooods, yes, buut nooot like yoou." The spider leaned forward. "Taaaller. With flying hooomes and louuud maaagic. Theeeey taught mee woooords, buut theey broooke the prooomise."

"What was the promise, exactly?" I asked.

"Thaaaat alllll whooo staaands in theeese trees are ouuuur fooood. That noo oone wouuld live in theiiir stoone hooome anymoooore. Thaaat my childreeen wouuuuldn't be huuunted."

"Oh," I said. Something in Mommy's body language said that last was the part that hurt her the most. "I think I know who's responsible. We're here because they hunted some of our flying homes, and took some of our family. We're here to take our homes, and the people they took, back."

Mommy tilted to the side, one of her legs crooking in a sort of *go on* gesture.

"We don't want to fight you, Mommy. These are your, um, trees. So, how about you let us pass, and we won't cross your forest again?"

Mommy considered it. "Buuut wee couuuuld eaaat youuu." She leaned forward and her mandibles shook.

I nodded. "You could. But we don't want to be eaten, so we'd fight. And then some of your children would be hurt. We're pretty tough, you know? If you let us pass without issue, then we might be able to do something about those people at the stone, if they're the people we think they are."

The giant spider tapped the tip of one long leg against one of the strings spanning the clearing with a bassy *thump*. "Yeees," she said at last, one claw running along a string to create the word. "Yooouu wiiiill saaaave myy chiiildren foor me."

"Um, yeah, we can do that," I agreed.

The spider bobbed up and down and clicked happily. Her children did the same, until the forest was filled with echoing clicks. "Gooood. Leave as sooon as yoouuu aaaaare dooone. Or beecoomme fooood."

With that, Mommy stepped back and turned around a large tree. The cohort that had accompanied her rushed ahead, grabbing her instruments in a flurry of motion before skittering after their mom.

The other spiders watched us for a few seconds more, then they tugged on strings and zipped up into the canopy above or climbed around trunks until, finally, we were alone in the forest.

I let out a long breath, relieved at the sudden absence of giant spiders. Still, the fact that they'd disappeared so quickly and quietly was somewhat unnerving.

Carefully, I stepped back and returned to my friends. The formation was still holding, but it was clear that the soldiers were beginning to relax, even if it was just a little. "That was stressful," I said.

"You did well," Bastion replied. "That large spider, Mommy? That would have been a challenge to face even prepared as we were, and a few of the other spiders seemed tough to fight as well."

Caprica nodded along with the assessment. "We're fine to carry on, then? I'm not entirely sure I heard everything it said correctly."

"She said we could. As long as we take care of the people at the stone home. Which I'm guessing is an important place nearby? There's supposed to be a tower, right?"

"Yeah," Amaryllis said. "The Lightning Watch. Weren't you supposed to ask the palace for information about that?"

Caprica cleared her throat to cover the red splotches growing on her cheeks. "We should head out, then. We don't know if we can trust the spiders not to try and grab a few of us while our guard is down."

"We'll change up the formation," Bastion said. "We'll be operating with fewer scouts, only those I trust to be able to sneak past the spiders. And we'll be moving slower. I doubt we'll reach the tower before tomorrow morning. Maybe even in the afternoon."

Caprica grimaced, but nodded all the same. "We have that amount of time, in theory. The *Royal Pride* is waiting on our communication to start its baiting maneuvers."

"If we can't cross the forest again," Awen said, "then how will we get back to the ships once we have the hostages?"

"Oh," I said. "That's a good question."

"We won't want to fight the spiders on the way back," Bastion said. "We might have to wait at the tower for the ships to come around and retrieve us. It'll mean a small change of plans."

"That sounds kind of dangerous," I said. The pirates would be on the lookout for ships, certainly. I didn't want them launching to fight the *Beaver Cleaver*, especially if I wasn't onboard.

Bastion started to order people around into a new formation, this one much shorter than the last, and I ended up next to Caprica, surrounded on all sides by watchful sylph soldiers. My friends were right behind us, of course.

We started to move, and this time, all eyes were looking for the signs of a sudden spider attack.

· Chapter Twenty-Nine ·

Mutually Assured Hugging

By early evening, the scouts were able to see the tower. I could only catch a few glimpses of it in the distance, and it looked . . . like a large tower. It was octagonal and had balconies running around some of the floors, but it was still distant enough that I couldn't make out much more about it.

We had no choice but to stop eventually and set up camp. We were still maybe an hour's walk from the tower itself, at least according to the scout who'd snuck up to it.

The camp we set up was different from what I was used to. The sylphs found some fallen branches from the huge trees around us and used those—along with some Earth magic—to create a palisade around our campsite. The smaller tents they carried were laid out in a circle around a larger one that sat in the middle, which my friends and I were currently standing within while the soldiers prepared for a big fight that we all hoped wouldn't happen.

"This is the tower," the scout said. He tapped on an octagonal shape he'd drawn on a sheet of looseleaf. "And this is the path I uncovered leading to it. As you can see, it's a switchback. It's difficult to tell from here, but what we see of the tower is merely the upper half. Most of it is hidden by this rise here."

I nodded along as I followed on his map.

"Where are their ships docked?" Amaryllis asked.

"Along here, ma'am," the scout said. He drew a circle with his fingertip, drawing out the base of the tower. "There are structures here for the ships. They're made of wood, probably sourced from this forest. They seem sturdy from afar. There are also buildings here and here." He tapped two spots.

"What sort of buildings?" Awen asked.

"I couldn't say with any certainty," the scout replied. "They seem to be newer constructions than the tower itself."

"Number of ships?" Bastion asked.

"Seven. Five look like Snowlander vessels, and the other two are definitely harpy ships. One of those might be the main diplomatic vessel. It's quite large and . . . ostentatious."

"Five Snowlander ships," Amaryllis muttered. "Does that match up with what we know of their attack on the delegation?"

"That's about the right number, yes, if we accept the accuracy of that ship's log from the *Remiges Crown*," Awen said.

Amaryllis nodded. "A good source, but the captain may not have managed to get an accurate number into the log. We should err on the side of caution and assume that they have more ships than that."

"And a large base of groundcrew working for them as well," Caprica said. "Seven ships, even if they're not all in use, is still a good-sized squadron. Any sign of the captives?"

"No, Your Highness."

"Guards?" Bastions asked.

"Few," the scout said. "I only saw three, and I'm uncertain if two of them were actually guards or just pirates stepping out for some air. They mostly seem to be sequestered within the tower, but it has parapets that allow them to see quite far into the forest. Anyone trying to move toward the tower from the south will have to move along these rocks. There's cover, but it's sparse." He traced a finger along the path again. I could imagine that someone standing atop the tower would have a great view.

"So, we can't sneak in?" I asked.

Caprica frowned. "Maybe not with our entire unit. The scouts can, certainly. I have full confidence in their ability to go unnoticed. Perhaps the royal guards we have as well, since they have skills to avoid detection."

The scout stood a little taller. "I'm certain my brothers-in-arms and I can reach the tower without being seen, Your Highness."

"I think I could make it," Calamity mused. "If nya give me some time and the guards aren't paying full attention."

"It's nearing evening," Caprica said. "Let's not do anything hasty. The *Royal Pride* will be passing by in the early morning, and our original plan is still the best chance we have at getting the hostages back. As long as we time things correctly, and the pirates take the bait, it might be all the distraction we need."

"Then we can have our ships launch just before we swoop in ourselves," Amaryllis said. "It'll take them two, maybe three hours to reach us here, I imagine."

"So, we wait here until morning and try to be well rested?" I asked. "That doesn't sound very heroic. Couldn't we do a teensy preliminary attack? You know, like set up some booby traps or tie their shoelaces together?"

Bastion rubbed at his jaw. "Moving in at dusk is too risky. Our soldiers, with a few exceptions, aren't trained for night operations, and we're all a little tired from the trek we had to endure today. Our best bet is still to wait for the *Royal Pride*."

I crossed my arms. I wanted to protest, but Bastion probably knew better, so we'd follow his advice and stay back. Besides, I kinda wanted to succeed without too much violence. If we barged up to the tower with overwhelming strength, then we could tell the pirates to surrender and just grab the prisoners and run.

A quick in-and-out, where no one needed to get hurt, and at the end of the day we'd all be big old heroes.

I liked the idea.

"In that case," Caprica said. "I have a few notes to send. I imagine you'd enjoy a warm meal."

The scout nodded. "That would be welcome, Your Highness," he replied.

"Good. Let's get everything sorted while we can. Tomorrow will prove to be a busy day, I imagine. Broccoli, could you follow me for a moment?"

I blinked, then nodded and followed Caprica into the deeper part of the tent where a section was walled off by a hanging curtain. There was a small bed behind that, mostly just a padded cushion with some blankets atop it, but it looked leagues comfier than sleeping on the ground.

Caprica rubbed at her face, and let her shoulders droop. "Are you okay?" I asked. I hadn't noticed any signs that she was stressed until just then.

She smiled. "I'm fine. It's a lot of work, but . . . well, I feel like I've been training for this my whole life. Anyway." She took a deep breath and shored up her reserves.

Then I hugged her.

"Broccoli?" she questioned after a few seconds, holding her arms out awkwardly.

"Back in my home world, everyone knew that thirty seconds of hugging could help you relax. I think it's because we need physical contact to feel safe. You know, like how doggies all sleep together in a big pile."

"I'll thank you for not comparing me to a dog," she said.

I squeezed a bit tighter. "Cats do it too," I said.

"Hmm . . ." She paused. "Broccoli, I think it's been more than thirty seconds."

"That's for humans," I said. "I don't know how long it is for buns or sylphs, so I'm being safe and doubling the dose."

"I suppose we'll need all the safety we can get."

I squeezed harder before finally letting go. I looked her up and down. "Are you feeling a little better?" I asked.

She nodded. "I am," she assured me. I wasn't sure if I believed her. Medication often had to be used over a long time to help someone feel better, and I think hugs were the same. I was going to prescribe her a dose of hugs, twice daily, from here on out.

"So, what did you want? Just hugs?"

She shook her head. "No, I wasn't looking for hugs. Though . . . thank you for that. I wanted to talk about something more . . . dangerous."

More dangerous than hugs? That didn't narrow it down at all; everything was more dangerous than a hug. "What is it?"

"Rainnewt," she said, and I felt my back straightening. "Under any other circumstances, his head would have gone to the block already."

"What?" I asked with a gasp.

She blinked. "What what?"

"You'd kill him?" I asked.

"Broccoli, he acted as if the lawbooks were a checklist of crimes to commit. Attempted regicide, terroristic threats, attempted mass murder, actual murder. That's not getting into all of the smuggling, conspiracy, identity theft, and the use of countless illegal spells. He's likely responsible for destroying dungeon cores, which alone would be enough to sentence him to death. What did you expect us to do with him?"

"I . . . don't know," I said, shifting my weight from foot to foot. "I guess put him in a cell and try to reform him?"

"I don't think there are enough hugs in the World for that," she said. "But it's all moot now. With him being part of the ransom demands from these pirates, the Harpy Mountains would throw a fit if we executed him now."

It sounded as if that was rather important. "You're not going to?"

"We don't want to spark a war. Not after we came so close to one because of Rainnewt already. The irony would be too much, I think, if a war started because of him even after we captured and foiled his plans."

"I guess," I said. "Do you think he planned on using the pirates and their hostages as a sort of contingency?"

"A lot of what Rainnewt was up to is still murky and unknown, but I think we can assume that most of it wasn't good. The telling thing is that this Commodore Megumi wants him freed. It does have the feeling of a contingency plan going off."

"Well, we're not going to give him back, are we?" I asked.

"We can't," Caprica said. Then she sighed. "He escaped."

I gasped. "He what?!"

That . . . No, how could he? We'd worked so hard to grab him! And he wasn't just in some little sheriff's office or something, he'd been taken in by the sylph army. They were supposed to be competent!

Caprica placed a hand on my shoulder and gave it a squeeze. "It's okay. We'll find him again. We have the best investigators in the country on his trail, and we've captured his co-conspirator already."

"Someone helped him?" I asked.

She nodded. "He couldn't have gotten out without help. As it turns out, he had more plans than we expected, including kidnapping some middling-ranked officer's family and holding them hostage unless they helped him escape. It worked."

"That's awful," I said. "I hope they don't get into too much trouble."

Caprica blinked. "Uh. I'll make sure of that, sure. I thought you'd be more concerned about his escape?"

"Oh, I'm very concerned," I said. "But . . . I don't think he'll come after me or my friends. Rainnewt struck me as very goal-oriented. We stopped him, but unless we meet again, he doesn't seem very vengeance-inclined." I tightened my fists. "But if we do meet him again, I think I might have to put my feelings aside to beat the stuffing out of him."

"Do you want a hug?"

I blushed, then nodded. "Yes please, I think I'd like that."

Caprica's hug was very technically correct and also very stiff. The princess clearly lacked hugging practice. But there was a lot of heart in it, so I hugged her right back and enjoyed the contact while it lasted.

"Thanks," I said once the hug ended. "I guess I should tell my friends?"

"You can. I'd suggest being discreet, though. The news isn't out yet — only myself, Bastion, and a few other guards know, and we're obviously keeping it quiet. It wouldn't do for the World to learn we've fumbled. Especially not the harpies."

I clasped my hand over my mouth. "They need Rainnewt for the hostages."

"And we're all out of Rainnewt to give," Caprica said. "Things will get rather heated, I think, if we can't save the day at the fort tomorrow."

I narrowed my eyes. "Don't worry, Caprica. If my friends and I are good at one thing, it's kidnappings. We have a *lot* of experience."

She opened her mouth to say something, then closed it. A moment later, she tried again.

". . . I am going to choose to believe that I was reassured by that."

· **Chapter Thirty** ·

With Catlike Tread

One of the soldiers tripped on some loose stones and his armor rattled as he caught himself against the cliffside.

Bastion half turned and made a gesture that I didn't need my translation abilities to understand meant "I said *be quiet.*"

In the soldier's defense, the path wasn't easy. We were walking more or less single-file along a trail picked out by a few of the scouts. It wound around the cliff edge below the tower, mostly keeping to outcrops and nooks where someone looking from the tower wouldn't be able to see our group moving.

The tower did as towers do, and towered above us. It was quite a bit larger than I'd expected, actually. The building's footprint must have been more than a hundred meters across, and it was shaped like a large octagon, with sheer walls only broken up by the occasional parapet that stuck out above.

The entire structure was clearly made from the same kind of stone we walked upon, though I imagined that there had been some magic involved in its construction, seeing as it was so remote.

Ahead of me, Caprica paused, then nipped into a depression against the cliffside where she set her shield down and took off her gloves. A moment later she was holding onto a long slip of paper.

"Anything good?" I asked as I came closer, stifling a yawn.

"Report from the *Royal Pride*. It's beginning its run now. Let's pray to the World that this works," she said.

I nodded along. "I'm sure they'll take the bait. It's big and juicy!"

Caprica snorted and pulled her gloves back on over her communication ring, then she picked up her shield and hefted it. "Come on, we still need to get into position ourselves."

As it turned out, our position was only a little ways away. The scout explained to us that it was the last point where we could reliably hide without being spotted by anyone who looked. Even then, the spot was rather tight with all of the sylph soldiers bunched in close to stay in the shadow of an outcrop.

I didn't mind so much; I got to bunch in close to my friends. "Do you think this will go well?" I asked.

"It might," Amaryllis said. "If we can move swiftly and with overwhelming force, things will go just fine, I suspect. These sylphs are well trained, I'll give them that. Probably better than any common pirate rabble."

Awen shrugged. "Ah, I don't know. But we have to try, right? If we don't, Sylphfree might end up freeing Rainnewt, and that wouldn't be any good."

A pit opened in my tummy. I still hadn't told my friends what Caprica had told me—that Rainnewt had already escaped. I probably should have, but there hadn't been a good time for it. We'd slept in a tent with walls thin enough that anyone could eavesdrop on us and we'd been walking since pretty much the moment we got up.

"So, who's this Rainnewt fella ny'all have been talkin' about?" Calamity asked.

"He's a fool of the highest order and someone whose head can't be separated from his body soon enough," Amaryllis said.

"Um. Rainnewt is a Riftwalker who destroyed a bunch of dungeons," Awen said. "But he also, ah, tried to start a war."

"A war between who?" Calamity asked.

"Everyone," I said. "The Trenten Flats, Sylphfree, the Nesting Kingdom, and even the grenoils down in Deepmarsh. He hurt a lot of people, framed innocents, and basically did terrible things just because he was too lazy to find a more peaceful solution to his problem . . . our problem, I guess."

"Huh." Calamity rubbed his chin. "Well, he sounds like the sort of person nya wouldn't mind getting into a hunting accident with."

I shook my head. "No, you wouldn't want to pick a fight with him. He's actually pretty strong. He even fought Bastion. Though Bastion's a better fighter, Rainnewt is a lot trickier."

"He fought the paladin?" Calamity asked. He glanced at Bastion, who was talking to some of Caprica's royal guardsmen at the moment. "Bet I could still take him."

Amaryllis snorted. "Maybe if he was tied to a post, blindfolded, and wearing only what he hatched with."

I giggled at the mental image of Rainnewt covered in egg goop. Amaryllis gave me a confused look, and I shook my head. "You're silly," I said.

She huffed a very clear *I am no such thing* kind of huff back at me.

"This Rainnewt guy work for any country?" Calamity asked.

"As far as we're aware, no," Amaryllis said. "It's very probable that he's an independent actor."

"Except that the pirates want him, so they have to have been working with him too," Awen pointed out.

"We'll be taking care of them shortly enough," Calamity asserted.

Bastion cleared his throat. "Quiet down," he said, his voice a low rumble that carried just far enough for us to hear. A few of the soldiers had also been chatting, and they clammed up right away.

I did the same, with a little zip-up-my-mouth motion that only had Bastion shaking his head in confusion. I guessed that zippers weren't a thing here yet.

"Check your gear, weapons at the ready," Bastion ordered, again in the same barely audible tone.

Was Ventriloquism a paladin skill?

I checked on Weedbane while Awen loaded up her crossbow, Amaryllis checked the straps on her holstered dagger-wand, and Calamity strung his bow. His weapon was the most well-worn in our bunch, but he looked really comfortable with it. It was a simple wooden recurve bow, with only a few flowers scratched onto the shaft as decoration. He set a quiver up against his hip with a couple of dozen arrows inside, each stuck through a bunched-up piece of cloth to prevent them from rattling around.

"Are you ready?" I asked.

He nodded. "Never hunted pirates before," he said. "A whole new sort of prey."

"Try not to hurt them too much," I said.

He blinked at me, then Amaryllis jumped in to explain. "She has a pacifist streak a flight wide. Even if the people we're fighting are clearly criminals."

"That'll make it a bit more of a challenge." He paused, then grinned. "I like challenges."

We were interrupted by Caprica who spoke up from the middle of the formation. "The *Royal Pride* reports they have been spotted," she said. "Just a few more minutes now and we'll know if our plan will work."

The next few minutes passed like molasses through an hourglass. I fidgeted, then tried to stop because I didn't want to waste any energy before we started.

Suddenly, one of our scouts appeared from behind a rock. I hadn't heard them moving at all, and I had the impression that I only noticed them because they didn't mind being noticed.

He joined the princess and the paladin, speaking to them in low tones. We were just close enough that if I twisted my ears their way I could eavesdrop a pinch.

"Your Highness, sir. I believe the pirates have taken the bait. Three of their ships are scrambling to cast off as we speak."

"Only three?" Caprica asked.

"They might not believe they need more," Bastion said. "Or, perhaps that's as many as they can have ready on short notice."

"Three out of seven isn't ideal," Caprica said. "But I suppose they'd leave some guards behind for their hostages. It's better than having to face off against the entire force, in any case. And it means less resistance for the *Royal Pride*. It might be able to outrun them."

"It also means fewer ships already in the air once our ships arrive," Bastion added.

Caprica nodded, then turned her focus back onto the scout. "Alert us as soon as their ships have taken off. We'll move then, and try to time it so that our attack coincides with the ships being out far enough that we'll have time to secure the tower before they can return."

"Yes, Your Highness," the scout said. He snapped a quick salute, then flew off over the rocks with a buzz that faded almost instantly.

"I guess we'll be heading out soon," I said. My grip on Weedbane tightened.

"Don't be so worried. We're only facing pirates," Amaryllis said.

"I think I'll be worried no matter what," I replied. There was no reason to assume that these pirates weren't going to be tough opponents. And our main priority was still finding and saving the hostages, whose fates were now in our hands.

"Buff time?" Awen asked.

I nodded, happy for the distraction, then I pulled out my tea set. I didn't have anything particularly useful, but I did have one tea that could soothe the nerves, and so I prepared a quick brew of that. It smelled nice, and when it was finally ready, I had a few soldiers looking at us longingly, so of course I shared.

Then, once the third kettle of tea was gone, I stuffed everything away and started giving out hugs liberally. The buff from that was tiny, but it might still help, and sometimes everything counted!

Plus, it was an excuse for more hugs!

Bastion perked up at about the same time as I was done snuggling all of my friends. "We're heading out," he said. "Stay low, move fast. Keep quiet if you can. Once we reach the tower, we'll be dividing into several groups. But before that, we need to secure an entrance. The scouts have determined the tower likely has only two entrances. We're going to use the one at the base of the tower; unfortunately, it's on the other side, so we'll need to circle around. Securing it will severely impact our adversary's ability to maneuver."

Caprica nodded. "Once inside, our primary objective, above all else, is securing the hostages. So clearing the route from the hostages—wherever they may be—to the first floor will be our second priority."

"Our third," Bastion continued right where Caprica had left off, "is crippling the pirates' operation. We don't have the ability to imprison such a large group ourselves. That means that we need to make it difficult for them to operate until a larger force can properly remove them as a threat later."

Caprica grinned. "Take out food supplies if you see them. We'll try to destroy whatever cisterns they have and pierce their fuel supplies as well. A small team will be sent to cripple their remaining ships. Cut important ropes, break flight mechanisms, poke holes in their balloons and ballast tanks."

"Remember, this is off the books," Bastion said. "Officially, we're not here unless this mission is a resounding success. For the moment, you are technically not soldiers of Sylphfree, but mercenaries working at your own discretion. That also means we can't afford to leave anyone behind. These pirates won't play by the same rules as a proper army would."

"Keep yourselves safe," Caprica said. I think she was really enjoying her byplay with Bastion. "Keep your brothers and sisters-in-arms safe as well."

The scout returned, perching next to the outcrop we were using for cover. "Your Highness, the ships are leaving."

I looked past him and saw that he was right: three airships were taking to the sky. Two of them looked like harpy-designed naval ships, and the third and largest was all boxy and square.

"Not all of them are Snowlander ships, then," Awen said. She sounded a smidge disappointed.

"Good," Amaryllis said.

"Let's move out, everyone," Bastion ordered.

We did as he said, filing out from behind the rock and moving at a quick jog toward the tower. The scout took the lead, walking a zigzag route that made it easier to scale the cliffside.

My heart was beating so fast in my chest that I could hardly hear anything else, even with all the ears I had. This was going to be something, and I wasn't sure I was entirely ready for it.

· Chapter Thirty-One ·

Octagon

The tower's base was another octagonal ring, with archways leading up to a crenellated terrace maybe ten meters off the ground that encircled the entire building. That's where the docks started. They were a series of long platforms, connected together and with wooden trusses rising from below to hold them in place.

The plateau the tower was on had to be somewhat artificial, because there was a wide space around the tower that didn't have any large stones on it, and the boulders on the edge were cut into as if someone had just . . . sliced through the stones without any resistance.

"There are the guards," Bastion said.

"Five of them," Caprica said after pulling her head back from around the boulder we had crept up behind.

"Six," Bastion said. "Four by the entrance, two above. There's one in the shadows of those crates. Might not be a guard, but it's another set of eyes."

I looked out myself, grabbing my ears to hold them down so that only the top bit of my head would be poking out.

I spotted three guards near the entrance, with two more up on the top of the base, looking bored behind the crenelations. Finding the sixth took a bit of squinting, but he revealed himself when my eyes caught the motion of him scratching his nose. Just as Bastion said, he was half hidden behind a stack of crates.

They were all human. Or close enough to human that I couldn't tell them apart from one another at this distance. For all I knew, they were catfolk like Calamity and I just couldn't see their ears from way over where I was hidden.

"The scouts might be able to take one or two out before they're noticed, but I wouldn't gamble on any more than that," Bastion said. "I'm open to ideas."

"We need to remove the ships from play as soon as possible," Caprica said. "Whatever we do to reach the tower, we should have a team split off right away to sabotage their remaining ships. We should probably avoid using fire, though. I didn't expect the docks to overhang the forest at all."

In Caprica's defense, the docks were on the other side of the rise as the one we'd climbed on. I guessed that they needed the additional space for some of the larger, missing ships.

"We don't want to destroy the docks themselves, either," Amaryllis added. "We can use them to pick us and the hostages up."

"Good idea," Caprica said. "So, clearing the docks is a priority."

Bastion considered that, then gestured up the length of the tower. "We can't do that if we don't clear all the floors in the tower above the docks, or else someone could toss spells and stones down at us."

"So we're not going to try?" Caprica asked.

"We'll try, but to do something like that, I'd prefer to have four times as many soldiers at my side," he said. "Ideally, we'll fulfill our primary mission objective and extract from there."

"Right, of course," Caprica said with a nod. "So, how do we move from here?"

Bastion's eyes narrowed as he thought, then he nodded. "We have a few decently capable mages, including you, Miss Albatross. If they each pick a target and hit them all at once . . . it'll be noisy, but some noise is better than risking a guard outright sounding the alarm."

"I'm in," Amaryllis said.

"After that, we'll grab those here who can't fly and move up to the balcony above the entrance," Bastion continued.

"I am significantly less in," Amaryllis amended.

"It'll be less guarded than the main entrance. I suspect the hostages will be kept below," Bastion said.

"Because it's easier to bring things down for them than up?" Awen asked.

"Because you can toss things onto their heads for a laugh?" Calamity added.

Bastion shook his head. "Because they have four guards at a door leading to nowhere in particular. It's likely the exit nearest the hostages, the one they would use if they were escaping."

He turned after saying that, and then picked out five sylphs from the soldiers behind us. Two of them were the royal guards attached to Caprica, and the other three seemed kind of random to me. I guess he had a way of knowing who could do what, or he'd just read their profiles or something.

I was having a bit of a hard time remembering all of the soldier's faces, and they mostly just called each other by their rank or by nicknames, which didn't help at all in getting to know them.

The five that Bastion had tapped moved to the front, and then he pulled Amaryllis closer too. After kneeling down, he started to doodle on the ground, and I recognized it as a top-down view of the tower's front. He drew X's where the guards were, then pointed to each soldier in turn to assign them to one of the guards. "We must neutralize them before they can react. Use a spell that flies as fast as possible and is guaranteed to silence them. You'll only have a couple of seconds to line up your shot on my command."

He allowed all of them to peek out for a second to see where their targets were, then all six of them started to prepare their spells.

"This is interesting," Calamity said. "We do something similar when hunting cockatrices." He unshouldered his bow and pulled an arrow out from his hip-sheath.

"What are you doing?" I asked.

"Just in case," he said with a smile.

"Go!" Bastion barked.

Amaryllis was the first to duck out to the side while a soldier followed after her, then the other four jumped up above the stone we were using as cover.

Six spells were cast in the same breath, sending beams of light, flashes of actinic electricity, and a few quick-moving blurs of mana toward the tower.

"No!" one of the soldiers hissed.

"See?" Calamity said. He bolted up the stone, planted his foot against it, and jumped into the air.

My friends and I rose to see what he was doing.

Calamity nocked an arrow, aimed, and fired, all while still in midair and with the kind of grace that made the whole thing look like it was easy for him.

Near the tower, five of the guards were on the ground, some shaking, some bleeding, and one covered in green goop. A sixth was still up, though, and running toward a bell on the far end of the entrance from where he was.

Calamity's arrow thumped into the guard's knee, and he went down with a scream.

"Move!" Bastion said.

We moved.

"Squad B, secure the prisoners, then rendezvous with us above. Squad C, carry the land-bound to the balcony above. Squad A, with me, we're clearing the floor," Bastion barked out commands so quickly that I had a hard time keeping up.

Four sylphs approached all of my friends, wings buzzing like cargo helicopters. "I'm good!" I told the one who moved over to me.

A group rushed ahead, pulling ropes out of their backpacks that they used to tie up the pirates by the front entrance. That had to be Squad B, then.

I ran until I was nearly at the base of the docks, then started pumping stamina into my legs and hopped twice before launching into the air. The momentum was enough to catapult me onto the landing above.

The sylphs landed around me, and then they fanned out into a line, weapons out and eyes peeled for trouble. My nonflying friends were dumped next to me with a bit more speed than grace before Squad C reformed into a line.

"All right, B, once you've secured the last prisoner, you're on sabotage duty," Bastion said. He gestured to the ships still moored in place. "Go make those inoperable, but remember, no fire. Squads A and C, you're with me. We're going to clear this floor, then work our way up. Squad D—that's Broccoli's Bunch—you're working with Princess Caprica and her guards. Clear the bottommost floors."

"Got it!" I said with a salute. I would have preferred Squad B, for Broccoli, but I could live with being Squad D.

We would need to come up with a cool name for our squad. The Destroyers? The Danger . . . somethings? Yeah! And we needed a uniform, or maybe just some pins, and of course we needed a secret handshake.

"Broccoli?" Amaryllis asked.

"Oh, sorry, yes," I said. "We're going down, right?"

"Yeah," Amaryllis said. "I think Caprica's in charge of our little squad?"

The other sylphs were moving out with alacrity, quickly following Bastion's instructions with the kind of almost-mechanical motions I'd come to expect from soldiers who'd trained for the moment a thousand times before.

Caprica nodded. "I suppose I do outrank everyone and I do have more training than most of you." She glanced at her two quiet guardsmen, a pair of sylph men who'd barely spoken a word at all in the last couple of days. "I just wish we were Squad C, for Caprica," she muttered so low that I wouldn't have picked it up without extra ears.

"So, how're we doing this?" Calamity asked. He tugged a fresh arrow out and held it pinched in the same hand as his bow.

"We go in now," Caprica said. "Bastion's squadron will clear this floor, so we'll go down as soon as we can, then we clear every room we come across. Awen, Calamity, can you take the middle? Broccoli, Amaryllis, at the rear, and my guards and I will take the front."

"Got it," I said. I made sure Weedbane was folded up. It wouldn't be handy while deployed inside of a building unless the tower interior was much more spacious than I expected.

We moved into the tower as a group through the large doorway, and I noticed something right away. The doorway was almost exactly as large as the corridor within. It was not spacious at all, with walls that were too close together, though the ceiling was on the taller side. The frequent archways didn't help any, since they squeezed the space in a little and had some space behind them where someone could conceivably stand.

"This place is weird," I said as I glanced over the heads of my friends ahead of me. The corridor was dimly lit by lamps hanging from the wall and burning a bit of oil.

"It's built for war," Caprica said. "Narrow corridors mean that one or two trained soldiers can defend an entire passage on their own. If the pirates had time to prepare, this is going to be challenging."

Fortunately, the corridor ended in a large room, this one with an even taller ceiling. The room was octagonal, with doors into rooms along the edges and eight more corridors leading outside. Right in the center was the entrance to a large spiral staircase with one path leading down to the floor below and another up to the next level. It looked like it rose up through the entirety of the tower, with doors leading off to each floor.

Bastion's squadron was already in the staircase, three sylphs looking up, three looking down, while the rest of the squadron barged into each room one at a time and checked it for pirates.

I saw them dragging one pirate out of what was obviously some sort of restroom. The man was screaming into the rope they'd tied over his mouth and he was walking awkwardly with his pants around his ankles.

I turned away before I saw something I shouldn't. Poor pirate. Being caught on the *toilet* of all places was just embarrassing.

"We'll stop anyone coming from above," Bastion said.

"Thank you," Caprica replied as she passed. "And the exterior?"

"The scouts will report it if anyone approaches," he said. "They'll be acting as runners between the squad leaders."

"Understood. We'll head down, then. Good luck," she said.

"And you, Princess," he said. Bastion gave her a rare smile and a quick salute.

Judging by the flush on Caprica's cheeks, she'd treasure that smile for a while. "All right, let's go!"

· Chapter Thirty-Two ·

Piracy's a Crime and Crime Doesn't Pay

We descended the staircase to the distant sound of fighting echoing down from above us. I imagined that Bastion and the other squads had encountered a few pirates already. We were luckier, at least so far. This part of the spiral staircase seemed free of any sort of guards or curious pirates, and as we reached the ground floor, we found the stairs ending at a final door.

One of Caprica's guards pressed up against the door and closed his eyes. "I hear three on the other side," he said. "More within."

"We'll have to assume they're hostiles," Caprica said. She adjusted her shield and then stretched the shoulder of her sword arm. "We'll try not to kill anyone, but if the choice is between you and them . . . Well, they're pirates."

I nodded reluctantly. I didn't like it, not one bit, but I understood where she was coming from. If I had to choose between my friends and some meanies, the choice wasn't hard to make. Just hard to live with.

"We'll stick together where we can," Caprica said. "Hopefully we'll be able to clear things room-by-room without too much trouble. Everyone ready?"

"Yup," Calamity said.

Awen nodded, and Amaryllis said, "I suppose so."

"I'm ready too," I said as I tightened my grip on Weedbane's staff.

Caprica gestured, and her guard carefully and silently opened the door, then stepped into the room as if he belonged there. We filed in after him.

Three pirates were loitering next to the door, and all three turned around and stared with slack-jawed surprise as we walked in.

"Hey, you're not—" the closest began.

Caprica's guard bashed him in the nose with the pommel of his sword, then swept his legs out from under him. The other guard flew straight toward the farthest of the pirates who was fumbling a knife out of a hip-sheath, which left the middle-most one for Caprica.

The princess grinned and her wings buzzed as she suddenly darted forward and rammed her shield into the pirate's stomach. He folded in half and fell onto his bum.

I looked around. As it turned out, the layout for this floor was similar to the one above. It was a large space with octagonal walls and doors to what I assumed were more corridors radiating outward. The passage leading to the exterior gate was wider than the rest of the doors, but otherwise it seemed as if maybe the entire tower was made of identical floors.

The ground floor had plenty of crates and boxes lying around, as well as cages and some couches. Those couches were occupied.

A dozen pirates were lingering around a big hookah with long tubes and little pipette thingies. They stared for a moment as three of their friends went down, then one of them slurred, "Invaders!"

"Oh good, they're all in one place," Amaryllis said. The air around her crackled.

"Wait," I said before I jumped up and onto one of the crates. The pirates were still a little distance away, so I was safe, probably. "Hello, everyone!" I called. "My name is Captain Broccoli Bunch, and you're all under arrest for piracy and kidnapping and for doing the kinds of stuff that pirates generally do. If you surrender nicely and let us tie you up, I'm sure we can make it so that no one needs to get hurt."

One of the pirates flung something at me, and I flinched aside, almost tripping off the edge of the crate. I needn't have bothered, though: There was a whistle, and an arrow struck the item out of the air. Both projectiles ricocheted off at wild angles—the arrow slammed into a couch, and the nasty, serrated knife smacked into the crate I was standing on.

"Don't seem like they're wanting ta surrender, Captain," Calamity said as he casually nocked another arrow.

"I guess not," I said. That was disappointing, but no one could say that I didn't try.

"There's just a few of 'em!" one of the pirates yelled. "Get 'em!"

I jumped back as the pirates ran across the room, some stopping to pick up clubs or short, curved swords. Most of the pirates, I noticed, were human, but there was a harpy and two sylphs there as well. One of the sylphs buzzed up into the air, then charged right at me, sword-first.

I batted the sword aside, then made myself small so that he flew right through where I had been a moment before, and then spun while returning to my normal height to bonk him across the back with Weedbane's staff.

His violently flapping wings caught on Weedbane and I heard a series of brittle cracks. Howling, he smashed face-first into the stone floor, blood splattering out from a broken nose. I winced, but there wasn't time to check on him, or even apologize.

The fight erupted into chaos. Awen's crossbow thunked and a pirate went down screaming, then Calamity sprinted along the outer edge of the room, followed by a pair of pirates while he fired arrows so fast his hands were a blur. They hit more often than not, too.

Amaryllis cast a big spell, and the corner of the room where the pirates had been relaxing exploded with questing arcs of bright-blue electricity that grounded themselves in the slower pirates.

They shouted and dropped their weapons as they went spasming onto the ground.

Caprica and her guards moved up, cutting off the pirates' charge with a wall of immovable shields and quick, expert takedowns.

Not to be undone, I started flinging cleanballs at the enemy. They wouldn't hurt anyone, but the pirates didn't know that, and they tended to jump out of the way to dodge, which left them prone for the others to take them out.

One of the doors to the side burst open, and I glanced over just in time to see six more pirates run into the room howling with their arms raised.

Awen eeped and spun, firing a bolt that thumped into one of the pirates who was wearing an ill-fitting breastplate. He flopped forward, arms windmilling as he lost his footing and sprawled into his buddies.

"Broccoli, distract them!" Amaryllis called out.

"Got it!" I said before I bounced over to the pirates. I landed on a crate before them, then flicked Weedbane out, the blade snapping in place with a very final, very dangerous sound. Then I pushed some mana into the weapon and it started to glow, with wisps of Cleaning magic flickering off the edges like barely contained fires. "Surrender, please!" I shouted.

The pirates scrambled to a halt, watching me warily.

After a moment of glancing around and finding my companions locked in combat elsewhere, the lead one firmed up and took a step forward. "Surrender? To one cute little bunny?"

I grimaced. "Surrender or . . . or I'll hurt you!"

He shot me a flabbergasted look with his one working eye. "Do I look like I fear pain?" he asked, gesturing with a scarred hand that was missing half its fingers.

I slumped a bit. "Well, no. Not really."

He grinned, and took a step forward—

But not before Amaryllis fired her splashy chain-lightning spell again, catching him full in the chest. Bolts of actinic blue coursed through his skin, leaping backward from his body and tearing into the five pirates behind him.

As they spasmed to the ground, I hopped forward and began whacking heads with the blunt side of Weedbane.

"Nice distraction," Amaryllis heaved out as she shook her arm, sparks jumping off of it.

"Eh?" I pouted. "I didn't even get to the distraction. You interrupted me."

She rolled her eyes, valiantly forcing her lips not to smile as sweat dripped from her feathery hair.

The last pirate went down with an almost comical *bonk* as Caprica smacked him with the middle of her shield. She stepped back, shield up and eyes peeled for trouble, but it looked as though we'd won.

"I . . . expected more," she said.

"More of a challenge, or more pirates?" Calamity asked. He stepped over to a pirate nursing an arrow wound in the meat of his shoulder and yoinked the arrow out. The pirate didn't enjoy that much and cursed Calamity, but the fight had been beaten out of them.

"I think I was expecting more of both," Caprica said.

"These must be the dregs," Amaryllis said. "Barely any armor, no proper weapons."

"I suppose so. Let's check the rooms around here, just in case." Caprica gestured to Calamity. "You and Awen take one of my guards and round these idiots up. Divest them of their weapons and tie them up near the center of the room. We'll decide what to do with them later."

"Did any of them surrender?" I asked. "If they did, we should be nicer to those ones."

"I don't think any of them took that option, Broccoli," Awen said. "Isn't that right, mister?" She poked a groaning pirate with the toe of her boot. "Broccoli tried to be nice and you tried to kill her. That's just bad manners."

I made a mental note not to anger Awen in the future. She seemed a bit vindictive sometimes. "So, we clear out the rooms now?" I asked.

"In case any of them are hiding more pirates, yes," Caprica said.

"And to loot the place," Calamity added.

We all looked at him.

"What? They're pirates. Taking from them isn't theft," he defended himself.

I nodded. That was true. Plus, looting sounded a bit fun when it was morally justifiable!

There were lots of crates in the room. A few were open at the top, revealing packed away furniture, and some had what looked like airship parts. One, fortunately on the opposite end of the room from where all the pirates had been hanging out, had a rack inside of it filled with long metal-tipped bolts that looked like they belonged on a very big crossbow. A lot of neat loot that the pirates had probably gathered up while being all pirate-y.

"Find some rope and get tying," Caprica said while her guards fanned out. "Amaryllis, Broccoli, come and help me, please."

The first room we poked into was more storage, this one filled with bags of grain and a few surprised rats.

The next looked like a barracks, and we caught one pirate snoring in a bunk bed. Amaryllis and I snickered as Caprica's guards poked him awake, then helped him to his feet and tied his hands together behind his back. He was confused the entire time and only really started waking up when we brought him back to where the other pirates were being held.

The next few rooms weren't much to look at. We found some pirate cooks in the kitchen, brandishing knives and looking rather fierce, but I was able to convince them to drop the knives without too much trouble. We sorta outnumbered them at that point.

The last room we barged into had us all pausing.

It was a large space. This area hadn't been subdivided into more rooms like the sleeping area, and it wasn't a big utilitarian space like the kitchen. Instead, the room was split down the middle by a corridor. On either side and at the end were big cages.

Within were some of the hostages.

In each cage was a huddled form of a bedraggled harpy, feathers bent and molting. A single dim light revealed pallid skin clinging tightly to bony joints, barely covered by stained and threadbare clothing.

The smell hit me a moment later, like rot and sewage, and I gagged before pushing some mana into a Cleaning aura around myself.

"It looks like they divided things by gender," Caprica said. She sounded detached, clinical almost. Her face didn't have any expression that I could see, which was wholly different from the little proud smile she'd had a moment before.

"Yeah," I said. I stepped into the room, then squinted around myself. We needed more light, so I started to cast lightballs and pushed them around.

That roused some of the captives. In the light, I could see sores and bruises on some of them. Others had bandages stained red and yellow. One man was missing most of his wing, lying on his back and seemingly unresponsive.

Unconsciously, I almost pulled my lights away so I wouldn't have to see. I didn't, though. I wouldn't give in.

I took a deep breath, then did the first thing I could to help. I smiled as big as I could, even if it was a little brittle, and called out, "Hi, everyone! I'm Broccoli, and I'm here to help." I flared out my Cleaning aura to start making things a little better.

More heads rose, and a few of the captives stood. They could still stand and walk . . . or at least, these ones could. That was good.

How long had they been here?

Suddenly, I felt terribly guilty about every minute we wasted. "Where are the keys?" I asked.

"We should organize things," Caprica said.

"We can do that once they're free," I said, a tiny smidge ruder than I wanted to. "Please, let's just . . . get everyone out." Out, fed, cleaned up a little, and flying back home as soon as we could manage it.

Even if I had to carry them all.

· Chapter Thirty-Three ·

Prisoner Swap

Calamity and one of Caprica's guards were told to keep an eye on the pirates. The pirates weren't fond of that, but those who complained the loudest were also those not nursing split lips, black eyes, or nasty arrow-wounds, so they were usually told to shush up by their friends—only none of the pirates used any language that polite.

It seemed like one of the requirements to be on this particular crew was having a foul mouth.

I was too busy to chastise anyone, though.

Awen ran to the kitchen and rooted around for stuff to feed people with. The easiest solution, as it turned out, was simple bread. The cooks had prepared a batch already, and there were some harder loaves that I imagined came from the day before. Some soup was bubbling away in a big cauldron and it smelled really nice too.

We gathered all of the bread into a few stacks, and Awen started to ladle soup into some bowls as well. Then we brought what we could into the room with the cells.

"Okay," I said as I inspected the room. More of the hostages were standing now. "We're going to get everyone out of here. Please, please be nice to each other. We have enough food for everyone. If you're hurt, go to . . . uh . . ." I turned to the remaining royal guardsman.

"Major Icearm," he said.

"Go to Major Icearm here, and he'll look you over. He knows some healing magic," I said. "I'm going to use some magic on you too, okay? Just to get you all cleaned up. And you can gather in the main room and eat, as I'm sure you're hungry."

Amaryllis and Caprica helped the hostages move out, first only one or two of the braver ones, then a trickle as they saw that we were handing out food and that my Cleaning magic, which I was pushing out at a steady stream that made the air sparkly-clean, wasn't hurting anyone.

I calmed down a bit as my Cleaning magic washed over them and the gunk evaporated from their feathers and clothing. Even those with wounds looked a little better after I had purified their bandages and cleaned out any infections.

But by their sunken eyes and hollow looks, I knew it would take more than a little cleaning and some bread for them to feel any peace.

"Who are you?" one of them asked.

I startled. That was the first word I'd heard out of any of them so far.

He was a younger blue-feathered harpy, maybe Amaryllis's age. He was wearing part of what looked like a uniform of some sort, black pants with a stripe running down the side and a sweat-stained button-up shirt that had probably once been white.

"I'm Captain Broccoli Bunch, and these are my friends," I said. "We're, uh, from the Exploration Guild, but we spend a lot of time trying to make the World a nicer place. And sometimes that means fighting pirates."

"The good captain here employed us to assist," Caprica said. "The sylphs you see are mercenaries, and nothing but mercenaries."

I nodded, because what else was I supposed to do, disagree? We hardly needed to confuse the ex-hostages more. "Let's get you all patched up," I said. We have some airships coming in soon, so we'll be able to evacuate everyone."

"What if they don't arrive?" someone muttered.

"What about the pirates?" asked another.

"How do we know you're telling the truth?"

There was a *snap-pop*, and everyone flinched except for Amaryllis, who had a talon raised. "World-damn it. We're here to rescue you, not play hatchery games. You're all harpies, aren't you? Now act like the proud birds you are and grow a little spine."

"Amaryllis, don't be too mean," I said. "They've been through a lot."

Still, her little admonition worked to settle them down. We hurried to give everyone enough to eat, and a few of the ex-hostages moved over to Major Icearm, who checked them out with a glowing hand that I imagined meant he was using some sort of healing magic.

Healing magic was supposed to be one of the things the sylphs were really good at, and it didn't surprise me that someone in the royal guard knew some. It seemed like a useful skill for a bodyguard to have.

It took a bit of time to get everyone out of the cells. A few needed help to stand, and those were the ones who Major Icearm fussed over the most. He even had to dip into his packs for some medicine and potions for them. Finally, though, we managed to get everyone back out to the main room.

We made sure to keep the pirates-turned-prisoners on one side and the freed harpies on the other. There was a lot of glaring across the invisible line between the two sides.

"Major, how are the delegates?" Caprica asked.

"Many are injured," the guard said. "Some seem to have been wounded back when they were captured—of course, all the pirates did was slap on some bandages and throw them in a cell. About half of the wounds were infected, but the good captain's cleaning helped in that regard." He nodded at me, then turned back to Caprica. "The worst is that one of them's lost his right arm from the bicep down . . . He doesn't seem fully aware, either." He grimaced, then schooled his face back to professionalism. "Others were beaten more recently. They all have signs of mana depletion. Chronic mana depletion, though I imagine it can't have lasted more than a few days at most. Some bedsores and stiff muscles, the usual side effects you'd expect to see in people allowed only limited movements."

"They're all wearing bracelets around their ankles," Amaryllis said.

I blinked, then turned to look at one of the nearest prisoners. Most were barefoot, which wasn't unusual with harpies. Even Amaryllis only wore a sort of wrap around the base of her talons. What *was* unusual was, as she said, that they all had bracelets around their ankles.

"Um, sorry, you, sir, can you come here please?" I asked one of the harpies. It was the same harpy who'd spoken up earlier.

He glanced around, uncertain, but came over all the same. "Can I help?" he asked.

I nodded. "What's that around your ankle?"

"Oh," he said. He raised his leg up, standing on the other with relative ease. "They put these on all of us when we arrived. They weren't gentle about it."

The anklet was made of thick, rusty iron, with a rivet punched through an eyelet holding it locked in place.

Amaryllis came closer and squinted at the device. "It's a magic item. It's casting something."

"It's casting light," he said. "We have a few people who know magic well enough, and they checked them out. It's casting a light spell, but the weave is really poor."

"A poorly cast spell, and I imagine the device is designed to cast upon touching someone," Amaryllis said. "Clever, I suppose."

"So it uses up all of someone's mana?" I asked.

Amaryllis shrugged. "That kind of device can't force your mana out of you. Here, touch it."

I reached down and touched it after the harpy whose leg it was on gave me a nod. The ring instantly started to glow a bit, tiny motes of light flickering off of it. It wasn't even as bright as a candle. I frowned, and with a smidge of concentration was able to stop it from glowing without removing my hand. "Um, this doesn't seem effective."

"Can you hold your mana back while sleeping?" Amaryllis asked me.

I had no idea. "I've never tried casting stuff while I sleep," I said.

"Exactly. I imagine it mostly drains mana while the wearer isn't paying attention, or while they're asleep."

The harpy boy nodded. "That's right. We wake up drained. You can rebuild your stores during the day, but . . . it's hard to focus on retaining your mana when you're hungry, and they only fed us every other day."

"The room with the cells was probably being drained the entire time," Amaryllis said. "The space would be filled with raw mana otherwise."

"You know your magic, ma'am," he said. "I'm Theodore Bluem, I was aboard the *Remiges Crown*. Did you come to find us?"

"We did," Amaryllis said. "I'm Amaryllis Albatross, I was part of a separate delegation to Sylphfree. When yours never arrived, we imagined something terrible happened, so we came to investigate."

"What *did* happen?" I asked.

Theodore glared at nothing in particular. "Betrayal happened. We ended up having to go farther north than intended. It was one of the ships, it kept drifting off course, and it signaled that something was wrong. Nothing big, just a stuck rudder. Combined with that storm and . . . it doesn't matter. The pirates came out of nowhere. To be honest, we could have taken them, except one of our ships turned on us."

"What?" I gasped. That was terrible.

"It makes sense," Amaryllis said as she stroked her chin. "The pirates couldn't have taken on as many ships as they did with the numbers they had, not without someone getting away."

"Wait, what happened to the ship that betrayed the others?" I asked.

Theodore shrugged. "I don't know. But Baron Vonowl came down here to gloat a few times. He's staying somewhere above, I think."

I turned to Amaryllis, and I think she caught my question before I even asked it. "I don't recognize the name. If he's actually a baron, then he's some low-ranked, unimportant one. I think I saw that name on the list, but that's it. Speaking of which . . . are any of the nobles with the captives here?"

Theodore shook his head. "They were taken away early on. We're the hostages that aren't worth much. I . . . don't know what they were planning to do with us."

"We should inform Bastion to keep an eye out," Caprica said. "In the meantime, let's get all of these people upstairs and away from the pirates down here."

"What are we going to do with the pirates?" I asked.

Caprica narrowed her eyes, then sighed. "Legally, we can't do anything. This isn't our land, and while there's some vague justification for coming in and freeing the hostages, we don't have any legal basis for carrying out proper justice."

"So no beheading the lot of them?" Amaryllis asked.

I slapped a hand over my mouth.

"No, nothing of the sort. I say we truss them up and toss them into the cages the captives were in," Caprica said.

I liked that idea a lot more.

We started moving the pirates over in little groups so that we could manage them if they tried anything. They weren't happy about being shoved behind bars, but when the alternative was being separated from their heads . . . they grudgingly listened to what we said.

Once they were all divested of weapons, tied up, and locked away, we got the captives sorted. Several insisted on grabbing some of the pirate's old weapons, and I didn't have the heart to stop them. If it made them feel better, then that was for the best. I could understand wanting to arm up after being in a cage for so long. They also ate through everything in the kitchen, at least what was easy to eat and didn't require any cooking. Major Icearm insisted that they eat slowly and carefully, but a few went ahead and stuffed themselves only to be sick all over again.

I wouldn't say they were in good shape for a fight, but adding them to our numbers was better than nothing. The fact that most of them were experienced airship crewbirds meant that maybe they could help us once the ships arrived.

We climbed back up to the second floor, where one of the squads was waiting for us. Their medic immediately jumped to help the harpies.

"Where's Paladin Bastion?" Caprica asked one of the nearby scouts.

"Above, Your Highness," he said. "Seventh floor."

Good," Caprica said. She turned to the squad leader. "Watch things here. Keep the harpies safe until rescue arrives. We're heading up."

"We're going to go poke at things upstairs?" I asked.

"Ah, isn't that what we always do?" Awen asked.

Calamity grinned next to her. "Man, I joined the right group of misfits, didn't I?"

· Chapter Thirty-Four ·

Employee Retention

We left the captives in the care of the squad who'd returned from handling the airships. I promoted Theodore, the harpy who'd spoken up first, as very-temporary leader of the harpies.

Mostly, the group needed their own spokesperson while we weren't around, and I think the sylph soldiers liked it when things operated with clear and distinct ranks. Promoting one of the ex-hostages wasn't very nice to the hostage in question. It was a lot of work for someone who looked like they needed a break, but Theodore seemed capable, and it would make it easier for everyone involved.

Once that was set up and done, my friends and I started climbing up the tower.

The first half-dozen floors we climbed weren't so bad. Every floor had a pair of sylphs guarding the entrance, and the third floor up from the ground was where Bastion's crew was keeping all the pirates they captured. We'd have to tell him about the cells on the first floor. It would make it easier to keep all the pirates in the same spot.

We eventually found Bastion and a very lightened squad near the twentieth floor. "Princess," he said.

"It's just Caprica, Bastion, you know that," Caprica said. "How are things going up here?"

"Well enough, but the need to garrison men every few levels means I've got fewer and fewer fighters in my assault group. I was right to be worried that we wouldn't have enough troopers to completely occupy this tower."

"We have a number of floors left, don't we?" Caprica asked. "My squad can assist you with those, if you want."

He nodded. "That would be welcome. How did things go on the first floor?"

"Well enough," Caprica repeated Bastion's own words back at him with a cheeky grin. "We freed a number of prisoners and captured a few pirates.

There are cells below, which we stuffed the pirates in. You might consider doing the same with any you've captured up here."

"Good idea. Were you able to confirm the retrieval of every captive?"

Caprica shook her head. "It seems as if the nobles and higher-ranking officers were kept elsewhere."

I bobbed my head in a nod. "We're ready to help find them," I said.

Bastion frowned, then looked up the stairs beyond him. "We can't afford to explore every room and also leave soldiers behind to guard them all as we've been doing. So, a change of tactics is in order."

"What're ya thinking of?" Calamity asked.

"We'll leave a number of troops on this level, creating a bottleneck, then proceed upward at a faster pace. It should be safe to leave some rooms unturned. We haven't encountered too much resistance past the second and third floors. I suspect that the pirates didn't have the numbers to fully utilize a tower of this size."

"Laid out, this tower has more room in it than most villages," Amaryllis said.

"Indeed. A number of the floors we crossed were simply empty. I think the pirates were mostly concentrated on the first half-dozen floors, with a contingent covering the uppermost levels and perhaps using the levels with balconies as watch stations."

"Um," Awen said. Everyone turned her way, and she straightened up at the sudden attention. "Maybe we should call the airships now? Ah, while we still can?"

"That's not a bad idea. We haven't cleared the tower yet, but it will be some time before the airships arrive," Amaryllis said.

Caprica glanced up to Bastion who nodded, then she reached under the neck of her shirt and pulled out a small amulet. "Give me just a moment and I'll send the communications officer there a missive."

While she got to work doing that, I leaned in toward Amaryllis. "Why doesn't everyone have one of those? It's like your bank ring, right?"

"While that would be nice, each device like that requires an enchantment mage who has two or more classes that work in tandem, or several enchanters working very closely together. The materials that go into each ring are precious, and while a bank can afford to rent bank rings, it only does so because no one else can compete to buy the frequency slots that the rings use. Caprica's amulet probably has a limited range, costs ten times as much, and it's likely something only high-ranking officers have access to. It's also a glaring security risk," Amaryllis explained.

"How's that?" I asked.

"It's a magical beacon designed to teleport small items. If it's left unsecured in such a way that anyone can send something along, then you risk having someone send something nefarious your way. Can you imagine a sharpened dagger appearing under Caprica's shirt?"

I nodded along. So, not quite like a cell phone, where the worst that could happen was some spam calls. "Isn't having something like that a risk for the military people too?"

"It is, which means you need added security with every device, and you'll want fewer of them on the market, so that fewer mages can discover how they work and how to tamper with them."

We had to cut that conversation off as Bastion and Caprica started to climb the stairs again, with the remaining sylphs following. We crept up the stairs to the next floor with a lot more caution than we'd shown so far. These floors hadn't been cleared at all, so there was always the possibility that we'd be ambushed, which meant stealth was in order. I wasn't used to it, but I got the general gist. Walk quietly, don't talk too much.

At the next landing, Bastion raised his hand in a fist, then leaned closer to the door. "Three contacts," he whispered. "One left, two right. I don't suspect they know we're coming. We break in on three." He made a few gestures to some of the nearest sylphs, then kicked the door open.

Bastion and the sylphs rushed into the room, and my friends and I came in next. By the time we'd stepped in, three pirates were on the ground, groaning as the sylphs pinned their arms into the smalls of their backs and pressed their faces into the floor.

"Wow," I said. "That was fast." It had only taken a second, and Bastion and the others had taken them all out. He didn't even look like he was winded.

"Fast is good on a battlefield," Bastion said as he scanned the rest of the floor. "You, you, and you. Bring these three down to the second floor. Report to the squad leaders for A and B, tell them that we'll be rotating people out from here on, then send three replacements up. Ah, and report Squad D's findings about the prison cells as well."

In short order, the three pirates were being led out of the room. We poked around to find any more of them, but came up with nothing other than some trash and a nice view out of the tower from one of the balconies. I hung over the edge, staring at the ground way, way below. It was impressive how high up we'd come already, but we were still only a bit past the halfway mark.

So we continued up the stairs. The next two floors were clear, and the one after that had only a single pirate, who seemed so confused by our arrival that he didn't even fuss when a sylph tied his hands together.

We continued on our way up, clearing the floors as we went until, suddenly, Bastion called us to a halt. "Two, coming down," he said.

Everyone tensed. An altercation in the stairwell would be tricky, to put it lightly. There wasn't much room to fight, and the steps made the footing somewhat precarious.

Calamity and Awen raised their weapons to cover the stairs. "I'll take the one on the right," Amaryllis muttered.

Then two harpies came walking down around the bend of the staircase. They froze and stared.

"Greetings," Bastion said. "Please surrend—"

Both of them spun around and started to run.

The one on the right squawked as a bolt and an arrow punched him in the right leg and he went crashing down onto the steps with a pained scream.

"Oh, not *their* right," Calamity muttered when Amaryllis glared at him.

A couple of the soldiers jogged after the downed harpy. Bastion took off after the other, wings buzzing and sword whispering out of its sheath. There was a crash above, a distressed caw, and the sounds of scuffling. I bounced after him. No way was I going to let one of my friends get hurt when I could help.

Turns out, Bastion was doing just fine. He had pinned the harpy to the ground with his elbow on one shoulder, his hand on the other, and his leg in an uncomfortable-looking spot between the harpy's legs. "Please stop squirming," he said. "Captain Bunch, some assistance."

"Oh, yup," I said as I jumped to it. Bastion had lengths of rope in his pack, all just long enough to tie someone's wrists together. I grabbed the harpy's one arm, then brought it to the small of his back while apologizing profusely for any pain I might have been causing. I didn't know that much about harpy anatomy when it came to shoulder mobility, and I didn't want to pull a muscle or something.

"Identify yourself," Bastion demanded.

"I—what?" He sounded dazed.

Bastion's voice sharpened. "What is your name?"

"I just work for the baron!"

"That sounds interesting," I said. "Did he send you down here?"

"Uh . . . yes! I mean, no! No, he didn't!"

"So, you came down here because you just felt like it?" I questioned.

"No! Not that either! I—let me go!"

The harpy struggled, completely failing to dislodge Bastion despite actually being the larger of the two.

Bastion lowered his voice to a tone I hadn't heard before: "Why. Were you. Descending. The. Stairs."

"Um, I'm just checking on the food! He ordered it an hour ago, and it hasn't arrived!" The man nodded to himself. "When he finds out, he won't be happy!"

Bastion raised an eyebrow, and I shrugged.

As our captive was face down on the floor, he saw none of that. I turned my attention back to him.

"Really?" I asked. "What will he be unhappy about? The food being late? The fact that you got captured? The sylph army overrunning the tower?"

The harpy went still. "All of . . . the above?"

"Oh. Well, that's really unfortunate for him. He's going to have a lot to be upset about," I said. "Can you tell us more about him, please?"

"I, uh, don't think that would be good for me."

"In what sense?" I asked.

"I wanna keep my job," he said.

"You . . . do know that the baron will probably be arrested today, right? He can't keep paying you if he's in jail."

The harpy stared blankly at the wall for a moment. "But I have three weeks of backpay."

I patted him on the shoulder. "That's rough. Come on, let's get you on your feet. I bet we can figure out a much nicer job for you. What sort of stuff did you do for the baron?"

"Me? Mostly just carried his complaints around. I can tidy up with the best of them, I do laundry, everything you'd expect a manservant to do."

My new pal told me a few choice things about the baron as I led him down the stairs towards the cells. The baron basically lived on the topmost floor of the tower, with the noble prisoners caged next to his quarters. He had a few guards, mostly harpies, but a couple of humans too, and he made it clear he really didn't like working with the pirates, though he said he had no choice about it.

The baron, from what I was hearing, wasn't the friendliest guy around.

"Thanks for sharing," I said to the harpy as I handed him off to a pair of sylphs. "Now, try to keep a positive attitude, and maybe make some friends while you're in your cell. Being forced to spend time with people is a lot more fun when you turn those people into friends!"

"Wait, what? I'm going to jail? But you said you'd have a job for me!" he asked as the sylphs took him by the arms. It looked like his pal had already been bandaged up and carried off as I walked him down.

I felt a little bad for the guy as he was dragged down the stairs.

"We need to pick up the pace," Caprica said as I returned to the group.

"Why's that?" I asked.

"The *Royal Pride* reported in. They had an altercation over the Trenten Flats with the three pursuing airships, but after our soldiers damaged one ship during a boarding attempt and gave another a bloody nose, the pirates turned tail. One of their ships is limping behind, but the other two were in better shape." Caprica waved a long strip of paper around, likely the one with the missive she'd received. "They'll be back here within the hour."

"And the *Beaver* and the rest of our fleet?"

"On their way," Caprica said. "But it might be half an hour before they show up, and then they'll need time to land and start boarding the rescued hostages."

"Oh . . . I'm starting to see some issues with our timetable here," I said. Hopefully, we'd manage to get everyone aboard safe and sound before the pirate lord returned. Something told me I didn't want to have to fight him.

· Chapter Thirty-Five ·

Upper Management

We rushed up the final few floors, following the directions I'd teased out of our harpy prisoner. Baron Vonowl was in for a rude awakening.

On reaching the floor where the harpy had told us the baron was hidden, Bastion gestured everyone to silence and approached the door to lean up against it. He listened for a bit, then came down the steps to where we all gathered. "Large floor. It sounds like a mostly open space. I can hear maybe a dozen people in there."

"That's a concerning number," Caprica said.

"We can probably take them, especially since we have the element of surprise on our side," Amaryllis said.

"That might still be tricky, though," I said as I glanced back up. The door was the very last one at the very top. I was a little surprised that the tower didn't have roof access. Or maybe it was elsewhere? In any case, that wasn't our problem at the moment.

Bastion shook his head. "We don't have time to worry much about anything. Our timetable is short. I'd much rather we not get caught out by the returning pirates while loading the hostages back onto the ships, so we need to move quickly. I'll take point, Caprica's guards can assist me on the flanks, everyone else comes in after. If you've been holding anything back, now wouldn't be an unreasonable time to use it."

Everyone shuffled in place, readying themselves, then Bastion launched himself up the steps, blowing the door with a boom. Caprica's guards were on his heels and the other soldiers rushed in right after.

I didn't wait long to follow.

The first thing I heard as I stepped in were panicked yells and the sharp ringing of steel on steel. The top floor was more of an open plan than most of the floors below had been. A good quarter of the space was used up by a set of large cages, pressed up against one wall and half-covered by curtains. I could see some prisoners inside. The rest of the space was one large living area.

Harpies and human pirates were rallying against Bastion and the royal guardsylphs, maybe a dozen of them in all. They looked competent at a glance, but entirely unprepared for the sudden fight, and a pair of them were already groaning on the floor.

I tightened my grip on Weedbane and moved to the side, taking my place in the impromptu line that was forming as we stretched out across the room.

The harpy guards and pirates we'd surprised were backing up toward a stairwell off to one side of the room—probably the roof access. Behind them was a harpy in a finely made suit of purple and blue cloth. He was red in the face and was shouting some rather rude things at us while backing up.

That had to be the baron!

My attention was snapped back to my immediate surroundings as I eeped and ducked under a sword swing. One of the guards was right in front of me, an angry scowl in full display as he tried to chop me into little Broccoli Bunch bits.

"Focus, Broccoli," Amaryllis bit off. She reached out with her dagger-wand and filled the room with crackling lightning that speared out toward a trio of guards. One went down convulsing, but the other two raised their hands and the magic splashed off a sort of shimmering shield of mana.

These weren't untrained pirates like the ones downstairs. They were a lot better at their job. But we'd still caught them with their metaphorical pants down. The guy I was fighting had a sword in one hand and a chair in the other, though unfortunately for him, he didn't seem to have the same experience with chair-combat as I did.

I caught the tip of Weedbane's blade between the bars of the chair he was using as a shield, then twisted sideways, ripping it from his grip. I took a step back, then spun Weedbane around and flung the chair right back at the guard, knocking away his sword in the process.

Then I kicked the chair as hard as I could, ramming the legs into his tummy so that he fell back wheezing.

Our foes were going down in quick succession, the surprise and the ferocity of our best fighters no match for them. Which is why I was surprised when the fighting suddenly came to a screeching halt as someone screamed.

"Stop!"

Everyone, minions and soldiers alike, froze up for a few seconds. Then the brigands ran backward to the staircase and pressed themselves up against the wall. The harpy who could only be Baron Vonowl was halfway up the steps, a buckler held with both hands. He was huffing and puffing, and looking like he couldn't decide if he was angry or scared.

"Just who in the World are you?" he shouted.

I glanced around, then met Caprica's eyes. She gave me a sort of *you explain this one* nod.

"Hello!" I said. "My name's Captain Broccoli Bunch, and my friends and I are here to rescue the people you kidnapped."

"What?" he asked.

". . . Uh. Which part did you not understand?" I asked.

"Do you have *any* idea who you're messing with?" the baron asked.

Calamity snorted. "An idiot with delusions of grandeur?"

"I'm pretty sure you're Baron Vonowl?" I asked. "In any case, you're the guy being protected by all of these guards while, uh . . ." I glanced over to the cages, where I could see a dozen or so harpies standing up. They were in better shape than the prisoners down below had been, dressed in finery and very nice outfits, though their clothes had ended up a little tattered from being imprisoned. "While these nice people over here are in cages, which kind of paints you in a bad light."

"A bad light? Do you have any idea what you're doing?" He swept a wing toward the cages. "Those fools who were born into undeserved power wanted to bumble their way into delaying an inevitable war instead of pressing our great nation's advantage!"

I blinked. "Uh. Yeah, no, we already negotiated peace, more or less. I don't think anyone actually wants that war to happen."

The baron seethed. "Then you're as great a fool as any of them! Our savior Rainnewt understood. He acknowledged our inherent value!"

"Okay, I think that's enough," Bastion said, interrupting what sounded like the beginning of a proper villainous monologue. He turned to the guards. "Lay down your arms and surrender, and we will be lenient. There's no need to die for someone like him."

A few of the baron's guards looked to each other, then back at us. At the moment, we were pretty evenly matched in terms of numbers. Then a couple of sylphs rushed into the room from downstairs to join us.

I could almost hear what the guards were thinking. The numbers might be even here and now, but that would change soon.

The first sword clattered to the floor, then another.

The baron screamed, then continued up the stairs. "Cowards!" he shouted.

Calamity's bow twanged, but the baron ducked behind the shield he held and Calamity's arrow thunked into it. Spells started to fly toward him, but his guards who'd decided not to surrender rushed forward, casting magical shields that shimmered and popped as they intercepted the magic that should have hit the baron.

Before any of us could catch up, Vonowl threw open a door at the top of the stairs and disappeared out of sight.

The guards who had decided not to surrender were punished for that choice as Bastion and the others met them with a sudden charge. "Captain, go after the baron," Bastion shouted.

"Got it!" I replied. I crouched for just a moment, then shot up and over the fighting to land on the staircase. I sprinted up the remaining steps, through the door, and onto the roof of the tower, vaguely aware that a few others were running after me.

The tower's roof was a flat space, with crenellations along the edges and a very slight incline that was probably there to make water run to the edge. A strong wind blew across the rooftop, and at a glance, I could see the open expanse of cloudy sky and the great forest that surrounded the tower.

There was also, I noticed immediately, an airship parked on the rooftop.

It was the same class as the *Redemption*, small and light with a soft balloon that was inflating itself even as I watched. The balloon was connected to a set of tanks that looked like they were recent additions to the rooftop.

The baron was onboard already, along with two other harpies who hadn't been below and who were hurriedly preparing the ship for launch.

"Hey! Wait!" I shouted before taking off toward the ship.

"I will do no such thing!" the baron said. "Look, Commander Megumi returns, along with the forces that will crush your pitiful rebellion!"

I paused, shoes scraping on the rooftop as I turned to see that he was right. Off in the near distance were two airships, both unfamiliar and both heading toward us.

In the other direction, over the forest and much, much closer, was the *Beaver Cleaver* and the rest of our little fleet.

The fleet was flying low over the forest, using the mountainous rise around the tower as cover, but that also probably meant that they couldn't see the pirate ships returning to the tower. I had to warn them!

But no, baron first.

I ran across the rooftop, and the baron saw me coming. "Hurry up!" he shouted to his accomplices, then grabbed a knife from within his doublet and slashed at one of the cords that was serving as an anchor. The ship tilted to the side and the other two harpies squawked.

One of them, thinking quickly, pulled on a lever and the other cords snapped off, leaving the ship free. It started to rise, even though its balloon still seemed a little underinflated. Then the engine started up and the tubes filling the bag popped out of their holes.

The entire ship lurched forward, careening over the side of the tower. Somehow, it was still rising despite the very early departure.

I reached the edge of the tower, planted a foot on one of the crenellations, and jumped.

I didn't exactly have a plan, but I figured this was as good a time as any to wing it.

The baron seemed quite proud of himself for his escape—at least until I crashed into the side of his ship. Weedbane, which I was holding in one hand, hooked onto the ship's railing and my feet thumped against the hull, absorbing some of the impact of my hit. I scrambled to find a hold with my other hand.

I glanced down for just a second, then refocused on hanging on. There was a long, long drop below.

Then the baron's face appeared above me. "You are a fool to even try to fight us, Captain. History will remember you only as an inconvenience."

"Uh, aren't you the bad guy?" I asked.

"There is no evil in setting the World aright! If it is necessary to use force to do so, then force must be used!" he declared.

I was about to point out that that sounded pretty textbook evil when the baron placed a taloned foot on my scythe. I scrambled up, grabbing the edge and planting a foot on the ship's hull to try to climb onto the deck.

Vonowl didn't stop his monologue and I was too busy not falling to interrupt him. I had one hand on the side of the ship, and one still clutching Weedbane, which was locked under his foot. "You're about to learn why the harpies are superior, though it won't be a lesson that'll stick for more than a few long seconds, I'm afraid."

I hissed as his talons came racing down for my hand and I let go of the ship, hanging with one hand from Weedbane. I could reposition, but I couldn't regrow fingers. But before I could find another hold, Vonowl flapped his wings and, with a grunt, pushed forward with his foot. My scythe unhooked from the railing.

I had a moment to feel everything in my tummy lurch before the ship started to fall upward and away from me.

I might have screamed a little.

Then someone rammed into me from the side and my vision was filled with black hair and buzzing fairy wings. "You're heavy!" Caprica complained into my ear.

Oh, right, I had friends who could fly.

I took a moment to breathe in and try to stifle my adrenaline, then I shrunk myself to make it easier for Caprica to sylphhandle me back to the top of the tower where I was greeted by Amaryllis, who smacked me upside the head for my recklessness.

I probably deserved that.

· Chapter Thirty-Six ·

The Enemy Always Gets a Vote

Amaryllis looked really cross with me. "Broccoli. Which one of us has wings?"

"Um, you?" I said.

Then she smacked me atop the head with her feathers again. "That's right," she said between smacks. "You could have died! Jumping to your death like that like a headless moron. Stupid bun! Stupid Broccoli!"

"Hey, don't smack the ears, they're sensitive!" I complained.

"I ought to test the sensitivity of your behind with a paddle if it means you won't try something like that again," she said. She sounded really angry. Then I noticed how wet her eyes looked, and I instantly felt terrible.

"I'm sorry," I said. I moved in close and gave her a hug. "I thought . . . well, I didn't."

She huffed. "Yes, not thinking is a habit of yours," she grumbled.

"I probably would have been fine! I could have made myself small, so I'd weigh less and wouldn't smack the ground as hard, and my ears can act as parachutes, and I'm good at jumping!" I babbled, but it didn't seem to be winning over Amaryllis much.

"This is very sweet and ny'all, but can nya two pay a bit more attention to what's goin' on?" Calamity asked.

I glanced up while still clinging to Amaryllis. After all, my heart was still beating fast from the spook of nearly falling and I needed the comfort. Calamity was right, though. The *Beaver Cleaver* and the rest of the fleet was coming around and so were the pirates.

"We don't have much time," Awen said. "We need to tell the fleet what to do before the rest of the pirates get here."

"Either turn around or face the pirates," Caprica said. "I don't imagine we can fight them while loading the hostages. That would be the height of irresponsibility."

"What about the baron?" I asked. I finally pulled out of my hug with Amaryllis and half turned to see where the baron's little ship had gone.

It wasn't too far off yet. I could still hear the rumble of its engines as it puttered along. The harpy crew aboard the ship seemed busy inflating the balloon from the reserves they carried onboard. It looked like they were just barely managing to remain buoyant in the air.

"They're heading west," Awen said. "Toward the Snowlands?"

"Technically we're in the Snowlands already, even if all they do is claim this space without inhabiting it," Caprica said. "But yes, the nearest city to the west of here would be Sissifin. Or maybe the pirates have a second base of operations, or the baron is aiming for somewhere entirely different. I don't think we have time to speculate."

She was right, the pirate crew was coming, and they'd know something was up. We wouldn't be facing pirates caught with their pants down and split apart across a dozen rooms where we could take them out in clumps this time, but a properly prepared group expecting a fight. And I bet that all the best fighters were aboard those ships. You didn't leave your best back at the base when you were going out to pirate something. Or so I assumed.

I looked to my friends. Bastion made it up onto the roof and glanced around, and he was soon followed by Caprica's guards, who ran up to stand near her. My friends were all here and no one was proposing anything.

I think it was mostly because we were all a bit tired. The last few hours had been . . . Well, it was all a lot.

"I have a plan," I said. The idea was still fresh, but it was there. And we needed to do *something*. Speaking up got everyone's attention. "Caprica, call off the fleet's landing, tell them to pull back and wait. If they do need to fight, then it'll be best if they're in the air already. Bastion, we need to move the prisoners up here. Or the floor right below us. We'll evacuate from the rooftop. Prepare some of the sylphs to take over the weapons of the ships below too. If the pirates decide to fly over the tower to attack the fleet, then we'll hit them from below. If they come to land . . . then we let them."

"And if they do land?" Caprica asked.

"Then they'll have to climb all the way up the tower to reach us," I said.

"Through a narrow, easily defendable stairwell," Amaryllis said. "Three or four sylph soldiers working in tandem could hold the stairs for a week."

"They'll be able to free the pirates we imprisoned," Calamity pointed out.

I shrugged. "Doing that will slow them down. We can't exactly move the prisoners with us. Besides, if we leave with all the hostages, especially after we sabotaged their ships, then it's an absolute victory for us, isn't it?"

"I'll send the message right away."

"They'll see the baron's ship flying away," Awen pointed out with a gesture in the baron's direction.

I chewed on my lip, then shrugged. "Okay. It's a loose end, but I never said my plan was perfect."

"It's good enough, I think," Amaryllis said. "Let's start moving people up. The hostages will have had a few minutes to relax and get their legs under them for the climb."

"We shouldn't rush them, they've been in cages for a while," I said. "But, uh, maybe hint that they should put as much effort into moving as they can."

Bastion clapped his hands. "All right, you heard the captain. Clear the roof, we don't need the pirates seeing us up here and figuring things out. Someone free the hostages on the level below us and push the baron's guards in their cages. Captain Broccoli, you're in charge up here for now. Once the ships arrive, start the loading process. Princess, I'm heading back down to direct things from there."

And with that, Bastion jogged to the edge of the roof and took the quick way to the ground floor. I almost gasped before remembering that he could fly.

Swallowing, I ran back inside and into the baron's lavish quarters, my friends bunching up behind me.

Some of the sylphs had already started freeing the noble hostages, and I noticed that they were complaining quite loudly already. That was something I could work with.

"Amaryllis, can you stay up here and help me with the nobles? Awen, Calamity, um, would you mind bringing the other hostages up from the bottom of the tower?" I asked.

Awen nodded, and Calamity gave me a sloppy salute. "Sure thing, Captain," he said before moving off.

I nodded to his back, then turned to the nobles. "Okay, everyone!" I said loud enough that my voice rang out above their grumbles and calmed them down for a moment. "My name's Captain Bunch, and I'm one of those responsible here. I need to talk to you all, so please listen for just a moment."

"A mere captain?" one of the harpies asked.

A snapping spark flickered next to Amaryllis, like a whip-crack, and the nobles flinched.

"Thanks," I muttered, then raised my voice again. "In a moment you're all going to be freed. We have rescue ships coming in to get you out of here, but there are a lot of pirates returning to the tower right now. We're going to evacuate everyone from the roof. So, please stand off to the side over there where you can, uh, relax out of the way. I'm sure the baron had some food up here, and we'll share that between everyone while the other hostages are brought up."

"Other hostages?" a harpy asked.

I nodded. "The crews of your ships, and all the others who the pirates captured. We're not leaving anyone behind, okay?"

The last of the hostages' cages was opened while I finished up my speech, so Amaryllis and I directed the nobles toward the far end of the baron's quarters. Someone had demolished a few walls, leaving only pillars behind, but some walls were left intact. It turned the upper floor into a space with lots of wide open nooks where plush sofas were waiting.

"That's mine!" one noble harpy said before she flounced over to a large seat and flopped down into it.

"Uh, it is?" I asked.

She sniffed, a very Amaryllis-like expression. "That . . . rotten-yolked good-for-nothing Baron Vonowl made a point of parading around all of the necessities we brought with us."

"Mm-hmm!" another agreed. "Did you think he commissioned that fine suit he was wearing himself? Of course not! The fatherless cur was merely lucky that our sizes were close. Though, perhaps they were closer before I went so long without food."

"We'll work on the food thing," I promised. I just wanted to wait for all of the baron's guards to be tossed into cages before we started to snoop around.

Once the nobles were settled out of the way, I left Amaryllis to babysit them while I searched for some food. Unfortunately, I was waylaid in my search by a sylph I recognized as one of the scouts. "Ma'am," he said with a quick salute. "We have issues."

"Issues, plural?" I asked.

He nodded. "We were seen, we suspect."

I gasped. "Oh no. Are the pirates heading toward us?"

He shook his head. "Their ships are moving lower. We suspect they're planning on connecting to the tower midway up, onto some of the middle-floor balconies."

I blinked. "They can do that?" I asked. "Wait, how do we know that's what they're planning?"

"Speculation, based on the height they're flying at, ma'am," the scout said.

It would be a pretty clever maneuver. "Where's Caprica?" I asked.

"The princess is still here," the scout said. He leaned to the side and pointed over to the other end of the room where Caprica was pacing.

"Thanks," I said.

"Any orders, ma'am?" the scout asked before I could go.

I considered what to say. It was weird to have people looking to me for orders. "Prepare for a fight," I said. "This is going to get complicated, I think."

The scout saluted, then darted off without making more than a whisper. I didn't have time to marvel at how cool the sylph scouts were though, not when things were about to get rather hairy in a not-fun sort of way.

"Caprica," I said. "What do we do?"

"First, we don't panic," she said. She was next to a thin slit of a window, the curtain covering it tossed aside so that we could see out. I noticed the *Beaver Cleaver* and one of the sylph frigates flying our way. "We'll have several minutes between the arrival of our fleet and the pirates, even if they're kicking things into high gear."

"Will that be enough time to evacuate everyone?" I asked. None of the hostages below had arrived yet. They weren't in great shape, and there were lots of steps. "Or are we not going to have a choice? We'll have to fight."

Caprica didn't look too pleased with the idea, but she turned to one of her guards anyway. "Find Bastion. Have every archer and range-specialized mage come up here. We'll launch what attacks we can from the rooftop."

"Would that work?" I asked.

"Against an entire airship? It would be a miracle if even one arrow hit someone past the gasbag, but there's a chance, and the pirates won't enjoy having arrows and spells whizzing past their heads," Caprica said. "It's the best we can do from here. Our rescue fleet will have to take care of the rest."

I stepped past her and looked out the window. Two of the pirate ships were relatively close to us now. Both were larger than any of the ships we had in our little fleet, and they were probably better-armed too. We might have had the numbers on our side, but that advantage wasn't great when we needed every ship we had.

I could now see the third pirate ship, lagging way behind, so it wasn't a worry just yet.

I squinted. The two closer ships weren't flying together, I noticed.

In fact, one of them was racing ahead of the other.

Almost as if it was coming straight for us.

Chapter Thirty-Seven

The Great Escape

We all watched as the pirate ship drew closer and closer without ever slowing down. Although the ship behind it still seemed to be heading for the middle of the tower, this one was gaining altitude, and was now higher than the top of the tower. We couldn't see the pirates aboard it, but I imagined a raging, raving group of very angry pirates eager to drop down onto us.

A big part of our plan relied on the pirates slowing down to approach their base at a reasonable speed, but it looked as if the captain of at least one of those ships had no intention of slowing down.

I wanted to stand and watch, but there was so much to do. I found myself making trips to help some of the hostages from the first floor up the stairs. I could carry someone light, and a lot of harpies were lighter than I was, so I bounced up the steps while hugging the weakest of them close.

Every time I reached the top floor, winded and a bit woozy from the climb, I took a minute to see how things were going. After three trips up—each one shorter, since the entire group was slowly making its way up the tower and every time I went down they were a few floors higher—I found Caprica writing furiously on a scrap of paper atop a desk that Baron Vonowl had probably stolen.

"How are things going?" I asked.

"We have a minute before everything starts going in a very complicated direction. There's no hiding the fleet now. I've set the two frigates on an intercept course. The *Lunch Box*, *Featherfall*, and the *Beaver Cleaver* will all wait a moment before approaching the rooftop to evacuate us. We'll be cutting all of this very close, Broccoli."

I patted her on the back. "We'll do our best," I said. That was all we could do. And I didn't want to see Caprica stressed out like this. It wasn't good for her health, and besides, with the growing number of people in the room, her tension might get to the others.

"The *Beaver* is slated to be the last to come and load people on," Caprica said. "That'll put it in a somewhat precarious position. The second pirate ship has slowed down, but I don't know why."

I shrugged. There could be a heap of reasons. Maybe its captain was more cautious, maybe they wanted to save on fuel, maybe they had some sort of clever plan. Worrying about it wouldn't help, not when there was so little we could do.

"It's here!" someone screamed.

I stood up, then ran to one of the windows.

The pirate ship was, in fact, at the tower. Well, above the tower. It was a long, sleek thing. Maybe a Snowlander ship, but if it was, then it was an older model than any I'd seen so far. Still, it was a big, intimidating ship, with a large turreted ballista platform on either side of its hull and thin platting covering the top half of its balloon and its sides. It was, without a doubt, a ship designed for fighting.

It was also dropping out of the sky at a rather disturbing speed.

"What?" I asked no one in particular.

Then the airship fired at the tower. I gasped, but the tower was huge and strong; there was no way a few ballista bolts would really damage it.

The projectiles slammed into the stonework, latching themselves in place like grappling hooks, and now I saw that each bolt had a line leading back to the ship itself. The ship dropped down past my vision, close enough that for a second as it fell I spied men sprinting up and down the deck, belting on swords and shouting orders at one another.

Then the lines went taut and I flinched away from the window as bits of stone broke away.

The ship lurched through the air, swinging violently toward the tower like a ball on a tetherball pole. Men reached out with poles to try to lessen the impact, and screams and curses echoed up as the ship collided with the tower. The balloon wobbled like a waterbed, some of the armor plating coming loose and plummeting to the ground below.

I stared in confusion as the pirates brought their ship under control. Why? Why risk so much by coming in at full steam, even going so far as to damage their own ship to stop in time? Compared to the other pirate ship, which was approaching at a more practical rate, they'd really only managed to save perhaps fifteen minutes with their maneuver.

Now it was a sitting duck for the two sylph frigates rushing over.

So why . . . ?

I put that out of my mind as the first pirate rappelled along the line toward the tower, leaping off toward the balconies below.

"We're being boarded!" I shouted. That got me a few confused looks, so I hastened to explain. "The pirates are landing on one of the balconies below! They'll be running up here soon!"

"I'll contact Bastion, it's time to secure the stairwell," Caprica said.

"I'll go help!" I shouted before rushing to the stairs. A few of the sylph soldiers loitering around formed up behind me.

Fortunately, we'd already brought the weakest of the hostages back up. Those who were still climbing were in better shape, though they would be winded by the climb and still had a few floors to go. I barreled down the stairs, and only stopped when I practically crashed into Awen. "What's going on?" she asked.

"Pirates!" I said.

"Yes, and?" she asked.

I shook my head. We were blocking the way and slowing people down, which was the opposite of what I wanted. "No, the pirates, they hooked onto the tower and are using ropes to land on a balcony. We need to move!"

The hostages and soldiers behind them heard me, and the stairwell filled with murmurs.

"Quick, quick, leave no bird or sylph behind," I said. "I know it's hard and I know you must be tired, but we need to move!"

The hostages picked up the pace, and following behind them were a heap of sylph soldiers who all seemed eager to help. I pushed myself to the side, determined to wait until everyone else had gone past so that I could take up the rear and help any stragglers. That's how I met Bastion, who was near the rear himself.

"Captain Bunch," he said. "I received the princess's message, but I imagine you might know more than I do."

I nodded. "The pirates hit the tower with harpoons. Then they used those to zipline onto one of the balconies. I think they're only a few floors below us."

Bastion glanced back over his shoulder.

"Sir, should we put up some defenses?" one of the soldiers asked.

"No, we need to keep moving. Get Squad B to set up defenses on the penultimate floor. We'll stall the pirates if they reach that far. Captain Bunch, do we still have roof-evac coming?"

I nodded. "I think so, yeah. The frigates are attacking the pirate ship. It was still stuck to the side of the tower when I saw it last."

"An easy target, then. What are they thinking?" he asked. "Unless . . . their priority is less about winning any battles in the air and more about getting revenge on those in the tower. Something's bizarre about this."

"Yeah, but we can figure that out later, I think," I said.

We raced back up the steps, quickly catching up to the hostages, who were really trying their best. Only a handful of them were in passable shape; the rest were still dealing with the aftereffects of mana depletion, malnourishment, beatings, sores, and sundry other injuries. The man who'd lost his wing was stumbling along with the help of the sylph medic.

Still, we were making good speed as we continued to climb. We were almost at the very top when I heard roaring screams echoing up from below.

I looked to Bastion, and he didn't appear pleased. "Go to Caprica, make sure she's on the first ship to go," he said.

"I'll ask, but I don't think she's going to agree to do that," I said.

He smiled. "I know. But I'd be remiss in my duties if I didn't at least try."

He spun around just before the landing onto the top floor and whipped his sword out. A few of the more experienced soldiers fanned out around him, effectively blocking off the entire stairwell.

"Good luck, and . . . I want a good hug later, so don't lose an arm or anything, okay?" I said, then bolted up the last few steps and into a room filled with arguing.

I paused, taking in the scene. A few harpies were talking in almost-shouts at Caprica and Amaryllis, who both looked entirely unamused by the situation.

"What's going on?" I asked.

I don't think anyone heard me over the shouting, so I filled my lungs up as best I could, placed my index and thumb in my mouth, then whistled.

That had everyone shushing up for a moment. "What is happening?" I asked.

"These fools want us to load up their furniture onto the airship before we load up anyone. They're *ordering* the other hostages to do as they say," Caprica said.

I looked at the nobles, then at the hostages around the room. A few of those who'd come from all the way down on the first floor looked cowed. A lot more of them looked like they were ready to toss the nobles out of a window whether they fit through the arrow slit or not.

"That's a great idea," I said. The nobles (though really, it looked like it was just one or two of them who were really making a fuss) straightened up. "Everyone, grab a chair or a table and get it up to the roof! The pirate ship is still below! If we throw things down, we might damage it!"

"Now, wait a moment!" a noble said.

He was drowned out by the scrape of furniture as everyone with any strength left grabbed whatever was closest and surged toward the roof access.

"Nice work," Amaryllis said as she came closer.

"I, ah, don't know if a chair will do too much to an armored airship," Awen said. "Unless it hits the prop, or some of the wing joints, I guess."

"It'll distract the pirates, at least," I said. "Have our ships arrived already?"

"Just one," Amaryllis said. "The *Featherfall* is connected on the side opposite the pirate ship. We don't want to give them an easy line of sight to us."

"And the sylph frigates?" I asked.

"Did a pass already, traded a few bolts with the pirates. They're flying to bleed off speed. I think they intend to park themselves above the hanging ship and fire down at it."

The room cleared of easy-to-grab furniture surprisingly quickly. A few of the rescued harpies worked together to grab end tables and such, while others just grabbed a cushion or two or maybe a tray that had been left behind.

The sylphs didn't grab anything themselves, but I suspect they were very much amused by the hostages' enthusiasm. Or maybe it was the way the nobles spluttered and protested without anyone actually paying them any heed.

"Once everyone's on the roof, we need help loading them onto the *Featherfall*," Caprica said next to the stairs.

"Oh, right, Bastion said that you should go on the first ship."

She just barked a very unprincesslike laugh. "No. Squad C, get on board the ship as well. Guard the harpies."

"That's a lot of people on board one vessel," Amaryllis said.

"We can rebalance things later," Caprica replied.

Everyone filed out of the room and onto the roof, myself included. While the room had felt claustrophobic, the roof felt . . . something else. I didn't know what word to use to describe the strange feeling of there being too many people standing next to an edge with too big of a drop.

The hostages had found a couple of stronger harpies to do the furniture tossing, and they seemed to be enjoying it immensely, though I did wish they'd hurry up.

The *Featherfall* sat heavy next to the lip of the tower, with a long gangplank extended out onto the tower roof itself. I don't think the plank would have passed even the most rudimentary of safety standards, but it worked to get people on board, even if it meant they were crossing in single-file.

Behind the *Featherfall* was the *Lunchbox*, which was working to counter a bit of a crosswind.

Everything was going . . . okay, actually. I tapped my foot with nervous energy. Half the hostages were loaded. The other half were getting there, though they still seemed to be having too much fun throwing down the furniture, and Squad C had simply opted to fly themselves onto the airship to help those who'd already crossed the gangplank.

Yup, things were going well. Now we just needed to wait for all the pirates to hit our defensive line, for the other two pirate ships to descend upon us, and for a few surprises to pop out of nowhere to mess things up for us.

Maybe being a captain was a bit more stressful than I'd expected it to be.

· Chapter Thirty-Eight ·

Pirate Property

The moment the *Featherfall* was at capacity, we drew the gangplank back. The ship's crew, along with Squad C, who were aboard, pulled the ship away from the tower and started to gain altitude.

All of us on the roof had to hunker down a bit as the ship turned and its propeller wash blasted across the rooftop. The captain wasn't playing around, and for good reason. The two pirate ships that had been lagging behind were catching up now, only a kilometer or so away. Technically within the longest range a ballista could realistically be expected to hit a target if given a dozen shots or so.

"The *Featherfall* will be heading back over the forest and around," Caprica shouted over the noise. "We don't know if we're going to have time to load up the *Lunchbox.*"

I winced. We still had about a quarter of the hostages left on the roof, not to mention most of our sylph soldiers.

"Then what do we do?" I asked.

Just then, there was a huge explosion from off to my side. I flinched back, arm rising to protect me from . . . nothing. The explosion had come from below us.

Someone cheered, and I jogged to the edge of the roof and looked down.

The big pirate ship that had been tethered to the tower was going down. Its rearmost section with the engine and all was pouring smoke and flames, and I blinked as I noticed an entire desk wedged halfway into the topmost part of its balloon, through the tin armor plating that covered it.

That wasn't the only hole marking the top, though it looked as if most of the furniture we'd thrown down hadn't done much more than dent the plating. I bet most of it just missed outright.

The two sylph frigates rumbled past the tower, both starting to gain altitude while they swung around toward the incoming ships.

"Okay," Caprica said. "We're bringing in the *Lunchbox* after all." She turned to a nearby sylph, who quickly raised some semaphore flags and started to guide the other cargo ship in.

The *Beaver Cleaver*, meanwhile, was moving up as well, stationing itself between the tower and the incoming pirates.

Things were still going all right. The ships we had were in decent shape all around. The pirate ships weren't. One of them had limped all the way over here, even.

We had the numbers advantage, and for the moment, the pirates would have to fly to us. That was great. What wasn't so great was that the remaining pirate vessels outweighed and outgunned our frigates, even with the damage they had taken. They were coming right at us because they knew they would probably win.

The evacuation needed to pick up the pace so we could disengage and flee.

I ran to help as the *Lunchbox* came close enough to toss out ropes. As a group, we grabbed hold of them and pulled, bringing the ship in close enough that the gangplank could be extended out to the lip of the roof.

"Move!" a soldier shouted to the hostages.

The remaining harpy hostages, who were mostly those in better shape, ran across the gangplank with very little heed to the fall. A line of sorts still formed though, bottlenecking us.

A distant set of thumps sounded out, and I looked over to see two bolts zipping past the pirate ships from our frigates. Two misses, but close ones, and the ships were already reloading.

"Squad B, get aboard!" Princess Caprica shouted.

"Princess—" one of her guards warned.

"I'm not leaving until everyone is safe and secured," Caprica snapped back. "If you have energy to complain, then you have energy to help."

Just then, a pair of sylph soldiers stumbled onto the rooftop from the roof access. They were both sporting fresh wounds. "The pirates are coming up, Your Highness," one of them said. "We need reinforcements down there."

Caprica froze for a moment, then glared around. "Squad A, you're the last out, go down, reinforce Paladin Bastion, but make it a fighting retreat to the roof. No heroics."

A few sylphs ran down the stairs, weapons out as they jumped to obey.

My friends and I glanced at each other, and we moved to the center of the roof, where we'd be right there to meet anyone coming up from below. The next few people who came up were more sylphs. Some bearing injuries, others looking tired and disheveled.

I kept glancing over to the battle in the air nearby. The frigates were trading ranged fire with the pirate ships. The smaller frigates were faster, so they were basically doing huge figure-eights in the air while also coming closer to the tower. That meant that after one ballista fired, they'd turn around sharply and bring the ones on the other side to bear.

Magic sparked and snapped in the air between the ships. Shields of thickened air burst apart, tossing projectiles aside, and walls of pure magic appeared for a split second to absorb tossed spells.

For every ballista bolt fired, there were a dozen spells traded between the ships.

From what I knew of spellcasting, the ballista bolts were probably still more effective. My spells, at least, tended to fall apart a short time after I released them, and they certainly couldn't reach over a hundred meters while remaining entirely cohesive.

I winced as a coordinated set of spells from the lead pirate ship slipped around a magical shield and rammed into the hull of one of the sylph frigates. Red flames detonated along the steel hull plating. Where they passed, the once-pristine surface was left pockmarked and rusty.

Not enough to really hurt the ship, but a spell that strong . . . Well, if it hit the main deck, it could send sailors flying or rip apart the rigging. There were a lot of parts to an airship that the ship couldn't afford to lose.

My attention snapped back to the moment as more soldiers barged onto the roof. This rush was a lot less organized than the previous ones. The soldiers didn't all seem injured, though they were a lot more panicked.

Then Bastion emerged onto the rooftop, looking as calm and fresh as ever, though his sword's length was dripping red. "Form a half circle," he commanded. "We're holding them off here. How long until the ship is loaded?"

I glanced back. The last of the hostages was getting aboard.

"We just need to load the soldiers on and we'll be ready to go," I said.

Bastion looked my way, then nodded. "Good. New plan, everyone on the ship! Get moving!"

"Will there be room for everyone?" Awen asked.

"I don't think that matters right now," Amaryllis said.

Boots clunked across the rooftop and sylphs took to the air, flying aboard the ship even as the last hostage was helped across the gangplank and the wooden board was pulled back. I wasn't worried for myself and my friends; we could ask someone to carry us over in a pinch.

Everyone started across the rooftop, even Bastion, who was walking backward along with a group of sylphs, so we were nearly at the ship when the pirates burst through the doors.

I heard Calamity's arrow whip past my head. The lead pirate attempted to evade it but was a hair too slow; he was struck in the neck and crashed to the floor.

The next one leapt over him but was caught in midair by Amaryllis's thunderbolt. He stumbled upon landing and Awen nailed him with her crossbow.

The third pirate slapped Calamity's next arrow out of the air, took another step, and was almost cut down by a beam of gold mana from a soldier, but the fourth pirate did something to disrupt it.

These weren't the same level of pirate as those we'd captured in the tower. They were pouring onto the roof now, each one bigger, burlier, and healthier than the pirates we'd seen before. I didn't have time to check all their levels, but glancing at a few revealed that they seemed a match for any of our own sylph soldiers.

The pirates spread out, advancing across the rooftop under our barrage of arrows, bolts, and spellfire. Sweat and blood stained their forms, but they advanced relentlessly, shielding and returning fire as they were able.

"Princess, get onto the ship," Bastion said.

"Not until you do," Caprica said.

Bastion half turned and locked eyes with Caprica. "Princess . . . No, Caprica. Allow me to overstep and say that . . . excuse me a moment—"

One of the pirates lunged across the distance between us, momentarily blurring out of my perception. Bastion whirled and slashed out, sending the pirate—with a jagged cut across his leg—sprawling across the tower.

Bastion turned back to Caprica. "As I was saying, I am incredibly impressed by what you've done today." He caught a thrown knife and threw it back. "I will be far less impressed if you die because you were too stubborn to get on that ship. Don't make me throw you on board."

Caprica flushed, and for a moment I thought she might still refuse out of principle. Then I touched her shoulder. "Head on over. We'll be fine," I said. "I can just jump over."

"Right," she said before turning.

Her royal guards let out twin sighs of relief and followed her across the gap to the *Lunchbox*.

Even as my allies retreated to the ship, they kept firing, holding back the pirates as much as possible. My own fireballs didn't do much against foes at their level of ability, but I cast them anyway.

The pirates had forced us up to the edge of the tower now. Only a few soldiers remained who still needed to escape, but we were practically in close combat now and it was looking like we might not be able to disengage.

I was caught off guard when the pressure from the pirates suddenly let up. The pirate mass parted down the middle, making room for a new figure to step up.

Immediately, I knew that this was Commodore Megumi, the Sky Killer, even if they didn't quite match what I imagined.

She was a handsome twentysomething woman, with wind-tousled blonde hair and pale brown eyes. Her long pirate-captain's coat was open at the front, and it seemed as if Commodore Megumi was a bit more comfortable with exposing skin than I was.

"Well, well," she said as she reached up and adjusted her hat. It was an all-right hat. A traditional pirate's hat made of red felt and with a skull and crossbones stitched on one side. She didn't look too strange beyond the pirate costume, but somehow I still felt nervous looking at her. The way Bastion tensed didn't help any. He hadn't seemed worried about all of the other pirates in the same way he was worried about the Commodore. Her eyes roamed over us. "So, you're the little rats who have invaded my home?"

I glanced at my friends, then back. "Um, I guess so. But really, you did kidnap a bunch of people, so it's only fair that we free them."

The commodore grinned, and the pirates around her edged back. "Cute," she said. Her eyes scanned me up and down. "A Cinnamon Bun Bun . . . A young woman with rabbit ears and not a single clue in her skull. You can only be Broccoli Bunch."

"You know me?" I asked. I felt strangely flattered.

"I've heard of you," she said. "You're the one who caused all that trouble for Rainnewt."

"So, you do know Rainnewt," I said.

She grinned. "In passing, yes. If you expect to trick any secrets out of me, I'm afraid I won't make it quite so easy. Rainnewt is the one with the penchant toward monologuing. I'm a little more down-to-earth."

"That's okay," I said. "Different strokes."

Commodore Megumi grinned. "I haven't heard that one in a while," she said.

"Broccoli, what is she saying?" Amaryllis asked.

I didn't dare glance back. "What do you mean?" I asked Amaryllis.

"I mean, what language is that?" she asked.

"Uh, I don't know?" I said. It sounded normal to me. But then, now that I was paying attention . . . had we been talking in English?

"Oh? So, that's one secret out of the bag. Oh well."

"You're a Riftwalker?" I asked.

She shrugged. "As are you. Though it shouldn't be a surprise. In a world such as this one, those of us from elsewhere have the greatest potential to disrupt the existing order. To thrive." She gestured to the pirates around her. "Look at this rabble. They're hardly impressive specimens. It's rare that you'll find anyone worth your time. We, I think, are the exception."

"Is this the part where you ask me to join your side?" I asked. This was feeling like familiar ground again, at least.

She chuckled. "Would you say yes?"

"Yes," I said.

Commodore Megumi stared at me, processed what I'd said, then squinted. "Wait, what?"

· Chapter Thirty-Nine ·

Bite the Gust

Wait, what?" Commodore Megumi asked.

"What what?" I asked right back.

"What are you two talking about?" Amaryllis asked right over my shoulder. "Do keep in mind that we can't understand a word of it."

I smiled back at her. "Well, she asked me if I'd join her side, and I said yes."

"You said *what*?" Amaryllis asked.

"That was her reaction too!"

Amaryllis pinched the bridge of her nose between the tips of her talons. "Broccoli," she muttered. "What do you *mean* you'd join her if she asked?! She's the bad guy."

"I know that," I said.

"I can understand you, you know," Commodore Megumi said.

I smiled over at her. "And that's okay. Anyway, what I mean is that I'd join her if she wanted to become a friend. Of course, friends don't let friends kidnap innocent people and hold them hostage. But . . . well, friends also help friends work through bad habits, like a penchant for piracy, and I'm sure that with some hard work and a few long conversations I'd win her over and she'd become a nice person and then we'd be friends and then we wouldn't have to worry about any of this piracy stuff."

"Why did you just say that? I can literally hear you," Megumi said.

I shrugged. "Why would that matter?"

"Because . . . are you an idiot?" she asked. "Obviously if I know your plan then it won't work."

"But it's a plan based on friendship and trust and niceness, all things that work best when you have open and honest communication," I pointed out. "Besides, I wasn't planning on being subtle about it. I'm never subtle about making friends."

"You don't make sense," Megumi said. She gestured grandly, encompassing the tower and the pirates atop it and the whole world around us. "Look at this World. Endless potential. A whole world that we can grasp and control and do whatever we want in, and you want to do . . . what? Play silly games with your friends and act like a hero?"

"That's . . . yeah, that's exactly what I want to do," I said. "Why wouldn't I? I've met so many nice people, seen incredible places and things, and I think this World is beautiful. Just look at this place! It's a huge tower that can dock airships, built by secretive snow-people and then abandoned for mysterious reasons, and surrounded by a hostile forest filled with colossal trees and giant spiders! There's so much to see and explore! Why would I want to ruin any of this by being mean and hurting people when I could make more friends instead?"

Commodore Megumi seemed stumped for a moment, then she frowned at me. "You sound a lot like Rainnewt," she said.

I blinked. "I what?"

"Hmph, now it's your turn to be confused, isn't it? You do sound like him. He would always go on and on the way you do, sounding so supremely certain of himself. Maybe whatever picks out Riftwalkers has a tendency to pick out people of your sort. But me? I'm not like that. I'm just here for the power, and I've admitted that to myself already."

"I don't think I'm like Rainnewt," I said. "Although, I guess we're both idealists. It's just that our ideals are very different. Are you sure I can't convince you to give up on the bad piracy? You could become an adventurer, or just sail around and have fun, or become the good kind of pirate that fights against corrupt people and stuff."

Megumi grinned. "I'm afraid not. I'm not an idiot, Captain Bunch, and I know how the world works. If you submit to an authority, you'll never have any power beyond what they allow you. You'll never be free. I'll be sticking with Rainnewt, I think. The two of us are equals, and he treats me as such."

I frowned, then raised Weedbane up between us. The blade swung out, then snicked into place. "I don't want to fight," I said.

"That's rich, coming from someone who invaded my base and wrecked half of my ships." She grinned, then raised a hand.

"Broccoli!" Amaryllis shouted.

I was grabbed from behind and flung back while Amaryllis created a staticky-shield between us and Megumi. A hard gust of wind slammed into the magical shield and I saw stray sparks of mana snap one the edges of the half-dome.

The *Lunchbox* creaked behind us as the wind continued to press against its side, and the gangplank scraped across the rooftop until its lip slipped off the edge and the board went tumbling away.

Megumi stood across from us, coat whipping around her as she continued to blow a storm our way.

"We need to move!" Amaryllis shouted.

The sylphs were tossing up shields, but they were barely doing anything against the constant wind. How much mana did Megumi have?

I allowed Amaryllis to drag me away, then I saw Awen being carried over to the *Lunchbox.* The last few sylphs on top of the tower were already heading over.

So I scooped Amaryllis up in a princess carry, let her fire off a spell over my shoulder, then jumped over to the airship to land on its deck with a *thump.*

"Cut us off!" Bastion shouted.

Ropes were snapped and the *Lunchbox* lurched away from the edge of the tower.

A howling downburst fell on us from above.

My legs flew out from under me as the ship jolted from the gale, then I was slapped to the deck as the balloon was blown down on top of me.

It felt like we were falling. I tried to scramble out from under the balloon, but I could hardly tell up from down.

"Engine to full!" a voice shouted, weirdly muffled through the material of the balloon.

The engine bellowed, vibrating the deck beneath me and audible even over the wind. The force pinning me to the deck increased.

Without warning, we seemed to tear free of the blasting wind, and the balloon jerked free from me, rising up above the ship to its proper station.

I pulled myself upright, gasping for air and looking around wildly.

We were much, much lower than before, just about brushing the tops of the trees.

The crew collected themselves, then ran around the deck, resetting sails and checking for damage while our flight steadied itself and we started to regain some altitude. The ship's engine was roaring below deck as it countered whatever that had been.

Had Megumi just shoved us straight down with a blast of wind? That was . . . strong.

And yet, if she'd wanted to kill us, it might have been as easy as just continuing to press us down until we crashed, or pulling us into the side of the tower so that the *Lunchbox* was dashed against the tower.

I smiled. There was some good in her still, which meant there was hope, even if Rainnewt had sunk his claws into her. Maybe we could talk some more? Oh! We could become pen pals! Did pirates get mail?

"Captain?" Caprica called out. The princess was standing on deck, feet spread to keep her balance.

"I'm here," I said as I stumbled to my feet, then I rubbed at my bum. I hoped that wouldn't bruise. "Is everyone okay?"

Caprica looked around the deck. Everyone seemed to be getting up, though a few of them were doing that strange little walk people do when they've just hurt something. "If they're not, then we'll see to it they get treatment," Caprica said. "Everyone will make it. My bigger worry is with the battle that's about to take place."

"Battle?" I asked.

I was under the impression that we'd just finished that.

Then Caprica pointed over my shoulder, and I turned around to see that our two frigates were busy circling around one of the pirate ships, the more damaged of the two. The other was racing ahead to intercept us.

"Oh," I said. "Where are the *Featherfall* and *Beaver Cleaver?*" I asked.

"Above them," Caprica said. "We're trying to gain altitude. Being beneath your opponent in an airship battle is a good way to lose in a hurry."

I nodded. That was . . . good news? Maybe? The *Beaver* was above the incoming pirate ship, so that lent it an advantage, right? I wasn't expecting such a big pit of worry to open up in my tummy, but if I was ever going to be stressed out of my mind, well . . . this is how it would happen.

"We're going to have to help," Caprica said.

"One thing at a time, Princess," Bastion said as he came over. "We just got out of one difficult situation. It wouldn't do to leap into another. Now, I'd usually order a VIP belowdecks, but I know you won't listen, so please just find a place to stand that isn't in the way and don't allow yourself to get shot."

Caprica nodded. "Yes, Bastion," she said.

I pulled her toward the rear where my friends joined me. Calamity was tapping the string of his bow impatiently, and Awen was reloading her crossbow, taking her time to refill the magazine below it with fresh bolts.

"I don't like this waiting," I said as I looked out. The *Lunchbox* was climbing, but it wasn't gaining altitude very quickly. The captain had directed the ship to go around the tower, toward the space where Commodore Megumi's ship had torn free of the tower and crashed to the ground. It looked like a number of pirates were swarming around the ship, putting out fires and picking themselves up. They were very close to the forest, so I hoped for their sake that they hurried up before the spiders came to investigate all the noise.

"Oh no," Awen said.

I spun around and looked up.

The injured pirate ship was close enough now to trade fire with the frigates, and its first target was the *Featherfall.*

The pirate ship was the same one that had limped back to the tower, the same one that the two frigates had taken potshots at. It had to be a tough ship if it was still airborne after so much constant punishment, and now it was firing huge bolts at the *Featherfall,* which it outweighed by a factor of three.

The *Featherfall's* crew, and probably all the soldiers and harpies onboard, brought up a screen of magical defenses. Wind spells, fireballs, magical barriers of different shades and sorts. The bolts crashed into the shields and through the first few barriers before losing enough momentum that they flew under the ship and fell to the ground.

They weren't always going to be so lucky.

The *Featherfall* fired back, but all it had to defend itself with was a rather pitiful set of ballistae. A few mages onboard fired some longer-ranged spells that either missed outright or splashed harmlessly against counter-magic.

Then the *Beaver Cleaver* came rushing in. Or it rushed as much as my strangely designed home could rush. "Someone's on my ballista battery," Awen said.

Caprica turned her way. "You built that thing?"

"Ah, yes?" Awen said.

"You have no idea how wildly illegal it is, do you?" Caprica asked.

"Awa? Really? I just wanted something to fight off pirates with."

"I suppose we'll see how well that works out," Caprica said with a nod.

"I wonder if they loaded on the explosive bolts," Awen wondered aloud.

Caprica whipped her head around. "The *what?*"

Awen didn't have time to answer. Above us, the *Beaver* opened fire. It took some squinting to make out Oda at the gun, with Sally next to her helping to aim. The air filled with a hail of bolts, which went wide, then they walked the bolts down toward the pirate ship.

The pirates, of course, intercepted with spells. I don't think they expected every other bolt to explode with a loud *crack-boom,* though, and for a moment the spells fizzled out and a number of bolts flew right through and slammed into the balloon's side.

A few plates of the pirate vessel's thin armor fell off, revealing the underneath. It looked as though there were multiple, smaller balloons within, or maybe it was just one well-compartmentalized balloon meant to take a bit of a beating.

In any case, it wasn't rated for Awen's special ammo.

As the glass-tipped bolts slammed into the ship and exploded, I could see the faint glimmer of glass shrapnel in the air and fist-sized holes punched through the armor where whatever gas the airship was using to stay afloat was starting to leak.

They, of course, had already started to turn to bring their ballistae around toward the *Beaver*, and the *Beaver* only had the one gun on that side, so it was going to be vulnerable soon.

"Caprica, can we charge that ship?" I asked.

"That sounds reckless," she said. Then she shrugged. "But we've been doing nothing but reckless things all day. I'll give the order. Get ready for some ship-to-ship fighting."

· Chapter Forty ·

If the Enemy Is in Superior Strength, Evade Them

Caprica, my other friends, and I all made haste to the rear of the ship. The *Lunchbox* had a proper wheelhouse, with a roof and windows overlooking the deck and sides of the ship, from which the airship could be directed without having the wind in our faces.

Actually, that was a pretty great idea. I'd have to ask Awen if we could do something like that on the *Beaver*. As it was, the *Beaver*'s wheel was right out in the open, so when it was windy, or when we rose high enough that it got fingertip-freezing cold, whoever was at the wheel just had to deal with it.

Behind the pilot stood the ship's captain in a well-trimmed uniform with his hands folded at the small of his back.

"Captain," Caprica said.

"Princess," the captain replied. "We're coming around now. At our current pace we should be sliding into formation with the *Featherfall* and the, ah, *Beaver* in a few minutes."

"I see," Caprica said. "Captain, do you believe it is possible that we could charge the pirate vessel?"

"Charge it?" he asked. "Your Highness . . . this isn't a warship."

"Exactly, so we can't just sit back and shoot. If we were close, we could start boarding procedures."

"Belay that." Bastion's voice rang through the cabin as he stepped in. "Captain, plot a course southeast, we're leaving the area."

"What?" Caprica asked.

Bastion spared her a glance. "We're not here to win an airship battle, Your Highness. Our objectives are complete. Leaving the area with as many ships intact as possible means that we have achieved our goals."

"But we could strike down that vessel," Caprica said with a gesture to the pirate ship still some ways above and away from us. I looked over to it with some trepidation. The *Beaver Cleaver* was circling around it, trying to keep Awen's repeating ballistae on target, but it was having a hard time.

The pirate ship wasn't exactly as maneuverable as the smaller ships harassing it, but despite being slower it still had more armaments pointing in more directions and was able to return fire toward every ship near it.

It was accumulating damage though. Even as I watched, a bolt from the *Featherfall* snuck past its magical defense screens and stabbed into a nacelle protruding out of the side. The engine burst into flames for a moment before a wash of what I imagined was water magic slammed into it from the deck and the fire was replaced by torrents of smoke.

The ship was studded with eight little nacelles, two of which were already either smoking or missing outright. Losing one more probably wouldn't be enough to stop it.

"What about the others?" I asked.

Bastion turned my way. "The signal was already sent and received. The frigates are moving to disengage, and the *Featherfall* and the *Beaver Cleaver* have both responded in the affirmative already. If the pirates give chase, then we'll turn around and deal with them, but part of combat on any scale is knowing when to cut away and retreat from an unfavorable position. We're in one of those at the moment. Let's not push our luck any more than we have."

Caprica's cheeks puffed, and I was reminded that she was a princess who didn't often get told no in such a stern way. I sighed. "Are you certain that the frigates will be able to escape on their own?" I asked Bastion.

"As certain as I can be," he replied.

"Then let's leave. We've done enough fighting for one day. The former hostages are safe, and the pirates will be left with damaged ships, no hostages, and dozens of injured."

Bastion nodded, then he looked to the ship's captain who nodded back. "Forty degrees to port, we're changing our heading south and east."

"Aye-aye," the pilot said before he turned the ship's wheel around a smidge and the *Lunchbox* started to turn.

I hovered by the windows, looking out at the ships that we were leaving behind . . . for the moment. The *Featherfall* broke off right away. I imagined they'd kicked their engines to the max, because they started to really gain some momentum as they flew past the pirate ship.

The *Beaver* executed a half turn, which meant that it couldn't fire back at the pirates for a moment, but then its big prop spun faster and the *Beaver* took off, gaining altitude even as the pirate ship found itself facing in the wrong direction to chase us.

Further out, the two frigates disengaged and cut over to meet us, leaving a damaged but still airworthy pirate ship behind.

The two remaining pirate ships hovered around. Clearly they hadn't expected the battle to end on such an anticlimactic note.

"I guess it's over," Amaryllis said. She let out a long breath next to me as if she was deflating a little. Awen giggled on my other side. She looked relieved too.

I grabbed my nearest friends, hands wrapping around their waists, and pulled them closer. The nearness made me feel a little better. "It's done, for now," I said.

I think Mister Menu caught on that the action was over, because no sooner had I spoken that than I was caught in a small flood of messages I'd missed out on.

Congratulations! Through repeated actions your Way of the Mystic Bun skill has improved and is now eligible for rank up!

Rank B costs 2 Skill Points!

Congratulations! Through repeated actions your Mad Millinery skill has improved and is now eligible for rank up!

Rank C costs 1 Skill Point!

Congratulations! Through repeated actions your Insight skill has improved and is now eligible for rank up!

Rank B costs 2 General Skill Points!

Congratulations! Through repeated actions your Archeology skill has improved and is now eligible for rank up!

Rank C costs 1 General Skill Point!

Congratulations! Through repeated actions your Hugging Proficiency skill has improved and is now eligible for rank up!

Rank C costs 1 General Skill Point!

I blinked at the wall of notifications. "Whoa," I said.

Calamity chuckled from somewhere nearby. "Got hit with the level-ups, huh?" he asked. "That's normal enough after nya worked so hard and took a few big risks."

"Yeah. I'd kind of forgotten that I would get so many level-ups. Or skill-ups, I guess."

And then Mister Menu flashed another pair of boxes up for me.

Bing Bong! Congratulations, your Cinnamon Bun Bun class has reached level 14!

Health +5

Resilience +5

You have gained one Class Skill Point

Bing Bong! Congratulations, your Wonderlander class has reached level 5!

```
Stamina +10
Magic +10
```

You have gained one Class Skill Point

"Oh, a double level-up!" I cheered. That was going to make a big difference!

Name	Broccoli Bunch
Race	Bun (Riftwalker)
First Class	Cinnamon Bun Bun
First Class Level	14
Second Class	Wonderlander
Second Class Level	5
Age	16
Health	155
Stamina	175
Mana	155
Resilience	70
Flexibility	85
Magic	30
Skills	Rank
Cinnamon Bun Bun Skills	
Cleaning	S - 07%
Way of the Mystic Bun	C - 100%
Gardening	D - 40%
Adorable	D - 100%
Dancing	D - 100%
Wonderlander Skills	
Tea Making	C - 19%
Mad Millinery	D - 100%
Proportion Distortion	C - 24%

General Skills	
Insight	C - 100%
Makeshift Weapon Proficiency	C - 75%
Archeology	D - 100%
Friendmaking	C - 89%
Matchmaking	D - 78%
Hugging Proficiency	D - 100%
Captaining	D - 100%
Cinnamon Bun Bun Skill Points	2
Wonderlander Skill Points	4
General Skill Points	3
First Class Skill Slots	0
Second Class Skill Slots	0
General Skill Slots	3

"Hmm, only one notification here," Amaryllis said. "Thundere's now at fifteen."

"Oh, you're ahead of me with your main class," I said.

"My secondary is still only at three," she protested. "Not too many opportunities to practice it, I'm afraid."

"Awa, I'm at thirteen and four," Awen said. "I think I'm still behind."

"Not by much," I said. "And with all the dings and dents on the *Beaver Cleaver*..."

She giggled. "Ah, yes, I guess having our ship damaged does have that silver lining."

I grinned back. It wasn't often I heard Awen being . . . well, not quite *snarky*, but clever with her words. I leaned my head to the side so that it was resting on her shoulder. "Urgh, now I'm going to have to decide what to upgrade and where to spend all of my points."

"Yes, I'm sure that's a terrible burden," Amaryllis said. "Come on, if you really need the help, we can sit down later and go over everything and pick out what skills would help you the most if improved."

"Thanks!" I said. "I'll make some tea, and we can make a nice evening of it."

"I doubt it would take all evening," Amaryllis said.

Caprica moved closer to us, and her eyebrows knit as she looked over us. "You're quick to dismiss all of the trouble we've just been through."

"Dismiss?" I asked. "We're not dismissing it, we're just focusing on what we can do now." I gestured to the pirate ships and the friendly ships flying away from them. The tower was slowly growing more distant. "That's done, right? We've kind of won."

"There's still lots of work to do. We need to transfer the rescued from ship to ship, as well as redistribute cargo. Then we need to decide where to go, how to communicate what happened, and to whom we should communicate with first."

I paused, then pulled back from my friends. The void seemed to bother Amaryllis and Awen, who looked at where I was, then looked at each other. I could almost *see* gears turning in their heads as they considered whether they should close ranks for hugging purposes or not. But then they were both just a smidge too shy for that.

I still had some work to do there!

"Come," I said to Caprica.

"Are you going to try and hug me again?"

"Do you want a hug?" I asked. "Because I don't mind delivering them."

She shook her head, and I didn't push. There was a time and a place to hug someone when they didn't think they needed one, and I didn't feel like this was the right place for it. "I'm just . . . . I don't know." She raised a hand and I noticed that it was shaking a little bit.

I grabbed her hand and held it between mine, warming her up as best I could. "I think it's all the adrenaline leaving you," I said. "It makes your heart *thump-thump* mad fast, but then when it's all done you get this big crash."

"You seem fine," she said. It was almost an accusation.

I grinned. "I'm not you, and you're not me, Caprica. There's more than one ingredient in a soup."

Caprica stared, confused for a moment before the horrible realization hit. "Broccoli, did you just make a play on words based on your name being a food?"

"Did it distract you?" I asked.

"Amaryllis was right," she said as if coming to a decision. "You're an idiot sometimes."

I giggled, then she joined in a moment later.

"Come on," I said. "Like you said, there's still a lot of work to be done. You need to look princess-y for the soldiers, and we need to figure out where and how to divide the rescued."

"The nobles are going to be trouble," she pointed out.

"Then we figure out which ones are the most trouble and split them from the people that'll encourage their trouble-ness," I said.

She nodded. "That easy, huh?"

"Well, no, but it's a good first step. Besides, I've noticed that keeping noble-sorts distracted tends to work great."

Her eyes narrowed as she looked at me. "Right," she said. "Let's get things in order, then. We need to ensure that each ship has enough medical personnel to watch over everyone. I don't think we have enough berths, but we can set up a simple rotation that'll give everyone a bit of time to rest until the ships arrive in Sylphfree. And I'm going to have to contact the port authorities to prepare to take in a number of refugees."

"Okay, let's get to work!"

· Chapter Forty-One ·

Booked for the Foreseeable Future

The *Featherfall* wasn't equipped to handle all the people we had on board. So we flew for a couple of hours before deciding it was safe enough to start transferring people from one ship to another.

That meant bringing the *Featherfall* and the *Lunchbox* in close to each other, then connecting the two together by means of a long gangplank and a bit of temporary rigging. It was a complex maneuver. The wind could shift at any moment and pull the ships apart or scrape them together, so the pilots had to pay very close attention and the crew on deck needed to be quick to act as well.

Fortunately, everyone was working together smoothly, and the transfer of the rescuees was progressing fairly well.

We had decided to move the least injured onto the *Lunchbox*. It was easier for them to move, and we didn't want to disturb the wounded harpies who were resting in the *Featherfall's* hold.

We also transferred some supplies and a few sylphs from ship to ship. Basically, we were turning the *Featherfall* into a temporary hospital ship, at least until the fleet arrived back in Sylphfree and could reach better accommodations.

"We'll be heading straight for the capital," Caprica said. "The *Royal Pride* should be waiting for us out ahead. It's also been damaged in the skirmish."

"We'll make quite the sight," Calamity said with a grin. "Half a dozen dinged-up ships, flying in tatters."

"But still victorious," Amaryllis pointed out. "We accomplished much with rather little. I think everyone will be able to appreciate that. Saving the hostages alone will earn us all a fair amount of goodwill."

Caprica nodded. "We're going to have to hope that the goodwill is enough to dampen some of the . . . less good will we'll be receiving from others. Some people will absolutely criticize this operation, saying we took enormous risks, acted outside of our prescribed authority, and raised international tensions by deploying the military in a foreign country. I think the fact that we were successful should quell most of the criticism, but we're still going to have a few complaints to deal with." She sighed and ran a hand through her hair. "Which leads to our biggest current issue. The Snowlanders."

"The Snowlanders?" I asked.

The princess grimaced. "Yes. We trespassed onto their land. Now, we had all the excuses in the World to do it, and we left without harming them, but I can imagine them using this as an excuse to stir up trouble."

"Would they do that?" Awen asked.

"Maybe. Maybe not," Caprica said. "The Snowlanders are usually very reserved, especially when it comes to more international affairs. Out of all the major nations on this continent, they are perhaps the most secluded."

"That doesn't mean that they approve of piracy," I said. "I bet all we have to do is tell them about all the mean things the pirates have done and they'll be really annoyed. Do they have a police force of some sort?"

Amaryllis nodded. "They do. The Snowlander army isn't as grand as that of the Harpy Mountains or Sylphfree, but what it lacks in numbers it makes up for in technological edge. Actually, that's how a lot of their things function. They make up for a small population by having an effective one."

"Oh, I can't wait to visit then," I said. It sounded so different from any of the places I'd been to so far. I wanted to visit all the cool places on Dirt, of course!

"That might happen sooner than you'd think," Caprica said. She straightened up a little, and I paid more attention. "Captain Bunch, Lady Albatross, Lady Bristlecone, Mister . . . Danger." She cleared her throat. "I have a mission for you."

"A mission?" I asked.

"Yes. I know this will mean basically no downtime between your preventing a war, today's assault on a pirate base, and now this mission, but I think it's important," she said.

Amaryllis huffed, but it was a huff that was at least a little curious. "Well, what's this mission of yours?"

"I need someone to visit the capital of the Snowlands. Both to deliver some correspondence on my behalf, and to discover how deep Rainnewt's grasp has reached. If he managed to turn one of the most advanced nations on Dirt against the rest of us, then we might very well be faced with an impending catastrophe. We need to know where the Snowlands stand, and if we need to act to stop anything terrible from happening. Also, Baron Vonowl needs to be brought to justice. We don't have the right to arrest him in foreign territory, but I'm certain a case could be made against him with the local authorities. Not only did he support pirates, but he kidnapped nobles from another nation and held them hostage within the Snowlands. That's a political disaster and a half for the Snowlands."

"That's a whole lot of stuff for us to do," I said. "But I wouldn't mind a trip to the Snowlands."

"You'll be compensated, of course," Caprica said. "I have a supply of discretionary funds that I brought along to pay for this expedition. I can give you most of those."

"Wait," Amaryllis interjected. "You want us to depart immediately? Now?"

"If possible, yes," Caprica grimaced. "I would prefer if we had time to plan, but I would like to get you on Vonowl's trail before it goes cold."

"I'm sure it'll be fine!" I grinned. "If my days weren't booked solid, I'd probably explode, like one of those deep-sea fish."

Amaryllis squinted at me. "What?"

"In any case," Caprica valiantly continued, "the money I can give you is a sum I have on hand that was meant to keep six ships afloat and functional for a couple of weeks. Not a vast fortune, but it should be enough gold to help."

"A little gold is nice, but this seems like a terribly dangerous mission," Amaryllis said. "And you're sending a group of explorers on a task better suited to a group of commandos and professional diplomats with the sort of pay that would barely cover the cost of chartering a few transport ships. Is the nation of Sylphfree having funding issues?"

Caprica flushed. "That's just what I can offer in physical gold now. Of course, I can give you a promissory note that would cover the rest. I'm not *cheap.*"

I held back a giggle, but stepped in before Amaryllis could really get going. I loved my best harpy friend, but sometimes she was a little avaricious when she saw the potential to make a heap of gold. "I think we wouldn't mind," I said. "I don't think we had any big business left in Sylphfree, did we?" I had to check in with Awen and Calamity!

"Perfect!" Caprica said. "In that case, we're going to have to arrange for a second air-to-air transfer, this time with the *Beaver Cleaver*. And . . . technically a change of command now that the admiral is leaving."

I laughed at that. In all the excitement, I'd kinda forgotten that Admiral Orange was in charge of this entire operation. I think she'd done a fantastic job of it, all things considered. "Oh! Is she going to get a medal?"

Caprica's nose twitched. "Uh . . . she might, actually. This kind of gung ho, semi-unlawful operation that still succeeds is exactly the kind of thing that elevated our most famous leaders to the status of heroes. It's very much the kind of thing that gets a slap on the wrist and a medal pinned to your chest."

I grinned. I kind of liked the idea of getting a shiny medal or two. I was sure people would take me more seriously if I had a few medals. I could even use them as hair clips!

Once the *Featherfall* had cast off from the *Lunchbox*, we continued to fly on for a little bit. Bastion said that it was wiser to get more distance between us and the place where we'd ended up stopping, in case the pirates were very quick to repair their ships and wanted to ambush us on our return to Sylphfree.

After all, it was pretty obvious which direction we were traveling in, so any pirate that wanted to intercept us would know more or less just to head toward Sylphfree.

Still, we had kind of messed up all of their ships. Two of them were still able to fly, but they were both heavily damaged, so they would probably have difficulty catching up to us. I hoped they wouldn't try anything. Our own fleet wasn't looking too sparkly and new at the moment either.

Eventually, we got the *Lunchbox* and the *Beaver Cleaver* to line up, and then one of the sylphs on board the *Beaver* flew over with a line to connect the two ships.

We brought the two ships closer together, the *Beaver*'s wideness actually coming in handy since we didn't need as long of a gangplank between the two. A few poles tied between the ships prevented them from accidentally ramming together too.

Then it was time to get supplies across.

Since the fleet was heading back home already and was just about a day's flight away, we got to load up the *Beaver* with all sorts of supplies. Food and water, of course, but also some things that Caprica thought might be handy, like extra clothes to keep us warm in the Snowlands, a few well-worn Sylph-free uniforms, and some medical supplies.

"You'll be able to disguise yourselves as merchants at this rate," Caprica said as she watched a crate being carried across. "I hope you won't need that kind of deception, but if it comes to it . . ."

"Yeah, better to have it and not need it, right?" I said as I stood next to the gangplank.

It was, unfortunately, time for goodbyes again. Those were always bittersweet moments. Bastion tore himself away from his endless work and endured a good hug. I knew he wasn't a very hug-y person, but he was a nice enough friend that he allowed me to give him a squeeze anyway.

While I stole Bastion for hugs, the others said their goodbyes to Caprica. I was happy to see that all of my friends were getting along, old and new.

Then I said goodbye to Caprica too, which involved more hugs!

"I'm going to miss this," she admitted, her voice low enough that only I could hear.

"Then I'll give you a few more for the road," I said as I squeezed tighter.

She laughed, and I found myself smiling. There was nothing to make you feel better quite like hugging someone who was laughing. "That reminds me. I'm going to have a package moved onboard the *Beaver*, into my former room. Open it once you're a little ways away, all right?"

"Sure," I said.

The hug ended, and then Caprica engaged with Amaryllis. A clinking pouch changed hands and Amaryllis smugly thanked the princess for her contributions before they paused and stared at each other. Then they hugged, and it was all I could do not to clap and do a little dance.

They were learning!

But, as with all goodbyes, this one came to an end. We crossed the gangplank back onto the *Beaver Cleaver*, with Calamity taking the lead (and showing a cat's disregard for heights as he did) before the rest of us followed.

"Welcome back, Captain," Clive said as he saluted us. The last of the sylphs onboard the *Beaver* were heading off, and a few were still carrying some final crates across.

"Hello, Clive," I said. "I saw that fight earlier, that was exciting!"

"Aye," the old sailor said. "A bit too exciting for my old bones, but the ship held himself together well enough, and we gave those pirates a reason to think twice with Miss Awen's contraption. Oda is quite enamored with the device."

I grinned. "How is he holding up?" I asked with a gesture to the *Beaver*.

"Well enough. A few scratches and maybe a scuff or two, but nothing that a lick of paint won't fix," he said. "He's ready for your orders."

"Great!" I said. "We're heading westward, away from the rest of the fleet. I think we'll have to fly fast at first, but once we're a ways away we can slow down and let the wind carry us on. How's our fuel situation?"

"Bunkers are three-quarters full," he said. "Enough to get us from one end of the Harpy Mountains to another, I'd judge."

"Brilliant! Let's wait until the last of the cargo is on, and then we'll take off. Awen, can you check to see if your turret's in tip-top shape? Amaryllis, check the charts please, we need to know where we're going. Uh . . . Calamity, maybe join up with the Scallywags, I'm sure they can show you a trick or two for sailing!"

The deck filled with the busy clonking of books moving about. I watched the last of the cargo get loaded on—including one large crate that went down to the room Caprica had used—and then I climbed up behind the wheel and helped Clive disengage us from the *Lunchbox*.

It was time to head off on another jaunt!

· Chapter Forty-Two ·

From Sylphfree with Love

After waving goodbye to the fleet and heading due west for a while, I finally let go of the *Beaver*'s wheel and let Calamity and Clive take over. Calamity was eager to learn how to pilot the ship, and Clive was a nice enough sort that he didn't mind teaching others his trade. In fact, I think he liked giving lessons about piloting airships.

As I left the poop deck, I ran into Awen, who smiled and gave me a little wave. "Hey, Broc," she said. "Do you mind helping me a little?"

"Of course not," I said. "With what?"

Her smile turned a little rueful and she gestured down at herself. She'd shucked off her coat at some point, leaving her in a blouse and sturdy trousers, both of which were now splattered with grease and oil.

"Oh," I said, giggling. "Sure, give me a second." A liberal application of Cleaning magic later, and Awen was as fresh as new.

"Thanks," she said. "I was just checking up on the engine. One of the pirate's bolts actually lodged itself into the engine compartment. It broke right through the wall and jammed itself into the housing of an air intake."

"Oh no!" I gasped.

"It's nothing too bad. I pulled it out and patched the hole. There was a weird whistle as soon as I opened the door into the engine compartment, so I knew something was up. Anyway, we'll have to get a new housing, but it's just a bit of tin, nothing too complicated, and it should work just as well now as it did before. It's not going to be an expensive fix. The hole in the hull is more annoying, because we just had it painted."

"I know," I commiserated. It really was annoying to have already collected a few scratches and scuffs right after the *Beaver* had been refitted, but there wasn't much we could do about it. At least the ship seemed to be in nearly perfect condition otherwise. Or . . . I hoped it was. "Is there anything else that's broken?"

"No. I think the engine was pushed a little harder than usual, but it's running fine. I oiled everything that moves and made sure that anything that wasn't supposed to be moving wasn't."

I laughed again. "You make mechanics sound easy when you put it that way."

"I don't find it all that hard," Awen said. "It's a little tricky, but it's just like a puzzle. The bigger and more complicated the machine, the more parts there are to the puzzle. Only they're all interconnected, moving parts that are very loud sometimes." She smiled. "That makes it more fun."

Awen loved her work, and it was just plain nice to see her enjoying what she did. I stretched until my lower back popped, then let out a big long sigh. "Ah, I think I need a nap," I said.

She nodded. "Today was tiring, wasn't it?"

I nodded at that. A glance at the sky suggested that it was still just the early afternoon, way too early for bed, but maybe not too early for a nap . . . Although I supposed that I should have been preparing supper for everyone. "Want to help me in the kitchen? More hands will make it lighter work."

"Sure," Awen said. "You'd think cooking would be like mechanics, but it's so much harder somehow."

"Well, cooking's like an art," I said. "You just need to know what does what and go with what you think feels right. At least, that's always worked out for me."

"I'm not good at art," Awen said.

I glanced at her, curious. "You're not?"

She shook her head. "No, I'm really not. My mother tried to get me to learn all sorts of art things, but I was never able to get the hang of any. Except music. But I can't make my own music, I'm just okay at playing the instruments and following along to what's written in front of me. I've tried to compose a little, but I don't know, it doesn't work."

I tapped my chin, then shrugged. "That's okay. Maybe try baking, then? That's less of an art and more of a science."

"That sounds fun. We could make cakes and things like that. Um, provided we install an oven on the *Beaver*, which sounds a little heavy."

"Right," I said. That would be tricky.

"Or I could bake in the engine room. Some parts get hot enough. All you'd need is to box them in, I think," Awen said.

"I don't know if that's a great idea. You'll end up with engine gunk in some bread, and I don't think that'd be healthy," I said.

Awen laughed. "Yeah, fair enough. Maybe a heat exchanger? But that would also be pretty heavy."

We discussed the possibilities of an airborne bakery as we made our way to the *Beaver's* lower deck and to the corridor lined by our separate bedrooms. I paused near the end. The door to the room we'd let Caprica take for herself was open a crack, which wasn't ideal. The ship rocked and turned sometimes, so having loose things meant that they'd roll around and bump into stuff. And if the door was open, anything could fly out.

"One sec," I told Awen as I pushed the door open. It felt a little rude to enter what I'd started to think of as Caprica's room, but in reality she hadn't left anything behind. There were some blankets on the cot and it was possible that she'd left some things in the few drawers tucked in the corner of the room, but otherwise the space was still empty, same as Bastion's room.

Except, of course, for the rather large crate left in the middle of the floor.

"Huh," I said as I stared at it. She'd mentioned sending this over, but I couldn't recall any details about *what* it was. It was just a box, about as wide as my shoulders and tall as my hips.

"Are those air holes?" Awen asked, leaning around me to see into the room.

There were, in fact, little holes drilled just under the hemp handles on either side of the crate. "That's a little weird," I said as I moved closer. I expected to find a note or something, but there was nothing, just a big old box.

Then the box shuddered and I jumped so high I smushed my ears against the ceiling.

"It's alive!" I squeaked.

Awen frowned and walked right up to the box, then placed a hand atop it to stop its wobbling. "What's in here?" she asked.

"It's me," the box said.

I blinked. The box was speaking in *Caprica's* voice. "Caprica?" I asked. "Are you in the box?"

"Yes?" the box said.

I looked to Awen who shrugged. "It's nailed shut," she said.

"Maybe it's a mimic," I suggested. "Caprica, can you prove that it's you? What's your sister's name?"

"Gabrielle or Sylvia? You haven't met my other sisters yet, as far as I know," Caprica said.

"Should we, ah, open the box?" Awen asked.

"I guess so," I said. This was a little strange. "You might want to go get Amaryllis and tell her that we have a stowaway onboard."

"I'm not a stowaway," Caprica said from within the box she'd used to sneak aboard our ship, kind of like how a stowaway would.

"If you say so," I said.

Awen looked at the box, then back up to me. "Right, I'm going to go fetch a crowbar," she said before leaving.

I sat on the edge of the bed and looked at the crate. I could just make out Caprica's eye through one of the air holes. "So, want to tell me why you're, uh, nailed into a box and onboard the *Beaver* without permission?" I asked. "Because you could have just asked us. You already have a room and everything."

"It's not your permission that's complicated," she said. From her tone, I could imagine her very unprincesslike pout. "It's my guards. It was complicated enough just getting on board in this box, you know, without a trail of guards and servants and all the usual train of sylphs that follow a princess around noticing."

"You wanted to sneak away?" I asked.

"Well . . . not just that," she admitted.

I frowned and thought about it for a bit. Caprica didn't seem to dislike her role as princess. She was a rather active one, and she sometimes pushed the boundaries, I imagined, but for the most part I think she enjoyed her life. Of course, there was . . . ah.

"Caprica," I asked.

"Yes, Broccoli?" she replied, voice a little muffled by the box.

"Did you do this so that Bastion would follow you and come to your rescue?" I asked.

The box was very, very silent. I could almost imagine it was a normal, stowaway-less crate. Finally, after a long wait, I heard a faint and very unconvincing "No."

"Uh-huh," I said.

Awen returned with a crowbar and an Amaryllis.

"What's all this about a stowaway?" Amaryllis asked. I pointed to the box and she stared at it for a moment. "Toss it overboard," she said. She sounded serious, but there was a hint of a smile in the corner of her mouth that suggested otherwise.

Caprica thumped the inside of her box. "Let me out," she said.

"Broccoli once used this phrase on me . . . I found it quite insulting at the time. Now, what was it? . . . Oh, yes." Amaryllis grinned. "What's the magic word?"

"Is it 'now'?" Caprica asked.

"No, it's 'please.' You should try it sometime, Miss Stowaway Princess."

"Please let me out?" Caprica asked churlishly.

Awen was holding back giggles as she moved around the box, jamming the end of her crowbar into the wood and forcing it up bit by bit. Whoever Caprica had convinced to help her into the box had really done a nice job nailing it shut.

"Ah, thank you!" Caprica said as she finally stood. The space in there wasn't all that much bigger than she was, so I imagined it wasn't a comfortable fit. Though it looked like she had a thin blanket squeezed into the bottom for padding.

"Care to explain?" Amaryllis asked.

"I thought you could use the help," Caprica said.

Amaryllis snorted. "Yeah, sure."

"She did it for love," I said. "It's kind of sweet . . . even if I'm pretty sure her plan won't work."

Caprica shot me a dirty look, but it faded soon enough.

"Anyway," I said. "Want to help us make supper?" I asked.

"Just like that?" she replied.

I stood up and got off her bed. "Well, yeah, what did you expect us to do? You obviously want to come with us, and I don't think any of us mind."

"I mind the heat this will bring," Amaryllis said. "The sylphs might decide that we've kidnapped one of their precious princesses."

I shrugged. "We'll deal with that when the time comes, right? Besides, maybe Caprica can write a nice letter home." I patted Caprica on the back. "Now, did you pack a change of clothes? Some gear? Did you bring more than just one blanket? You know, you should always bring a towel with you when stowing away, it's only polite."

Caprica seemed a little overwhelmed for a moment, and I almost hugged her on reflex, but she shored up her resolve and stood taller. "I'm all right. I didn't bring any clothes, but I'm certain I can endure these for a day or two. And I stashed a spare shield and sword under the bed, just in case."

"Cool!" I said. "Anyways, did you want to help Awen and I in the kitchen? We don't know what we're making yet, but I bet it'll be really tasty!"

· Chapter Forty-Three ·

Cultural Considerations

And here we go!" I said as I placed down what Awen and I had cooked.
It wasn't anything too complicated, just a big stew with whatever spices smelled nice, plus chopped-up carrots, parsnips, turnips, radishes, and beets. All root vegetables that apparently grew aplenty in the Sylphfree mountains, judging by the stores we had of those. We also added some lentils to add some thickness to the stew and tossed in some mushrooms as well to make it taste a little meatier.

I wasn't sure of the taste yet, but my tummy was very insistent that I have a bowlful. Every sniff made it growl and grumble.

We pulled out a few extra chairs from the bedrooms so that there would be room for everyone at the dining room table.

The *Beaver Cleaver* was flying on a slow, meandering path westward, the wheel and sails locked and the engine shut down for the moment while the wind gently pushed us along. We couldn't leave the wheel unattended forever, but for one meal? We could manage that.

"That smells fantastic," Calamity said as he spun his chair around and sat on it backward. Next to him, the Scallywags, Joe, Sally, and Oda, pulled up their own seats. It was nice to see them getting along.

Steve, Gordon, and Clive found seats mixed in with the rest of us, and soon enough I was taking people's bowls and ladling in a healthy portion for everyone. Airshipping was busy, hard work, so the crew needed their bellies full.

Empty tummies lead to empty minds, I always found.

I served myself last, checked the cauldron (which was down to half, so not everyone would get thirds, which was a shame), then passed around some still-fresh bread before I sat down. "Eat up!" I called—though some of the crew were already digging in.

What followed was a couple of minutes where the only sounds were happy noises and the *clink-clink* of spoons scraping against bowls. Eventually though, the initial hunger passed and Calamity, who was the first to empty his bowl, pointed across the table with his spoon. "So, is the princess supposed to be here?" he asked.

"Nope," I said. "She snuck on board."

"That's a gross oversimplification," Caprica said.

"But it's right?" I asked, a little confused. I paused to grab another spoonful of carrot.

"You know, back in my day we used to just toss stowaways overboard," Clive said. I looked at him, horrified, and he went on to clarify. "They were harpies, they could glide down safely enough."

That still seemed a bit extreme, and not terribly nice, even if the stowaway wasn't supposed to be there. "Well, let's not throw Caprica overboard," I said.

"Yes, she might be somewhat useful," Amaryllis said.

"Somewhat?" Caprica grumbled. "I'll have you know that I'm more than just *somewhat* useful, thank you very much."

"Girls, don't fight," I admonished. "Not at the dinner table, please. Or anywhere else."

"It wasn't a fight, Broccoli. Or even an argument. Just stating simple, verifiable facts," Amaryllis said. She smiled slyly as she took a sip of water.

Caprica glared across at her, then seemingly decided to be the bigger person and also to let everyone know that she was being the bigger person by sniffing haughtily and looking away.

"So, is this normal?" Calamity asked.

"Kidnapping noblewomen?" I asked. "I don't think it's normal, but it is strange that it's happened twice."

"Wait, was Amaryllis the first time?" he asked.

"Oh, awa, that was me," Awen said. "And it wasn't so much kidnapping as, um, Broccoli helping me to run away from home."

"Huh, all right," Calamity said. "Ny'all are a weird bunch, you know that?"

I laughed, and the mood at the table lightened up a bit, not that it was ever dark to begin with. Though it *was* getting darker outside. The *Beaver's* dining room had a floor-to-ceiling window to one side that gave us a stunning view of the expanse of sky and land below, all of which was turning the burnt orange of near-night.

Soon enough it was time for dessert, which wasn't anything too fancy. Sylph chocolate bars, which were more like chocolate bricks that we had to scrape with a knife and that I imagined would break the teeth of anyone who tried to bite it.

Caprica showed us a neat trick with some fire magic that warmed the interior of the bar up and turned it soft enough to be sliced apart with a butter knife.

Once dessert was had, everyone sat back and enjoyed a mugful of warm tea. We discussed night rotations (I volunteered to take the first half of the night's watch, since I was wide awake from all the chocolate) and generally planned our flight to the Snowlands.

We were currently so far north that to get to the capital, Stormtower, we would actually need to head south around the Deepcloud Mountains, then straight west for a long ways. It was going to take two days, at least, and that was if the wind was with us.

No one here had flown across this part of the World before, but Clive warned that the winds around any mountains could be tricky, so we'd have to watch our heading and maybe fight the wind for a little while.

On the more positive side of things, we had bunkers full of fuel, and more fuel aboard the *Redemption* if we needed it. Our pantry was full of yummy stuff to eat, and the company was fun to be around.

With food taken care of, I said I'd do the washing up (which was basically just magic practice), and then the crew dispersed. Those on break lingered and those who had to take care of things went off to see to them.

That meant that in the end, I was left mostly alone with Amaryllis and Caprica in the little kitchen space we had. I cleaned our plates off and secured them in our rattle-resistant plate racks.

"What do you know about the Snowlands?" Caprica asked.

"Why? Do you intend to lecture us?" Amaryllis asked right back.

"Girls," I warned.

"Sorry," Amaryllis said after a moment. "Do go on."

Caprica nodded. "What I meant to ask was . . . Well, I know a little about them, but not too much. I've met a few Snowlanders, but only rarely, and their nation is far enough away from Sylphfree that we don't have much business with them. I imagine you might have seen them more often, Amaryllis, seeing as how you're basically neighbors."

"There's a strip of land between the Harpy Mountains and the Snowlands. It ostensibly belongs to the Trenten Flats, even if their claim on the region is . . . tenuous at best," Amaryllis said. "In any case, no, I really don't know much about them. Most of their technology is ahead of ours, and they're not keen on sharing, but otherwise . . ." She trailed off. "You could ask Awen about their machinery. She'd know more than I do."

Awen was off checking on the engine at the moment, so that discussion would have to wait.

"I don't think a people's technology is everything there is to know about them," I said. "What's their culture like? Are they friendly? Shy? Reclusive? I haven't met anyone from there, so I wouldn't know where to start. What do Snowlanders even look like?"

"Oh," Caprica said. "Well, I can share a little about their culture, but I think you're operating under a misunderstanding."

"Huh?" I asked.

"It's a fair one to make. Most nations have formed around a dominant core of a certain species, with representatives outside of that species being rare, although hardly unheard of. In Sylphfree we have the mole folk, who make up a sizable percentage of the total population, even though they are quite different culturally. I think the Trenten Flats are a little more diverse when it comes to its population. The leadership and majority are both held by cervids, but a number of enclaves and cities exist with other peoples. Calamity's kin being one large group."

"Oh," I said. "Are the Snowlands like that as well?"

She nodded. "The nation is split nearly evenly between two groups who have coexisted for a very long time."

"That's cool!" I said.

"Cool?" Caprica asked.

"It's a Broccoli-ism," Amaryllis explained. "It means both interesting, neat, and cold at the same time. I suspect it's because she comes from a place that's very cold."

I blinked. How had my translation magic stuff translated "cool" just then? "Yeah, anyway, tell me more about the Snowlanders. Are the two species similar, or are they super different?"

"It's less a scenario like the Harpy Mountains with its dozens of clans and old families," Amaryllis said. "And more something akin to . . . Well, actually I think it's rather unique. The larger of the two groups—thought not by very much—are called the Cold Mountain Dwarves, and the smaller group are the Snow Forest Elves."

I dropped a bowl.

Fortunately, it was a tin bowl (because anything easy to break would be silly on an airship) and all it did was clang onto the floor, then do a warble-wobble until it settled. "Dwarves? Elves?!" I asked.

"Yes?" Caprica said. She was leaning way back, and I realized that maybe I hadn't been using my indoor voice there.

"Sorry, but . . . yeah, I wasn't expecting that."

"Why are you surprised?" Amaryllis asked.

"I just am," I said. "Are they Tolkien elves?"

"What?" they both asked at the same time.

I shook my head. "Sorry, I mean, tall, pretty, very long-lived? Lithe?"

Amaryllis nodded. "That seems to describe them. Though I don't know about their lifespans."

"They're quite long-lived," Caprica said. "But there are relatively few of them, overall."

"Awesome! And are the dwarves small stocky fellows with big beards?"

"So you have heard of them," Caprica said. "Are there any in your homeland?"

"No, but I wish there were! Oh, now I can't wait to arrive. Are the elves snooty? Do the dwarves care a bunch about their beards?" I asked. These were, of course, very important questions. When I set out to play fantasy tourist I didn't expect to actually meet elves and dwarves.

"I . . . don't know about snooty. They're certainly a proud and noble race," Caprica said. "As for the dwarves, yes, they do tend to have beards."

"This is *amazing*. I am so excited." I could barely contain myself.

"We can see that," Amaryllis replied. I think she was a little teensy bit weirded out, but she didn't understand, so it wasn't her fault. "In any case, the Snowlanders are big on respect and decorum. Moreso even than Sylphfree."

"And at the same time, they're also exceptionally laid back," Caprica said."

"I think I can manage that," I said. "How do you think they'll react to our mission? Is it even a mission?"

"Chasing down Vonowl?" Amaryllis said. She avoided calling him a baron, I noticed. "If they know what's good for them, they'll surrender him to the Harpy Mountains for justice without too much of a fuss."

"Or they might not. It's hard to tell. We might have more luck dealing with an intermediary. There are a number of humans in the Snowlands, especially in their port cities where Endless Swell ships can come in to dock. They might be able to simplify our quest for us."

"I'm sure things will work out," I said. "In the meantime, we're still a couple of days out, aren't we?"

· Chapter Forty-Four ·

The Storm Tower

The first sight of Stormtower wasn't the tower itself. That was because Stormtower and the Storm Tower were two different things, confusingly named the same thing. Stormtower—one word—was the capital city of the Snowlands. The Storm Tower was the big tower in the city's center.

As our second night away from the fleet progressed, I could slowly begin to make out a spot of red and orange in the distance, an oasis of light in the darkness of night.

My watch ended, I took a long nap, and when I woke up and returned to the deck, the sun had risen. That distant spot had grown much larger, but still, that wasn't the Storm Tower, and it wasn't even Stormtower. Instead, it was a small city, maybe half the size of Goldenalden, with a sprawl of small homes with big gardens around them and big, wide roads crisscrossing each other.

The city was without walls, though there were small towers all around it, each one thin and narrow and quite tall, with a capped roof of green copper over a lookout post.

What was most interesting of all though, at least to me, was the road leading away from the city and toward the actual Storm Tower.

It was a wide road that wove between large hills, broad enough that it could have been a six-lane highway back on Earth. On either side of it was a thin strip of homes and businesses and all sorts of buildings.

It was like a long, extended city reaching out and away from the first larger city and all the way over the hills and to the coast.

That's where the city of Stormtower was, right on the edge of a bay that I couldn't see the other side of.

The Storm Tower itself . . . kind of just took my breath away.

A monument of stone, iron, and glass, the tower dominated the horizon. The base of it was perhaps twenty times as wide as the Beaver Cleaver was long, occupying an area best measured in dozens of acres. From this foundation, the tower soared up in a cascade of terraces and monolithic walls, rising straight up through the lower wispy clouds that drifted in off the bay. Above that cloudy mantle, the tower gathered itself into a dome, which was further crowned with a narrower tower that itself could've rivaled Big Ben.

It was practically a man-made mountain, and the sprawling complex that radiated out from its base was just as stunning. Countless interlocking buildings flooded out for a kilometer in every direction, every one of them no less than ten stories in height, many of them stretching up to skyscraper level in their own right. Roads entered the complex and vanished into vaulted, tunnel-like passages. The original ground was long since built over, but the wooded courtyards hundreds of feet in the air felt like slabs of hills had been installed in place of some of the roofs.

Buildings had been built on top of other buildings, reinforced, and then more buildings had been built on top of those again. It all combined into an organic layer-city with no defined edge, seeming to be bursting apart at the seams. There were some castle-like buildings of stone, others made of glass and wrought iron, some still only shells of new construction, surrounded by a forest of scaffolding.

It was clear, at a glance, that this place hadn't been built in a day. The tallest of the buildings, to the north of the Storm Tower's main . . . tower part, had a skeletal structure and walls of glass. It almost looked like a modern skyscraper, except that it was made of wrought iron with decorative curves and its base was all interlocking stone.

Farther along the coast, to the south of the tower, was a third city. This one seemed less built for people and more for industry. Big factories sat next to the bay, spewing coal smoke into the air from long chimneys, and a huge port extended over the water where more traditional ships were docked.

Was the reason this city was so far from the others to keep the smoke and smog away? Or was it to keep the dwarves and elves apart? What about that big road, with all of the homes built alongside it? And the tower! Oh, I had so many questions, but no one to ask.

The air was filled with ships. Little zippy ones that flew past us at blazing speeds and bigger lumbering giants that barely looked like they were moving at all. Most of the ships circled the main tower, but a number of them hovered over the more industrial area, where I could see airship docks where stuff was being loaded on and off of waiting ships.

We flew past an airship whose entire side was made of two bulbous, glass-covered cars filled with little figures on seats. At a glance it looked like they were reading newspapers or chatting. Were those airbuses?

Our approach was noticed soon enough, and a small ship not much bigger than the *Redemption* came to a hover nearby. A small figure stood on its deck and pulled out semaphore flags to signal us.

I raced to our second deck to reply, of course. They wanted to know if we had a transceiver, and when I said that we didn't, they used their flags to ask if we were there on business or Tower business.

After a very quick conference with Caprica, we decided on Tower business, and the ship told us to follow them and that our berth was five-zero-one.

I relayed that to Clive, but he didn't know what it meant any more than I did. Still, we did as instructed and followed what was clearly some sort of air-traffic-direction ship closer to the tower.

There was a system in place that decided who could approach and when, but we weren't privy to whatever that system was, so we had to wait and do as we were told.

"Whoa," Awen said. She'd been on the deck ever since we could see the city, a magic-made spyglass in hand the entire time so that she could better see what was going on and take a look at the ships we passed. Her attention, and mine, was now on the Storm Tower. A slice of the dome at the top could slide open.

It revealed that the whole of the massive tower was hollow, and the interior was lined by a circle of docks and gantries and catwalks and big cranes that could unfold from the walls to grab onto ships.

I imagined that maybe the largest airships around couldn't fit into the tower, but most of those we saw weren't much bigger than the *Beaver*. And ships of that size . . . Well, I imagined that the tower could hold hundreds of those.

I couldn't just stare with my jaw slack, though. There was piloting to be done, and even with Clive at the wheel and everyone in top form, it wouldn't do for the captain to slack off.

As we approached the tower, a signal must have been sent by our pilot boat, because a magical beam of green light appeared before the *Beaver*, tracing a route through the tower's doors and into its depths.

"I guess we follow that," I said. For some reason, I hadn't expected there to be magic around such an industrious city, but of course, there was no reason for them to have abandoned magic.

We moved in, going perhaps a lot slower than we could have, but slow was safe, and the inside of the tower, even if it was so grand it probably had its own weather, was still a busy place.

Ships were moored against the walls, loading and unloading cargo, being repaired, or just sitting and waiting. The tower's interior was lit by big searchlights and a thousand torches hanging above the catwalks, but the space was still relatively dark compared to the bright morning sun outside. Actinic splashes of light flared up every so often, and when I looked for the source I found a team of workers with what looked like welding equipment working on a ship to one side.

The space was cacophonous. Clangs of metal on metal, distant shouts, even a lot of music of a few different genres competing for loudness. Combined with all of the moving parts, and the many strange and new scents, it made for something of a sensory overload, and I found myself fighting back dizziness, so I refused to take it all in and instead focused on what was ahead of me.

The various berths had numbers above them, but it wasn't organized all that easily for me to understand. Each number seemed to correspond to a space, but that space was somewhat changeable since some ships were bigger than others, and it looked as if the landing areas could change size, with the clamps and gantries and cranes all being built on huge rails pressed up against the walls that let them shift from side to side.

Eventually, though, the green line ahead of us led us down, to a space five levels off the ground—or at least the ground within the tower. Clive did a bit of expert flying, spinning us around so that we could enter the berth back-first.

I saw figures on the sidelines, both short and squat and tall and lithe and those in between, all working to adjust the space where the *Beaver* eventually came in for a landing. Clamps thumped gently against the ship's hulls, then Clive set the engine to idle and we pulled in all of our sails, letting the retreating clamps pull us into our mooring.

Finally, once we were properly locked in place, a catwalk unfolded from the berth and came to rest a pace above the rightmost deck. The end of the catwalk had a ramp which the Scallywags hurried to drop.

We had arrived at Stormtower. Well, at the Storm Tower part of Stormtower.

A figure was approaching across the catwalk, each step eliciting a clang and a bang, so I rushed to meet them at the end of the ramp while tugging my captain's hat on straighter.

The person was . . . someone. I couldn't immediately tell if it was a dwarf or an elf. He was a bit shorter than I was, and rather on the stocky side, but he had a thin face and pointy ears, as well as thick but long hair tied up in a ponytail dangling out the back of his hard hat. And, of course, he had a beard. It was a rather neatly trimmed one that only went down to his sternum, but it was clean and had a few little beads woven into it. "Greetings!" he said with a deep bass of a voice. "And welcome to the Storm Tower. Permission to come aboard?"

"Hello," I replied. "And permission granted. Welcome aboard the *Beaver Cleaver.*"

He grinned and stepped up onto the ship. "Thank you. Are you the captain of this strange vessel?"

"Yeah, that's me. I'm Captain Broccoli Bunch, and this is my crew and friends," I said with a gesture to everyone, because no one was staying below deck and missing this. "Pleased to meet you, ah, sir?"

"Thorin Rootbreaker, Clerk of Landing Floor Five, at your service, Captain. Now, I know my records like I know my beard, and I don't recall a ship called the *Beaver Cleaver* scheduled to head to my docks today or any other day."

"Ah, that's because we haven't told anyone," I said.

Amaryllis stepped up and curtsied to Thorin Rootbreaker. "I'm the one who usually cares for the ship's paperwork, sir dwarf. I'm Amaryllis Albatross, the first mate."

Amaryllis was my first mate? I supposed she was!

"Which forms do we need to fill out for an impromptu landing, and how much are the standard docking fees?" Amaryllis asked.

"Before all that," Thorin said. "I'm mighty curious to know what brings you here. Your ship doesn't look fat with cargo, and that there's a Tower-made skiff you've got grabbed in your midships."

Amaryllis made a disgusted face. "We're here on political business, I'm afraid. One of the *Beaver*'s guests is a noble who has affairs to take care of here. You know how it can be."

"Ah, I do, I do," Thorin said. "Well, in any case, no one will be calling a Rootbreaker a penny pincher. Standard fare's good enough. Your ship's unusual, but not stranger than some of the hulls we see here, and besides, this berth isn't going to be filled for another week. That does mean you'll be needing to find accommodations elsewhere for this ship of yours between now and then. Can't be giving away promised places."

"I'll be sure to keep that in mind," I said.

"Good as iron, then," Thorin said. "The administration's at the tower's base."

"Thank you," I said. "Um, Mister Rootbreaker, if we wanted to find out about another ship? Like a ship that might be docked at the tower, is there any place we could ask about it?"

Thorin frowned, big bushy eyebrows meeting in the middle of his brow like two blind caterpillars bumping into each other. "Oh, sure, administration ought to be able to do that for ya. Looking for a friend?"

I wouldn't call Vonowl a friend unless his personality improved a fair bit. "Not quite. I'm just looking for someone."

"Well, good luck to ya, then. Now, will your ship be needing fuel? Provisions? Some elbow grease to get it up to snuff?"

· Chapter Forty-Five ·

Hustle, Bustle, Toil & Trouble

Initially, I thought finding the baron would be somewhat easy. I don't know why I thought that, it just felt like the kind of thing that wouldn't be too hard.

Whatever city he hid in, he'd probably insist on being in the nicest part of it. That seemed to match his personality.

The problem was that I couldn't have expected Stormtower to be . . . the way it was, really.

While the outer wall of the Storm Tower wasn't all that thick, it was still filled with curving corridors, staircases that climbed up and down, and plenty of storage spaces, offices, and little breakrooms.

What caught my attention the most, though, wasn't the strange verticality of the space, but the people within it.

Dwarves were stomping about like busy bees, both men and women. (At least, I thought they were women? The beards made it hard to tell. I'd have to find a way to politely ask about dwarven genders at some point.) Next to them, and usually moving with both more speed and grace, were elves.

They were tall and lithe, with chiseled, noble features and very nice chins on average. The elves weren't in a class of their own though, or if they were, I didn't notice it right away. Dwarf and elf worked together, and there didn't seem to be that big of a difference in their jobs. Sure, I saw more dwarven mechanics, but there were some elves in overalls covered in grease stains as well, and while the elves looked more comfortable in their office attire, plenty of dwarves had button-up shirts open at the front so that they could stuff the tips of their beards away.

"Awa, there's so much to look at," Awen said. Which really summed up my problem, even if she was talking more about all the ships parked away around us.

"I know," I said. "This place is enormous. And it's not even the entire city or anything, I bet the rest of the complex is even more packed with stuff and people and things."

"As far as I'm aware, the tower complex is where most of the governance is," Caprica said. "The two satellite cities are for housing and industry, respectively. Though what I read about the Storm Tower and what I'm seeing now . . . Well, my history books didn't do justice to the scale of this place. This is a wonder of engineering."

"It's pretty big, yeah," I agreed. I bet someone could fit a whole Eiffel Tower in the middle of this place and still have room to park a few ships. "Where do we even start?"

Amaryllis hummed. "I think we start with the obvious. We'll go pay our docking fees, then ask about the baron's ship. If it's here somewhere, then all the best. We won't have to search for him across the continent."

Spending time in an administration building while visiting a whole new place didn't sound super fun, but Amaryllis was probably right about its effectiveness. So the five of us (Amaryllis, Awen, Calamity, Caprica, and me) all headed out of the docks. With a few helpful directions from some locals and some time spent trying to understand the tower's signage, we bustled our way into a big administrative center just off the main tower but still within the huge complex.

There were windows overlooking a pretty view of the sea and the industrial sector just to the south of the Storm Tower, but we weren't there for the view.

Amaryllis took the lead, bringing out a few papers and permits that a young elf man looked over quickly. She managed to convince him that the *Beaver* didn't need an inspection and that we weren't carrying any cargo to sell, so we obviously didn't need a cargo manifest. We were here on business, not to sell stuff.

Finally, the question I was listening for came up. "We're also looking for someone while we're here," Amaryllis said. "A harpy noble by the name of Baron Vonowl. He might have arrived here on a skiff, perhaps a day ago."

"Do you have any more details than that?" the admin asked. "We have skiffs aplenty here."

"It was a Snowlander ship," Awen added. Then she rattled out a few specifications: its balloon size, approximate tonnage, the propeller and engine models. I didn't know she'd gathered that much information about his ship just at a glance.

Unfortunately, that didn't really help much. At least, not until we got lucky. The admin turned as a dwarf in a suit trundled by. "Hey, have you heard of a harpy crew coming in on a Snowlander skiff lately?" he asked.

The dwarf paused. "Yeah, sure, yesterday morning?"

We all perked up. "Did you see them, mister dwarf?" I asked.

"Mmm, yes," the dwarf said. "They parked in the morning and only bothered to send someone to pay the docking fees in the afternoon. Not against the rules, but certainly annoying."

"What did the person who came in here look like?" I asked.

"Harpy," the dwarf said. He rubbed at his beard. "Hmm, lots of feathers. Some wings. Looked a mighty lot like that harpy sir right there," he said, pointing to Amaryllis.

"'Sir'? I'll have you know I'm a woman," Amaryllis huffed.

"Ah, my pardons. Hard to tell, what with, you know." He gestured vaguely toward his lower face, and I took it to mean that Amaryllis didn't have a very womanly beard.

"You can tell by the hips and the breasts," the other admin said matter-of-factly.

"I'll keep that in mind," the dwarf replied. "In any case, just a normal harpy. Looked mighty nervous and sweaty about it though."

That didn't sound like Baron Vonowl. I suspected that if he had come here to take care of his own paperwork, he would have made sure to have everyone here knew who he was. He was . . . maybe not memorable, but certainly loud. "Do you know where the ship's crew is now?" I asked. "Did they leave an address or something? They can't be staying in their ship like we are, it's just a skiff."

The admin and the dwarf conferred for a bit, then the admin wandered off. We had to wait a couple of minutes, but he returned with a file that he was leafing through. "Your friend is staying at the Grand Mami Hotel," he reported, before very nicely giving us some directions.

"Thank you," I said once everything was done. "Um, one more thing. Did you happen to hear anything about someone called Rainnewt?"

"Rainnewt?" the admin asked. He squinted, then his eyes widened and he smiled. "Yes, he's on that poster over there."

We all turned to see a wall off to one side that was covered in posts, local ads, and official reports for everyone to see. One of those had a rather well-drawn image of Rainnewt on it.

It was right under a large label that said WANTED.

I walked over to the wall and read the whole poster. Under the wanted part was the image of a serious-faced Rainnewt, and below that, the list of crimes he was wanted for. Conspiracy, theft, impersonating an officer of the law, kidnapping.

There was a nice reward for his capture too.

I wondered if I could cash that in. We did capture him, after all. Sure, it was across the continent from here, and he'd gotten away after already being imprisoned, but technically . . .

"What did he do?" I asked.

The administrator shrugged. "That poster has been up there for months. I don't know."

It seemed as if we had another little mystery on our hands. Something else to discover about Rainnewt, and probably more stuff to add to his long list of misdeeds.

"We can ask more about that later, after we've found the baron," Amaryllis said.

"Maybe before," Caprica said. We turned to her, and she crossed her arms. "We don't have any authority here. If we walk up to the baron to confront him, there's quite literally nothing we *can* do. At least legally. This isn't like our last . . . legally dubious situation either. This is the capital and the heart of the Snowlands. They won't take kindly to any hostile actions."

"That makes sense," I said. "But then, what do we do?"

"Kidnap the baron?" Calamity suggested. "I'm quick with a rope. I can have him hog-tied in a second or less. Then nya just have to carry him back to wherever."

"That . . . isn't how it works," Caprica said.

Calamity shrugged, as if to say, *Well, I tried.*

"Any options, then? Other than something so evidently criminal?" Amaryllis asked.

"Ask nicely?" I tried.

"Yes Broccoli, but *who* do we ask nicely?" Amaryllis asked. "We don't really have any connections here, do we?"

"Um," Awen said.

We all turned toward Awen, whose cheeks took on a cute shade of pink at the sudden attention.

"I think I know someone here. Well, someone who knows someone I know. Awa, what I mean is . . ." She took a deep breath to recenter herself while we listened. "My uncle came here a few times, starting a long time ago, when the tower wasn't finished being built yet. His airship is very, very old, like . . . one of the first, probably, and it was partially built here, though it's had so many parts replaced that . . . well, never mind. My point is, he had a bunch of friends in the Snowlands. He told me stories about them."

"And those friends might be willing to assist us?" Caprica asked.

"Maybe?" Awen tried. "There is an Exploration Guild here. And they probably have a club for old people."

"That isn't a bad idea," Amaryllis said. "It's a place to start, at least. And the kind of old person that hangs around at the Exploration Guild is exactly the kind of person that likes getting into a bit of trouble."

"That doesn't sound like what I envisioned at all," Caprica said.

Amaryllis sniffed. "You were expecting us to go through all the right and proper channels? Caprica, this isn't Sylphfree, and we're not diplomats. We don't know what the proper channels would be, or if they even exist."

"We're troublemakers," Calamity said with a devilish grin.

I shook my head. "We're nothing like that. Just friends trying to fix a few little problems and see some amazing stuff while we're at it. I think Awen's idea is the best one so far. We'll get to meet some people who can help, and then we can figure out where we want to go from there."

Finding the Exploration Guild proved to be surprisingly easy. I flagged down an unhurried-looking dwarf in the halls outside the dock administration place, then asked them where we could find the guild.

It turned out to be at the top of what locals called the "little tower," which was a smaller tower built closer to the coast. That was still a very long walk away though, not that anyone minded. We got to tour the Storm Tower and play tourist as we crossed the entire massive complex.

I just wished the place was a little more tourist-friendly. They really needed more signs explaining things. Like the main complex had an interior train system where people who needed to get around could hop aboard one of the moving platforms—they had benches and rails to grab on to—so that they could move around without having to walk, but we didn't know which platform to ride on, so we had to just hoof it.

I wasn't complaining. It meant I got to see all the strangely dressed people moving around, many of whom paused to look at us as we passed by. Also, we discovered that the locals had a thing for street food.

It didn't taste very good. Everything from the sausages they had to their drinks was super bitter and smoky. I imagined the dwarf palate wasn't anything like a human one, because I saw plenty of them seeming to enjoy their snacks.

Finally, after a good bit of wandering around, we made it to the Exploration Guild.

· Chapter Forty-Six ·

Living History

The Exploration Guild's entrance was . . . I don't think "impressive" really covered it. The entrance was to one side of a huge, long room that reminded me a little of a subway station, with an arched ceiling covered in little tiles and two lanes of interior train tracks for the trolleys that people seemed so fond of in here.

There were plenty of shops and workstations and offices pressed into the sides, but the Exploration Guild's entrance towered above them all. Huge pillars the height of the entire wall stood on either side of a set of double doors so massive you could march an army through it.

My friends and I stepped into the guild proper, a little cowed by how vast everything was within. The floor was all huge squares of beautifully swirling marble, and the entrance hall had golden plinths that stopped at waist-height to display all sorts of things. Adventuring tools, strange statues, little objects whose use I couldn't guess at.

The hall echoed with our footsteps, and I wondered why the sounds from the main halls of the tower weren't carrying in. Magic of some sort? That wouldn't surprise me, this place *felt* magical. There were huge maps on the walls, paintings of strange places, ancient-looking artifacts, and . . .

I stared, drifting to a stop. Amaryllis realized I was no longer with her, and turned back, only to stare as well. Then Awen followed our gazes, only to jerk back in shock, and by that point even Calamity and Caprica had turned to see what all the fuss was about.

Hanging in pride of place on a wall, enclosed in a frame made of dark wood engraved with intricate little flower patterns, was a painting of six men. I recognized two of them right away, even if I hadn't seen them in a while. To the left was a grenoil gentleman, head tilted back, spectacles perched on the end of his broad nose.

It was Raynold, who I had last seen in the company of . . .

"Uncle Abraham?!" Awen squeaked.

I don't think it was seeing an oil painting of her uncle that shocked her so much as it was the fact that in the painting her uncle, and all the other men with him, were shirtless.

The Abraham in the picture was a lot younger than the man I remembered. He had a few gray hairs at the temples, but his hair, including the bristly bush covering his upper chest, was mostly the same blonde as Awen's.

Next to him was a young harpy who looked slender, especially compared to the barrel-chested dwarf flexing next to him. At the far end of the image was a tall elf with his arms raised above his head, biceps bulging, and below that elf was a sylph gentleman who looked to be working hard to make his abs stand out.

"Wow," Amaryllis said.

"I can feel the testosterone," I said.

"That there's some fine-looking specimens," Calamity agreed. "But, ah, what's got Awen all bothered?"

"That's her uncle," I said while pointing to Abraham.

"Really?" Calamity asked. He looked between Awen and her uncle. "I guess the hair matches but the old man's got a bit more muscle to him."

"I guess," I said. I tilted my head to the side to examine the painting from a different angle. It was really striking. Behind them was a big cliffside and a coastline that seemed familiar. Something was being built atop the cliff. "Maybe we should get an oil painting done of our group too," I said.

"Broccoli, if you suggest that we do it shirtless I'm going to have words with you," Amaryllis said.

Awen walked up to the frame, then squinted at a plaque set at its base. "Abraham Bristlecone, Eustace Mountainstorm, Raynold Weatherwick, Tharval Boltbinder, Wesley Vonowl, Willowbud Wintersdawn."

"Vonowl?" I asked, my attention snapping to the harpy in the painting. When I'd seen the baron during the fight he'd been clothed, but it was still pretty clear that this wasn't the baron, although . . . maybe there was some family resemblance? The harpy in the painting had brown-white plumage and rather big eyes, the same as the Vonowl we were chasing. It was possible they were related.

"That's . . . a strange coincidence," Caprica said. "Eustace Mountainstorm . . . the Mountainstorm family are lesser nobles in Sylphfree. I think they were big supporters of the Exploration Guild in the past, but I've never heard of this Eustace. How long ago was this made?"

"Is that the Storm Tower in the background?" Amaryllis asked.

I looked at the background again, then nodded. "Yeah, yeah, the coast looks right. Except, well, there's no tower, just the foundation."

"So, this was made before the tower was finished, which doesn't help in dating it as much as you might think. A project as big as the tower could take decades," Caprica said.

"Awa, Uncle Abraham has white hair, and his moustache is . . . more. Um, he went off to have big adventures a long time ago, so this could be forty years old, or more," Awen said.

That was a while ago. "No airships," I said as I looked at the sky in the painting.

"Airships are older than forty years," Amaryllis said. "But the business isn't ancient. There are people around who were our age when the first airships sailed and who are still around. Trust me, I'd know that much."

My friends quieted down and stood straighter as an elf wandered over. He was in a button-up shirt and vest and looked properly respectable. "Hello, can I assist you?" he asked. His eyes lingered on the lapels on my and Amaryllis's chests. "Oh, you're members of the guild? The Deepmarsh branch?"

"We are," I said with a grin. "We're here looking for information, but then we got distracted by, ah, that." I gestured to the painting.

"The founding fathers?" the elf asked.

"They started the guild?" I asked. "Whoa! That's cool."

"They did, indeed," the elf said. "We have a few books and biographies that cover the history of the Exploration Guild, if you wish to peruse them."

I nodded. That would be kind of cool. I hadn't expected the guild I joined more or less on a whim to have much of a history, but I should have. Pretty much everything has a history.

Awen raised a hand. "Is there a biography of Uncle Abraham?" she asked.

The elf blinked. "Uncle Abraham?"

"Awa!" Awen said. "That's my uncle," she said while pointing to the painting. "I . . . didn't expect to see anything like this here."

"Hey, are any of the other founding fathers here?" I asked. It would be nice to meet them, I figured. Maybe they'd have stories about Abraham that Awen could listen to? Her uncle was a great storyteller, but his stories were always very . . . spectacular.

"Certainly, in the lounge on the fourth floor," the elf said. "Are all of you members?"

"Only Amaryllis and I are," I said. "Can the others come as guests?"

"Certainly. You'll merely have to sign in to our guest book. And of course, I'll need to see your identification as well."

We moved through the entrance hall and to the back where there was a counter and, to the side, an elevator with a wrought-iron cage and a complicated lever-based mechanism next to it. The elf accompanying us pulled out a guest book, and stepped aside for the others to sign it.

He watched as Awen signed her name, then nodded, then Caprica did the same and finally Calamity.

That's when things went a little weird. The book rattled once Calamity was done signing, and his name turned red, the ink hissing and spitting. "Uh," Calamity said.

"Please sign your true name, Mister . . . Calamity Danger," the elf suggested, leaning over to read what Calamity had written.

Calamity glared. "But that's my name, isn't it?"

The elf smiled. "You can use whichever name you wish, but we would prefer it if you wrote your birth name here."

Calamity grumbled, grabbed the pen, then wrote another name down. Curiosity got the best of me and I stretched up to read the name he'd placed. Claire Dogfriend.

"Um," I said.

"I don't wanna talk about it," he muttered.

I shrugged. "Okay, Calamity."

He nodded once, and then stalked toward the elevator and the rest of us followed. The elevator rose up slower than I could crawl, but I supposed it was still pretty novel to people here. My friends seemed amused by it, Awen most of all. "I wonder if it works with a counterweight, or if it's all engine power. Oh, and look at those tabs on the side. It looks like they're designed to break the elevator's fall if it fails."

We crossed the second floor, which looked like an office floor, with a bunch of desks laid out and staffed by dwarves and elves, then the third floor, which looked like something between an armory and a blacksmith's shop.

Finally, we arrived on the fourth floor, which had another small lobby with a long corridor. A floorplan on one wall suggested that many of the rooms were conference rooms and planning spaces, but the biggest space was taken up by a lounge and bar.

"You mentioned knowing someone here," Amaryllis said to Awen.

"Only from uncle's stories," she said. "He talked about a dwarf called Bolty and an elf called Buddy."

"That must be Tharval Boltbinder and Willowbud Wintersdawn from that painting," Caprica said.

"That's what I was thinking too," Awen said. "Uncle likes his nicknames. It annoys a certain kind of person, and makes easier friends with another sort. At least, that's what he told me."

"That's a cute trick," I said. "But I wouldn't want to anger anyone . . . Although, you're all my friends already . . . so."

"Don't start giving us nicknames, Broccoli," Amaryllis said.

"We call Broccoli Broc sometimes," Awen said.

"Yes, but she might start getting *creative* with our nicknames," Amaryllis said. "And that's the last thing anyone wants."

I giggled. "Didn't your sister call you Amy?"

"Amy is fine," Amaryllis said with a serious nod. "But nothing past that."

"Prickly," Caprica muttered.

"Do you want her calling you Capy?"

Caprica flinched. "I don't think I'd ever allow someone to call me that, no."

"Not even Bastion?" I asked.

Caprica's face shifted, her expression dropping to something entirely neutral that wouldn't give away her feelings while also turning tomato red.

"Ah, I'm sorry," I said as I pulled her into a side-hug. "I didn't mean to tease you too hard."

Amaryllis patted Caprica on the back.

We arrived at the lounge while Caprica was still steaming in embarrassment. The place was closed off by a large pair of double doors that we pushed open to reveal a great big room with glossy wooden floors. Floor-to-ceiling bookcases took up the walls on either side of the doors. The far wall had a big fireplace with a roaring fire within, and there was a bar against another wall, plus a few dozen chairs all around. The exterior wall was all windows, with a spectacular view of the northern coast and part of the bigger tower to the east.

A few heads rose at our arrival. Mostly older men and women, but there were a handful of people closer to our age sitting at the bar.

I felt a little awkward as my friends and I lingered by the entrance and kind of just stood there, uncertain of where to go for the moment. Still, I was the nominal leader, so social stuff was my job, wasn't it? "Ah, hello everyone!" I said. "We're looking for some people called Bolty and Buddy?"

There was a long pause, then a roar of laughter erupted from one side, where a big stout dwarf was lounging in the depths of a recliner. He shuffled forward in the seat until he was right on the edge, then smacked a hand on his knee. "Who gave you that name, missy?" he asked.

"Um, my uncle did," Awen said. "Abraham, Abraham Bristlecone."

The dwarf bounced off his seat. "Bud! Did you hear that?"

"I heard," a familiar-looking elf said. He looked just like the elf in the oil painting. "I'm not deaf, you old dwarf."

"I'm not old, you decrepit tree-hugger," the dwarf snapped back. Then he grinned widely. "Come over here, I need to take a good look at the lot of ya! And you need to tell me how Abe's doing!"

· Chapter Forty-Seven ·

Passing the Torch

Chairs were pulled up, cushions were fluffed, and the old dwarf shouted across the room to the barkeep, who brought us all big mugs of frothing ale.

I sat myself down across from what I imagined were some of Abraham's old adventuring buddies and held onto my mug politely while it fizzed.

"So!" the dwarf said. "We're all sitted and we've got some talking juice. Introductions are in order."

"Civilized as ever," the elf said. He bowed a little from his seat. "I'm Willowbud Wintersdawn. Miss Bristlecone, I was one of your uncle's companions on his many travels throughout the Snowlands and beyond. The dwarf here is Tharval Boltbinder."

"I can introduce myself, Bud," Tharval said. He took a long pull from his mug—or was it a pint?—then wiped the froth from his bristly moustache with the back of his sleeve. "But the elf's not wrong. We were both good pals with Abe. Why, it feels like he ran off to another great adventure just yesterday."

"Awa, when did you last see Uncle?" Awen asked. She took a long pull from her mug, matching Tharval.

I looked at my own beer, then gave it a sniff. It smelled bitter and tangy. Not necessarily a bad smell, but a bit strange and spicy. Not spicy in the "hot" sense, but in the sense that there were a number of spices mixed into the beer.

Shoring up my bravery, I took a big gulp, then both coughed and spat at the same time. It was so bitter! I noticed Amaryllis hiding her smile behind a sip of her own mug. Calamity, meanwhile, was drinking along at a decent pace.

I think Caprica was the only one who agreed with my taste buds about the beer's flavor.

Tharval laughed, both at my reaction and I think just out of sheer good humor. "Ah, the last time I saw Abe . . . Was it two years back, Bud?"

"Already?" Willowbud asked. He leaned back, then nodded. "Yes, it would have been the summer before last. He brought that ugly ship of his in for repairs."

"The *Shady Lady*'s a fine vessel," Tharval said.

"It was outdated before it left the shipyard that built it," the elf retorted. "It's a wonder it can fly at all, especially with Abraham at the helm."

"She's a beauty, a piece of aeronautical history," Tharval argued.

Willowbud nodded. "Exactly. She belongs in a museum."

"Ah, I got to fly on the *Shady Lady* a few times," Awen said. "And I worked on her a little. There was always something broken."

"That's because Abe couldn't keep his toenails fixed, never mind an entire airship!" Tharval guffawed. He clapped a hand on his lap while tipping his tankard back. "Ahh, but those were the days. Back before we were stuck in this windy old tower, when we wandered the World looking for trouble."

"And causing trouble when we couldn't find any," Willowbud said. He grinned, and something about the smile aged him a bit, gave him more of an edge. "We still have something of a reputation, even after a few years of sitting on our laurels and reaping the benefits of our . . . what were they calling them? Youthful indiscretions?"

"Bah! Don't remind me," Tharval said. "Besides, we've got these impressionable kids to impress, don't we?" He reached over, swiped my mug, and took a swig of it. I didn't complain.

Awen swallowed a mouthful of her own beer, then smiled. "Um, what sort of things did you do with Uncle Abraham? He used to tell me stories, but I never knew which ones were, uh, real. I think he softened them a little because I was young."

Willowbud hummed. "That sounds like Abe, yes. You could never tell if he was being truthful or not. He'd say the most farfetched things and then they'd turn out to be entirely true, even if they sounded wild. Why, I remember, he once approached me and Eustace about a colony of snow dryads in the western Tallwoods who needed help because of a cave-in."

"Oh, I remember that," Tharval said. "Ain't that how we met?"

"It was, yes," Willowbud said.

I moved to the very edge of my seat. "What happened?" I asked.

"Let me do the telling," Tharval said. "Bud here could bore through a meter of stone with his voice alone. So, here Abe comes, with this strange frog man, a reedy little harpy boy, and a runaway sylph knight—"

"No, Wesley joined us later," Willowbud said. "And Raynold was busy with something else. That . . . lizard cult incident."

"Anyway," Tharval continued, ignoring him. "He comes over to us deep in the Snowlands. Now, this was just after us elves and dwarves finally got our heads on straight and decided to stop murdering each other over dumb insults."

"A regular occurrence," Willowbud said.

Tharval chuckled. "So Abe shows up and he starts asking around for help with these snow dryads. Mostly asking the elves, since they're the local experts when it comes to hugging trees."

"Of course," Willowbud interjected, "the snow dryads were a myth. Everyone knew they didn't exist, so Abe sounded like a lunatic. But he managed to convince me to help him anyway."

"Bud here was running away from a marriage," Tharval said with a chuckle. He looked at his tankard and saw that it was empty, then he leaned over and took Caprica's. "Oi! Someone get this sylph lady some of that sweet elven wine," he called out to the bar. "And some fruit juice for the bun."

Willowbud glanced to Tharval. "That's awfully considerate. You're not going to force them to drink your usual dwarven swill?"

"Bah, you remember how Eustace used to complain about everything us proper folk cooked up? If it wasn't slathered in honey, the sylph won't touch it."

I held back a giggle at Caprica's conflicted look. I think she couldn't decide whether to agree or take insult. In the end, she rolled her eyes slightly and didn't comment at all, especially not when a younger elf came from the bar with a fine crystal goblet for Caprica and a big cup of what smelled like a strawberry-banana smoothie for me. It even had a straw!

"So, ah, what happened after Abraham asked you for help?" I asked.

"Ah, right. So he asks this mulch-for-brains for help," Tharval said with a gesture to Willowbud. "And he had the first good idea of his entire life. That is, to find an expert. Now, that turned out to be me."

"Tharval here had just been kicked out of his guild for accumulating too many misdemeanors, and he was hard-pressed and looking for work," Willowbud said.

Tharval harrumphed. "They said that it would take a thousand years of development to make an airship. And I said that they were a bunch of rock-headed morons. Anyway, Abe comes over and hires me to go look for these snow dryads. To be honest, I thought he was crazy, but he was also mighty persuasive and, in any case, I needed the coin. I didn't much care if he thought the moon was made of cheese, so long as I got paid." Tharval laughed. "I was pretty shocked when I got out to the site, and there they were, a whole town of snow dryads living underground."

"I didn't know dryads could live underground," I said. I remembered Oak and a few of the other dryads I'd met. They'd seemed pretty happy to live outside, like trees usually did. Did they even eat anything?

"Snow dryads, as it turns out, are more based on fungal bodies than the dryads we're all mostly familiar with," Willowbud said. "They live in large caves beneath the Tallwoods, where they carefully tend pools of water to keep the humidity as high as possible, allowing them to cultivate lichen that they use for clothes and tools. They're quite interesting, though they're also very quiet and isolationist. So it's no wonder we thought them a myth."

"And Uncle Abraham found them?" Awen asked.

"More like they found him," Tharval said. "Or did they find Eustace?"

"It was Eustace, yes. He and Abraham were exploring the edge of the Tallwoods when Eustace went off course. He ran into some snow dryads, and eventually they managed to ask him for help. In any case, the dryads had a problem."

"A cave-in," Tharval said, quite seriously. "They weren't keen on digging often, so most of their cave homes were all natural. But even a natural cave needs some proper reinforcement. One of their tunnels collapsed and a number of 'em were stuck. Fortunately, they're dryads, and standing still for a few days doesn't bother them all that much."

"So, how does the story end?" I asked.

"Bah. I went over and blew the hole open with some explosives. After we chopped up some trees and built trusses, of course. Didn't want to worsen things. It all ended well. I think some folk are still keeping in touch with the snow dryads, aren't they?"

Willowbud nodded. "A few. They make interesting fermented wines and are experts at growing certain mushrooms in their caverns. They're difficult to trade with, since there's little they want or need, but a few academics make a point to stay in touch and study their environment."

"Ah, did you join Uncle from then on?" Awen asked.

"Join? Bah, he hardly has a monopoly on anyone, does he? The madman just likes dragging like-minded folk into his schemes, but we dragged him into ours just as often." Tharval grinned. "What about you lot? Dragging folk around into trouble just like Abe, huh?"

Awen started to shake her head, then froze. "Um. No, we're just trying to help people and that, ah, sometimes means we end up in strange places."

"Yeah," I agreed. "We're three-quarters of the way to circling the entire continent already! We made a heap of friends along the way, and we helped some people with things too. Plus we get to explore new places. It's great!"

Tharval grinned. "Been on a few little adventures yourself, huh?"

My friends and I nodded. "Yup!" I said. "Right now we're tracking someone called Baron Vonowl. He helped a terrible person kidnap some nobles and used that as a way to try to free that terrible person after we got them arrested in Sylphfree. He tried to blow up a peace summit to start a war between the Trenten Flats, the Harpy Mountains, Deepmarsh, and Sylphfree."

Tharval and Willowbud both blinked as they parsed all of that, then Tharval took another swallow from his tankard. "Well, that's something. This Baron Vonowl, any relation to Wesley Vonowl?"

We shrugged, but it was Amaryllis who answered. "We don't know. But we suspect so. It might be a situation like Awen here being related to Abraham. A nephew or younger cousin, maybe?"

Willowbud rubbed at his chin. "That's possible. Wesley passed away about . . . four years ago. He was . . . Well, harpies age a lot faster than elves or dwarves."

"Eustace moved on too," Tharval said, his voice rather grave. "We lose friends as we go. But most of us have made sure to leave a legacy behind." He gestured around. "This guild, the Storm Tower, so many new ideas and fresh ties and opportunities for the next generation." Then he straightened and cleared his throat. "Bah, what's it matter? You're looking for this Vonowl fellow, yeah?"

"Yeah," I repeated.

"Might be that we can help you," Tharval said. "We may be semi-retired, but that doesn't mean we're so old that we can't jump into an adventure or two."

Willowbud smiled. "That'll set some nerves alight, seeing the two of us looking for trouble again."

"Good! We can even blame Abraham for it, like in the good old days!" Tharval said.

"Awa, you blamed Uncle Abraham for stuff?" Awen asked.

"Oh yes, he's a wanted man here," Tharval said. He grinned. "He's responsible for the greatest theft ever to occur in the Snowlands, something he somehow did while halfway across the continent."

"We really ought to give those paintings back," Willowbud said. I followed his gaze across the room to where a row of paintings in nice frames hung on the far wall. "No one will bother him for it," Willowbud reassured Awen. "After all, he can easily prove that he wasn't here when the crime happened."

"Mm-hmm," Tharval said. "Now . . . I'm getting the sense that you want our help for your trouble, which means payment." He smacked his knee. "And I only accept payment in stories. Now, spill! What have Abraham's niece and her friends been up to?"

· Chapter Forty-Eight ·

Boltbound

And then," I said, having to speak up a little over Tharval's hooting laughter. The dwarf was a great listener. Well, no, he kept interrupting and liked to add his own tall tales to the mix, but he was a great *audience*, which counted for a lot when telling a story. "Then we went to meet these grenoil mafia people, and they were quite mean. We ended up scuffling with them in the streets, but Cholondee landed right next to us."

"And that's how the dragon ended up ruling the city's underground?" Willowbud asked. He wasn't as boisterous or loud as Tharval, but he was still attentive, and I think a little bit drunk, judging by the rosiness of his cheeks.

I nodded. "Yeah! I don't know what's happened since, but I haven't heard of Port Royal burning down or anything, so it can't be that bad."

"That's a good sign," Tharval said with a nod. He was tipsy too, with ruddy cheeks and a bright red nose, but he wasn't slurring his words any, even though the floor next to his seat was a sea of empty tankards. He must have drunk his weight in beer already.

Willowbud grinned. "You girls, and sir, seem to have been on your share of adventures."

"We've only been adventuring for a couple of months," Awen said. "I don't know if we've had time to really, ah, get into the spirit of it the way Uncle has."

"Bah, it's not the time spent adventuring that matters, it's the experience of it!" Tharval said. "You judge the quality of an adventure by how many people you saved, what discoveries were made, and the number of angry noblefolk left in your wake."

I giggled at that, especially at the look Caprica gave that he didn't notice. "Is that how you calculate things here?"

"I doubt they can codify it accurately," Amaryllis said.

"What?" Tharval said. "No! Of course we can. The number of people saved is easy to verify most of the time, and discoveries are obvious. As for the noblefolk, well, we keep a record of who's gotten the most angry letters written about them."

"And scathing news articles, of course," Willowbud said.

Amaryllis shook her head. "Won't that undermine the Exploration Guild in the Snowlands?"

"Bah! The real people of the Snowlands know that it's all a big game for us. The nobles will spit and bluster and complain, and for every big complaint they make, another toast is raised in every pub across the nation."

"What Tharval means to say," Willowbud said, "is that the Exploration Guild, at least in the Snowlands, has proven to be . . . politically divisive, at times. But we have the will and have had the momentum to push for sweeping changes, which were very unpopular with those who were already established, and immensely popular with everyone else."

"What kinds of changes?" Caprica asked.

Willowbud smiled. "Well, I could talk about it for hours, but we got several large infrastructure projects pushed through. We trained explorers, opened several schools, successfully championed new reforms for education, and bankrolled several inventors and clever businessmen who were starting beneficial ventures."

"We dragged this entire country into the future, though it was kicking and screaming all the way," Tharval said. "And some stuck-up old farts complained the entire time, even as they reaped the benefits."

"That sounds annoying," I said.

Willowbud shrugged his shoulders. "It meant several huge changes to the status quo, and not every noble house and clan survived the changes. Their reasons to complain made sense, on a small scale. They were losing prestige, livelihoods, traditions, and power. In the end, though, I think it was all for the best. The Snowlands were a harsh place, once. We needed those traditions to survive. Now we're thriving, and there's no need for the old ways. Ah, but now it's us who are the old ones stuck in the past, aren't we, Tharval?"

"Speak for yourself, elf!" Tharval grumped. "I've got a century left of drinking and whipping these young brats into shape, mark my words in stone."

"Ah, speaking of whipping whippersnappers," I said while holding back a giggle. "Do you think you could help us?"

"With your baron problem?" Tharval asked. He tugged at his beard with all of its tresses and beads.

I wasn't going to say anything, but I was a little envious of his beard. It looked really fun to stroke and pull at, and if I were ever to grow a beard (which would be a little weird), I'd want it to be as fantastic as Tharval's.

"Awa, we could use the help," Awen admitted. "We don't know anyone from Stormtower, and the baron has a huge lead on us. We don't know what he's up to, but . . . but it's no good, I'm sure. Rainnewt worked hard to make a lot of trouble for a lot of people, and I just know that he'll be doing the same kind of thing here—and the baron works for him."

"Actually, we noticed a wanted poster with Rainnewt's face on it," Amaryllis said. "We might want to investigate that too. We know there's a link between the baron and Rainnewt, so if Rainnewt was doing something troublesome here, then that might give us more clues to work with."

I nodded along.

Tharval smacked his knees, then jumped to his feet. "All right! I'm tired of sitting back and drinking and collecting dust. Come on, Buddy, we're going to my shop."

"I doubt we'll find answers there," Willowbud said as he stood.

"No, but we'll find eager young fools of the best sort who'll jump to find the answers for us," Tharval said with a grin. "Besides, Abraham's niece seems to have inherited all of the mechanical wit that he lacks. She'll like the place."

"What kind of shop is it?" Awen asked.

Tharval's grin was almost wolfish. "The best kind! Where inventions that ought never see the light of day are hammered into being from the crooked minds of . . . ah . . ." He paused, arms half raised as he searched for what to say next.

"Wide-eyed drunks?" Willowbud volunteered.

"That's exactly it," Tharval agreed. "Are you coming, or are you going to sit here and wallow some more?"

"I do like a good wallow session," Willowbud admitted. "It's a good way to introspect."

Tharval sniffed. "Only an elf would volunteer to waste time like that. I swear, if you lot had the drive of a proper dwarf, the World would be a different place. Bah! Probably for the best that you're all lazy, tree-loving snobs."

The insults came on thick, but all they did was make Willowbud grin. "And you lot hardly do anything but work. I think I could make any dwarf happy by letting them bang a hammer on a rock and giving them a barrel of beer a day."

"Damned right!"

My friends and I followed the strange pair as they left the lounge and headed to the elevator. "Ah, will we all fit?" Caprica asked.

"Well, I'm not the one to be blamed for taking up too much room if we can't," Tharval said with a chuckle. "Come on, just squeeze in tight. Can hardly call yourselves proper adventurers if you haven't had your friend's knee in your nose at least once."

I was pretty sure we were breaking some safety codes as we squeezed in. Then Tharval ripped a panel off the side of the control level and flicked a little switch. "What's that do?" Calamity asked.

"Makes us move faster, and gets us to the floors under the guild," Tharval said. "They're off-limits, of course." Then he yanked the elevator lever down, as if that wasn't a concern, which I supposed it wasn't for him.

The elevator lurched, then started downward. I was expecting it to drop super fast, but it was . . . about as fast as a normal elevator, maybe? We zipped down a few floors, then past the lobby area where that nice reception elf looked up at our passing.

I blinked as we lowered down through a long, dark space, and then, finally, a bigger room came into view. This must have been closer to the middle of the complex that housed the towers, because the room was huge.

If it wasn't for all the gantries and huge machines all over, it might have been able to fit the entirety of the *Beaver Cleaver*. As it was, parked around the workshop were several airships . . . sorta. They were much smaller than any ship I'd seen, even smaller than the *Redemption*. Little more than planks and metal beams with engines and props and sometimes balloons hovering above.

A constant whirring sound filled the space, sometimes accompanied by a loud *clang* as metal met metal.

Big fans were pumping in fresher air from outside, which I imagine was necessary since there were a number of things on fire and the air was currently filled with the scent of oil, smoke, scorched metal, and industrial chemicals.

Heads turned toward us as the elevator slowed its descent and finally stopped. There were about half a dozen people in the workshop. Half were dwarves, but there was an elf and two . . . half-elves? They looked a bit tall for dwarves and too beardy to be elves.

"I'm back!" Tharval said as he opened the elevator door and hopped out. "How's the work going?"

"Sir!" one of the half-elves said as he jogged over. "Pleased to see you again, Mister Boltbinder. Things have been going well. Did you want a report?"

"Later," Tharval said. "Unless there's anything liable to explode while we're here?"

"Ah, I don't think so," he said.

"Then we're good! We've got company. This here's Awen Bristlecone, my best mate's niece, and these are her companions. They're explorers from here and there."

"Hello!" I said with a friendly wave.

My friends joined in with a chorus of polite greetings to the collection of . . . what were they, exactly? Inventors? Workers? They seemed to be tinkering with a bunch of different things, and while I wasn't a mechanically inclined person like Awen, even I could tell that most of the dozens of projects sitting around were unfinished.

"These lads and lasses," Tharval said as he gestured to the tinkerers, "are some of the brightest minds in this World-forsaken tower. I don't get out as much as I used to, but I have folk in all the schools that keep an eye and ear open for people with actual talent. Then I invite them over to my workshop."

"What do they work on?" Awen asked. "It looks like there's a lot of, um, things going on all at once."

"Hmm? Oh, they'll work on whatever needs improving, tinkering, or reinventing. Once in a blue moon one of 'em will come up with an actual good idea," Tharval said, his chest puffing out in pride.

"It's a better deal than it sounds like," the young man who'd greeted Tharval said. "We get room and board and can spend all day focusing on our pet projects. That's not something that we'd get to do if we needed jobs to keep fed. We get to practice all day, level our skills, and learn from one another. Occasionally, we even get to learn something from Mister Boltbinder."

Tharval nodded. "The kind of thing I wish I had when I was their age."

"That's impressive!" I said. "What kinds of things are you working on now?"

That was both the wrong and right thing to ask. Right because it started about five conversations at once, with lots of jargon and gesturing, and wrong because it started five conversations at once and I could barely follow one of them.

"Quiet down!" Tharval grumbled. "These folk are looking for someone in the tower, and I figured you lot might know where to start."

"Uh . . ." the same guy started. "Sir, we uh . . ." he trailed off, exchanging glances with his fellows. They gave uncomfortable shrugs.

He turned back to us. "We may not be of much help. Can't rightly say we . . . pay much attention to the goings-on in the tower." He gestured expansively around himself. "We, well, we don't get out much."

It seemed as if Tharval's plan had run into something of a snag already.

· Chapter Forty-Nine ·

Stop, Drop, and Shop

I can't believe it," Willowbud said. Then he frowned. "Actually, I take it back, I can believe it quite easily."

Tharval huffed mightily. "Now, don't get uppity with me, elf," he said.

"Pointing out your mistakes doesn't make me uppity," Willowbud said. "Now, if you *want* me to be uppity, I can show you what that's like, and trust me, neither of us will forget that experience."

I raised my hand. "Let's not fight, please," I said. "Um, I don't know why you're being angry with Mister Tharval, Mister Willowbud."

Willowbud straightened. "I'm not angry, Miss Bunch, merely . . . exasperated. Tharval seems to have brought us down here under false pretenses. He didn't bring you here because you would find help here, but rather to show off whatever he's been tinkering on lately."

"Now don't go slandering my name," Tharval groused. "I didn't . . . well, I didn't *only* bring them down here to see this stuff! I really thought we could get some help from these tinkerers!"

"Hey, don't go blaming us for your inability to think things through," chided one of the aforementioned tinkerers.

Tharval huffed, hands on his hips. "It was just a slipup, I ain't gone senile yet."

"True." Willowbud nodded. "You've been slipping up as long as I've known you. It has nothing to do with age."

The dwarf rolled his eyes.

Willowbud nodded again. "Well, I suppose we can afford to lose some time inspecting whatever greasy thing you've put together now."

Tharval chuckled. "There's always time for that!"

And so we were given a tour of the shop. Tharval pointed to all sorts of neat gizmos and inventions, many of which turned out to not work as intended or to be wildly impractical, but he seemed no less proud of those.

"Invention is about discovering things that work, and part of that is discovering what *doesn't*," Tharval proclaimed.

Soon, he and Awen became enmeshed in an increasingly complex and technical discussion that I tried to follow but soon lost track of. It was clear that while Awen was holding her own, the old dwarf's own knowledge dwarfed hers.

I had to hold back an inappropriate spout of giggles as I realized the pun I'd just thought up.

The tinkerers, of course, returned to their tinkering, and I suspected that they were working with some extra pep since their sorta-boss was right there in the room with them.

Eventually the tour ended, and we were all left near the elevators while Tharval looked a little contrite. "So, Bud, how are we gonna find that baron for these brats, hmm?"

Willowbud looked unamused. "*You* are the brat here," he said. "Now . . . ah, no, this isn't so simple a thing that I can just snap my fingers and fix it. The guild might be able to assist, though. We have a number of people with . . . certain talents when it comes to the gathering of information."

I gasped. "Spies?" I asked.

"I think they'd usually rather avoid that label," he replied.

"But it's so cool!" I said.

"Regardless," he said after a moment. "How about you all come back to the guild tomorrow . . . Actually, how long have you been searching through the Storm Tower for the baron?"

"We only arrived a few hours ago," Amaryllis said. "We parked our ship at the dock, then after registering it we came to the guild."

Willowbud nodded. "Then take some time for yourselves. You'll need to eat soon, I imagine. And the Storm Tower has some of the best shopping around. Part of being a good explorer is developing a love for exploration, and that's something you can cultivate even in a civilized place like this tower."

"Don't know that I'd call it civilized," Tharval said. "But the elf's right. Give us a day, and we'll figure this out, we will. And in the meantime, the tower's got a number of fine smiths and shops. Plenty of adventurous folk around here to keep them busy too."

"I don't recall ever seeing all that many elven or dwarven adventurers," Amaryllis said. "I think I might have noticed some in Port Royal, but otherwise . . ."

"Oh, we'd see some in Greenshade sometimes," Awen said. "Um, usually coming from or heading west?"

Tharval nodded. "West's where the adventuring's at. Not in Pyrowalk, but past that. And to the south a ways too. There's the north as well, if you're keen on freezing off your extremities for months on end only to discover a new kind of dwarf-eating lizard that they'll name in your honor after you're eaten by one."

"I wouldn't mind shopping," I said. I glanced to my friends, and while there wasn't unanimous cheering and excitement, no one seemed to think it was a bad idea either. "I think we could use some time to refresh some of our equipment, and besides, I think most of us need a bit of new clothes."

My own equipment was . . . not that bad, actually. I'd kept it clean, of course, but at the same time Cleaning magic wasn't Maintenance magic, and I'd noticed a few things getting a little threadbare in spots. The leather straps holding my armor together were looking a bit stretched too, and I suspected that I'd hit a teensy growth spurt lately, because my skirt had climbed almost to my knees!

"Awa, that does sound nice," Awen said. "I've always wanted to explore the Storm Tower. So many interesting devices come from here."

"It wouldn't be a waste of time," Amaryllis agreed. "And we do have a fair amount of gold we can afford to spend, even after taking into account docking fees and the like."

"I've barely got a copper to my name," Calamity said with a grin.

I bumped my shoulder against his. "Don't worry about that! You're due some payment for helping us, and besides, you're our friend, no?"

"Thanks!" he said. "In that case, I need me some new clothes. These are starting to look ratty, especially with the company I've been keeping." He tugged on the front of his shirt which was a little worse for wear. It was clean, of course. Even if he didn't seem to put much effort into cleaning it, he was still in my proximity often enough that my Cleaning aura probably scrubbed away any sweat stains, but that aura didn't do anything for the holes in the fabric or the bits that were stretched.

I looked to Caprica, who shrugged. "I'll come along," she said. "Though I don't think I need much, and I don't know if they'll have anything for sylphs."

"You're also poor," Amaryllis said. Her lips were a thin line, but I knew she was holding back a smile from the way the corners of her eyes turned up.

"Poor?" Caprica asked. Then she blinked. "Oh."

Had she brought any gold with her when she snuck onboard the *Beaver*? I couldn't recall. That might be a shock to the system, going from being a princess of a really rich place to a poor girl who had to sneak onboard ships.

I gave her a hug, of course.

"Why are you hugging me?" she asked, though she didn't make any move to remove me.

"Poor person hug of solidarity," I said.

"Broccoli, *you're* not poor. You're the captain of an airship with more gold on board than some entire villages have," Amaryllis said.

"Oh," I said. "Well, ah, we should go?" I said as I tried not to feel so awkward. Caprica was giving Amaryllis a *look* and I chose not to get between them. I figured they actually liked each other, but in that sort of friendly-rival way that included lots of little digs and veiled half insults.

Not my favorite flavor of friendship, but I'd take it!

Tharval and Willowbud bid us a nice day, and Willowbud told us to show up at the guild again the next morning. Then the five of us shuffled into the elevator and rode back up to the guild's lobby.

The nice reception elf pointed us toward the shopping center, which happened to not be all that far from the guild. It was just on the other side of the interior train station, which did require that we leave the guild, go down a floor, then come back up one on the other side.

The interior of the Storm Tower was essentially a maze of warrens, alleys, little side-passages, stairwells, and then the occasional cavernous room. It wasn't organized in any way that I could decipher, and no one had bothered putting up helpful maps for lost tourists.

Basically, it was a great place for exploring and adventuring because it was so easy to get lost in!

Of course, since we were looking for something specific and not for a fun adventure, I ended up asking some nice locals for directions . . . several times.

We found the shopping area eventually. An endless row of stores and shops, all squeezed in next to each other on one side of a long corridor. On the other side were benches and thick windows looking out toward the industrial area and the cliffs below the tower.

"Oh, where do we start?" I asked as I spun around. "Should we do every place in order? Or run around back and forth, or just ask around and go exactly where we need to? Do you think they have ice cream?"

"Let's do things in order," Amaryllis said. "That seems like the simplest way to go about things. And the best way to keep us from getting separated and lost."

I clapped my hands. "Right! If anyone gets separated then, uh . . . let's all meet up at that place right there." I pointed.

"The food stand?" Amaryllis asked.

"Yeah, that way you won't go hungry while waiting," I said. It looked like they were selling sausages and beer, which felt a little strange for a food stand to sell, but it *was* run by a dwarf.

The first shop right on the corner was a discount and used armor store. It was called *Half-Elf's Half-Off Emporium*, and it was filled from front to back with mannequins along the walls, each wearing full or partial sets of armor.

The place had so much stuff and so little room that my friends and I basically filled the shop to capacity.

It was fun, though. We poked at various armors (most were for elves, unsurprisingly) and got into a giggle fit when we discovered some sets had very pronounced codpieces.

Nothing looked like it would fit any of us, since elves had very long legs and tall chests in general, though a few pieces looked more human-sized. The proprietor was a younger gentleman, a bit shorter than I was and quite stocky, but with the long ears I'd expect from elves and very fine features, including a nice pointy chin.

I got to talking to him and he said that there was a growing population of half-elf half-dwarves in the Storm Tower. For all that the two races had some pretty big cultural differences, it didn't mean that love couldn't flourish between them.

The next shop was a general store that sold mostly tools and crafting supplies. I would have skipped it, but Awen's eyes lit up when she saw it. Gnome Depot didn't have much that we needed, but Awen still walked out of there with a few bags full of supplies for the *Beaver* and for her own projects.

After Gnome Depot, we ran to a little shop called Arrow Smiths, where the owner, a grumpy dwarf, fussed over Awen and Calamity's bows. He ended up giving Awen's the thumbs-up of approval, but Calamity didn't get off so easily.

"I've had this thing for years," he said.

"Oh, and it's a fantastic piece," the dwarf said. "Clearly handmade, but well done, even if it wasn't made by a true professional. Well-maintained too."

"Well, I made it myself," Calamity said a little sheepishly.

"Oh-hoh. Well, you did all right. I imagine you're not a professional, though. We have bows here that'll improve your aim tenfold and will have each arrow hitting like a lightning bolt!" He started to show off his wares and it didn't take long for Calamity to be won over by the idea of something shiny and new.

We ended up spending a few gold coins on a much nicer bow, one with a wheel and cam system that was made of metal and wood and seemed a whole lot more complicated to use and maintain, but Awen said that she wouldn't mind helping Calamity figure it out.

Grinning, we left the shop and continued on our rather expensive outing!

· Chapter Fifty ·

Facial Hare

Huh," I said.

"Huh," Awen agreed.

"Hmm?" Caprica asked.

"Are you all really just going to stand there and stare?" Amaryllis asked. She fluttered a wing toward the shop. "There's nothing stopping you from going in."

"Yeah, but it's *weird*, isn't it?" Calamity asked.

The shop in question was right next to Arrow Smiths. It was a smaller shop, with two big windows sandwiching a doorway. The shop's name was above that, written on a simple, discreet plaque: *Substitute Stubble, Prosthetics & Artificial Replacements*.

Through the windows we could make out mannequins. Some had wooden or metallic arms and legs, fitted for both dwarves and elves, but most of the mannequins were just wooden heads on little stands. And all of them had fake beards.

"Well, I wanna check it out," I said before I boldly stepped up and into the shop. A bell jingled above the doorway, and I was hit with a weird mix of smells, a combination of oils and shampoos. It reminded me a little of the barber shops I'd sometimes visited back on Earth when my dad needed a haircut.

The shop was divided into two sections. A small area to one side sold bodily prosthetics of various makes and models, and a few signs promised yearlong guarantees, free adjustments, and a bonus can of oil with every purchase of a magitech arm-clamp or buzzsaw hand.

The rest of the shop was all about the fake beards. There were long ones, short ones, beards split into thirds, and partial fake beards, as well as beard extensions, goatees, muttonchops, and beards that were shaped in all sorts of fanciful ways.

"Hello, sir," someone said from the front. An older dwarf stepped out from behind a counter. He had an apron that fell to his knees and a pointy-sharp beard with beads around the moustache. Also, one of his legs clacked and was very obviously artificial. "How can I help you?"

"Ah, I was just looking," I said.

"Oh, no need to be shy," he said as he adjusted a pair of spectacles. "I see that hairless chin of yours and the envy in your eyes. You, good sir, are in want of a magnificent beard!"

"Uh. I guess?" I said. They *were* pretty magnificent.

"Fantastic. Now, I'm curious, and if the memory pains you too much, then feel free to tell me to shut my old gullet up, but how did you lose your beard?" He squinted at my face, and I had the impression he was really inspecting my cheeks and chin.

"Ah, well, I never had one to begin with," I said.

"Hmm," he said. Then he shook his head. "Shame."

"Well, I was a human girl, and we don't usually have beards. Uh. Now I'm a bun girl, and I haven't seen one of those with a beard either."

He blinked. "Oh. You're a woman. My apologies, miss, for misgendering ya. It's hard to tell, you see."

"It's fine," I said with a little wave. "Um, are any of these beards . . . girl beards?"

"Hmm? Why, yes, obviously," he said. "Nearly half of them. The ladies have beard-related accidents just as often as the men do, of course."

"Right, of course," I said, despite not seeing any difference between the beards. Presumably there was some cultural or perceptual thing I wasn't picking up on, or maybe couldn't pick up on. "What's the most common beard-related accident?" I asked while my friends filed into the shop.

"Oh, getting caught in gears is common enough. Burns happen too. Usually that'll just clip a bit off the end, though. A shame, but nothing too unusual. Something for your friends to rib you about, but it happens to the best of us. Now, these prosthetics are for more serious injuries to the beard. The poor souls who go through something harrowing and awful and who come out of it bereft of their whiskers and facial hair." He frowned and shook his head. "I do what I can to help, having been there once myself." Then he stroked his own magnificent beard.

"Wow, that's really kind of you," I said. "Is this the only, ah, prosthetic beard shop around?"

"Hmm? Only the finest! There are a few others, but none as spectacular or with such a fine quality of faux-beards as you'll find here. Now . . . are these your companions, miss?"

"Ah, yup!" I said. "They're here to help me shop for a beard . . . Uh, unless you guys want a beard of your own?"

Awen giggled and shook her head. Amaryllis looked unimpressed, and Caprica was visibly confused at the very idea. Calamity though, stepped up. "Hey, can you make moustaches?"

"A moustache? Of course, miss."

"Ah, no, I'm a . . . never mind," Calamity said with a sigh. "Yeah, a nice moustache would do."

"You can't grow your own?" I asked him.

He shrugged. "Not really. But I always wanted one. Maybe one that matches my ears?" He wiggled his cat ears and the old dwarf squinted up at them.

"Hmm, might have something that fits. The miss first, though!" He turned his attention back onto me. "Now, what kind of beard are you looking for? One for special occasions? A worker's beard?"

"Ah, I don't know much about beard culture. What do you think would be best?" I asked.

"Well, something to bring out your femininity, of course. Maybe something simple and traditional. Just a few braids and maybe a bead or two. Nothing less than a foot, though. Now, a proper beard reaches down to the belly button, of course, but on taller folk that sometimes looks a mite strange. Maybe . . . hmm."

He mumbled to himself as he limped between the stands and shelves of beards, then he returned with a few samples.

Grinning, I followed him over to a seat at the back with a large mirror before it. The dwarf had me try on a couple of beards real quick, but he whipped them away almost as soon as they were on. Finally, after a dozen, he held one against my face and nodded. "Not a bad option, don't you think?"

The beard was just long enough to reach my upper chest, with a pointy middle and a few simple braids along the sides. The moustache was properly thick, with something for me to grab and curl on the edges. It was also the same shade of brown as my hair.

"We can get some beads to match your eyes. You'll have every beau from here to Sissifin complimenting your whiskers."

"I'll take it!" I said.

The beard was held in place by a set of discreet straps that ran around and over my head and were thin enough to be hidden by my hair. In the end, the beard looked perfectly natural and hung on without any painful tugging.

Broccoli's Beard

New Skill Acquired: Tinkering Proficiency

Rank: D

Oh! A skill! I didn't know that Mad Millinery could work on wearing a beard, of all things. Beards weren't hats, were they? Though I supposed they were technically headwear? I needed to see if sunglasses would give me a skill too, though something told me it wouldn't work that way, exactly. "Hey, I got a Tinkering Proficiency skill from the beard," I said.

"Oho, you have a gear-based skill? That's uncommon enough. And yes, obviously beards make you a better tinkerer."

Now Awen was looking at my beard with an indecipherable expression on.

"Did you want one?" I asked her.

She hesitated, then shook her head. "No, it's okay," she said.

Once I was bearded up, I stood aside while the old dwarf helped Calamity find a suitable moustache. He ended up with a big bushy thing that sat like a hairy caterpillar on his upper lip. It looked a bit silly, but it also gave Calamity the air of an outdoorsman.

We paid for the dwarf's services and the facial hair, then headed out to explore the rest of the shops.

"It's going to be tricky, eating with this thing," I said as I stroked my beard. Of course, I was starting to think about food. We were shopping, and grabbing something unhealthy to eat was part of the shopping experience.

But, since there wasn't a place to sit down and eat at just yet, we continued to window-shop for a bit. I tried not to tug at my beard while we walked around, which was surprisingly hard.

We ended up in another clothes store where we perused all of the things they had, but for the most part they were either way too big or way too small for any of us. I did end up buying a few pairs of knit socks that looked very comfy.

I had a weakness for fluffy socks.

Then we ran into a little novelty store. They had cameras, and a setup that allowed them to develop photos in an hour. Pinned to the walls were all sorts of photos of dour-looking dwarves and serious elves, all in those sorts of shades of brown and black.

We filed in, and an excited elf explained photography for us. Or rather, for my friends. I was familiar with the idea already, even if the way he described it made it seem novel and new.

In the end, we all settled into a spot at the back of the shop, squeezing in tightly so that all of us could fit into the frame. Then we ignored the nice elf's advice to look serious and smiled big and bright as the camera went off.

He took a few pictures, just in case, and we paid up before heading off. Given that it would take an hour to develop the pictures, we had some time to eat!

We found a coffee shop a little ways off, but there was a huge line leading up to it, so we continued until we found a restaurant that was run by a tall, wiry man of dark complexion. It took me a moment to realize that he was an ostri, of all things. They were selling ostri specialties from the Ostri desert, which Awen was pretty excited for.

"Their food tastes great," she said. "Just, ah, the names are strange."

The restaurant's name was interesting too. *Come Here to Eat Ostri Food.* It . . . Well, it certainly told anyone passing by what to expect. We ended up sitting at a round table, with some chairs stolen from nearby.

I had *cactus leaves with hurty weed sauce*, which was surprisingly spicy, but also flavorful, and the others had a mix of things, from *spicy bird cooked over fire* to *flatbread with meat and burning sauce.*

Once we were appropriately stuffed, it took some serious effort and will-power to get up and waddle out of the restaurant. I also discovered that eating with a beard was probably a challenge for people who didn't have Cleaning magic. The fine hairs caught on every non-solid food and I ended up with half my meal tucked away in my moustache instead of in my tummy.

I sniffed out a bakery on our way back to the photo shop, and as it turned out, there was a teeny tiny bit of room in me to squeeze in some cake along with a hot citrusy tea-like drink.

By the time we returned to the photo shop, all five of us were groaning with effort and our bellies were bulging from all the food we'd stuffed our-selves with, but it was worth it!

We each got a copy of our new team photo, and I carefully slid mine into a pocket. It would, I suspected, make for a nice memory in the distant future. A way to look back and show our respective kids how much fun we'd had and who our friends were.

I was looking forward to that future, but more so, I was looking forward to the now, when we were still having all that fun.

"Oh, look, they sell flowers over there," Caprica said. "Do you think I could get something for Gabrielle?"

"Let's go see!"

<h1 style="text-align:center">· Chapter Fifty-One ·</h1>

<h2 style="text-align:center">Dress-Up Games</h2>

I noticed Awen was fixated on her copy of our team photo as we walked along. She was staring at the image, her expression something I couldn't quite read while her thumb ran up and down the edge, careful not to rub against any of the smiling faces on the photograph.

"Are you okay?" I asked, voice pitched low so that I wouldn't disturb the others.

Caprica, Amaryllis, and Calamity were in the middle of a spirited argument about whether or not eating rodents was okay. Calamity and—surprisingly—Caprica both seemed to agree that the occasional mouse was a fine snack, while Amaryllis disagreed quite sternly.

Awen looked up, then her expression changed, becoming a shy little smile. "Yeah," she said.

"Are you sure?" I asked. I only had to move my arms up a tiny bit for her to walk right into a hug. "You looked . . . I don't know."

Awen booped her head against my shoulder, and soon we had to break apart the hug because walking-hugs were an advanced-level hug tactic and it wasn't easy to keep up. "It's okay. I was just . . . this is a really nice painting."

"Photograph," I corrected softly. "And yeah, it is! We're all real smiley. Did you see the expression on the elf's face when we didn't just stand there all gloomy and dour?"

"My cheeks still hurt from holding the smile," Awen admitted.

"Ah, but it was worth it, yeah?"

She bobbed her head in a nod. "Yes. A lot of things have been worth it lately." She looked at the photo one last time, then carefully tucked it into the envelope it came in and placed it in her bag. When she looked back my way, there wasn't any shyness in her smile. "Thanks, Broccoli."

"Huh?"

"Awa, guys, I don't think we'll find any mice to eat here, um, so maybe it doesn't matter?" Awen said as she walked around me and toward our other friends, putting an end to their argument as she did so.

Not to be left out, I skipped over to my friends and grabbed the nearest two—which happened to be Amaryllis and Calamity—from behind for a quick hug. "Yeah! If we find any mice then we'll see what they taste like, okay? Unless they're cute talking mice. Those we'll make friends with."

"Emergency ration friends?" Calamity asked. He licked his lips.

"No," I said chastisingly. "Friends don't eat friends."

"Says you," he shot back. "Bunnies are part of a cat's diet, you know. Roasted on an open flame, maybe with some spices. Tasty!"

"We just ate, why are we talking about food again?" Caprica asked.

"Because explorers think with their stomachs," Awen said. "At least, my uncle used to say that a lot of his adventures happened because of his lower brain, so that's what I think he meant." She nodded.

Amaryllis smacked herself in the face with a wing. "World, why," she muttered.

"What?" I asked her.

"Never you mind," she said. "Look, clothes."

I turned, following her pointing talon to a store across the hall from us. It was actually quite large, one of the bigger stores we'd crossed, and the interior was filled with mannequins and racks upon racks of clothes. The sign at the front named the place *Every Body Needs Clothes* and it seemed as if they specialized in clothes for every body type and species. "Oh, let's go!"

"Yes, you and Awen and Caprica and Calamity . . . Wait, all of you except for me need clothes," Amaryllis said. "Why am I surrounded by people who only have one outfit?"

"I have at least two," I said.

"I have a large wardrobe," Caprica said.

"Not on the *Beaver* you don't," Amaryllis said. "And Broccoli, one set of adventuring clothes and one nice suit for special events doesn't count as a full wardrobe."

I shrugged. "You don't need to convince me! Come on, I wanna play dress-up with unlimited funds!"

"Unlimited—Broccoli, don't waste all of our money on pretty clothes. No more than a dozen gold each. Ten, even!" Amaryllis said as she ran after me.

Her budget turned out to be really generous, though. Most clothes here only cost a few coppers, with the much nicer things priced in silver. The Stormtower economy must have been booming if all of its stuff was priced so cheap. Or something like that. I wasn't an economist. In fact, at the moment, I was the opposite: a consumer.

"Who do we shop for first?" I asked.

"Calamity needs it most," Caprica said. "He looks like a ruffian."

"But I *want* to look like a ruffian," Calamity said.

"In that case, you've succeeded in a spectacular way," she said.

I clapped my hands. "Ruffian chic!"

"That's not a thing, Broccoli," Amaryllis said.

"It could be," Awen suggested.

We ended up scrounging for all sorts of things across the store, with more and more clothes piling up onto Calamity's outstretched arms until we could barely see the tips of his ears over the heap.

Then we shoved Calamity into some changing booths and giggled while he cursed and stumbled around inside. He came out with various outfits, all of which we nixed, denied, or agreed with him that they just didn't suit him. Formal didn't work on Calamity. Putting him in a nice suit left him looking like someone playing dress up in their dad's clothes, and he didn't look comfortable.

In the end though, he found something that he liked.

"You can't wear a vest *and* a sleeveless leather jacket," Caprica said.

"Why not?" Amaryllis asked. "It leaves his wings . . . arms, free."

"Yeah, check out my cannons!" Calamity brought his arms up and flexed. He did have rather bulgy muscles on his upper arms. Probably from using a bow so much; that had to require a lot of upper body strength.

His new outfit was fairly simple, but clean: a short-sleeve button-up shirt with a little blue tie around the neck and a black vest over the shirt. And atop all of that, a beige leather coat, also without sleeves.

He finished the look with a pair of white pants made of a tough, denim-like material, and topped it all off with a white cowboy hat—with ear holes.

If it wasn't for my Cleaning, I might have suggested that he forgo wearing so much white.

"I think it suits you," I said.

"I'm liking it," he replied as he adjusted his hat.

So that was that. Somehow, without needing to communicate it, all of our attention turned toward Caprica, who blinked and suddenly had the kind of expression I'd expect from a bunny that tripped out of a bush and into a wolf pack. "What?" she asked.

In the end she was pushed into the changing room with another small mountain of clothes. It was only a small mountain because there weren't that many things sized for a sylph, otherwise we might have been there all day.

We pushed Caprica a little bit out of her comfort zone, her comfort zone being things in smart military cuts with stiff shoulders. We were looking for something casual, not something that could pass as a commander's outfit.

Still, Caprica had her tastes, and she settled on a simple outfit. Pants—"You don't wear skirts when you intend to *fly* anywhere"—that were on the tighter side, some slip-on shoes, and a nice blouse under a button-up cardigan. With the sleeves rolled up, she could pass for an off-duty librarian instead of an off-duty princess-commander.

It was cute!

"Who's next?" I asked.

"Awa," Awen awa-ed, and so she was picked to be next. We did the same thing, pulling her across the store and showing her all sorts of outfits. It was easy to shop for Awen. If something was too much, her face would go red, and if she liked it she would give a little nod.

In the end, we pushed her into the changing room with only a few items. She stepped out of it wearing a blue dress and a nice leather jacket. The only problem was . . .

"Wow," Amaryllis said. "That's . . . a very short skirt and a lot of leg."

"Ah," Awen said. She tugged the hem down, which didn't do much.

"If you want, we can go back to that picture place. Send Rose something to remember you by," Amaryllis teased.

Awen spun and ran back into the changing room and only came out ten minutes later, her blush significantly less incandescent. She had a nice, rather modest dress on, though she'd kept the jacket. It had pockets, after all.

"Okay! Amaryllis next!" I said.

"Why not you next?" she asked.

"Because you were too slow," I replied before grabbing her by the talon and pulling her back into the racks. Amaryllis, as it turned out, had a very particular idea of what "casual" meant, and I ended up having to jog after her as she flitted around the store and tossed clothes back for me to catch.

I didn't know that one of my best friends was such an avid shopper, but here we were, with a heap for Amaryllis to pick through and discard. She ended up only going into the changing room with one or two items.

When she stepped out she was wearing a white . . . shirt-thing. It wasn't an item of clothing I'd ever seen on earth before. It had short sleeves on the inside, but a long, shawl-like piece of cloth came out from around the collar and swept down over the wings.

She was also wearing a tracksuit.

There was no mistaking it. Her pants—white, the same as her strange shirt—had stripes on the side and were tucked into a pair of large, talon-accommodating shoes.

She looked surprisingly modern, actually. "Well?" she asked.

I nodded and gave her a thumbs-up. I was going to tell her she looked cute, but she probably wouldn't appreciate that. "You're very attractive."

"Moron," she said before pouting off.

"My turn!" I cheered.

My friends seemed to make a point of dragging me all over the store, deliberately suggesting the most absurd outfits they could, but the joke was on them. I loved spending time with them, even if it meant playing the part of a doll.

"Broccoli, I want to show you something," Amaryllis said. Next to her, Caprica was nodding seriously. Then unfolded a pair of pants. "These, my dear Broccoli, are pants."

"Uh," I said.

"They're very practical," Caprica went on. "See, they're like two skirts, but together."

"I know what pants are?" I tried.

Amaryllis huffed a sort of *I don't believe you* huff. "We'll see about that."

I was shoved into the changing room with a lot of outfits, and then I spent the next while trying things on and stepping out to see what worked and what didn't. Of course, my friends made me take my beard off after the first outfit, but I vowed to put it back on after! Some of the stuff was . . . not as modest as I was used to, and after stepping out with a shirt that exposed my tummy and rather tight shorts, I found that Awen was having a hard time breathing. She was also covering Calamity's face with her arm.

Amaryllis pushed me back into the changing room, and I looked over everything until I found something I thought would be comfy. A nice teal sweater with some vertical lines, a clean button-up shirt, and some pants with flared legs. They reminded me a little of my mom's bell bottoms.

"Oh, that works," Amaryllis said as I stepped out.

Caprica nodded. "Very comfortable."

I grinned. "Then I'll take it!" I said.

I insisted that we take some time to put everything away while also tossing around a bit of Cleaning magic, just because it seemed like the nice thing to do. It paid off in the end when the cashier gave us a little discount.

And so, with more comfy clothes on, we headed out . . . probably to find even more food to eat.

· Chapter Fifty-Two ·

Late to Bed and Late to Rise

We ended up waking up late.

I don't know why, but after coming back to the *Beaver* after a whole day spent shopping, all of us loaded down with bags and bags of stuff, the tiredness walking about had just . . . evaporated, and it had been replaced by a sort of manic energy that had the bunch of us throwing an impromptu party.

Not a very loud one. Though there was music! Clive had a harmonica, and the Scallywags had fashioned some drums out of bits and bobs laying around. As it turned out, that was about all we needed to get a sing-off of sorts going.

Awen even ended up coming out of her shell a little to, as she put it, "put a few years of singing practice to use."

Caprica also had a rather pretty voice, but all the songs she knew were about how grand and mighty the sylphs were, which was kinda funny, but not as funny as the songs Abraham had taught Awen about adventurers and getting into trouble.

There wasn't just singing, of course. We also discovered some late-night stalls in the megadock that sold bitter dwarven food, and Calamity and the harpy boys went out and returned with a little keg of strong dwarven ale that got shared around.

By the time we all flopped onto bed it was well past midnight, so I wasn't too surprised when I woke up just shy of noon feeling a bit creaky and dehydrated.

I stumbled out of bed, got undressed from the night before, then redressed in my new comfy clothes before making my way to the dining room.

"You look like your egg was left out in the sun too long," Amaryllis said from the dining room table. She was twisting a spoon in a bowl of gray goop. "I made oatmeal. Enough for . . . well, everyone, I suppose." She gestured to a big pot nearby that was filled near to the rim with oatmeal.

"Huh," I said. "Did you forget the oatmeal expands when it cooks?" I asked.

She didn't deign to answer me, instead choosing to take another mouthful.

"Thanks for the breakfast," I said as I served myself a bowl. It was a little bland, especially compared to all the savory and bitter things I'd eaten the night before, but maybe that was for the best. It would help settle my tummy.

Could have been improved with some maple syrup, but I chose not to complain.

"So, what're we doing today?" I asked.

"Not shopping again, that's for sure," Amaryllis said. "We might have a surprisingly full coffer of gold from all that work we did for Sylphfree, but we still made a dent in our reserves spending the way we did."

"Will we be okay?" I asked.

She waved the concern away. "I'll let you know when we need to tighten the belt. Truth is, we made nearly enough working for Sylphfree to buy an entire airship, crew and all. What we have right now should keep us going for a year or more if we're careful."

"Oh, that's good to hear!"

"Only if we're careful," she repeated. "If we keep spending gold like we did last night, that year's going to be shortened to a month."

I laughed. "We'll be a little more discreet, then! Besides, if we want more, it feels like adventuring and exploring's been pretty good money so far."

"Only because we picked up some . . . strange missions. Don't go thinking most explorers get into the kind of trouble we do," Amaryllis said.

I shrugged. "Tharval and Willowbud seem like the kind of people that would do fun things too."

"They're exceptions to the rule," she said with a mighty huff. "But, speaking of those two, we should probably visit them and see if Willowbud was able to find any info about Vonowl."

I nodded along and scooped up another spoonful of oatmeal just as Awen zombied her way into the room and collapsed in her usual seat. She didn't move, and I suspected that she had fallen back asleep, so I left her to it. "Do you think all of us should go?" I asked.

"We hardly need five people to pick up a bit of intelligence," Amaryllis conceded. "Maybe just the two of us? It'll give the others a chance to recover." She nodded her head toward Awen, who had started to snore very faintly. It was more of a whistle-y breath than a snore, really.

I licked my bowl clean while Amaryllis gave me a disgusted look, then I cleaned the rest of it off along with my spoon before placing both in front of Awen to use when she finally woke up again.

"All right! Let's head out. I bet we can make it back before the others wake up completely," I said.

Amaryllis snorted, and soon we were climbing up onto the main deck. Surprisingly, that was where we ran into Calamity. "Howdy," he said with a tip of his new hat. "Didn't reckon anyone would be up yet."

"Good morning," I said. "I didn't expect to see you up either. You don't look hungover at all."

He grinned. "I've spent a good part of my life in hunting groups. They might be unwashed and uneducated sorts, but nya never partied harder than with hunters after a big hunt."

"I guess that makes sense. Amaryllis and I were heading over to see Willowbud and Tharval."

"Ah, the old guys? Did nya need me along?"

I thought about it, then shook my head. "How about you stand guard on the Beaver while we're ashore?"

He tipped his hat. "Can do. You two stay safe out there."

I gave him a quick goodbye hug, then hooked one arm with Amaryllis's wing as we moved off the *Beaver* and across one of the movable catwalks of the docks. The space wasn't quite as busy as it had been when we returned the night before, but it was still noisy. The way the massive dock was built meant that every sound echoed through the entire space, so a single hammer's clang would reverberate over and over again across the chasm in the center.

It was even worse now that the ceiling was closed up for the night. I imagined they did that to keep the rain and weather out.

Arm-in-wing, Amaryllis and I left the docks and promptly got lost as we took a turn too early and ended up in part of the Storm Tower we didn't know—admittedly, that part of the Storm Tower would be "most of it." Fortunately, some helpful elves were kind enough to point us toward the trams, where we hopped aboard and zipped across the complex toward the Exploration Guild headquarters.

We were greeted by the same nice reception elf, who gestured us to the elevator when we asked about Willowbud and Tharval. "Your little group certainly has livened those two up," he said offhandedly.

"Really?" I asked.

"Oh yes. It's nice to see them reliving their best days a little. Although it's also somewhat worrying. I don't recall having seen Willowbud don his armor in nearly half a decade," he said.

"Maybe he was just seeing if it still fit," I suggested.

The receptionist didn't seem to believe that any more than I did. Still, we got in the elevator and rode up to the floor with the lounge. On entering, we discovered Tharval and Willowbud in the middle of an argument. But it seemed like one of those friendly sorts of arguments, the kind that friends rehashed every so often.

Willowbud was, indeed, in armor. It was all steel plates made to look like interlocking leaves with finely etched patterns across the entire surface. The edges were covered in a greenish metal that I suspected was tarnished copper, but it looked purposefully done. Every gesture moved pieces of the armor in and out of each other with a mesmerizing degree of articulation.

"Hi!" I said as I came closer. Tharval was also in heavy plate, though he looked like a really old cast-iron fireplace more than anything. "Nice armor, Mister Wintersdawn."

"Thank you," Willowbud said. His tone suggested that he'd just won a point in whatever argument he was having with Tharval. "See? Miss Bunch thinks that my armor is 'nice.'"

"Nice enough for your funeral, more like. Besides, what does she know about armor, huh?" he asked that last one directly to me.

"Um," I said. I wasn't even wearing my armor at the moment. "Not very much, I guess. Are you guys arguing about armor?"

"Tharval here insists that this piece isn't good enough," Willowbud said with a hand pressed to his breastplate. "Even though it has served me quite well over the years and was made by a very close friend."

"Oh. Well, if it has sentimental value, then maybe," I began.

"*I'm* that close friend!" Tharval said. "And I say it's not good enough! You're insulting me and everything I ever built by ambling about in that rusty half-baked mess."

"Um," I said. Now I wasn't sure what to think.

Willowbud sighed and tried to explain. "He's embarrassed, you see."

"I am not! Though you ought to be, wearing that thing."

"Because," Willowbud continued as if Tharval hadn't spoken. "This suit of armor was one of his earlier creations, and he has improved greatly as a smith and artist since. But I still think it's a fine piece, and I hardly need to commission a new one."

"I'll give you a good price, I already said!"

I held back a giggle. "Ah, so it's a bit like . . . you're walking around showing people the equivalent of Tharval's first ever poems and he's embarrassed about them?"

Willowbud ruminated on the analogy for a moment before smiling. "Yes, exactly."

"Oi! It's nothing like that!" Tharval griped.

"I think the armor you made is very pretty," I told Tharval.

He pointed a fat finger at me. "Don't you start, little miss."

I worked hard to hold back my smile, but it wasn't an easy thing to do. "All right, I won't say anything," I said.

"Your pointless argument aside," Amaryllis stepped in, "did you discover anything about Baron Vonowl?"

"A few things," Willowbud said with a nod. "As it turns out, he is, in fact, related to our old companion. Wesley Vonowl was his grand-uncle. After Wesley founded the first Harpy Mountain branch of the Exploration Guild, he went on to marry and essentially retired from the more demanding side of the exploration work. He spent most of his time after that doing administrative tasks."

"That's the *harder* side of things," Tharval muttered. "Give me an unexplored ancient dungeon any day over a stack of unsigned papers."

"Anyway, his family used their ties to the guild to grow somewhat more prominent, from what I gathered. Which is only fair I suppose. The barony came soon after, and the new Vonowl is its head."

"Interesting," Amaryllis said. "Yes, I can see someone using a high rank within the Exploration Guild as a way to propel themselves into lesser nobility. That would make this Baron Vonowl's grasp on his position somewhat tenuous."

"That may be so," Willowbud said. "In any case, I did discover he's staying at the Grand Mami Hotel."

Right, that's what the clerk had said. He waited expectantly, but Amaryllis and I only gave him a blank stare.

". . . It's one of the smaller towers sticking out of the main Storm Tower complex. Though its tower is mostly for show and for when diplomats arrive aboard private shuttles. Most of the hotel is within the complex."

"Bah, they don't care about that. They care about catching this moron," Tharval said. He punched his hands together, knuckles striking with a clang. "We're gonna catch him and string him up by his toes."

"I don't even know if harpies *have* toes," Willowbud said.

"But you do! Maybe I ought to string yours up instead, huh?"

I had the impression that working with these two was going to be an experience.

· Chapter Fifty-Three ·

Abomination Against Engineering
and Good Sense

So should we just visit the hotel then?" I asked.

"Without the others?" Amaryllis replied. "That seems needlessly risky."

I nodded. "You're right, it's more fun with friends."

Amaryllis didn't even react. I guess she was used to my views on friendship by now. "Of course," she said, turning to the old guys, "I'm assuming from the way you two are geared up that you intended to come?"

Tharval snorted. "What, you came here begging for our help, you know? Think we'd just let you walk into the lion's den on your own? Bah! You folk are so green it hurts to see. I can't imagine any of you making it out of a fight with your heads still connected to your shoulders."

"But my head's more connected to my neck than my shoulders," I said.

"I don't think we came here begging for help, as you so eloquently put it," Amaryllis said, a bit tetchy. "We came here asking for some basic assistance. Besides, we're not useless in a fight. All of us are in our second tier."

Tharval sniffed. "That's the bare minimum to become . . . not even an explorer. More like the person who carries the explorer's bags."

"Now, don't be that way. We both know that different guilds have different entry requirements. Not all of them are as rigorous as the Stormtower and Snowlander Exploration Guilds."

"Is it hard to become a member here?" I asked.

"Most are in their third tier, and if they are not, then there's a yearlong training course that we usually insist upon," Willowbud said. "It takes prospective members to a couple of local dungeons whose difficulties are easy to manage so that new members can learn the ropes, so to speak."

"Hmph, maybe the other guilds have the right idea to it. Take raw recruits and toss them into the smelter. If they don't melt right away then they might be worth forging into something usable. I dare say half the new members we get are a bunch of flower-sniffing morons who don't know their boot from their ar—"

Willowbud patted Tharval on the head. "That's quite enough. I'm sure Amaryllis, Broccoli, and their friends aren't that sort. They made it all the way here, didn't they?"

"Hmph. Get your hand off my head, you—"

I clapped my hands, both to distract them from the oncoming scuffle that I felt was about to start, and because I was a little excited. "You can come and see the *Beaver Cleaver*! That's our airship. He's the best ship that's ever flown!"

"He?" Tharval asked. "Ships are meant to be fine ladies."

"Well, I think the *Beaver*'s a he," I said. "But honestly, I don't know how to tell, really. Which bit of the ship gives away its gender?"

"Well, what's the figurehead look like?" he asked.

"Oh, there's two! They're both furry ducks with top hats."

The dwarf didn't seem to know what gender "fur-covered duck" was, so he dropped the subject with a grunt. With that done, we left the guild as a small group, Willowbud taking the lead once we were out of the guild proper with Tharval trotting along with the two of us.

"So, I noticed that you don't wear any proper armor," he said to Amaryllis.

"I'm the team's mage," she replied. "And I'm a harpy besides. Armor weighs us down."

"You can't be the team mage if someone pokes a few holes through your gut," Tharval said. "Now, what you need is some proper plate and to give up on all that silly flying business. If you were meant to fly under your own power you'd manage it just fine, but seeing as you can't, then you might as well strap on a few thumb-thick steel plates."

Tharval regaled us with the advantages and glories of proper plate armor while trampling over Amaryllis's objections and ignoring any cultural misapprehensions she might have about it. It was a little rude, but also kind of funny to see Amaryllis trying and failing to get a word in edgewise. Her huffs grew increasingly huffy as we went.

Eventually we reached the docks, and in far less time than it had taken us to get to the guild. Willowbud knew all the shortcuts, it seemed. Once we arrived, we circled around the edge of the tower, and Tharval finally changed tracks.

"Now, this place took twenty years to build, you know! Had to grab steel from seven different mines and stone from two quarries. It wasn't just getting the materials here that was hard, though. We needed to invent entirely new ways of building things just to get this place started. Not to mention all the stigma of building a place like this."

"Stigma?" I repeated. "People didn't want to build the tower?"

Willowbud fielded that question. "Our nation, young as it is, is rather divided in some ways. The elven people are used to living aboveground in large, open communities, but the dwarven folk escaped the cold of the north by making their homes below the earth. There were, and still are, entire groups that don't like leaving their underground fortresses."

"Most have reconsidered things," Tharval said. "The Storm Tower's the shining jewel of the Snowlands. It's hard not to want to be close enough to appreciate its luster. Besides, you don't think a building this grand could be built without reinforcing the ground beneath, do you? There's nearly as much tower underground as there is above."

"Whoa," I said. "How big is it, really? Because this place is huge already. It might be the biggest dock I've ever seen."

"Hmm, no, the docks back home are larger. Or some of them are," Amaryllis said. "But none of them are enclosed. The best we have are airship ports tucked away in crags and between mountains. Even the shipyards tend to be partially open." She gestured over the side of the nearest guardrail to the depths at the bottom of the tower. "It looks like you have entire factories here."

"Just for assembling," Tharval said. "Most of the proper manufacturing is done by the coast and brought over by train. Then the shipwrights put things together down there."

"You know, for some reason, I never expected to see dwarves on airships," I said.

Tharval chuckled. "Oh, we're awful at flying!" he said, seemingly quite proud of the fact.

"I wouldn't say awful," Willowbud said. "Dwarves hold the records for longest flights, highest heights reached, and even the records for fastest flight."

"May Roberry the Rocket rest in peace," Tharval said solemnly.

"Dwarves are hardy folk," Willowbud continued. "Tough and surprisingly nimble, and of course generally quite mechanically inclined. But, ah, we elves have certain biological advantages."

"Tall bastards," Tharval grunted. "Sneaky and quick too."

"We are more dexterous, as a rule, and perhaps better suited to the work of piloting modern airships," Willowbud said. "Most Snowlander craft have mixed crews, though, taking advantage of both races' natural advantages."

"Oh, that's clever," I said. "But, ah, I don't recall seeing many Snowlander ships about. And people say that the Snowlanders are a little isolationist."

Willowbud considered that, then nodded. "That's probably not wrong. As a rule, we've been focused on building a better World for ourselves, creating ways to be more impervious to the cold, and more recently there's been a great push toward discovering new machines and contraptions."

"Lots of pride to be found if you're the first to invent some new thingy-whatsit," Tharval said. "Especially if it actually has a use of some sort. Now, which one of these tugs is your ship?"

I squinted across the docks, then pointed. "That one!" I said. It was still on the fifth level where we'd left it. I could see tiny forms on the deck, some of the Scallywags, maybe? It was hard to tell from so far away.

Tharval peered at the *Beaver* then back to me and Amaryllis. "What in the World is that?"

"Uh, our ship?" I said.

"It's got too many hulls!" he said.

"I think it's a neat design."

"Let me see this thing from up close," he grumbled before stomping off. We had to jog to keep up; the old dwarf was surprisingly fast when he wanted to be. When we did catch up, he was waiting next to the catwalk leading onto the *Beaver*'s deck. "Well, are you going to give me permission to come aboard and poke at this thing?" he asked.

I laughed. "Sure. Welcome aboard, Tharval, and you too, Willowbud!"

The two stepped onto the *Beaver*, though Tharval didn't linger on the main deck for long. He practically teleported to the rear, staring at the space between the decks and muttering up a storm. He even threw up his arms a couple of times.

Awen walked onto the deck, looked a lot more awake than when we'd left. "Broccoli!" she said. "And Amaryllis."

"Nice to see I'm still mentioned," Amaryllis muttered. Awen blushed, then smiled slightly and hugged Amaryllis first.

"You're my friend," she beamed before turning to me and Willowbud. "Hello, Mister Willowbud," she said with a slight bow.

"Hello, Miss Bristlecone."

"Awa, please just call me Awen? You were Uncle's friend, so I guess that kind of makes you, um . . ."

"A family friend?" I asked.

"I suppose so," Awen said.

Willowbud chuckled warmly. "Why, thank you. I'd gladly consider myself your friend. Ah, but speaking of friends, Tharval might start taking things apart if we don't stop him."

That got Awen to stand up straighter. "He's going to do *what*?"

We found Tharval in the *Beaver*'s engine room, poking at the engine with a wrench that Awen quickly yoinked out of his hands. "Interesting configuration you've got here. Terribly inefficient, but I'll give you points for being different."

"The *Beaver* is a very nice ship," Awen said. "He flies . . . well, and is very comfortable, even if he has a few little deficiencies."

Tharval hmphed. "Well, the engine's much larger than what you'd need if the ship only had one of its two hulls, but probably too small for the twin setup you have. And I can't imagine the bracing between the two being up to spec. There's a bridge between the two halves. A bridge! It's a wonder this thing isn't falling apart under the strain of flight."

"I keep him well maintained," Awen shot back.

Tharval snorted, but he couldn't deny that. The engine itself was covered in a nice layer of oil, but Awen had every tool tucked away in its place and she'd asked me to help her clean it once some time ago, so the engine compartment was basically spotless.

"Awa, did you want to see, ah, my repeating self-loading anti-air emplacement?" Awen asked. "It's illegal in most countries, from what I've been told."

That necessitated a detour to the cargo hold, where Awen's repeating crossbow turret was still folded into the ship. Tharval hemmed and hawed over it, then started pointing to bits and pieces that weren't well made, or parts that could be improved if approached from a different angle or with a different method.

I left them to it while I ran off to fetch Caprica and to see if anyone else wanted to come track down Vonowl with us. I found the princess in her room, dressed in a long blouse that we'd bought the day before and which I supposed could count as a nightshirt.

"Is everyone else awake?" she asked. Caprica looked like she had used every spare minute of rest afforded her, and like she could still use another couple of hours.

"We have been for a bit. Amaryllis and I went to fetch Tharval and Willowbud, and we're going to invade a hotel later!"

"Oh. Well, let me get dressed in something more appropriate for that kind of event, then," she said.

"Okay! Join us on the deck when you're done!"

Calamity was easy to convince. There was trouble around, and he liked the idea of that, I suspected. And so, within a few minutes, the whole bunch of us were ready.

· Chapter Fifty-Four ·

Doorbuster

So, how are we going to do this?" I asked.

"Do what?" Amaryllis asked right back. The bunch of us, plus our new friends Tharval and Willowbud, were ambling along through one of the upper-level corridors of the Storm Tower. The elf and dwarf both seemed to know where they were going, so the rest of us just followed along, even if that meant going up stairs, then down stairs, then across catwalks, then through maintenance passages, and even ducking through the back rooms of a shop at some point—much to the consternation of an employee who wasn't aware that one of their walls could pop out to reveal a secret passage.

It was neat how well the two knew their way around, but I supposed they *had* been around while the tower was built, so they had the home-field advantage.

"I mean, how are we gonna capture Vonowl? Do we barge into the hotel and demand that he surrender? Do we go in all sneaky-like and try to catch him unaware? Maybe we can ask the nice hotel people to help us get him . . . or the police. Does the Storm Tower have police?"

"Not really," Tharval said. "We have guards. They're hired by the tower directly. They might help, but I doubt it. We never get along well with them."

"We might have if you ceased antagonizing them," Willowbud said.

"Bah! They're a bunch of rock-headed fools who sold out for a bit of gold."

"Is that so wrong?" Amaryllis asked.

Tharval nodded. "Of course it is! Sure, you need a bit of gold to keep the belly full and your toes warm at night, but there's more honest ways of doing it. Are they pursuing a dream? Fighting for what they think is right? Nah, just walking around with little sticks and looking tough. Ain't right. Now, a proper explorer? They have *principles*. They're going out there to see what hasn't been seen yet, to discover things. Same for a proper tinkerer. They're making new things, pushing what they know. It's art, and it's a whole lot more valuable than looking tough for a fraction of an ounce of gold every hour."

"Is it so important to have principles?" I asked.

"Don't you have any?" he asked.

I ran my hand through the length of my prosthetic beard as I thought. "I don't know. I just want to make friends, explore the World, and be happy. I don't know if that's complicated enough to be a whole ideology."

"Well, it's the start of one, at least," Tharval mused.

"Don't encourage her," Amaryllis said. "She'll start a religion."

I nodded. "Huggism," I said.

"I think I need to point out that while Sylphfree gives its citizens the freedom to express themselves and have whichever religious beliefs they want, we also firmly believe in the separation of religion, state, and military, and therefore I cannot join you in this particular endeavor," Caprica said.

"But we have hugs!" I said.

"That is a rather tempting offer," she admitted with a serious nod. Then her lips quirked up and I giggled along with her.

"I'd join Huggism," Awen said. "It sounds nice."

"We'd do snuggle hour every day, and eat cookies," I said.

"I'm not sure if you understood what I was trying to say," Tharval said. "But I appreciate your enthusiasm, kid."

I set aside my dreams of becoming a High Priestess of Hugs as we arrived at the hotel. I was expecting it to be a grand place, with big stairs and chandeliers and one of those super long counters, maybe with some elves and dwarves in fancy red uniforms behind it, but instead I found something entirely different. The hotel lobby was relatively small, with rounded walls all around and several plant-filled boxes along the sides.

A small podium sat in the center where a staff member waited, and behind them was a spiral staircase leading up.

"Hello," the reception dwarf said when our group ambled in. "And welcome. How might I help you?"

"Hmph, where's that Vonowl guy?" Tharval grumped.

"What my companion here means to say," Willowbud cut in smoothly, "is that we're looking for Baron Vonowl. We have a meeting with him."

The reception dwarf didn't seem convinced. He glanced over to my friends and I, and I gave him my most disarming smile, which I hoped would distract him from the fact that we were all armed. "Right, well, the good baron is staying in the penthouse suite, but he's not currently in his rooms."

"He isn't?" Willowbud asked.

"No, he left the premises a few hours ago, along with some of his guards," the reception dwarf said.

"Do you know where he went?" I asked. Did we miss him because we stayed up late partying and then slept in? I didn't expect there to be actual consequences to placing fun before work!

"Yes," the dwarf said. He pointed out the door, and we all followed where he was pointing. "He left through there, and took a right."

Those were all the directions he had, which . . . well, it wasn't quite as helpful as I might have hoped, but it was something. "Thanks," I said. Then I looked to the others, hoping for some sort of idea of what to do next.

"I say we ransack his room, figure out where he went, and maybe confiscate anything nice he has," Calamity said low enough that his words didn't carry.

"We can't do that," I said. "It's mean, and a crime, and just . . . not very nice."

"Well, we do need to know where he went, and there might be some hints in his room. I, for one, don't want to spend the afternoon running around this entire tower just for the *chance* of running into Vonowl," Amaryllis said.

I pursed my lips, but she might have been right. Willowbud convinced the receptionist that we were just going to go upstairs to check for Vonowl's staff outside his room—maybe one of his guards or servants had stayed behind and could take a message for us—then we climbed up the spiral stairs to the floors above. As it turned out, each floor above the lobby was split into several small rooms, and the further up we went, there were fewer rooms per floor.

The entire hotel was basically a small tower rising out of the larger Storm Tower complex, and the topmost floors stuck out of it and probably had really nice views.

Baron Vonowl himself was staying in the topmost floor, the penthouse where the entire floor was a single suite. I imagined it was a huge pain in the butt for the staff that had to carry food and stuff all the way up there. My legs were rather warm from climbing up so many steps, and all I was carrying was myself, not a trayful of whatever.

"So," I said as I came to stand before the doors into the penthouse. "Should we knock?"

"Going to try to pass yourself off as a traveling preacher?" Calamity asked.

"I could," I said. "But I think Baron Vonowl might be, uh, what's the word for someone that's not compatible with a religion?"

"A heretic?" Amaryllis asked.

I frowned. "No, in Huggism, we prefer the term 'snugglepunk.'"

"Please stop inventing lore for your dumb idea," Amaryllis begged.

I had to hold in a laugh as I tapped my knuckles against the door. My friends spread out a little, with Willowbud and Tharval staying pretty close by. The dwarf stifled a yawn.

Someone opened the door a crack and a chain pulled taut, keeping it shut while a harpy man looked out. "Is this room service?" he asked. Then he looked over our group and the door started to shut.

I was about to say something when I felt a gust of wind blast past me. When I blinked next, the door was rebounding off the wall, the security chain had exploded into fragments that were skipping along the wood flooring, and the insensate harpy on the other side was gently being lowered by Willowbud while Tharval, now in the penthouse, finished his yawn. "Well, are you kids going to stay outside all day?"

I had kind of forgotten, what with how nice they were, that Tharval and Willowbud were experienced explorers. They hadn't retired from adventuring due to age or injury—they'd quit while they were ahead, at the top of their game. They were bursting with levels, skills, and capital-E Experience.

So, I shouldn't have been surprised that they could simply step outside the realm of physical limits. But I was. My brain couldn't keep up with the information my senses were feeding it. It took an act of will to get my head back in the game.

For better or worse, my friends were equally stunned. Caprica seemed to be handling it best, probably because she had grown up surrounded by paladins who were about as cool.

Calamity jerked forward, seemingly trying to recover his equilibrium. "This guy really likes his luxury stuff," he noted, running a hand along a porcelain vase. The whole place was spacious and richly appointed, with grand windows overlooking the top of the Storm Tower and the World beyond. In a place like the tower, where I imagined most homes were on the smaller side, having lots of open space was probably a great luxury.

Calamity poked at the keys of a piano, producing a few random notes while I checked on the guard that Willowbud had knocked out.

"Bah, nice place," Tharval said as he looked around. "No sign of that fish of a baron though."

The penthouse had a great big entryway, with an open kitchen space to one side, a living room on the other, and what I imagined were bedrooms down a corridor past the living room. Caprica helped me drag the guard to the living room (he still had a pulse, but it looked as if Willowbud had cast a spell of some sort to make him loopy), where we put him on a couch so he could rest for a bit.

"All right," Amaryllis said. "Calamity, check the kitchens, Caprica, come with me to the bedrooms, Awen, Tharval, do you think you two would be able to spot hidden compartments?"

"Ah, maybe?" Awen said.

"Obviously," Tharval replied.

Amaryllis nodded. "Good. Broccoli, keep an eye out on the door. Mister Willowbud, I wouldn't presume to tell you what to do."

"Hey now, but you'd presume for me?" Tharval groused.

"Yes," Amaryllis said without explanation, then she headed off toward the bedrooms, Caprica following after her while hiding a smile.

I grinned at Tharval's harrumph and Willowbud's smug smirk. "Don't forget to look in the bathroom!" I called out, just in case.

I swished Weedbane around a few times while standing next to the closed door in an attempt to limber my muscles in case someone barged in. If I was going to be on guard duty, then I wanted to take it seriously. Mister Willowbud looked at me, amused, but didn't comment on anything.

"Awa, we found something!" Awen said as she returned from the bedrooms.

"There was a hidden compartment?" I asked as I turned.

"Um, no, these papers were just on a desk in the office," Awen said as she waved a stack of papers about.

Amaryllis poked her head out of one of the bedrooms. "Well, what is it?"

Awen looked at the pages, scanning them quickly. "It looks like a contract? For, ah, weapons. Lots of them."

Willowbud walked to Awen and looked at the pages from over her shoulder. "I recognize that company. They're dwarven smiths. Tharval would know more about them, though."

"He's cracking a safe," Awen said.

There was a loud *thunk* from the far end of the penthouse where she'd come from, then a lot of really rude words.

"He might be having a hard time with it," Awen admitted. "But I found this in the meantime, and I thought it might be a hint?"

"Good job, Awen!" I cheered.

"Yeah, nice work!" Calamity said from the kitchen, where he was holding a butter knife covered in jam in one hand and a large slab of bread in the other. I gave him a look, and he shrugged. "I was looking for hints too. And I discovered a hint that I was hungry."

Well, at least we hadn't wrecked the place.

There was another big *thump* from the office and the guard on the couch groaned.

I winced. Maybe if we left discreetly, the hotel wouldn't be too angry with us?

· Chapter Fifty-Five ·

Moral Fiber

We gathered up all the clues we could find, as well as the contents of the baron's safe, and spread them out on the dining room table.

It wasn't much, really. A few dozen papers, including some forms, and neat stacks of gold coins, banknotes, and little ingots with numbers and seals stamped onto them.

"So . . . we're not going to steal the money," I said.

"Why not?" Calamity asked.

"Because stealing is wrong," I explained. He didn't seem entirely convinced, but I felt like Caprica and Amaryllis, at least, were on my side. Willowbud too. Awen seemed ambivalent about it, and Tharval was just as willing to pocket the gold as Calamity was.

"Setting aside the gold for the moment," Amaryllis said. "We need to consider the other things on the table here." She stabbed a talon at one of the pages. "This is the order for weaponry that Awen found, and I, for one, think it's rather concerning."

Tharval tugged the page out from under Amaryllis's grip and squinted at it. "Hrm, I know this group. They've got a shop in the tower, not too far from here. Bunch of money-grubbers with no artistic sense, but they know how to hire good folk and pay them what they're worth. This is an order for four hundred automatic repeating crossbows. That's enough to outfit an army."

"Closer to two battalions of an army," Caprica said. "But those are the kinds of weapons you'd want to keep out of the hands of angry civilians. They're easy to learn how to operate and are difficult to fight against. A strong enough soldier will brush off a bolt and someone like a paladin wouldn't be easy to hit in the first place, but still . . ."

"I wouldn't dismiss these things so easily, missy," Tharval said. "These aren't little sylph bolt throwers. These are proper dwarven bows. They'll punch through rock and fly faster than a lightning bolt."

I hoped he was exaggerating a lot there.

"Four hundred of those is concerning," Awen muttered.

We all nodded.

"I dunno, ny'all. If it was to equip hunters or the like, it wouldn't be that big a deal. It's mostly concerning because of who might be getting them," Calamity said. "Anything we can do about that contract?"

Tharval squinted at it, then grinned. "Well, says here he'll be needing to pay in installments, and they're not cheap. So if we take that there gold, he won't be able to afford a single one, let alone four hundred."

"So what you're saying is that the morally correct thing to do is to take his gold," Calamity said while nodding to himself.

"We're not taking the gold. Stealing is *wrong*," I repeated.

"As wrong as breaking and entering, subduing that guard back on the couch, and . . . well, we stole from his pantry already," Calamity pointed out.

I pouted. He was right, but I still didn't want to push things. Doing one bad thing didn't give you the right to do another, no matter how easy it could be to dance around the logic. "We're not taking it. Please?" I said.

Tharval and Calamity rolled their eyes, proving that they were pretty alike in at least one way. "All right, what else do we have?" Amaryllis asked, changing the subject. She tapped a small pile of pages. "These are the docking forms for Vonowl's ship. It's in a private exterior dock now, which might explain why we never spotted it within the tower."

"Private docks are fairly common, though they're far more expensive than the tower docks. They're the only option for larger ships, and certain well-to-do persons like to keep their ships away from the common airships," Willowbud said.

"And some hobbyists rent out private spots to park their ships in," Tharval added, "so that they can tinker with them in peace. It's a common enough practice. There's airship racing and endurance runs and a number of sports that require a ship, usually a small one that can operate solo or with a minimal crew."

So it was kind of like people who had boats on Earth. There were some people who had lots of money and who bought a yacht, and then some people who just kept a little boat as a sort of very expensive hobby.

Not the kind of hobby my family was into, or that we could afford. Our budget was more suited to gardening and long walks.

"That doesn't seem like very useful information, although maybe we can impound the vehicle before he makes another escape," Caprica said.

"That's a good idea," Amaryllis said. "But there's more. See, he has two other ships that he's paying the docking fees for. Their names are . . . a series of letters and numbers. They're barges. I think Pyrowalkian?"

"Terrible ships," Tharval grumped. "No artistry, mass-produced chaff that's as likely to fly as it is to fall apart around your ears. Cheap, though."

Amaryllis huffed a *we're better than that* kind of huff. She was very proud of harpy-made ships. "Maybe the good baron is running out of funds. Or he just doesn't care about the quality of his ships. In either case, he has two more ships he might use to escape with."

"Give me their names, please," Willowbud said as he tugged out a little notebook from a pouch around the waist of his armor. "I have enough sway, I think, to have the vehicles interdicted before they can leave. Or at least have them be part of a surprise inspection before takeoff."

"Ah, I know a person or two that handles that kind of thing as well," Tharval said. His smile was downright predatory. "We can make sure that the inspection is quite thorough. They'll find *something* that's not up to one of those damnable codes."

"You don't like safety regulations?" Awen asked.

"I like them when they stop others from being morons. I don't like them when they get in the way of my genius," Tharval said.

I suppressed a giggle.

"So, what do we do now? Are there any other hints we can work with?" I asked. Some of the papers hadn't been touched.

"Well, these are letters back to the Harpy Mountains. Some of them are correspondence that might hold a few secrets, I haven't had time to read them all. The rest are letters to family. His mom is worried about him." Amaryllis rolled her eyes, but I thought it was rather sweet.

Even bad guys could have nice moms.

"Maybe we ought to write her ourselves," Calamity said with a grin. "Tell her what her boy's been up to. I mean, sure, we're gonna try to get him arrested and all, but there's nothing like a disappointed parent to put your mood down. Trust me, I'm an expert at that."

"At disappointing your parents? Or feeling down?" Amaryllis asked.

Calamity paused, then shrugged. "Both?"

"As interesting as that idea is," Caprica said, "it seems a little too infantile for my tastes. Perhaps we can come up with a plan to actually deal with Vonowl before we start thinking about adding insult to injury."

"Ah, he's going to come back here, right?" Awen asked. "This is his room."

"Unless someone warns him," Amaryllis pointed out. "He's shown that he's willing to run before, so we can assume that he might try to run again."

I nodded. "In that case, we'll go and confront him."

"And where would we go for that, exactly?" Amaryllis asked. "I can think of several places he might be, and that's not including the possibility that he's in transit or that he has friends in the Storm Tower who can shelter him."

"I don't know, I didn't spend too much time with him, but he doesn't seem like the type of person to have a lot of real friends," I said.

"Wow, that's . . . painful coming from you," Amaryllis said.

I felt my cheeks warming up a little. That *had* been kind of a mean thing to say, hadn't it? Maybe I was turning into a mean kind of person? Were my friends bad influences?

No, that couldn't be it.

"A-Anyway," I said. "Maybe we could split up, go to all the most likely places to find him?"

"And then what, have only one or two of us there to confront him?" Caprica asked. "I don't doubt the combat prowess of anyone here, but the baron will likely have guards with him, and he might be in a public place where starting a fight could lead to some trouble with the locals that would be best handled as a group."

I reached up and tugged on my droopier ear as I thought, but before I could come up with anything, Calamity had an idea.

"Let's first stop that weapon shipment," he said. "Even if we don't get the baron, we'll have to stop it in any case, and we can tell the folk selling those crossbows to fetch the baron for us. Two birds with one arrow."

My friends and I glanced at each other, and when no one had a better idea, we decided to give it a go. Tharval agreed to lead us to the munitions store listed on Vonowl's order form.

We filed out of the hotel—after I made sure we put all the money back. We also made sure the guard on the sofa was okay. He had come to a while ago, and Calamity untied one of his arms and gave him the leftovers of what he'd made in the kitchen as a snack so he wouldn't go hungry while untying himself.

We happened to encounter the reception dwarf on the way down. "He wasn't there," I said with a shrug.

"I . . . yes, I'm aware," the dwarf said. "I heard some commotion above?"

"Nothing much, we didn't break anything, I don't think." I smiled to reassure him. "Don't worry! If there's any trouble, you can direct it to the Exploration Guild."

"Ah, yes, of course," he said before squeezing himself out of the way.

We continued on down the stairs for a bit, and Amaryllis piped up almost as soon as we were out of the receptionist's hearing range. "Wow, Broccoli, that was almost devious."

"Huh?"

"Shoving all the blame onto the guild like that," she said. "When you started talking, I was worried you'd just admit to ruining Vonowl's rooms."

"But we didn't ruin them," I said.

"I left a mess in the kitchen," Calamity said.

"I cut up the mattress to see if there was anything hidden in it," Caprica said, then saw all of our expressions. "What? I read about it in a novel."

"Ah, we kind of . . . broke the wall around the safe," Awen admitted.

"And the safe too!" Tharval added.

I pressed my hands over my face. "I'm a liar. A liar and a manipulator."

Amaryllis patted me on the back. "It's okay, as long as you're not lying to or manipulating me."

"I wouldn't!" I said. "Not on purpose, anyway."

We left the hotel without any of my friends commenting on my realization that I was slowly turning into a terrible person. Fortunately, we soon started to talk, and I was able to put that out of my mind for the moment. Maybe I was just being a bit silly and overdramatic. A bit of breaking and entering and theft wasn't *that* big of a deal, was it?

With Tharval and Willowbud leading our group, we descended another staircase, boarded a trolley filled with so many people that some were hanging off the side, and continued on deeper into the Storm Tower on a circuitous route toward the weapons company.

When we arrived at our destination, we paused and took in the front of the shop.

It was a grand thing, with a massive ballista on a platform to one side and several oversized swords and spears behind glass on the other.

Above, in hard iron letters, was the name Thorade's Munitions.

· Chapter Fifty-Six ·

Pay for It

We walked into Thorade's Munitions and discovered the front lobby was empty.

Or at least, empty of people. There were lots of things to poke at and see. The walls had racks and racks of different tools of war. Most of these were crossbows and the like, with one wall displaying individual bolts with a variety of mean-looking heads.

There was a counter to one side laden with teeny-tiny miniature ships that had teenier-tinier ballistae on them, clearly as the focal point of the models, as if to show prospective ship captains the kinds of armaments they could buy here for their own ships.

"Oh," Awen said. She pointed to something and I followed her finger to a wall with diagrams.

"What is it?" I asked.

"That kind of repeating crossbow mechanism? That's what's at the front of the *Redemption*," she said. "It must have been made here."

"Hrm," Tharval said. "That's the little skiff tied up in your airship? Then that's possible. Thorade's Munitions makes cheaper gear, but the quality isn't terrible. Plenty of smaller ships carry a couple of their emplacements."

That made some sense, I figured. "Do you know anything else about them?"

Tharval stroked his beard, then shook his head. "Not much. Respectable midlevel crafters. Good at mass-producing things. Not the most ingenious bunch, but they've made a decent thing or two."

Right, that made sense. The dwarves especially seemed really fond of mechanical workings.

Just then, a dwarf stepped into the room from the back. They looked a bit frazzled, with tufts of beard sticking out this way and that. They paused on seeing us, scanned over our entire group, then locked their attention onto Amaryllis.

Then, they let out the kind of sigh that only someone working in customer service could before muttering, which sounded like *"another one"* under their breath.

"Hello!" I said, summoning up as much good cheer as I could. "You look a bit busy, but, ah, we had a question or two."

"Hello, and welcome to Thorade's Munitions. We *are* a little busy at the moment," they said, trailing off leadingly.

"We're looking for a Baron Vonowl," I said.

They winced.

"To arrest him."

That cheered them right up. "Oh, really?" they asked. "Well, I can't imagine what the good baron has done, but I can lead you right to him."

I blinked. "Wait, he's here? Now?"

"Yes indeed!" The dwarf seemed unable to contain his grin. "Please, follow me!"

He began striding toward a door labeled EMPLOYEES ONLY.

I traded glances with my friends. Awen and Caprica looked surprised, while Amaryllis was grinning viciously and Tharval rubbed his hands together.

"Well, let's not keep the poor kid waiting," he said. "We came here to stop Vonowl from buying weapons, and the easiest way to do that is to deal with him before he can buy them, isn't it?"

That got us moving.

As soon as we crossed the doorway, the nice veneer of the storefront disappeared. Pretty stone flooring was replaced by metal grating and the walls lacked any decorations other than posters of scantily clad dwarves using their beards to cover themselves up and gazing at the viewer in ways that made me blush and look away.

The main factory floor of Thorade's Munitions was a busy, loud space, with dozens of dwarves and a few elves working big, complex machines. It smelled nice, though. A lot of the ballistae they made had wooden frames, and a whole section of the shop floor was dedicated to woodworking, so despite the dusty air, the scent of freshly sawn wood was pleasant.

We passed a machine that seemed entirely built to raise up an anvil-sized hammer and sent it down onto a car-sized anvil, and another that consisted of a whirling mess of interlocking gears and spokes just asking for someone to stick their fingers in.

I imagined that they didn't have much by way of safety regulations in the Storm Tower. Or if they did, those weren't being applied here.

We found the baron, as well as a pair of harpy guards and a small gaggle of unhappy-looking dwarves, standing at the back of the shop.

Baron Vonowl was kicking up a fuss, wings flapping as he hurled a lot of not-very-nice words at a shorter dwarf, one with a long dark beard densely woven with beads. The dwarf's stern face and twitching eye told me they didn't appreciate the Baron's spittle-heavy style of debate.

"Thorade!" the dwarf guiding us said. "We have more guests." They were clearly working hard to mask some of the glee in their voice.

Thorade, who seemed to be the one Vonowl was lecturing, looked over our group with brows knit and mouth set in a frown. Then they spotted Tharval and Willowbud and their eyebrows rose up.

"I'm quite busy at the moment," the baron said. "I'm sorry, but your business with Thorade will have to wait." He looked me right in the eye, then turned back to the dwarf he was talking to.

Did he not recognize me?

I was a little upset, actually. I thought I was a pretty memorable kind of person. Oh well, that was okay. Maybe not being recognized just then was for the best?

"I'm sorry, Mister Thorade," I said. "We didn't mean to intrude or anything."

Vonowl snapped back around and glared at me.

Oh! He recognized my voice!

"You moron!" Vonowl spit out, "Can't you see that this is a lady?"

Or maybe he hadn't. I was having a lot of highs and lows at the moment. "Um . . . actually, I'm really bad at telling dwarves' genders apart."

He sniffed, then pointed to Miss Thorade's shoulders. "The hips and shoulders on a female are wider. They're very slightly shorter as well. And, of course, the hair of a female dwarf's beard is curly, whereas that of a male tends to be straighter. How can you not know this?"

"That's . . . actually really helpful, thank you," I said.

"As thanks you can leave me to my business," he said offhandedly before turning back toward Miss Thorade.

"Um, actually, our business is with you," I said. "See, uh, we want to arrest you? Please?"

The baron paused, then turned to give me a stare. "You what?"

"You really don't recognize me?" I asked. "Last we saw each other was at that big tower with all the pirates working with you. You'd kidnapped a bunch of nobles and stole a few ships, and I was there with my friends and the sylph army? This was only like, a few days ago."

Vonowl narrowed his eyes at me, his feathers ruffling up. Thorade threw some sharp glances between us, and my friends all spread out behind me.

Miss Thorade gave the baron a very hard stare. "Pardon me, Baron, but when you mentioned that you wanted my equipment for the purposes of pirate defense, did you mean defending against piracy, or were you planning on using our bows to defend the pirates?"

"Are you accusing me of lying?" he snapped at her. "Don't listen to these fools. The noble house of Vonowl would never stoop to piracy." He turned back to me. "And you! What is this slander? Arrest me? I've done nothing wrong."

"Well," I began, "You did kidn—"

"Stop lying!" he cut me off. "You whiny little rabbit-eared child! I strive only for the betterment of harpykind, and I won't let you stand in the way of that! If you're talking about arrest, then I ought to have you imprisoned for defaming my good name!"

"Oh, shut up," Amaryllis said. "Your name's good for nothing."

He squinted at her. "Who are you?"

That got Amaryllis to bristle quite prettily. "Me? I'm Amaryllis Albatross, you feather-brained incompetent."

I had never been happier in my life to hear Amaryllis drag someone into a bickering contest. Very deliberately, I refocused on Miss Thorade. "Sorry, you don't mind if we arrest him, do you?"

The dwarven lady tugged at her beard, but then shook her head. "No. My Business Sense was hinting that I wouldn't be paid by this man. Though you *are* distracting my workers."

That was true; I noticed a number of heads poking up from around and above the various machines in the shop. It seemed that even dwarves were keen on being busybodies when there was good gossip about.

"We're sorry for the likely loss of this contract," Willowbud said. "Is there anything we can do to help?"

"You're Willowbud, aren't you?" she asked. "And that makes the irritable grump next to you the infamous Tharval."

"Infamous is still famous, whelp," he grumbled at her.

She sniffed. "I heard that you're insane, with the occasional flash of genius only a madman would dare to have."

"Hear that, Bud? I'm a genius."

"Yes, that was the part of the statement that really caught my ear," Willowbud replied. "In any case, we should take the baron somewhere a little more discreet, I think."

"Where?" I asked. "We don't exactly have cells on the *Beaver.*"

"Bah, we have cells at the Exploration Guild," Tharval said with a dismissive shrug.

There was a pause.

"Um, why?" Awen asked. I thought it was a very sensible question to ask.

"Because some of us aren't good with our drinks," he said. And that seemed to be enough explanation for the rest of my friends. Except for

Amaryllis, of course, who didn't hear what Tharval had said. Her argument with Vonowl had devolved from a catty back-and-forth to a tirade of insults that was gaining in loudness with every mention of someone's hatching and the quality of their plumage and ancestry.

I patted her on the back. "Hey, it's okay, we're going to arrest him now."

"Arrest implies a certain amount of legal authority," Caprica said. "This is more of a . . . citizen's detention."

"But we're not citizens here," Awen said.

"A . . . non-citizen detention." Caprica amended. "You know what, I'm just going to work hard to not think of things in legal terms for a while. I feel like doing that might be bad for my mental health."

"That's the spirit, Princess," Calamity said.

Seeing as how we were more or less all in agreement, I turned to the next potential source of problems. The baron's guards. "Hi," I said to the two. "I know that you're basically being paid to take care of the baron here, but we kinda need to take him away for a while. And we'd much rather not have to fight."

The two bodyguards looked to each other, then to our group. I imagined that even though we were mostly a friendly bunch, we might have been a teensy bit intimidating, under the right light.

"Also, your boss is broke," Calamity added. "Unless nya got paid in advance? No? Oh, that stings. Well, live and learn, huh?" That was enough for the guards to put down their weapons.

I walked up to the baron, and then patted him on the shoulder. He flinched back. "Don't touch me," he said.

"Oh. Well, okay. But only if you agree to walk ahead of us and not kick up a fuss. You've done some very mean things, and I think we should do something about that."

"If you want, my boys can whip up a pair of cuffs or fetch some ropes real quick," Thorade said.

"You'd betray me, Thorade? After I brought you so much business?" Baron Vonowl asked.

"You haven't paid me yet either," she said.

I made an itty-bitty mental note to make sure I paid people in the future, because it seemed like not doing so led to people being rather unhelpful.

The baron protested quite a bit as we tied his wings up against his sides (Amaryllis suggested against tying them to his back, harpy shoulders not being the same as human ones, apparently). We considered gagging him for a while, mostly because he was being extremely vocal about . . . well, every-thing, but that felt a little rude, especially when the only thing we could gag him with were the socks that Calamity volunteered with rather more glee than might have been appropriate.

With the baron all tied up, we pushed him along ahead of us. Willowbud apologized to Miss Thorade, who charged us a token sum for the ropes, and then we were off.

Crossing the Storm Tower with a rather unwilling, tied-up baron in our midst, one who constantly shouted about how we were scoundrels, kidnappers, and other more vile things, was a little tricky.

We tried to stick to less popular routes, but that only helped so much.

What helped a lot more was the strange amount of authority Willowbud could exude whenever he wanted. I had to wonder if it was a skill, especially when we ran into some guards and he persuaded them that this was all Exploration Guild business and that they should keep on doing their jobs . . . but elsewhere.

"Once we have you in a cell," Amaryllis said to Vonowl. "We're going to have *all* sorts of questions for you."

· Chapter Fifty-Seven ·

Polite Friction

The elf receptionist at the Exploration Guild didn't even bat an eye when we came in dragging a seething noble and asked to put him in a cell. He merely asked if we wanted to be discreet about it or if one of the more public cells was fine.

I thought it was a little weird that the Exploration Guild had a secret dungeon, but it also had a secret workshop that we'd seen already, so really it wasn't all that surprising.

Baron Vonowl continued to protest as we dragged him through a sliding bookcase—we had to get one of those on the *Beaver Cleaver*!—and plopped him down in a cell.

The rest of us gathered on the far wall of the prison space, none of us really comfortable with all the strange devices and racks and sharp implements lying on tables and hooked to the walls. At least the room was well lit, even if the light was all red and flickery and felt a lot like it was chosen more to set the mood than to make it easy to see.

Tharval gestured to the baron, then turned toward Willowbud. "Well, do your thing," he said.

"My thing?" Willowbud asked.

Tharval tugged at his beard. "That's right. Your thing. Get the idiot to tell us what we want to know."

"Ah, that thing," Willowbud said with a nod, then he shook his head. "I don't want to do that thing. There are children here."

"We're not children," I said. I was sixteen, which was pretty firmly not the age of a child. My friends were all about that age too. Calamity might have been the oldest . . . or maybe it was Caprica, it was hard to tell. In any case, none of us were children.

"Regardless," Willowbud said, and I felt as if I'd just been dismissed. "We won't torture the good baron, use any hard social skills on him, or push him too hard. We aren't as cruel as that."

"You're cowards, then," the baron snapped from inside his cell. He was rubbing his wrists and glaring out at us. "You mush-brained cretins! You think that you can just dump me in some cell and forget about me? Fine then. Do that. I won't be the first of us locked away, and I won't be the first to find his way out of a cell either."

"Are you talking about Rainnewt?" I asked.

"Do you think you can convince me to talk?" he asked right back.

"Honestly, I wonder if we could convince you to stop talking," Amaryllis said. That had the baron glaring even harder. He really didn't like Amaryllis.

"Disgusting, no-good brat. You have no idea how good you had it, do you?"

"Is this coming from a baron?" Amaryllis asked. "Please, tell me how awful your life as lesser nobility was. Did someone with more clout than you mock you? Wait, no, someone probably just pointed out the truth, and you couldn't handle it."

"As if you'd understand, little Albatross princess! You and your filthy family sit near the top, driving our fine nation to ruin!"

I stepped up between the baron and Amaryllis. "Okay, guys," I said. "Insulting each other won't help any, I don't think. It's not very friendly behavior."

"Shut up, you half-breed."

I blinked, then decided to let that pass. The baron wasn't in a very nice place in his life at the moment, and while that wasn't a reason to forgive being mean, it did explain it a little. "All right, all right, enough with the name-calling and the insults, please? Amaryllis, you're a good girl, don't be like that. And Baron Vonowl, it's not very noble of you to fling insults around."

"What would you know about nobility?" he asked.

"Well, I've hugged a bunch of them," I said.

The baron blinked, a little confused by that for some reason.

"Ah, should we ask him questions while he's here?" Awen asked.

"Isn't it good enough that he can no longer be used by Rainnewt to cause any harm?" Caprica asked. "The time he spends in a cell is time he can't be disruptive."

"But what if he did something disruptive already?" Awen asked. "He was buying weapons, but what if he bought other stuff already? And besides, where were those weapons going in the first place?"

We all turned toward the baron, who took a small step back at our collective look. "Well, Mister Baron Vonowl," I started. "Do you think you could tell us a thing or two about all that?"

"I'm not telling you anything," he bit out.

"What if we say please?" I asked.

Ding! For repeating a Special Action a sufficient number of times, you have unlocked the general skill: Politeness!

I jumped as Mister Menu—who I hadn't seen in a while—popped up in front of me as a little blue box.

"Broccoli?" Awen asked.

"I got a skill," I said.

"Interrogation?" Willowbud guessed. "Though we haven't really started with that yet, it's a useful skill to have. I could give you some tips."

"No, Politeness," I said.

That stumped the elf.

"What kind of harebrained skill is that?" Amaryllis asked. "Refuse it, of course."

"You can do that?" I asked. I could've avoided all the trouble with Cuteness! "I've never refused a skill before, they just slot right in."

"World spare me," Amaryllis said. "No wonder you're so . . . Anyway, Politeness doesn't seem like the most useful of skills, Broccoli. You're hardly impolite to begin with."

"I know some people who could have used the skill," Caprica said. "But I do agree, it doesn't seem immediately useful. Is it a class skill?"

"No, a general skill," I said with a shake of my head.

```
Politeness
Rank F - 0%
```
The ability to appear as a polite, respectable person when desiring to.

"The description isn't all that helpful," I said before repeating it aloud.

"That really doesn't seem like a very good skill for you, Broccoli," Awen said.

"Yeah, but I haven't gotten a new skill in so long," I said. "Why this one now? Shouldn't I have gotten this the first time I said *please* and *thank you*? Wait, do I not say those often enough? Have I been impolite until now?"

Awen patted my head. "You're not impolite, Broccoli," she said.

"Okay, okay," I said. "It doesn't matter, I guess I'll just level it passively in the background, and maybe it'll turn into something handy!"

```
Ding! Four of your current skills are eligible for Merg-
ing: Dancing, Tea Making, Matchmaking, and Politeness!
```

"Oh!" I said before I tried to grab Mister Menu in a quick hug. He, of course, ducked out of the way.

"What is it now?" Amaryllis asked.

"Why do you people spend time with this clown in your midst?" Baron Vonowl asked with a gesture at me.

"She's our leader," Awen explained.

The baron reeled back. "*She's* the one in charge? Are you all really that stupid? Why would you let her be the leader? She's incompetent!"

I deflated a bit, mid-lunge to catch Mister Menu. That was very mean.

"She's competent enough to capture *you*," Caprica pointed out, which did a number on the baron's self-esteem, judging by how he flinched back.

"Ignore him," Amaryllis said. "He's proven time and time again to be an idiot."

"Nya shouldn't listen to idiots," Calamity said with a nod. "It's why so many folk ignore me."

I nodded along too. "I won't let the mean words bring me down, I'm not fragile or anything. Anyway! I got a merge skill! It's Politeness, Dancing, Tea Making, and Matchmaking together."

"What's the end result of that?" Amaryllis asked. "Four skills merging all at once is quite something."

"Uncommon, though not unheard of," Willowbud said. "You seem to have a lot of social skills if you have enough that they can combine that way."

"Ah, thanks," I said. "I didn't really make any effort to pick social stuff, though."

I poked at Mister Menu to see what the confluence of all those skills would be.

`Do you wish to Merge Dancing, Tea Making, Matchmaking, and Politeness to unlock the Social Butterfly skill?`

"Huh, it's the—um?" I paused when Amaryllis tapped my shoulder.

"Not in here," she said. "Hold off on that for a little bit? We can talk about it and pick a good option once we're back on our ship. You have more than just friends in this room." She nodded her head toward the baron stewing in his cage.

"Oh, right," I said. I adjusted my clothes to make sure they fit on right, then smiled at the baron. "So, are you ready to talk yet?"

"You haven't even started the torture," he rolled his eyes. "All that you've done is reveal your complete lunacy."

I wondered if harpies had a species-wide disposition toward insults, or if it was more of a cultural thing. No wonder they'd been having such a long-standing argument with the sylphs.

"We're not going to do anything like that," I said. "We just want to know a few things. Why you were buying all those crossbows, where you were sending them, what the plan was with kidnapping all those nobles, what your relationship with Rainnewt is, that sort of thing."

"We know why he kidnapped the nobles," Amaryllis said. "It was to force the sylphs to release Rainnewt from custody."

"Ah, but they kidnapped them before Rainnewt was captured," Caprica pointed out. "And Rainnewt didn't strike me as someone who thought he was likely to be captured, so it probably wasn't a preemptive plan."

Amaryllis frowned, then nodded, conceding the point. "Fair enough. Then it was either for the ransom money, or for the potential to destabilize things."

"Or he just did it because he could," Calamity said. "This guy doesn't strike me as smart enough for long-term plans."

"Are you trying to get me to divulge things by insulting me? You're a million years too young for that to work, dog."

"Dog?" Calamity asked as he stood a little straighter. His ears twitched. "I'm not a dog, I'm a cat, you overfluffed turkey."

"You know nothing!" Baron Vonowl said. "And once the proper authorities find out what you've done to me, you'll be finished. There will be no room for fools of your caliber in the future that Rainnewt and I are ushering in, and even if you remove me, the plans we've set in place will continue! We don't need those weapons to ruin that wedding, and we don't need my presence to ensure that everything nonetheless goes according to plan. Do you think us unable to deal with a few minor setbacks?"

"Wedding?" a couple of us asked at the same time.

The baron's mouth clicked shut, and he looked away. Pouting didn't become him, but he was doing it anyway.

We poked and prodded at him a little more, but from that point on, he just shrugged his shoulders and refused to speak.

Eventually we gave up. There was no pushing the baron past a certain point. Willowbud said he could take care of the baron for a while here at the Exploration Guild, but we couldn't really hold him forever. We didn't have the right, and what we were doing was a teensy bit super not-okay legally.

"So, what wedding was he talking about?" I asked.

"It would have to be an important one," Amaryllis said. "Caprica, any ideas?"

"I don't know of any approaching royal weddings, I can tell you that much. None of the bigger nobles, either. Maybe an earl or two? Weddings aren't uncommon, but I imagine Rainnewt would be after something big."

"Don't look at me," Calamity said. "Most of the weddings I've been to have been more about the shindig than anything else."

"Well, maybe we can ask around?" I asked. "The baron bought hundreds of weapons, that seems like a lot for a minor noble's wedding."

Something was up, and we didn't know nearly as much as we needed to, even if we did have the baron in custody. It was starting to feel like no matter what we did, it just wasn't enough.

· Chapter Fifty-Eight ·

The Wedding Trackers

We regrouped in the parlor on the floor above, where the older members of the Exploration Guild were gathered around, drinking and reminiscing and doing whatever it was old folk did when they were put together in a room and left to their own devices.

"So, what does that leave us with?" Caprica asked.

"It leaves you with a potential location," Willowbud said. "An unspecified wedding, presumably somewhere on the continent."

"Har har," Amaryllis said, clearly unamused. "We're not exactly tied into the social networks of most countries, so if it's going to take place in the Trenten Flats or the Harpy Mountains, then we won't know for a good long while."

"Ah, we do have a timetable," Awen said.

We glanced at her.

"The weapons need to arrive, right? So we know that Rainnewt's plan probably involved waiting for them to get there. When were they going to be shipped?"

"It looked like the baron was hard at work nagging the manufacturers to move faster," Caprica said. "Good point, Awen, that does give us a small window. We know this wedding probably isn't tomorrow. The further out it is, the farther away the wedding will be, to account for the weapons' necessary travel time."

"Not *that* helpful," Calamity said. "Uh, no offense meant, Awen. Good idea and all, just we still don't know the when."

"We could ask the crew of the ships the baron hired. That'll give us a more accurate picture," Amaryllis said. "Unless those guys have already left town. Or if they were planning on transferring the goods to another ship along the way. Still, it might still give us a rough heading. Not every port has direct routes to every location, so we can probably assume the most convenient routes are the ones Vonowl was planning on using. That barely narrows it down, though."

Willowbud shrugged. "We'll continue to question the baron."

"Bah, bring him to the forge, I'll roast that chicken for a few hours and then we'll see if he talks," Tharval said.

Willowbud patted the dwarf on the head, which seemed to really insult him. "No, Tharval, we won't torture the idiot noble, no matter how tempting. When our adversaries sink, we swim."

I listened to the conversation going on around me, the back and forth and the friendly bickering, and I just soaked it all in. It was tense, but not bad.

While my friends talked, I debated over Social Butterfly.

The skill seemed really nice to have. It was what I aspired to be, in a way. A person who could make friends easily. Maybe I didn't want to rely too much on a skill for that, but it didn't seem too dishonest to have a bit of help. After all, my other skills also helped me make friends.

Cleaning helped by making it so that I wasn't stinky when I met new people, for example, and that was important for socializing and I wouldn't consider it a cheat.

Losing some of my other skills for Social Butterfly would hurt a little, though. Matchmaking's . . . matchmaking part wasn't super interesting to me, but the way it helped with small fire spells was nice. Tea Making was a great buffing skill, even if I probably didn't use it to its full potential.

Really, the biggest loss would be Dancing. It was, strangely enough, one of my main combat skills. It allowed me to have surer footing and to dance around opponents and predict their moves. It was super useful!

Then again, I did have Way of the Mystic Bun now, which did something similar.

Merging the four into Social Butterfly would also free up some class skill slots. Dancing was a Cinnamon Bun Bun class skill, Tea Making was a Wonderlander skill, and both Matchmaking and Politeness were generals. With one new skill I'd open up three slots for new, shinier skills.

And then there was the winged elephant in the room.

Would Social Butterfly eventually give me butterfly wings?

I looked at Caprica, who had big, fluttery faerie wings on her back. They were pretty, a translucent, pale-blue film stretched over spar-like veins. They reminded me a little of stained glass. Careful and delicate and obviously very magical. Caprica might have been a rather tiny woman, but she still had to weigh too much for those wings to give her lift without magical assistance.

Maybe?

High school physics class had been a while ago. Still, I remembered that thing about bee wings not being able to lift them up, even though they clearly did anyway. Maybe this was something like that? Or maybe it was just magic.

In any case, I wouldn't mind being a bun with wings!

"Broccoli?" Awen asked.

"Hmm? Oh, sorry, I was distracted by something. What's up?" I asked.

"Ah, we were going to go get some food," Awen said. "Me and Calamity." She waved a little piece of paper around, a menu. "Did you want something?"

"Oh? I'll go with you!" I said. "Need to get my daily skips in any way, and I could use a walk."

"Sure!" Awen said with a genuine little smile. "I wouldn't mind having you along."

I bounced out of my seat and followed Awen to the door, where Calamity was waiting while spinning his hat around on one finger. "Nya coming along too?" he asked. "Less to carry, then!"

I laughed. "I mostly want to move a bit."

"That's fair. I don't mind a pinch of planning, but some of our friends back there like talking more than they like moving, I think. Amaryllis and Caprica both."

"They're not so bad," I said.

He shrugged. "I've known worse. Just I'm more of a doer, nya know?"

"Mm-hmm!"

Was I a doer?

Do you wish to Merge Dancing, Tea Making, Matchmaking, and Politeness to unlock the Social Butterfly skill?

"Yeah," I said to Mister Menu. I *was* a doer, and that meant taking concrete steps toward being the best friend I could be. Mister Menu popped away with a soap-bubble *plop*, and I felt myself shift slightly with my next step. My balance felt oh-so subtly different, as if the bounce in my step had changed in quality.

Where do you wish your new skill to be placed? Cinnamon Bun Bun, Wonderlander, or General Skills?

Oh, that was something to consider, wasn't it?

"Wonderlander," I muttered. I was planning on getting this skill up a few levels, so that only made sense!

New Skill added!

Skills consolidated!

Skill Points refunded!

Oh! I had to check on the difference that made for my skills!

Name	Broccoli Bunch
Race	Bun (Riftwalker)
First Class	Cinnamon Bun Bun
First Class Level	14
Second Class	Wonderlander
Second Class Level	5
Age	16
Health	155
Stamina	175
Mana	155
Resilience	70
Flexibility	85
Magic	30
Skills	Rank
Cinnamon Bun Bun Skills	
Cleaning	S - 08%
Way of the Mystic Bun	C - 100%
Gardening	D - 40%
Adorable	D - 100%
Wonderlander Skills	
Mad Millinery	D - 100%
Proportion Distortion	C - 29%
Social Butterfly	F - 00%
General Skills	
Insight	C - 100%
Makeshift Weapon Proficiency	C - 77%
Archeology	D - 100%
Friendmaking	C - 92%

Hugging Proficiency	C - 100%
Captaining	D - 100%
Cinnamon Bun Bun Skill Points	2
Wonderlander Skill Points	5
General Skill Points	3
First Class Skill Slots	1
Second Class Skill Slots	0
General Skill Slots	4

That was a lot of room for new skills, and I got back that one skill point from Wonderlander that I could now use on my brand-new skill! Well, once I got it up a smidge. But that wouldn't be too hard, I figured. I was nothing if not social, so I'd have plenty of opportunities to grind that out. I excitedly checked out my new skill.

```
Social Butterfly
Rank F - 0%
The ability to flit from conversation to conversation and
make the best of any social situation.
```

Oh, that sounded like just the perfect skill!

Now all I needed to do was to start doing cool stuff so that I'd eventually unlock cooler skills too!

"So," I said, trying to practice my new skill, "what did everyone order?"

"Ah, mostly Tharval suggested that we try this one place nearby," Awen said. "It's a dwarven pub? Um, he ordered steaks."

"I want me some of that steak too," Calamity said. He licked his lips and I could almost see the drool there. "These dwarves know how to eat."

"Willowbud also suggested this elven place. It's a saladhouse," Awen said. "I thought you'd like that better."

"Oh, yes, I guess that'd be better," I agreed a little sadly. Steak was nice, but it wasn't worth the tummy ache. Still, I had to start testing other foods. I couldn't live off of just pastries, pastas, veggies, and fruit.

Well, I suppose I *could*, but variety was the spice of life, and eating tons of yummy things made me a happy bun. I was always at my happiest when surrounded by friends and with my tummy so full I could barely walk.

That was hard to achieve with salad.

On arriving at the Exploration Guild's lobby, we were greeted by the same reception elf as usual. He nodded to us cordially. "Heading out?" he asked.

"Just to grab some food," I said. "I guess we're all a little hungry."

"If you wish, we have people we can send out for that. The more experienced members can be a little demanding at times, so we keep a few very young members around to foist all the undesirable tasks onto."

"Ah, no, it's okay," I said. "But thanks!"

"No problem," he said. "If you're ever looking for suggestions on where to eat, then just ask, I'm usually well-connected."

"You are?" I asked. Then I paused. "Hey . . . you wouldn't happen to know of any weddings going on soon?"

"Weddings? A number of them, yes. Did you mean of Exploration Guild members?"

I shook my head. It wouldn't be someone in the Storm Tower. "No, I meant more . . . someone important outside of this country, maybe? Like in the Harpy Mountains, or in the Trenten Flats? Like a king getting married or something, maybe?"

The receptionist's eyebrows perked up. "Well, let me see. There's an eligible princess in Pyrowalk who has become famous for refusing suitors. I suppose it's possible she might have found someone agreeable. But that's far to the east. There's a rich noble's daughter missing from Mattergrove that's sparked some controversy. And there's a duke in the Trenten Flats due to be married."

"Oh, that one!" I said.

He nodded. "The wedding is in nine months, I think."

"Oh . . . maybe not that one," I deflated.

"The only other wedding I've heard of recently is the big one in Port Royal."

I perked up. "Port Royal? In Deepmarsh?" I'd been there! Twice, even. It was where I'd joined the Exploration Guild and first met Amaryllis.

"That's the one, yes. The grenoil city, though it has turned into something of a city-state recently. The Deepmarsh government still taxes people and runs amenities, but there's a dragon ruling over the city as well. Several of them, in fact. It's one of them who is getting married, from what I've heard."

I felt an electric shock zap through me, and a look to Awen showed she was as wide-eyed and surprised as I was.

Spinning around, I launched forward, ignoring the elevator to bounce up the stairs a flight at a time.

"Hey! Wait!" Calamity called as he ran after Awen and me. "What's going on?"

At the top, I burst into the room with the rest of my friends, the door cracking against the wall next to me. "Guys!" I said.

"Are they outta steak?" Tharval asked.

I took a deep breath. "Booksie's getting married!"

· Chapter Fifty-Nine ·

Beauty and the Dragon

Wait, really?" Amaryllis asked.

"Who's Booksie?" Caprica asked as well.

I took a second to calm my pitter-pattering heart. "She's a bun friend of mine! We helped her on her first, uh, sorta dates! I think it must be her wedding that's being targeted! It has to be! And Rainnewt would know about it because it's happening in Port Royal!"

"Wait, back up a moment," Amaryllis said. "Where did you learn about this wedding?"

"The receptionist. Oh shoot, the food."

"Never mind that," Amaryllis said. "You heard that Booksie is getting married? To Rhawrexdee? When's the wedding?"

"Well, not exactly that, but I *think* that's what's happening. It makes sense. Well, some sense. It's a bit fast for a wedding, if you ask me. But yeah! We need to go to Port Royal."

Amaryllis huffed a *calm your horses* huff. "That hardly sounds like a confirmation to me. More like a suspicion, at best."

"Well, yeah, but if it's real, then I wanna be there. I bet she'd allow us to attend." I gasped. "We could be bridesmaids!"

"You're getting about twenty steps ahead of yourself," Amaryllis said. "First we need to confirm if there's really a wedding going on, and if it actually *is* Booksie's, then . . . Well, Port Royal isn't next door."

Awen and Calamity stumbled into the room behind me. "What?" he asked.

"You think Rainnewt will go after this Booksie friend of yours?" Caprica asked.

"Maybe," I said. "It would make sense."

"Is she important?" Caprica asked.

"She owns a nice little bookstore," I said.

Caprica didn't look impressed.

"But her boyfriend is Rhawrexdee, and he's a whole entire dragon," I added.

"A dragon," Caprica said, her tone seemingly completely dead. "A *dragon*. As in a large, fire-breathing, magic-wielding, apex predator, sylph-snacking *dragon?*"

"Yeah," I said.

"And he's marrying . . . a bun?"

I nodded. "I think they're very cute together."

"No, we don't know how they make . . . things work," Amaryllis said, without actually enlightening anyone about what she actually meant. She patted down her feathers and shook her head. "In any case . . . I don't know what to think about this. If you're correct, Broccoli, then it might mean some serious trouble."

"I don't know, if Rainnewt is trying to kill a dragon, I say let him," Caprica said.

"Caprica!" I gasped. "How could you say that?"

The princess just seemed entirely confused. "What do you mean? What part of that was so controversial? Either Rainnewt succeeds, in which case one less dragon will terrorize the skies, or he fails and is turned into dragon chow."

"Hmm," Tharval grunted. "Wouldn't want to fight a dragon myself. Though . . . I might be able to think of a way or two to make the fight a little more fair."

"Yes, you keep thinking about those things, as long as they stay thoughts," Willowbud said.

I ignored the two of them for a moment. "Caprica, Rhawrexdee is a friend. So is his sister Cholondee, and even their mom, though I don't know her as well."

"They're dragons, Broccoli," Caprica said. "Do you know how most interactions between a sylph and a dragon end?"

"Uh, no?" I asked.

"It ends in the dragon's stomach." She crossed her arms. "Dragons have their own language, you know. And in their tongue, we're known only as 'snacks.'"

I recoiled. I didn't know that. My autotranslate let me speak and understand Dragon perfectly, but it didn't provide any kind of explanation for the words. While speaking it, I could easily call a sylph a snack and not even realize it. But . . . yeah, that kind of etymology might make sense for a dragon. When I'd met Rhwarexdee way back in Rosenbell, he *was* planning on burning down the town and eating the townspeople, which are objectively mean things to do. Still . . .

"I . . . I don't know," I admitted. "But I think that maybe even dragons can grow past their own instincts for princess-kidnapping and town-burning.

It might not come naturally to them, but I think that dragons can become friends too. You just need to try!"

"Well, we have a history of trying with dragons," Caprica said. "Goldenalden is dragon-free, and has been for two generations now. Whenever a lizard so much as looks at one of our peaks, we teach them a valuable lesson about the strength of sylphs. It took centuries to rid ourselves of the last dragons who wanted to make our mountains their home. Unlike the harpies, we never settled for appeasing them."

"So, you've never met a dragon yourself?" I asked.

"Of course not," she said.

"Well, maybe you should? I'm sure they're not as bad as you think. They might be . . . a little bad, sometimes, but they can be reasoned with." I winced. My argument wasn't very convincing when the other side was basically "but they ate us."

"Caprica's cultural hang-ups aside, we do need to address this," Amaryllis said. "If Rainnewt crashes that wedding in particular, then it might start exactly the kind of war we've been trying to avoid all this time. I can picture it now already. He hires some mercenaries—sylph, cervid, harpy, whatever—arms them with the best Snowlander crossbows they can afford, and they make a mess of the wedding, which, if it does occur in Port Royal, will be attended by dignitaries from all over. Then the dragons will retaliate, and they might not be as . . . precise with their retaliation as we would hope."

"Precise?" Calamity asked.

"If they think Rainnewt is in a particular city, they might just burn the whole thing down and wait for him to come out of the ashes," Amaryllis said. "For a creature of their scale . . . that might make a crude sort of sense. They're not sized for the cities of most civilized people. They can either ask the authorities to work with them, which has a small chance of success, or they can burn everything and wait to see if that worked."

"That's . . . not good," I said. It was something of a massive understatement.

"Very not good, yes," Amaryllis agreed.

Caprica nodded. "My point stands then, dragons are no good."

I pouted. "But Rhawrexdee let us fly on him. Did you ever fly while riding a dragon before? It's really cool!"

"I'd rather fly with my own wings, thank you very much," Caprica rebutted.

"I think we should go," Awen said. "We should be there. To stop Rainnewt if he tries something, and to be there for Booksie if not."

"I'm down for a dragon wedding," Calamity said. "Bet they've got great food."

Caprica gave him a very stern look, and Calamity winced out an apology.

Amaryllis rubbed at the bridge of her nose. "Fine. Yes. We should try to be there, even if I'm not sure what we could do to help. We'll have to cross through the Harpy Mountains to get to Port Royal, in any case. So we might be able to toss the baron out to some proper authorities while we're there as well. Or . . . No, that's not clever. Let's inform the authorities of the Harpy Mountains now, then let them come pick him up. I'd rather not have to keep him onboard the *Beaver* if we can avoid it."

"We can keep him here," Willowbud said. "It wouldn't be a big imposition, and I'm certain that after a few days of commoner food our dear baron will crack. But I don't know if you have a few days to wait."

"Adventure doesn't wait for you," Tharval complained. "Best you kids get going. You've got half a continent to cross to get to Port Royal. Hmm . . . Is that place still filled with frogs?"

"You mean grenoils?" I asked. "Yeah, it's mostly them, but I don't think it's very nice to call them frogs."

"Bah, one of my best friends was a frog," he dismissed. "But Willowbud's right. You've brought enough excitement around here. About time you scamper off to the next spot of trouble. And get that weird ship of yours out of my docks while you're at it."

I didn't let Tharval dismiss us so easily. He got his share of hugs, and then I glommed onto Willowbud too.

We might have been in something of a sudden hurry, but there was no point in rushing out the door and not saying our goodbyes properly.

"Stay safe out there," Willowbud said. "It's a long flight from here to Port Royal, and there's plenty of room for things to go sour along the way."

"They'll be fine, you worrywart. They've got each other to rely on, don't they?" Tharval said.

I nodded. The dwarf was right. As long as we had each other, we'd figure things out.

With a final few hugs (to spread Huggism, of course), we left the Exploration Guild and headed back onto the confusing streets of the Storm Tower.

"We're going to have to come back here," Amaryllis said.

"Hmm? Why's that?" I asked.

"Because we haven't seen half of what this place has to show. It's not fair that we have to leave so soon."

I laughed. "I didn't think that you'd get so caught up in the spirit of adventure," I said.

"I did join the Exploration Guild for a reason beyond the pragmatic, I'll have you know," Amaryllis said. "Now that I think about it though, we're rather terrible members."

"We are?" I asked.

"Broccoli, we haven't taken a mission from them in months," Amaryllis said.

I blinked. That was true. "We were busy with other things, I guess. Maybe some of the stuff we did could, ah, retroactively count as exploration?"

"I could draw up a sloppy map of the plains, and maybe of that pirate tower," Calamity said.

"See," I said. "That could count, right?"

Amaryllis rolled her eyes. "Well, whatever. We *have* been doing important work, so I doubt anyone would actually begrudge us the time spent outside of exploring. Plenty of people treat guild membership as a sort of privilege instead of as a career."

"Ah, I think what we're doing is a lot like what Uncle did," Awen said. "He just went around and found things. At least, that's how a lot of his stories started. With him hearing strange rumors and then heading out with an expedition to find out what they were about."

"Well, I want to go around and find people that need friends, and see cool things, and meet cool people," I said.

"Hmph," Amaryllis said. "I suppose I want to discover new magics and make a name for myself."

"Ah, I guess . . . I just want to become strong," Awen said. "And maybe see a bit of the World, the way Uncle did."

"Are we doing mission statements?" Caprica asked. "Is this some kind of rousing speech?"

"Just play along!" I said as I bumped hips with her. "It's fun!"

"Fine then. I suppose I want to see the World a little as well. Away from the obligations and restrictions of my lineage. And . . . I wouldn't mind growing stronger either, to impress a certain someone."

I grinned big. Caprica wanted to impress Bastion! So cute!

"Well, ny'all have got some fancy wants and such," Calamity said. "But I'm just along to eat new foods, see new sights, and beat the stuffing out of new stuff. Oh, and make it rich. That too."

Amaryllis huffed, unimpressed. "The least complicated of us, aren't you?"

"Ny'up!"

I laughed, then bounced ahead of my friends, ears and beard flopping with every step. I'd had a lot of fun in the Storm Tower, and in the Snowlands overall, but yeah, I was ready to keep moving.

I wondered, for a moment, if I was getting some sort of wanderlust addiction. That would make it hard to settle down in the future.

But then, I could just live the rest of my life aboard the *Beaver Cleaver*, surrounded by friends and always on the hunt for the next adventure.

That sounded like a blast, actually.

"Broccoli, wipe that smile off your face or it'll get stuck that way," Amaryllis said.

"Hah! I don't care!" I proclaimed. "Come on, you could stand to smile some more too, you big grump!"

"Ah, this is nice," Awen said.

And it was!

About the Author

RavensDagger is a Canadian writer who wants to make people smile. The best way to do that, he has found, is by pecking away at the keyboard and hoping for the best.

RESPAWN YOUR CURIOSITY

follow us on our socials

podiumentertainment.com

@podiumentertainment

/podiumentertainment

@podium_ent

@podiumentertainment